James Edg~~
and
Jean Jessop H
Point Loma Branch Library

SEP 1 1 2003

P9-CJI-730

WITHDRAWN

The
CAVE

ALSO BY JOSÉ SARAMAGO IN ENGLISH TRANSLATION

Baltasar and Blimunda

The Year of the Death of Ricardo Reis

The Gospel According to Jesus Christ

The Stone Raft

The History of the Siege of Lisbon

Blindness

The Tale of the Unknown Island

All the Names

Journey to Portugal

JOSÉ SARAMAGO

The
CAVE

Translated from the Portuguese
by Margaret Jull Costa

James Edgar
and
Jean Jessop Hervey
Point Loma Branch Library

SEP 1 1 2003

HARCOURT, INC.
New York   San Diego   London

© José Saramago e Editorial Caminho, SA, Lisboa—2000
English translation copyright © 2002 by Margaret Jull Costa

All rights reserved. No part of this publication may be reproduced or
transmitted in any form or by any means, electronic or mechanical, including
photocopy, recording, or any information storage and retrieval system,
without permission in writing from the publisher.

Requests for permission to make copies of any part of the work
should be mailed to the following address: Permissions Department,
Harcourt Inc., 6277 Sea Harbor Drive, Orlando, Florida 32887-6777.

This is a translation of *A Caverna*

www.HarcourtBooks.com

Library of Congress Cataloging-in-Publication Data
Saramago, José.
[Caverna. English]
The cave / José Saramago; translated from the Portuguese
by Margaret Jull Costa.—1st U.S. ed.
p.   cm.
ISBN 0-15-100414-5
I. Costa, Margaret Jull. II. Title.
PQ9281.A66 C3813 2002
869.3'42—dc21   2002002355
Text set in Dante MT
Designed by Linda Lockowitz

Printed in the United States of America

First U.S. edition

A C E G I K J H F D B

For Pilar

What a strange scene you describe
and what strange prisoners,
They are just like us.

—Plato, *The Republic*, Book VII

The
CAVE

The man driving the truck is called Cipriano Algor, he is a potter by profession and is sixty-four years old, although he certainly does not look his age. The man sitting beside him is his son-in-law, Marçal Gacho, and he is not yet thirty. Nevertheless, from his face too, you would think him much younger. As you will have noticed, attached to their first names both these men have unusual family names, whose origin, meaning, and reason they do not know. They would probably be most put out to learn that "algor" means the intense cold one feels in one's body before a fever sets in, and that "gacho" is neither more nor less than the part of an ox's neck on which the yoke rests. The younger man is wearing a uniform, but is unarmed. The older man has on an ordinary jacket and a pair of more or less matching trousers, and his shirt is soberly buttoned up to the neck, with no tie. The hands grasping the wheel are large and strong, peasant's hands, and yet, perhaps because of the daily contact with soft clay inevitable in his profession, they also suggest sensitivity. There is nothing unusual about Marçal Gacho's right hand, but there is a scar on the back of his left hand that looks like the mark left by a burn, a diagonal line that goes from the base of his thumb to the base of his little finger. The truck does not really deserve the name of truck, since it is really only a medium-sized van, of a kind now out of date, and it is laden with crockery. When the two men left home, twenty kilometers back, the day had barely begun to dawn, but now the morning has filled the world with sufficient light for one to notice Marçal Gacho's scar and to speculate about the sensitivity of Cipriano Algor's hands. The two men are traveling slowly because of the fragile nature of the load and also because of the uneven road surface. The delivery of merchandise not considered to be of primary or even secondary importance, as is the case with plain ordinary crockery, is carried out, in accordance with the official timetables, at mid-morning, and the only reason these two men got up so early is that Marçal Gacho has to clock in at least half an hour before the doors of the Center open to the public. On the days when he does not have to give his son-in-law a lift but still has crockery to deliver, Cipriano Algor does not have to get up quite so early. However, every ten days, he is the one who goes to fetch Marçal Gacho from work so that the latter can spend the forty hours with his family to which he is entitled, and, afterward, Cipriano Algor is also the one who, with or without crockery in the back of the van, punctually returns him to his responsibilities and duties as a security guard. Cipriano Algor's daughter, who is called Marta and bears the family names of Isasca, from her late mother, and Algor, from her father, only enjoys the presence of her husband at home and in bed for six nights and three days every month. On the previous night, she became pregnant, although she does not know this yet.

The area they are driving through is dull and dirty, not worth a second glance. Someone gave these vast and decidedly unrural expanses the technical name of the Agricultural Belt and also, by poetic analogy, the Green Belt, but the only landscape the eyes can see on either side of the road, covering many thousands of apparently uninterrupted hectares, are vast, rectangular, flat-roofed structures, made of neutral-colored plastic which time and dust have gradually turned gray or brown. Beneath them, where the eyes of passersby cannot reach, plants are growing. Now and then, trucks and tractors with trailers laden with vegetables emerge from side roads onto the main road, but most of these deliveries are done at night, and those appearing now either have express and exceptional permission to deliver late or else they must have overslept. Marçal Gacho discreetly pushed back the left sleeve of his jacket to look at his watch, he is worried because the traffic is gradually becoming denser and because he knows that, from now on, once they enter the Industrial Belt, things will only get worse. His father-in-law saw the gesture, but said nothing, this son-in-law of his is a nice fellow, but very nervous, one of those people who was born anxious, always fretting about the passage of time, even if he has more than enough, in which case he never seems to know quite how to fill it, time, that is. What will he be like when he's my age, he thought. They left the Agricultural Belt behind them, and the road, which grows dirtier now, crosses the Industrial Belt, cutting a swath through not only factory buildings of every size, shape, and type, but also fuel tanks, both spherical and cylindrical, electricity substations, networks of pipes, air ducts, suspension bridges, tubes of every thickness, some red, some black, chimneys belching out pillars of toxic fumes into the atmosphere, long-armed cranes, chemical laboratories, oil refineries, fetid, bitter, sickly odors, the strident noise of drilling, the buzz of mechanical saws, the brutal thud of steam hammers and, very occasionally, a zone of silence, where no one knows exactly what is being produced. That was when Cipriano Algor said, Don't worry, we'll get there on time, I'm not worried, replied his son-in-law, only just managing to conceal his anxiety, Of course you're not, but you know what I mean, said Cipriano Algor. He turned the van into a side road reserved for local traffic, Let's take a shortcut down here, he said, if the police ask us why we're here, just remember what we agreed, we had some business to deal with at one of these factories before we went into town. Marçal Gacho took a deep breath, whenever the traffic on the main road got bad, his father-in-law would always, sooner or later, take a detour. What worried him was that he might get distracted and decide to make the turn too late. Fortunately, despite all his fears and his father-in-law's warnings, they had never yet been stopped by the police, One day, he'll realize

3

that I'm not a little boy any more, thought Marçal, and that he doesn't have to remind me every time about how we have business to deal with at one of the factories. It did not occur to either of them that the real reason behind the continued tolerance or benevolent indifference of the traffic police was Marçal Gacho's uniform, that of a security guard working at the Center, rather than the result of multiple random lucky breaks or of stubborn fate, as they would doubtless have said if asked why they thought they had so far escaped being fined. Had Marçal Gacho known this, he might have made more of the weight of authority conferred on him by his uniform, and had Cipriano Algor known this, he might have spoken to his son-in-law with less ironic condescension. It is true what people say, the young have the ability, but lack the wisdom, and the old have the wisdom, but lack the ability.

Once past the Industrial Belt, the city finally begins, not the city proper, for that can be seen beyond, touched by the caress of the first, rosy light of the sun, and what greets one are chaotic conglomerations of shacks made by their ill-housed inhabitants out of whatever mostly flimsy materials might help to keep out the elements, especially the rain and the cold. It is, as the inhabitants of the city put it, a frightening place. Here, every now and then, and in the name of the classical axiom which says that necessity knows no law, a truck laden with food is held up and emptied of its contents before you can say knife. The modus operandi, which is extremely efficient, was devised and developed after a prolonged period of collective reflection on the results of earlier attempts whose failure, as immediately became apparent, was due to a total lack of strategy, to antiquated tactics, if one could glorify them with that name, and, lastly, to a poor and erratic coordination of forces, which amounted, in practice, to a system of every man for himself. Since the flow of traffic was almost continuous throughout the night, blocking the road in order to stop one truck, which was their first plan of action, meant that the assailants fell into their own trap, for behind that truck came others, bringing reinforcements and immediate help for the driver in distress. The solution to the problem, quite brilliant, as the police themselves privately acknowledged, consisted in dividing the assailants into two groups, one tactical, the other strategic, and in erecting two barriers instead of one, the tactical group swiftly blocking the road after one sufficiently isolated truck had passed, and the strategic group, a few hundred meters farther up the road and informed of this action by the predetermined signal of a flashing light, equally rapidly setting up a second barrier where the ill-fated vehicle would have no alternative but to stop and allow itself to be robbed. No roadblock was required for the vehicles traveling in the opposite direction, the drivers themselves would stop when they saw what was going on up ahead. A third group, the rapid intervention force, was responsible for dissuading any bold attempt at solidarity with a rain of stones. The barriers were built out of large boulders transported on stretchers, and, afterward, some of the actual assailants, swearing blind that they had had nothing to do with the robbery, would help to move the boulders onto the hard shoulder, It's people like them that give our area a bad name, we're honest folk, they would say, and the drivers of the other trucks, anxious to have the road cleared so that they would not arrive late at the Center, merely responded, Yeah, sure. Cipriano Algor's van has been saved from such incidents en route mainly because he nearly always travels through these areas by day. At least, up until now. Indeed, since earthenware crockery usually appears on poor tables and tends to break fairly easily, the potter is not entirely safe, for, who knows, some woman, one of the many who struggle to make ends meet in these shantytowns, might one day say to the head of the household, We need some new plates, to which he will doubtless respond, No problem, I sometimes see a van driving past with Pottery written on the side, it's bound to have some plates on board, And some mugs too, the woman will add, making the most of the favorable tide, All right, some mugs as well, I won't forget.

Between the shacks and the first city buildings, like a no-man's-land separating two warring factions, is a large empty space as yet unbuilt on, although a closer look reveals on the ground a criss-crossing network of tractor trails and areas of flattened earth that can only have been created by large mechanical diggers, whose implacable curved blades pitilessly sweep everything away, the ancient house, the new root, the sheltering wall, the place where a shadow once fell and where it will never fall again. However, just as happens in our own lives when we think that everything has been taken away from us, only to notice later that something does, in fact, still remain, so here too a few scattered fragments, some filthy rags, some bits of recycled rubbish, some rusty cans, some rotten planks, a piece of plastic sheeting blown hither and thither by the wind, reveal to us that this territory was once occupied by the homes of the excluded. It will not be long before the city buildings advance like a line of riflemen and take over this plot, leaving only a thin strip of land between the outermost buildings and the first shacks, a new no-man's-land that will remain until it is time to move on to the third phase.

The main road, to which they had now returned, had grown wider, with one lane reserved exclusively for heavy vehicles, and although the van could only by some flight of fancy be included in that superior category, the fact that it is undoubtedly a vehicle transporting goods gives its driver the right to compete on equal terms with the slow, mastodonic machines that roar and groan and spew out choking clouds of smoke from their exhausts, and to overtake them with a swift, sinuous agility that sets the crockery in the back rattling. Marçal Gacho glanced at his watch again and breathed more easily. He would arrive on time. They were already on the outskirts of the city, and although they still had to drive down a few winding streets, take a left, take a right, another left, another right, right again, right, left, left, right, and straight ahead, they would finally emerge into a square and, from then on, all their difficulties would be over, for a straight avenue would carry them to their destinations, to where the security guard, Marçal Gacho, was expected and to where the potter, Cipriano Algor, would leave his cargo. At the far end, an extremely high wall, much higher than the highest of the buildings on either side of the avenue, abruptly blocked the road. It did not actually block the road, this was just an optical illusion, there were streets that ran alongside the wall, which, in turn, was not a freestanding wall, as such, but the outer wall of a huge building, a gigantic quadrangular edifice, with no windows on its smooth, featureless façade. Here we are, said Cipriano Algor, we made it and with ten minutes to spare before you have to go in, You know very well why I can't be late, it could affect my position on the list of candidates for resident guard, Your wife isn't exactly wild about the idea of you becoming a resident guard, It would be better for us, it would make life easier, we'd have a better standard of living. Cipriano stopped the van opposite the corner of the building, it seemed that he was about to respond to his son-in-law's remark, but instead he asked, Why are they demolishing that block of buildings, They must have finally got the go-ahead, What for, They've been talking for weeks now about a new extension, said Marçal Gacho as he got out of the van. They had stopped by a door above which hung a notice bearing the words No Entry Except for Security Personnel. Cipriano Algor said, Maybe, There's no maybe about it, the proof is there, the demolition work has started, Sorry, I didn't mean the extension, but what you said before about living conditions, now I won't argue with you about it making your life easier, not that we have much to complain about, since we could hardly be classed among the unfortunate, Look, I respect your opinion, but I have my own views too, and when it comes to it, you'll see, Marta will agree with me. He took a couple of steps and then stopped, doubtless realizing that this was not the correct way for a son-in-law to say goodbye to a father-in-law who had just given him a lift in to work, and he said, Thanks, and have a good trip back, See you in ten days' time, said the potter, Yes, see you then, said the security guard, at the same time waving to a colleague who was also just arriving for work. They went in together and the door closed.

Cipriano Algor started the engine, but did not immediately drive off. He looked at the buildings that were being pulled down. This time, probably because the buildings to be demolished were not particularly tall, they were not using explosives, that swift, modern and highly spectacular process that, in a matter of seconds, can transform a solid, organized structure into a chaotic heap of rubble. As one would expect, the street at right angles to this one was closed to traffic. In order to deliver his merchandise, Cipriano Algor would have to go behind the back of the block under demolition, drive around it, and then straight ahead, the door at which he would have to knock was on the corner farthest from where he was now, at the other end of an imaginary straight line that cut obliquely through the building Marçal Gacho had just entered. Diagonally across, the potter thought to himself to make the explanation shorter. When he comes to pick up his son-in-law in ten days' time, there will be no trace left of these buildings, the dust of destruction now hovering in the air will have settled, they may even have excavated the great pit in which they will dig the trenches for the foundations of the new building. Then they will erect the three walls, one of which will run parallel with the street along which Cipriano Algor will shortly have to drive, the other two will seal off on either side the land gained at the cost of the street running through it and of the demolished buildings, obliterating the façade of the building he can see now, the door for the security personnel will have to be moved, and, after a matter of days, not even the most keen-eyed observer, viewing it from the outside, still less from the inside, will be able to distinguish between new and old. The potter looked at his watch, it was still early, on the days when he drove in with his son-in-law he always had a two-hour wait before they opened the reception area he was heading for, plus all the time he would have to wait

8

before it was his turn, But at least I have the advantage of getting a good place in the line, I might even be first, he thought. Not that he ever had been, there were always people who got up earlier than he did, some of them had probably spent part of the night in the cabins of their trucks. They would go up onto the street when it was growing light and have a cup of coffee, a sandwich, even, on cold, damp mornings, a drop of brandy, then they would stand around talking, until about ten minutes before the doors opened, when the younger drivers, as nervous as apprentices, would rush down the ramp to take up their positions, while the older ones, especially if they were parked toward the rear of the line, would saunter back, chatting quietly, taking one last drag of their cigarette, because underground, if any engines were running, smoking was forbidden. It wasn't quite the end of the world, they judged, so there was no point in rushing.

Cipriano Algor started up the van. He had got distracted by the buildings under demolition and now wanted to make up for lost time, a ridiculous expression if ever there was one, an absurd idiom with which we hope to disguise the harsh fact that no time once lost can ever be made up or recovered, as if we believed, contrary to this evident truth, that the time we thought forever lost might, after all, have decided to hang back and wait, with the patience of one who has all the time in the world, for us to notice its absence. Stimulated by the sense of urgency born of these thoughts about who would arrive first and who would arrive later, the potter quickly drove around the block and straight down the street that ran parallel with the other façade of the building. As invariably happened, there were already people waiting outside for the doors to be opened to the public. He pulled over into the left-hand lane, into the access road for the ramp that led down to the basement, he showed the guard his supplier's identity card and joined the line of vehicles, behind a truck loaded with boxes which, to judge by the labels on the packages, contained objects made of glass. He got out of the van to see how many other suppliers were ahead of him and thus calculate, more or less accurately, how long he would have to wait. He was number thirteen. He counted again, no, there was no doubt about it. Although he was not a superstitious person, he knew about that number's bad reputation, in any conversation about chance, fate, or destiny, someone always chips in with some real-life experience of the negative, even fatal influence of the number thirteen. He tried to remember if he had ever been in this place in the line before, but the long and the short of it was that either it had never happened or else he had simply forgotten. He got annoyed with himself, it was nonsense, utterly absurd to worry about something that has no real existence, yes, that was right, he had never thought of that before, numbers don't really exist, things couldn't care less what number we give them, it's all the same to them if we say they're number thirteen or number forty-four, we can conclude, at the very least, that they do not even notice the position they happen to end up in. People aren't things, people always want to be in first place, thought the potter. And it isn't enough simply to be there either, they want the fact to be known and want other people to notice, he muttered. The basement was deserted apart from the two guards who were posted at either end, watching the entrance and the exit. It was always the same, the drivers left their vehicle in the line as soon as they arrived and went up to the street to have a coffee. Well, if they think I'm going to stay here, said Cipriano Algor out loud, they're very much mistaken. And as if he did not after all have anything to unload, he put the van into reverse and left the line, That way I won't be number thirteen, he thought. A few moments later, a truck came down the ramp and stopped in the place that his van had vacated. The driver got out of his cabin, looked at his watch, I've still got time, he must have thought. And as he disappeared up the ramp, the potter, after some rapid maneuvering, parked behind the truck, Now I'm number fourteen, he said, pleased with his own cunning. He leaned back in the seat and sighed, he could hear the hum of traffic in the street above, usually he joined the other drivers to have a cup of coffee and buy the newspaper, but he didn't feel like it today. He closed his eyes as if withdrawing into himself and immediately began to dream, it was his son-in-law explaining to him that when he was appointed resident guard the whole situation would change overnight, he and Marta would no longer live at the pottery, it was time to start a family life of their own, Try to understand, what will be, as the saying goes, will be, the world doesn't stop turning, and if the people you depend on for your living promote you, you should raise your hands to heaven in gratitude, it would be silly to turn our backs on fate when fate is on our side, besides, I'm sure that your greatest wish is for Marta to be happy, so you should be pleased. Cipriano Algor was listening to his son-in-law and smiling to himself, You're just saying all this because you think I'm number thirteen, you don't know that now I'm number fourteen. He woke up with a start to the sound of car doors slamming, the signal that unloading was about to begin. Then, still not fully emerged from his dream, he thought, I haven't changed numbers at all, I'm still number thirteen, I just happen to be parked in the place of number fourteen.

So it was. Almost an hour later, his turn came. He got out of the van and went over to the reception desk with the usual papers, the delivery note in triplicate, the invoice for the actual sales from the last delivery, the quality statement that accompanied each shipment and in which the potter took responsibility for any production defect found during the inspection to which the crockery would be submitted, the confirmation of exclusivity, again obligatory with every shipment, in which the potter undertook, subject to sanctions in the event of any infraction, to have no commercial relations with any other establishment regarding the sale of goods. As was customary, a clerk came over to help him unload, but the assistant head of department in charge of reception called to him and said, Just unload half the shipment and check it against the delivery note. Surprised and alarmed, Cipriano Algor asked Half, why, Sales have fallen off a lot in the last few weeks, we'll probably have to return anything of yours that we've got in the warehouse too because of lack of demand, Return what's in the warehouse, Yes, it's in your contract, Oh, I know it's in the contract, but since the contract also forbids me to have any other customers, would you mind telling me where I'm supposed to sell the other half of the shipment, That's not my problem, I'm just carrying out orders, Can I speak to the manager, No, it's not worth it, he wouldn't see you. Cipriano Algor's hands were shaking, he looked around him in bewilderment, to ask for help, but he saw only indifference on the faces of the three drivers who had arrived after him. Despite this, he made an appeal to class solidarity, Can you believe it, a man brings along the fruits of his labor, having dug the clay, mixed it, and shaped the crockery that they ordered from him, then fired it all in the kiln, and now they tell him they're only going to take half of what he's made and are going to return everything of his that's in the warehouse, I mean, where's the justice in that. The drivers looked at each other and shrugged, they weren't sure how best to respond nor to whom they should respond, one of them even got out a cigarette to make it clear that he was having nothing to do with it, then remembered that he couldn't smoke down there and, instead, turned his back and removed himself from events by taking refuge in the cabin of his truck. The potter realized that he could lose everything if he continued to protest, he tried to pour oil on the troubled waters that he himself had churned up, after all, selling half was better than selling nothing, things would probably sort themselves out, he thought. He turned submissively to the assistant head of department at the reception desk, Could you just tell me why sales have dropped so sharply, Yes, I think it was the launch of some imitation crockery made out of plastic, it's so good that it looks like the real thing, with the added advantage that it's much lighter and much cheaper, But that's no reason for people to stop buying mine, earthenware's earthenware, it's authentic, it's natural, Tell that to the customers, look, I don't want to worry you, but I think that from now on your earthenware products will be of interest to collectors only, and there are fewer and fewer of them nowadays. The counting was done, the assistant head of department wrote on the delivery note, Received half, and said, Don't bring in any more until you hear from us, Do you think I should go on making things, asked the potter, That's up to you, I really couldn't say, And what about the returns, you've still got to return to me what you've got here, his words were so full of despair and bitterness that the assistant head of department made an attempt to sound conciliatory, We'll see. The potter got into the van and set off so abruptly that some boxes, no longer secured now that half the load had been taken out, slithered across the floor and slammed into the rear door, Oh, let it all break, who cares, he shouted angrily. He had to stop at the bottom of the exit ramp, regulations demanded that he show his card to that guard too, pure bureaucracy, no one knows why, after all, someone who enters as a supplier will leave as a supplier, but there are apparently exceptions, a case in point being Cipriano Algor, who was a supplier when he came in and now, if those threats are carried out, is just about to cease being one. It must all have been the fault of the number thirteen, destiny isn't taken in by people trying to make what came first come afterward. The van went up the ramp into the light of day, there's nothing to be done now but to go home. The potter smiled sadly, It wasn't the number thirteen, the number thirteen doesn't exist, if I had been the first to arrive, the sentence passed would have been just the same, give us half now and then we'll see.

The woman in the shantytown, the one who needed new plates and mugs, asked her husband, So did you see that pottery van, and her husband replied, Yes, I made him stop, but then I let him go, Why, If you'd seen that driver's face, you would have done the same.

13

The potter stopped the van, rolled down the windows on both sides and waited for someone to come and rob him. It is not uncommon for certain states of despair, certain of life's blows, to force their victim into dramatic decisions like this, if not worse ones. There comes a point when the confused or abused person hears a voice saying in his head, Oh well, might as well be hanged for a sheep as a lamb, and, depending on the particular situation in which he finds himself and the place where the situation finds him, he either spends his last bit of money on a lottery ticket, or places on the gaming table the watch he inherited from his father and the silver cigarette case that was a gift from his mother, or bets everything he has on red even though he knows that red has come up five times in a row, or he climbs alone out of the trenches and runs with his bayonet fixed toward the enemy's machine guns, or he stops this van, rolls down the windows, opens the doors, and waits for the people from the shantytown to attack with their customary clubs, their usual knives, and anything else they deem appropriate to the occasion, If the people at the Center don't want them, then the robbers might as well have them, was Cipriano Algor's last thought. Ten minutes passed without anyone approaching to commit the desired armed robbery, a quarter of an hour went by without even a stray dog wandering onto the road to pee against a tire or sniff the van's contents, and a whole half hour had elapsed before a dirty, evil-looking individual came over and asked the potter, Have you got a problem, do you want some help, I can give you a push if you like, it might be the battery. Now given that even the strongest spirits have moments of irresistible weakness, which is when the body fails to behave with the reserve and discretion which the spirit has spent long years teaching it, we should not be surprised that this offer of help, especially coming from a man with every appearance of being a common thief, should so have touched Cipriano Algor's heart that it brought a tear to his eye, No, thanks very much, he said, but then, just as the helpful Cyrenian was moving off, he jumped out of the van, ran to open the rear door, at the same time shouting, Sir, sir, excuse me, come back. The man stopped, So you do want some help, he asked, No, no, it's not that, What is it, then, Will you do me a favor. The man came over and Cipriano Algor said, Take these six plates and give them to your wife, it's a present, and take these six soup plates too, But I didn't do anything, said the man doubtfully, It doesn't matter, it's as if you had, and if you need a water jug, have this one, Well, I could actually do with a water jug at home, Then take it, take it. The potter piled up the plates, the flat ones, then the bowls, then put the latter on top of the former, placed them in the curve of the man's left arm, and since he was already holding the water jug in his right hand, the beneficiary had no other way of showing his gratitude than proffering the commonplace words thank you, which are as often sincere as they are not, and the surprise of a little bow of the head not at all in keeping with the social class to which he belongs, which just goes to show that we would know far more about life's complexities if we applied ourselves to the close study of its contradictions instead of wasting so much time on similarities and connections, which should, anyway, be self-explanatory.

When the man who looked like a highwayman but turned out not to be, or had simply chosen not to be on this occasion, had vanished, somewhat perplexed, back into the shantytown, Cipriano Algor set off again in his van. Not even the sharpest eyes would have noticed any difference in the pressure exerted on the van's suspension and tires, for, in matters of weight, twelve plates and one earthenware water jug mean about as much to a goods vehicle, even only a medium-sized one, as twelve white rose petals and one red rose petal would mean falling on the head of a happy bride. It was not by chance that the word happy emerged just now, indeed that is the least we can say about the expression on Cipriano Algor's face, for looking at him, no one would think that the Center had bought only half of his delivery. Unfortunately, two kilometers later, when he entered the Industrial Belt, the memory of that cruel commercial setback returned. The ominous sight of those chimneys vomiting out columns of smoke made him wonder which one of those hideous factories would be producing those hideous plastic lies, cunningly fashioned to look like earthenware, It's just not possible, he murmured, you can't copy the sound of it or the weight, and then there's the relationship between sight and touch which I read about somewhere or other, something about eyes being able to see through the fingers touching the clay, about fingers being able to feel what the eyes are seeing without the fingers actually touching it. And as if that were not torment enough, Cipriano Algor went on to ask himself, thinking of his old kiln at the pottery, how many plates, jars, mugs, and jugs could those wretched machines produce per minute, how many things could they make to replace pitchers and quart pots. The result of these and other questions that remain unrecorded was that the potter's face once more grew sad and dark, and the whole of the rest of the journey was one long cogitation on the difficult future awaiting the Algor family if the Center were to persist in its new evaluation of products of which the pottery was perhaps only the first victim. All honor to him, though, for he richly deserves it, at no point did Cipriano Algor allow his spirit to be filled with remorse for having been generous to the man who, by rights, if all that has been said about the people in the shantytowns is true, should have robbed him. On the fringe of the Industrial Belt stood a few small, very low-tech factories, which had somehow survived the giant modern factories' hunger for space and their multiplicity of products, but there they were, and seeing them as he passed by had always been a consolation to Cipriano Algor when, at certain anxious moments of his life, he had started to ponder the future of his profession. They won't last long, he thought, and this time he meant the small factories, not the pottery profession, but that was only because he had not taken the trouble to reflect for long enough, as often happens, we confidently say that it's not worth trying to reach any conclusions merely because we decide to stop halfway along the path that would lead us straight to them.

Cipriano Algor drove swiftly through the Green Belt, not glancing even once at the fields, the monotonous sight of those vast expanses of plastic, dull by nature and made dingier by dirt, always had a depressing effect on him, so imagine how it would be today, in his current state of mind, if he were to turn his gaze on that desert. Like someone who had once lifted the blessed tunic of some altar saint in order to find out if it had legs like you and me or was supported by a pair of rough-hewn posts, it had been a long time since the potter had felt tempted to stop his van and go and see for himself if there were real plants growing beneath the coverings and panels, plants that bore fruits one could smell, touch, and bite into, with leaves, tubers, and shoots that one could cook, season, and put on a plate, or if the overwhelming melancholy of what lay outside had contaminated with incurable artificiality what was growing inside, whatever that might be. After the Green Belt, the potter turned off along a secondary road, where there were the few spindly remains of a wood, a few poorly cultivated fields, a large stream containing dark and fetid water and, around a corner, the ruins of three houses with no windows now or doors, their roofs half fallen in and the rooms inside almost devoured by the vegetation that always irrupts out of the rubble as if it had been there, just waiting for that moment, ever since the first trenches were dug for the foundations. The village began a few hundred meters beyond, it consisted of little more than the road that passed through it, the few streets that flowed into it and an irregularly shaped main square slightly to one side, where a disused well, with its water pump and its great iron wheel, stood in the shade of two tall plane trees. Cipriano Algor waved to some men who were standing there talking, but, contrary to his custom when he came back from delivering goods to the Center, he did not stop, he had no idea what he wanted to do at that moment, but he certainly didn't want to have a chat, even with people he knew. The pottery and the house where he lived with his daughter and his son-in-law were at the other end of the village, out in the country, some distance from the other buildings. When he drove into the village, Cipriano Algor had slowed down, but now he was driving even more slowly, his daughter would just be putting the finishing touches to lunch, it was about that time, What shall I do, shall I tell her now or after we've eaten, he was asking himself, Best to do it afterward, I'll leave the van by the woodshed, since I wasn't going to do any shopping today, it won't occur to her to go and see if I've brought anything back with me, that way we can eat in peace or, at least, she can eat in peace, I won't, and then I'll tell her what happened, or perhaps later on this afternoon, when we're working, it would be just as bad to find out before lunch as immediately after. The road curved around where the village ended, some way beyond the last building you could see a large mulberry tree, at least ten meters high, and that was where the pottery was. The wine has been poured and we must drink it, said Cipriano Algor with a weary smile, and thought how much better it would be if he could just vomit it up. He swung the van toward the left, up the slight slope that led to the house, and halfway up he sounded the horn three times to announce his arrival, he always did this, and his daughter would think it odd if he failed to do so today.

The house and the pottery had been built on this large plot of land, doubtless once a floor for threshing or treading, in the middle of which Cipriano Algor's potter grandfather, who bore the same name as he did, decided, on some distant day of which there remains neither record nor memory, to plant the mulberry tree. The kiln, set slightly apart from the house, had been an attempt at modernization by Cipriano Algor's father, who had also been given the same name, and had replaced another ancient, not to say archaic, kiln, which, seen from outside, looked like two cone-shaped logs placed one on top of the other, the smaller one on top, and of whose origins there was no memory either. The present-day kiln had been built on those antique foundations, the same kiln that fired the batch of crockery of which the Center took only half, and which, cold now, waits to be loaded up again. With exaggerated care Cipriano Algor parked the van beneath the wooden lean-to, between two piles of dry firewood, then he thought that he might just go and have a look at the kiln and thus gain a few minutes, but he couldn't really justify doing this, there was no real reason to do so, it was not like on other occasions when he came back from the city and the kiln was working, on those days he would go and peer inside the muffle and estimate the temperature by the color of the incandescent pots, to see if the dark red had changed to cherry red, or the cherry red to orange. He stood stock-still, as if the courage he needed had got left behind somewhere en route, but it was his daughter's voice that obliged him to move, Aren't you coming in, lunch is ready. Intrigued to know what was keeping him, Marta had appeared at the door, Come on, the food's getting cold. Cipriano Algor went in, gave his daughter a kiss and then locked himself in the bathroom, a domestic utility that had been installed when he was still an adolescent and which had long been in need of enlargement and improvement. He looked at himself in the mirror, but found no new line or wrinkle on his face, It's probably somewhere inside me, he thought, then he ran the tap, washed his hands and went out. They ate in the kitchen, sitting at a large table that had known happier days and more numerous gatherings. Now, since the death of the mother, Justa Isasca, of whom we will perhaps have little more to say in this story, but whose first name we give here, since we already know her surname, the two of them sit at one end of the table, the father at the head, Marta in the place vacated by her mother and, opposite her, Marçal, when he's home. How did your morning go, asked Marta, Oh, the usual, replied her father, bending over his plate, Marçal phoned, Oh, yes, and what did he want, He said that he'd been talking to you about us going to live at the Center when he's promoted to resident guard, Yes, we did talk about that, He was annoyed because you said yet again that you didn't think it was a good idea, Well, I've had a change of heart since then and I think it will be a good thing for both of you, And what brought about this sudden change of heart, You don't want to work in the pottery all your life, No, although I enjoy what I do, You should be with your husband, one of these days you'll have children, and three generations of clay-eaters is quite enough, And you're willing to go with us to the Center, to leave the pottery, asked Marta, Leave, no, never, that's out of the question, So you're going to do everything yourself, are you, dig the clay, knead it, work at the bench and the wheel, fire the kiln, load it, unload it, clean it, then put everything in the van and go off and sell it, may I remind you that things have been difficult enough even with the help Marçal gives us on the few days he's here, Oh, I'll find someone to help me, there are plenty of lads in the village, You know perfectly well that no one wants to be a potter any more, the ones who get fed up with the country go to the factories in the Industrial Belt, they don't leave the land in order to work with clay, Yet another reason for you to leave, You don't think I'm going to leave you alone here, do you, You can come and see me now and then, Oh, Pa, please, I'm being serious, So am I, love.

Marta got up to clear away the plates and serve the soup, which it was the custom in their family to eat after the main course. Her father watched her and thought, I'm just complicating matters with this conversation, I'd better tell her now. He didn't, his daughter was suddenly eight years old, and he was saying to her, Look, it's just like when your mother kneads the bread. He rolled the block of clay backwards and forwards, pressing it and stretching it out with the heels of his hands, then he slapped it down hard on the table, squashing and squeezing, then started all over, repeating the whole operation, again and again and again, Why do you do that, his daughter asked him, So that there aren't any lumps or air bubbles left inside, that would be bad for the work, Is it the same with bread too, With bread you just have to get rid of the lumps, the air bubbles don't matter. He put to one side the compact cylinder into which the clay had been transformed and began kneading another lump, It's high time you learned, he said, but immediately regretted his words, Don't be ridiculous, she's only eight, and so he said instead, Go outside and play, go on, it's cold in here, but his daughter said that she wanted to stay, she was trying to make a doll out of a scrap of clay that kept sticking to her fingers because it was too soft, That clay's no good, try this piece, that way you'll be able to make something, said her father. Marta was looking at him anxiously, it wasn't like him to sit with his head bent over his plate to eat, as if, by hiding his face, he was also trying to hide his worries, perhaps it was the conversation he'd had with Marçal, but we talked about that and he didn't look like he does now, or perhaps he's ill, he seems worn out, drained, that day my mother said to me, Be careful, don't push yourself too hard, and I said, The only strength you need is in your arms, the technique's all in your shoulders, the rest of your body doesn't have to do anything, Oh, don't give me that, even the hairs on my head start to ache after an hour of kneading, That's just because you've been feeling a bit tired lately, Or perhaps it's because I'm getting old, Don't say things like that, Mama, you're not old, who would have thought it, though, only two weeks after that conversation, she was dead and buried, such are the surprises that death springs on life, What are you thinking about, Pa. Cipriano Algor wiped his mouth with his napkin, picked up his glass as if he were about to drink, only to set it down again without raising it to his lips. Tell me, go on, said his daughter, and in order to make it easier for him to get things off his chest, she asked, Are you still worried about Marçal or is something else bothering you. Cipriano Algor picked up his glass, drank down the rest of the wine in one gulp and replied quickly, as if the words were burning his tongue, They only took half of the shipment today, they say that fewer people are buying earthenware crockery, that some new imitation plastic stuff has come onto the market and that the customers prefer it, Well, that's hardly unexpected, it was bound to happen sooner or later, earthenware cracks and chips, it breaks easily, whereas plastic is more resistant, more resilient, The difference is that earthenware is like people, it needs to be well treated, So does plastic, but you're right, not nearly as much, And the worst thing is that they've told me not to deliver any more crockery until they ask for it, So we'll have to stop work, No, we can't stop, because when the order comes, we'll have to have the plates ready to deliver that same day, we can't just fire the kiln up after we get the order, And what do we do meanwhile, We'll have to wait, be patient, but I'll go for a drive around tomorrow and see if I can sell anything, Don't forget you did that only two months ago, so you won't find many buyers, You're not trying to discourage me, are you, No, I'm just trying to see things as they are, you yourself just said that three generations of potters in a family is quite enough, You won't make a fourth generation anyway because you're going to live at the Center with your husband, Yes, I should go, but you must come with me, Look, I've already told you that I'll never go and live at the Center, Up until now, it's been the Center that has fed us by buying the fruits of our labor, and it will go on feeding us when we live there and have nothing more to sell, Thanks to Marçal's salary, There's nothing wrong with a son-in-law supporting his father-in-law, It depends on the father-in-law, Oh, Pa, there's no point being proud at a time like this, It's not pride, What is it then, Something I can't explain, it's more complicated than mere pride, it's something else, a kind of shame, but I'm sorry, I shouldn't have said what I did, It's just that I don't want to see you go without, What if I started selling to shops in the city, it's just a matter of getting authorization from the Center, after all, if they're buying less from me, they can't really stop me selling to someone else, You know as well as I do that the shops in the city are having a real struggle just to keep their heads above water, everyone does their shopping at the Center, more and more people want to live at the Center, Well, I don't, What are you going to do if the Center stops buying our crockery altogether and the people around here start using plastic utensils, Let's hope I die before that happens, What, like Mama, She died at the potter's wheel, working, if only I was lucky enough to do the same, Don't talk about dying, Pa, The only time we can talk about death is while we're alive, not afterward. Cipriano Algor poured himself a little more wine, got up, wiped his mouth with the back of his hand as if the rules governing good table manners no longer applied once you had left the table, and said, I've got to go and break up some clay, we're running out. He was just about to leave when his daughter called to him, Pa, I've just had an idea, An idea, Yes, I'll phone Marçal and ask him to talk to the head of the buying department and try to find out what the Center's plans are, whether the reduction in demand is just a temporary thing or if it's here to stay, you know how well his bosses think of Marçal, So he says, If he says so, it's because they do, retorted Marta impatiently, adding, But if you don't want me to, I won't phone, No, go on, phone him, it's a good idea, besides, it's the only one we've got at the moment, although I doubt that a head of department at the Center will be prepared, just like that, to discuss his plans with a second-rank security guard, I know them better than he does, you don't have to work there to know what kind of stuff these people are made of, they're so full of themselves, besides, a department head is just another minion carrying out orders from above, he might even try to fool us with explanations that aren't true, just to make out how important he is. Marta listened to this whole long tirade, but did not respond. If, as seemed obvious, her father was in-tent on having the last word, she wasn't going to rob him of that pleasure. When he went out, she thought only, I must try to be more understanding, I must put myself in his place and imagine what it must be like suddenly to have no work, and to have to leave his home, his pottery, his kiln, his life. She repeated the last words out loud, His life, and her eyes immediately filled with tears, she had put herself in her father's place and was suffering what he was suffering. She glanced around her and noticed for the first time how everything looked as if it were covered in clay, not with clay dust, but with the color of clay, with all the many colors of the clay dug from the clay pit, a color left behind by three generations who, every day, had stained their hands with the dust and water of the clay, and she glanced outside too, at the bright ash gray of the kiln, the last, fading warmth that lingered from when they had last emptied it, like a house abandoned by its owners, but which waits patiently, and tomorrow, if all this is not over with once and for all, there will again be the first flame from the wood, the first hot breath of air that encircles the dry clay like a caress, and then, very gradually, the slight tremor in the air, the rapidly increasing glow, the dawning splendor, the dazzling irruption into flames. I will never see that again when we leave here, said Marta, and her heart contracted as if she were saying good-bye to the person she loved most in the world, although at that moment she could not have said which of them she meant, whether her dead mother, her suffering father, or even her husband, yes, it must be her husband, that would be logical, since she is his wife. Then she heard the dull thud of the mallet breaking up the clay, as if the sound were rising up from beneath the floor, but those blows sounded different today, perhaps because they were driven not by the simple need to work, but by impotent rage at losing that work. I'm going to phone Marçal, muttered Marta to herself, if I carry on thinking like this, I'll end up as sad as Pa. She left the kitchen and went into her father's bedroom. There, on top of the small table on which Cipriano Algor kept an account of income and expenses, was an antiquated-looking telephone. She dialed one of the numbers for the switchboard and asked to be put through to security. Almost at the same moment, a man's voice said abruptly, Security, the speed with which he had answered did not surprise her, everyone knows that in matters of security even the most insignificant of seconds counts, May I speak to security guard Marçal Gacho, Marta said, Who's speaking, It's his wife, I'm calling from home, Security guard Marçal Gacho is on duty at the moment, he can't come to the phone, In that case, could you give him a message, You're his wife, Yes, my name's Marta Algor Gacho, you can check in your records, Then you should know that we don't take messages, we merely make a note of who called, Could you just tell him to phone home as soon as possible, Is it urgent, asked the voice. Marta thought for a moment, was it urgent, no, it wasn't, it certainly wasn't a matter of life and death, there were no serious problems with the kiln, still less a premature birth, but in the end she said, Yes, it is rather urgent, I'll make a note, said the man, and hung up. With a sigh of weary resignation, Marta replaced the phone on the rest, there was nothing more to be done, it was out of their hands, security could not survive without thrusting their authority in other people's faces, even in a trivial case like this, so banal, so mundane, a wife phoning the Center because she needs to talk to her husband, she wasn't the first and she certainly wouldn't be the last. When Marta went out into the yard, the thud of the mallet no longer sounded as if it were coming from under the ground, it came from where it came, from the dark corner in the pottery where they kept the clay extracted from the clay pit. She went over to the door, but did not go in, I phoned, she said, they'll pass the message on, Let's see if they do, replied her father, and without another word, he began laying into the largest block of clay in front of him with the mallet. Marta withdrew because she knew that she should not go into a place deliberately chosen by her father in order to be alone, but also because she too had work to do, a few dozen jugs, large and small, waiting to have handles attached to them. She entered by the side door.

M arçal Gacho phoned back later that afternoon, after finishing his shift. He replied to his wife's comments with a few disconnected phrases, with no show of sadness, concern, or anger at the commercial lack of courtesy of which his father-in-law had been the victim. He spoke in an absent voice, a voice that seemed to be thinking about something else, he said, Yes, hm, yes, I understand, maybe, I suppose that's to be expected, I'll go as soon as I can, not always, absolutely, yes, I understand, no need to repeat it, and he finished the conversation with his only complete sentence, which bore no relation to what they had been talking about, Don't worry, I won't forget the shopping. Marta realized that her husband must have been speaking in front of witnesses, work colleagues, possibly a superior come to inspect the dormitory, which was why he had to put on an act, in order to avoid arousing any awkward or even dangerous curiosity. The organization of the Center had been conceived and set up according to a model of strict compartmentalization of its various activities and functions, which, although they were not and could not be entirely separate, were only able to communicate with each other via particular channels that were often hard to disentangle and identify. Obviously a mere second-rank security guard, both by virtue of the specific nature of his job as well as by virtue of his infinitesimal importance in the ranks of minor personnel, one being an unavoidable consequence of the other, is not, generally speaking, equipped with the necessary discernment and perspicacity to notice such subtleties and nuances, which are, indeed, almost volatile in their nature, but Marçal Gacho, despite not being among the most astute of his colleagues, has in his favor a certain ferment of ambition, with, as its known goal, promotion to resident guard and, eventually, of course, to first-rank security guard, and we do not know where that ambition might lead him in the near future, still less, in the distant future, if he has one. By keeping his eyes and ears open since the day he began working at the Center he soon learned when and how it was best to speak, or not speak, or simply to dissemble. After two years of marriage, Marta thought she had a pretty thorough knowledge of the husband she had ended up with in the game of give and take which is what married life almost always comes down to, she bestows all her wifely affection on him, and were it in the interests of the story to delve more deeply into their private life, she would be quite prepared to declare vehemently that she loves him, but she is not given to self-deception, and, were we to insist, it is even likely that she would ultimately admit that he sometimes seemed to her too prudent, not to say calculating, always assuming that we wanted to take our investigations into such negative areas of the personality. She was sure that her husband would have been annoyed by their conversation, that he would already have started worrying about the prospect of meeting the head of the buying department, and not out of an inferior's timidity or modesty, the fact is that Marçal Gacho has always prided himself on his declared dislike of drawing attention to himself except in the line of duty, especially, as someone who thinks he knows him well might add, when such attention will not be to his advantage. In the end, Marta's good idea had only seemed good because, at that particular moment, as her father had said, it was the only idea available. Cipriano Algor was in the kitchen, he could not possibly have heard the isolated, disconnected fragments of conversation spoken by his son-in-law, but it was as if he had read them all, and filled in the gaps, in his daughter's weary face, when one long minute later, she emerged from the bedroom. And since it wasn't worth putting his tongue to work over such a small matter, he did not waste any time and asked simply, So, and she was the one who was forced to state the obvious, He'll talk to the head of department, although Marta needn't have bothered to say that either, a shared glance would have been enough. Life is like that, full of words that are not worth saying or that were worth saying once but not any more, each word that we utter will take up the space of another more deserving word, not deserving in its own right, but because of the possible consequences of saying it. Supper passed in silence, as did the two hours spent in front of the indifferent television, and at some point, as has often happened in the last few months, Cipriano Algor fell asleep. He was frowning angrily, as if he were admonishing himself even as he drifted off for having given in so easily to sleep, when, in all fairness and justice, his feelings of annoyance and upset should have kept him awake day and night, the former so that he could absorb the full impact of the offense, the latter so as to make his suffering bearable. Exposed like that, disarmed, his head lolling back, his mouth half open, lost to himself, he presented a poignant image of hopeless abandon, like a bag that has broken and spilled its contents all over the road. Marta was staring fervently at her father, with passionate intensity, and she was thinking, This is my old father, the forgivable overstatement of someone still in the early dawn of adulthood, one should not refer to a man of sixty-four, albeit rather low in spirits like the man in question, as old, that might have been the custom in the days when teeth began to fall out at thirty and the first wrinkles to appear at twenty-five, but nowadays, it is only from eighty years onward that old age, authentic and unambiguous and from which there can be no return, nor even any pretense at a return, begins, de facto and unapologetically, to deserve the name by which we designate our last days. What will become of us if the Center stops buying our products, who will we make crockery for if it is the Center's tastes that determine everyone else's tastes, Marta was wondering, it wasn't the department head who decided to buy only half our goods, the order came down to him from above, from his superiors, from someone who cares not a jot if there is one potter more or less in the world, what happened might well be just the first step, the second step will be to stop buying altogether, we'll have to be prepared for that disaster, yes, prepared, although I'd like to know quite how one prepares oneself to be hit over the head with a hammer, and when Marçal gets promoted to resident guard, what will I do with my father, I can't possibly leave him here all alone in this house with no work to do, I just couldn't do that, cruel child, the neighbors would say, or worse, I would say the same myself, things would be different if Mama was still alive, because contrary to what people say, two weaknesses don't make for a still greater weakness, but for renewed strength, well, that's probably not true and never has been, but there are occasions when it would be nice if it was, no, Pa, no, Cipriano Algor, when I leave here, you will come with me, even if I have to use force, I don't doubt that a man can live perfectly well on his own, but I'm convinced that he begins to die as soon as he closes the door of his house behind him. As if someone had shaken him brusquely by the arm, or as if he sensed he was being talked about, Cipriano Algor suddenly opened his eyes and sat up properly in his chair. He rubbed his face with his hands and, with the slightly confused look of a child caught in flagrante, he muttered, I must have dropped off. Whenever he woke up from one of his brief naps in front of the television, he always said the same thing, I must have dropped off. But tonight is not like every other night, which is why he added in a murmur, It would have been far better if I hadn't woken up at all, at least while I was asleep, I was a potter with work to do, With one major difference, that any work you do while you're dreaming doesn't produce any real results, said Marta, So it's exactly the same as when you're awake, then, you work and work and work, and one day, you emerge from that dream or that nightmare only to be told that what you did was worthless, But it wasn't worthless, Pa, It feels as if it was, Today was a bad day, tomorrow we'll be able to think more calmly, and we'll see if we can find a way out of this problem they've created for us, Yes, we'll see, and yes, we'll think about it. Marta went over to her father and kissed him fondly, Go to bed, go on, and sleep well and rest that head of yours. At the door of his room, Cipriano Algor stopped and turned around, he seemed to hesitate for a moment, then said, as if trying to convince himself, Perhaps Marçal will phone tomorrow, perhaps he'll have some good news for us, Who knows, Pa, who knows, said Marta, he certainly seemed very keen to help.

Marçal did not phone the next day. That day, which was Wednesday, passed, Thursday and Friday passed, Saturday and Sunday passed, and only on Monday, almost a week after the incident with the shipment of crockery, did the phone ring again in Cipriano Algor's house. Despite what he had said, the potter had not gone out and about looking for buyers. He occupied the slow hours with small tasks, some of them unnecessary, like meticulously inspecting and cleaning the kiln, from top to bottom, inside and out, joint by joint, tile by tile, as if he were preparing it for the biggest firing in its history. He kneaded a lump of clay for his daughter, but he did not give the task the scrupulous attention he had lavished on the kiln, in fact, he made such a botched job of it that Marta, behind his back, had to knead it again to get rid of the lumps. He chopped firewood, swept the courtyard, and on one afternoon, during a three-hour interlude of fine, monotonous rain of the sort people used to call mizzle, he spent the whole time sitting on a log in the woodshed, sometimes staring straight ahead with the fixity of a blind man who knows that even if he turns his head in the other direction he will still not see anything, at other times studying his open palms, as if looking for a route in those lines and crossroads, either the shortest or the longest, generally speaking, choosing one or the other depends on how much or how little of a rush you are in, not forgetting, of course, those cases when someone or something is pushing you from behind, and you don't know why or where they are pushing you. On that afternoon, when the rain stopped, Cipriano Algor walked down the street to the main road, unaware that his daughter was watching him from the door of the pottery, but he did not need to say where he was going, nor did she need to ask. Stubborn creature, Marta thought, he should have gone in the van, it could start raining again at any moment. Marta's concern was only natural, it was what one would expect from a daughter, because the truth is that, no matter how often people in the past may have made statements to the contrary, the heavens never were to be trusted. This time, though, even if the drizzle does slither down again from the uniform grayness covering and encircling the earth, it won't be one of those drenching rains, the village cemetery is very close, just at the end of one of those streets leading off the main road, and Cipriano Algor, despite being of a certain age, still has the long, rapid stride that younger people use when they're in a hurry. But be they old or young, let no one ask him to hurry today. Nor would it have been wise of Marta to suggest that he take the van, because we should always visit cemeteries, especially bucolic, rural, village cemeteries on foot, not in accordance with any categorical imperative or with some ruling from above, but out of respect for mere human decency, after all, so many people have gone on walking pilgrimages to worship the shinbone of some saint that it would be inexplicable if we were to choose any other mode of transport to go to a place where we know beforehand that what awaits us is our own memory and perhaps a tear. Cipriano Algor will spend a few minutes beside his wife's grave, not in order to pray prayers he long ago forgot, nor to ask her to intercede for him up there in the empyrean, always assuming that her virtues carried her to such high places, with the one who some say can do anything, he will merely protest that what they did to me is simply unjust, Justa, they mocked my work and the work of our daughter, they say there's no interest any more in earthenware crockery, that no one wants it, and therefore we too are no longer

31

needed, we are a cracked bowl which there is no point in clamping together, you had better luck while you were alive. There are small puddles along the narrow gravel cemetery paths, the grass grows everywhere, and in less than a hundred years' time, it will be impossible to know who was buried beneath these mounds of mud, and even if people do still know, it's unlikely it will be of any real interest to them, the dead, as someone has already said, are like broken plates on which it is no longer worth placing one of those equally outmoded iron clamps that were used to hold together what had become broken or separated, or, as in the case in question, and using different words to explain the simile, the iron clamps of memory and regret. Cipriano Algor approached his wife's grave, she has been under there for three years now, three years during which she has appeared nowhere, not in the house, not in the pottery, not in bed, not beneath the shade of the mulberry tree, nor at the clay pit beneath the scorching sun, she has not sat down again at the table or at the potter's wheel, nor has she cleared out the ashes fallen from the grate, nor seen the earthenware pots and plates set out to dry, she does not peel the potatoes, knead the clay, or say, That's the way things are, Cipriano, life only gives you two days, and given the number of people who only get to live for a day and a half, and others even less, we can't really complain. Cipriano Algor stayed no longer than three minutes, he was intelligent enough to know that the important thing was not to stand there, with prayers or without, looking at the grave, the important thing was to have come, the important thing is the road you walked, the journey you made, if you are aware of prolonging your contemplation of the grave it is because you are watching yourself or, worse still, it is because you hope others are watching you. Compared with the instantaneous speed of thought, which heads off in a straight line even when it seems to us to have lost its way, because what we fail to realize is that, as it races off in one direction, it is in fact advancing in all directions at once, anyway, as we were saying, compared with that, the poor word is constantly having to ask permission from one foot to lift the other foot, and even then it is always stumbling, hesitating and dithering over an adjective or a verb that turns up unannounced by its subject, and that must be why Cipriano did not have time to tell his wife everything that was on his mind, apart from that business about it being unjust, Justa, but it may well be that the murmurings we can hear coming from him now, as he walks toward the gate leading out of the cemetery, are precisely what he had meant to say. He had stopped muttering to himself by the time he passed a woman dressed all in black who was coming in through the gate, that's how it has always been, some arrive and others leave, she said, Good afternoon, Senhor Cipriano, the respectful form of address is justified both by the age difference and because that is the custom in the country, and he replies, Good afternoon, the only reason he does not say her name is not because he does not know it, but because he thinks that this woman, dressed in heavy mourning for her husband, will play no part in the somber future events about to unfold nor in any account of them, although she, for her part, intends going to the pottery tomorrow to buy a water jug, as she is telling him now, I'll be around tomorrow to buy a water jug, I just hope it's better than the last one, the handle came off when I picked it up, it smashed to smithereens and the water went all over my kitchen floor, you can imagine the mess, although, truth be told, the poor thing was getting on a bit, and Cipriano Algor replied, There's no need to come to the pottery, I'll bring you a new jug to replace the one that broke, absolutely free, as a present from the manufacturers, Are you just saying that because I'm a widow, asked the woman, No, certainly not, just think of it as a gift, we've got a number of water jugs in stock which we might never sell, Well, in that case, Senhor Cipriano, I gratefully accept, Don't mention it, Getting a new water jug for free is quite something, Yes, but that's all it is, something, Right, then, I'll expect you tomorrow, and thank you again, See you tomorrow. Now, given that thought, as explained above, was now running simultaneously in all directions and given that feeling was keeping pace with thought, it should come as no surprise to us that the widow's pleasure at receiving a new water jug without having to pay for it should, from one moment to the next, have eased the unhappiness that had forced her out of the house on such a grim afternoon in order to visit her husband's final resting place. Of course, despite the fact that we can see her still standing at the entrance to the cemetery, doubtless rejoicing in her housewife's heart at that unexpected gift, she will still go where grief and duty called her, but once there, she will not perhaps weep as much as she thought she would. The afternoon is slowly growing dark, dim lights are beginning to come on in the houses next to the cemetery, but twilight will nevertheless last long enough for the woman, without fear of will-o'-the-wisps or of ghosts, to be able to say her Our Father and her Hail Mary, may peace be with him, may he rest in peace.

When Cipriano Algor had left the last building in the village behind him and looked toward the pottery, he saw the outside light come on, an ancient lantern in a metal case hanging above the house door, and although not a night passed without its being lit, this time he felt his heart lift and his spirits soften, as if the house were saying to him, I'm waiting for you. Barely palpable, pushed hither and thither at the whim of the invisible waves that drive the air, a few tiny drops of rain touched his face, it will not be long before the mill of the clouds begins sieving out its watery flour again, with all this rain I don't know when the pots will dry. Whether under the influence of that twilight calm or of his brief evocative visit to the cemetery, or even, which would be an appropriate reward for his generosity, because he told the woman in black that he would give her a new water jug, Cipriano Algor is not, at that moment, thinking about the disappointment of not getting something or about fears of losing something. At such a time, when you are walking over the damp ground and the outermost skin of the sky is so close to your head, no one could possibly say anything as absurd as Go back home with half your shipment unsold or Your daughter will one day leave you all alone. The potter reached the top of the road and took a deep breath. Silhouetted against the dull curtain of gray clouds, the black mulberry tree looks as black as its name suggests. The light from the lantern does not reach its crown, it does not even touch its lowest branches, only a very feeble light carpets the ground as far as the tree's thick trunk. The old kennel is there, it has been empty for years now, ever since its last inhabitant died in Justa's arms and she said to her husband, I never want another animal in my house. Something glitters in the dark entrance to the kennel, only to vanish at once. To find out what it was, Cipriano Algor crouched down to peer inside, having first walked up and down in front of it. The darkness inside is total. He realized then that his body was blocking the light from the lantern and so he moved slightly to one side. There were two glittering objects, two eyes, a dog, Or a genet, but it's more likely to be a dog, thought the potter, and he's probably right, there is no credible record of wolves in this area, and the eyes of cats, whether domestic or wild, as everyone knows, are just that, cats' eyes, or, at worst, one might think they were those of a small tiger, but an adult tiger would never fit inside a kennel that size. Cipriano did not mention cats or tigers when he went into the house, nor did he say a word about his visit to the cemetery, and, as for the jug he is going to give to the woman in black, he realizes that this is not a matter to be dealt with now, so what he said to his daughter was this, There's a dog outside, then he paused, as if expecting a response, and added, Underneath the mulberry tree, in the kennel. Marta had just had a wash, changed her clothes and sat down to rest for a moment before beginning to prepare supper, she is not, therefore, in the most receptive frame of mind to consider the places that lost or stray dogs might pass through or stop off in, You'd better just leave him, if he's the kind of animal who simply dislikes traveling at night, he'll be gone by morning, she said, Have you got something there I can give him to eat, asked her father, A few leftovers from lunch, a bit of bread, he won't need water, plenty of that fell from the sky, Fine, I'll take it out to him, If that's what you want, Pa, but you know he'll never leave our door again if you do, You're probably right, and if I was in his position, I'd do exactly the same. Marta put the leftover food on an old plate that she kept on the ledge by the fireplace and poured a bit of soup over it, Here you are, and mark my words, this is just the beginning. Cipriano Algor took the plate and was already halfway out of the kitchen when his daughter asked him, Do you remember what Mama said when Constante died, that she didn't want any more dogs in the house, Yes, I remember, but I'm sure that if she was still alive, I wouldn't be the one taking this plate of food out to that dog she didn't want, replied Cipriano Algor, and he left without hearing his daughter's murmured comment, You may be right. The rain was falling again, it was the same deceptive drizzle, the same fine dancing dust of water that masks distances, even the whitish figure of the kiln seemed ready to up and leave, and the van looked more like a phantom coach than a modern vehicle with an internal combustion engine, even though it is not, as we know, of recent make. Beneath the mulberry tree, the water was sliding off the leaves in large, infrequent drops, now one, now another, at random, as if the laws of hydraulics and of hydrodynamics, still in operation outside the precarious umbrella of the tree, did not apply there. Cipriano Algor put the plate of food down on the ground and took a few steps back, but the dog did not leave its shelter, You must be hungry, said the potter, or perhaps you're one of those dogs with too much self-respect, perhaps you don't want me to see how hungry you are. He waited another minute, then withdrew and went back into the house, but he did not completely close the door. He could not see much through the crack, but he managed to make out a black shape emerging from the kennel and going over to the plate, and he noticed too that the dog, for it was a dog and not a wolf or a cat, glanced first at the house and only then lowered its head to the food, as if it felt that it owed this degree of consideration to the person who had come out in the rain, defying the elements, to satisfy its hunger. Cipriano closed the door properly and went into the kitchen, He's eating, he said, If he was that hungry, he'll have finished by now, said Marta, smiling, Yes, you're right, her father smiled back, always assuming that the dogs of today are the same as the dogs of yesteryear. Theirs was a simple supper and quickly served. When they had finished, Marta said, Another day with no news from Marçal, I can't understand why he doesn't phone, just to say something, a word would do, it's not as if I was expecting a long speech, Perhaps he hasn't had time to talk to the head of the buying department, Then why doesn't he at least tell us that, You know perfectly well that things aren't easy over there, said the potter, in unexpectedly conciliatory mode. The daughter looked at him, surprised more by the tone of voice than by the meaning of the words, It's not like you to make excuses to justify Marçal's actions, she said, Well, I like him, You may like him, but you don't really take him seriously, The person I can't take seriously is the security guard that the nice, friendly lad I used to know has turned into, Now he's a nice, friendly man, and working as a security guard is no less dignified or honest than working at any other equally dignified, honest job, But it isn't just any other job, What's the difference, The difference is that your Marçal, as we know him today, is all security guard, he's a security guard from his head to toes, and I suspect that he's even a security guard in his heart, Pa, please, you shouldn't talk like that about your daughter's husband, You're right, forgive me, today shouldn't be a day for criticism and recrimination, Why not, Because I went to the cemetery and because I gave a water jug to a woman in the village and because we have a dog outside, all of which are events of great importance, What's all this about a water jug, The handle came off in her hand and the jug was smashed to smithereens, These things happen, nothing lasts forever, But she had the decency to admit that the jug was old, and that's why I thought I should give her a new one and pretend that the other one was flawed, well, why pretend, I'll just give it to her anyway, there's no need for explanations, Who is this woman, She's Isaura Estudiosa, the one who was widowed a few months back, She's still a young woman, Now, look, I'm not considering getting married again if that's what you're thinking, If I did think that, I wasn't aware of it, though perhaps I should have, then you wouldn't have to stay here all alone, since you refuse to come and live with us at the Center, Really, I have no intention of getting married again, still less to the first woman I meet, as for the rest, I would be grateful to you not to spoil my evening, Sorry, I didn't mean to. Marta got up, cleared away the plates and the knives and forks, folded up the tablecloth and the napkins, it would be a great mistake to assume that the craft of potter, even, as in this case, when the pottery produced is fairly crude stuff, even when carried out in a small, graceless village, as you may already have deduced this one to be, is incompatible with the delicacy and good manners that distinguish the present-day upper classes, who have forgotten or been ignorant since birth of the brute nature of their own great-great-great-grandparents and of the bestial nature of their great-great-great-grandparents. These Algors are quick to learn what they are taught and are capable of putting it into practice in order to drive it home, and Marta, who belongs to the latest generation and is, therefore, more favored by developmental aids, already had the great good fortune of going to study in the city, well, those large centers of population have to have some advantages over villages. And if she ended up being a potter, it was because of her conscious and manifest vocation as a modeler, although her decision was also influenced by the fact that she had no brothers who could carry on the family tradition, not forgetting the last and most important reason, the powerful bonds of filial love that would never allow her to adopt some kind of God-will-provide-if-you're-lucky attitude toward her parents in their old age. Cipriano Algor had turned on the television, only to switch it off again shortly afterward. If anyone had asked him what he had seen or heard between turning the television on and switching it off, he would not have known what to say, but he would simply have refused outright to answer if asked a different question, You seem very distracted, what are you thinking about. He would say, What do you mean, I'm not distracted, merely in order not to confess his childish concern for the dog, whether it would still be safe in the kennel or if, hunger satisfied and energies restored, it would have continued on its way, in search of better food or of a master who lived in a place less exposed to gales and fine rain. I'm going to my room, Marta said, I've been putting off doing some sewing for ages now, but I really must get it done tonight, No, I won't be staying up much longer either, said her father, I feel worn out, even though I haven't done a thing, You did, you kneaded some clay and you serviced the kiln, You know perfectly well that that piece of clay will have to be kneaded again and that the kiln hardly needed a stonemason to work on it, still less a wet nurse to take care of it, The days are all the same, it's the hours that are different, when a day comes to an end it always does so with its twenty-four hours all present and correct, even when those hours contained nothing, but that's not the case with either your days or your hours, Ah, Marta, philosopher of time, said her father and kissed her on the head. His daughter returned the kiss and said, smiling, Don't forget to go and see how your dog is, For the moment, he's just a dog who happened to turn up here and who decided that the kennel would provide a good shelter from the rain, he might be ill or injured, he might perhaps have a collar with the phone number of the person we should call, he might belong to someone in the village, they probably beat him and he ran away, and if that's the case, he won't still be here tomorrow morning, you know what dogs are like, their master is still their master even when he punishes them, so don't go calling him my dog just yet, I haven't even seen him, I don't even know if I like him, Ah, but you know that you want to like him, and that's a start, So now you're a philosopher of feelings too, are you, said her father, Assuming you do keep the dog, what will you call him, asked Marta, It's too early to think about that, If he's still here tomorrow, that name should be the first word he hears from your mouth, Well, I won't call him Constante, that was the name of a dog who won't be coming back to his mistress and who wouldn't find her if he did, so perhaps it would be appropriate to call this one Lost, There's another even more appropriate name, What's that, Found, That's no name for a dog, Neither is Lost, Yes, you're right, he was lost and now he is found, that's what we'll call him then, See you in the morning, Pa, sleep well, Yes, see you in the morning, and don't sit up too late sewing, you'll strain your eyes. When his daughter had gone to bed, Cipriano Algor opened the door into the yard and looked over at the mulberry tree. A steady drizzle was still falling and there was no sign of life inside the kennel. I wonder if he's in there, thought the potter. He provided himself with a false excuse not to go and look, That's all I need, getting soaked to the skin for the sake of a stray dog, once was enough. He went to his room and lay down, read for half an hour, and then fell asleep. In the middle of the night, he woke up and turned on the light, the clock on his bedside table said half past four. He got out of bed, picked up the flashlight he kept in a drawer and opened the window. It had stopped raining, he could see stars in the dark sky. Cipriano Algor switched on the flashlight and pointed the beam at the kennel. The light was not strong enough to be able to see inside, but Cipriano Algor did not need to, two glittering lights would do, two eyes, and there they were.

Ever since they sent him back with half the load of crockery, which, it should be said, has not yet been unloaded from the van, Cipriano Algor has, from one moment to the next, ceased to deserve his reputation, gained over a lifetime of much work and few holidays, as an early-rising worker. Now he gets up when the sun has already risen, he washes and shaves more slowly than is strictly necessary for an already closely shaven face and for a body accustomed to cleanliness, he has a light breakfast but takes his time over it, and finally, with no visible lifting of the low spirits with which he got out of bed, he goes to work. Today, however, having spent what remained of the night dreaming about a tiger that came and ate from his hand, he threw off his blankets as soon as the sun had begun to paint the sky with light. He did not open the window, merely opened the shutter door just a crack to see what the weather was like, at least that is what he thought, or what he wanted to think that he thought, but the fact is that he was not in the habit of doing so, for this man has lived long enough to know that the weather is always there, sunny, as today promises to be, or rainy, as it was yesterday, indeed, when we open the window and raise our nose to the air above, it is merely to find out if the weather is doing what we want it to do. To cut a long story short, when he peered outside, what Cipriano Algor wanted to know was if the dog was still there waiting for them to give him another name or if, tired of waiting fruitlessly, it had gone off in search of a more diligent master. All that could be seen of the dog was a pair of floppy ears and a snout resting on its crossed front paws, but there was no reason to suspect that the rest of its body was not inside the kennel. He's black, said Cipriano Algor. When he had taken the dog the food last night, it had seemed to him that the dog was indeed that color, or, as someone will doubtless remark, that absence of color, but it had been dark, and if in the dark even white cats are gray, the same, in even darker circumstances, could be said of a dog seen for the first time beneath a mulberry tree when a fine, nocturnal drizzle was dissolving the line separating beings from things, making those beings more like the things which, sooner or later, they will all become. The dog is not really black, although his snout and ears almost are, the rest of his body is a more general gray, with an admixture of other tones from dark to solid black. Given that the potter is sixty-four years old with all the usual visual problems that age brings with it, and that he stopped wearing glasses because of the heat of the kiln, one cannot really blame him for saying, He's black, since the first time he saw the dog was at night and in the rain, and, now, distance makes the early-morning light seem misty. When Cipriano Algor finally goes over to the dog, he will see that he will never again be able to say, He's black, but that he would be guilty of grave misrepresentation were he to say, He's gray, especially when he discovers that the dog has a thin white blaze, like a delicate cravat, that goes from his chest to his belly. Marta's voice rings out from the other side of the door, Pa, wake up, the dog's waiting for you. I am awake, I'm just coming, replied Cipriano Algor, immediately regretting those last few words, it was puerile, almost ridiculous, for a man his age to get as excited as a child who has been brought a long-dreamed-of present, when we all know that, on the contrary, in places like this, the more useful a dog is, the more it is valued, an unnecessary virtue in toys, and as far as dreams and their fulfillment are concerned, a dog could not possibly satisfy someone who, that same night, had dreamed of a tiger. Despite this self-administered dressing-down, Cipriano Algor did not take excessive care this morning when getting washed and dressed, he merely pulled on his clothes and left the bedroom. Marta asked him, Shall I make him something to eat, No, afterward, food would only distract him at the moment, Go on, then, off you go and tame your wild beast, He's not a wild beast, poor thing, I've been watching him from the window, Yes, I had a look at him too, What do you think, Well, I don't think he belongs to anyone around here, Some dogs never leave their backyards, they live and die there, apart from those cases where they're taken out into the country to be hanged from the branch of a tree or finished off with a bullet in the head, That's hardly the kind of thing I want to start the day with, thank you, No, you're right, it isn't, so let's start the day in a less human but more compassionate way, said Cipriano Algor, going out into the yard. His daughter did not follow him, she stood in the doorway, watching, It's his party, she thought. The potter took a few steps and, then, in a clear, firm voice, although not too loud, he pronounced the chosen name, Found. The dog had already looked up when he saw him, and now, hearing the name he had been waiting for, he emerged fully from the kennel, a slim young dog, neither big nor small, with a curly coat, he really was gray, gray tending to black, with that narrow white blaze, like a cravat, dividing his chest in two. Found, the potter said again, advancing a few more steps, Found, come here. The dog stayed where he was, he had his head up and was slowly wagging his tail, but he did not move. Then the potter crouched down so that his eyes were on the same level as the dog's, and this time he said in an intense, urgent tone of voice, as if giving expression to some deep personal need of his, Found. The dog took one step forward, then another, not stopping this time, until he was within reach of the arm of the person calling him. Cipriano Algor held out his right hand, almost touching the dog's nostrils, and waited. The dog sniffed a few times, then stretched out his neck so that his cold nose brushed the tips of the fingers held out to him. The potter slowly moved his hand toward the dog's nearest ear and stroked it. The dog took the final step, Found, Found, said

Cipriano Algor, I don't know what your name was before, but from now on your name is Found. It was only then that he noticed that the dog had no collar and that his fur was not just gray, it was covered in mud and bits of vegetation, especially his legs and belly, a clear sign that he had taken a difficult route across fields and open countryside, rather than traveling comfortably by road. Marta had joined them, she brought a plate with a little food on it for the dog, nothing too substantial, just enough to confirm the meeting and to celebrate the baptism, You give it to him, said her father, but she said, No, you give it to him, I'll have plenty of other opportunities to feed him. Cipriano Algor put the plate down on the ground, then got up with some difficulty, Oh, my knees, what I wouldn't give to have even the knees I had last year, Does it make that much difference, asked his daughter, At this time of life even a day makes a difference, the only saving grace is that sometimes things improve. The dog Found, and now that he has a name, we really shouldn't use any other, not dog, which we slipped in just now out of force of habit, nor animal nor creature, which serve to describe anything that does not form part of the mineral and vegetable kingdoms, although now and again we might still have to resort to these variants in order to avoid boring repetition, which is the only reason why, instead of Cipriano Algor, we have sometimes written potter, or man, old man, and Marta's father. Anyway, as we were saying, the dog Found, having cleaned the food off the plate with two licks of his tongue, providing clear proof that yesterday's hunger had still not been satisfied, raised his head like someone waiting for a second helping, at least that was how Marta interpreted the gesture, which is why she said, Be patient, lunch comes later, make do with what you've got in your stomach, but it was a hasty judgment, the kind that so often emerges from the human brain, for despite his continuing hunger, which he would be the last to deny, it was not food that was preoccupying Found at that moment, what he wanted was to be given some sign as to what he should do next. He was thirsty, but he could obviously go and quench his thirst in one of the many puddles of water left around the house by the rain, yet something held him back, something which, if we were talking about human feelings, we would not hesitate to call scrupulousness or good manners. Since they had put his food on a plate rather than making him grub for it in the mud, then surely the water should be drunk from some special receptacle too. He must be thirsty, said Marta, dogs need a lot of water, There are plenty of puddles over there, said her father, he's not drinking from them because he doesn't want to, If we're going to keep him, we can't let him go drinking water from puddles as if he had neither house nor home, obligations are obligations. While Cipriano Algor occupied himself making various seminonsensical utterances, the sole aim of which was to accustom the dog to the sound of his voice, but in which deliberately, and as insistently as a refrain, the word Found was repeated several times, Marta brought a large, earthenware bowl full of clean water, which she placed beside the kennel. In defiance of all skepticism, which is more than justified after the thousands of stories one has read and heard about dogs and their exemplary lives and sundry miracles, we must, nevertheless, point out that Found again surprised his new owners by remaining exactly where he was, face to face with Cipriano Algor, apparently waiting until he had finished what he had to say. Only when the potter had stopped speaking and made a gesture as if to dismiss him did the dog turn around and take a drink. I've never known a dog behave like that before, Marta remarked, The worst thing, after all this, replied her father, would be for someone around here to tell me that the dog belongs to him, Oh, I don't think that will happen, I'd guarantee that Found doesn't come from these parts, sheepdogs and watchdogs don't do what he did, After lunch, I'll go and ask around, You could deliver Isaura's water jug too, said Marta not even bothering to hide a smile, Yes, I'd already thought of that, as my grandfather always said, never put off till tomorrow what you can do today, replied Cipriano Algor, his gaze elsewhere.

Found had finished drinking his water and, since neither the potter nor his daughter seemed to want to pay him any attention, he decided to lie down at the entrance of the kennel where the ground was not so wet.

After breakfast, Cipriano Algor went to choose a water jug from the store, placed it carefully in the van, among the boxes of plates, so that it wouldn't fall over, and then he got in, sat down and started the engine. Found looked up, he obviously knew that such a noise always precedes a departure, which is immediately followed by a disappearance, but previous experience must have taught him that there is a way of preventing such calamities from happening, at least sometimes. He got up on his long legs, frantically wagging his tail, as if he were wielding a whip, and, for the first time since he had come seeking asylum, Found barked. Cipriano Algor drove the van slowly toward the mulberry tree and stopped a little way from the kennel. He thought he understood what Found wanted. He opened the door on the passenger side and held it open, and before he'd had time to issue an invitation, the dog was already in. Cipriano Algor had not intended taking him along, he had simply thought he would go from house to house asking if anyone knew such and such a dog, with this color coat and this appearance, with this cravat and these moral virtues, and while he was describing these various characteristics, he would pray to all the saints in heaven and to all the devils on earth, please, by fair means or foul, to make whoever he asked say that they had never in their life owned or heard of such a dog. Having Found there in the cab with him would eliminate the monotony of describing him and save him repeating himself, he would just have to ask, Is this dog yours, or is it yours, my friend, depending on the degree of intimacy with his interlocutor, and await the response, No, or Yes, if the former, he would pass rapidly on to the next house in order not to allow time for emendation, if the latter, he would carefully observe Found's reactions, because he wasn't the kind of dog to allow himself to be taken away on false pretenses by the mendacious demands of some would-be master. Marta, who, at the sound of the engine starting up, had appeared at the door of the pottery, her hands covered in clay, wanted to know if the dog was going too. Her father said, Yes, he is, and a moment later the courtyard was as deserted and Marta as alone as if this were the first time this had happened to either of them.

Before going to see Isaura Estudiosa, the origin and provenance of whose surname, by the way, as with those of Gacho and Algor, remains a mystery, the potter knocked on the doors of twelve neighbors and had the satisfaction of hearing all of them give the same answer, It's not mine, No, I don't know whose it could be. A tradesman's wife took such a liking to Found that she made a generous offer to buy him, an offer immediately rejected by Cipriano Algor, and in the three houses where no one replied he could hear the violent barking of canine guards, which allowed the potter, by some tortuous reasoning, to conclude that Found could not possibly belong there, as if, according to some universal law for domestic animals, it was written that where there is one dog there cannot be another. Cipriano Algor finally stopped the van outside the house of the woman in black and knocked on the door, and when she opened it, he said good morning rather more loudly than was natural, the person to blame for this sudden vocal confusion being Marta with her preposterous idea of marrying off two old widowed people, a description deserving of the severest censure, it must be said, at least as far as Isaura Estudiosa is concerned, for she can be only forty-five at most, and if, for the sake of accuracy, one had to add a few more years, you would never think it to look at her. Oh, good morning, Senhor Cipriano, she said, I've come to keep my promise and bring you your water jug, Thank you so much, but you really shouldn't have bothered, after our conversation in the cemetery yesterday, it struck me that people and things are much the same, they have a certain life span, they last for a while, then, like everything else in the world, they come to a sudden end, On the other hand, one water jug can be replaced by another water jug just by discarding the shattered remains of the old one and filling the new one with water, but that's not the case with people, it's as if with the birth of each new person, the mold they emerged from was broken, which is why everyone is different, Well, people don't emerge from molds, of course, but I think I know what you mean, That was just the potter in me talking, pay no attention, here you are, and I hope the handle of this one doesn't fall off quite so soon. The woman put out her hands to take hold of the body of the water jug, then clutched it to her and thanked him again, Thank you so much, Senhor Cipriano, and it was then that she saw the dog in the van, That dog, she said. Cipriano Algor felt a shock go through him, it had never occurred to him that Isaura Estudiosa might be the dog's owner, and yet she had said That dog as if she had recognized him, with a look of surprise on her face that could have belonged to someone who has at last found what they were looking for, you can imagine with what reluctance Cipriano Algor asked, Is he yours, hoping that she would say no, and you can imagine too his relief when he heard her answer, No, he's not mine, but I remember seeing him wandering around a couple of days ago, I even called to him, but he pretended not to hear me, he's a lovely dog, When I got home yesterday after visiting the cemetery, I found him huddled inside the kennel we've got under the mulberry tree, the one that belonged to another dog we had, Constante, anyway, it was getting dark and all I could see were these two eyes shining, He was obviously looking for the right master, Well, I don't know if I'm the right master for him, he may already have one, that's what I've been trying to find out, Where, here, asked Isaura Estudiosa, and without waiting for an answer, she went on, I wouldn't bother if I were you, that dog isn't from around here, he came from a long way away, from another place, from another world, Why do you say another world, Oh, I don't know, perhaps because he seems so different from other dogs nowadays, You've hardly seen him, What I saw was enough, in fact, if you don't want him, I'll have him, If it was any other dog, I might let you, but we've already decided to take him in, assuming we don't find his owner, of course, So you really want him, We've even given him a name, What's he called, then, Found, A good name for a lost dog, That's exactly what my daughter said, Well, if you want to keep him, don't go looking for an owner, But I have a duty to return him to his owner, that's what I'd like someone to do if I lost a dog, If you do, though, you'll be going against the wishes of the dog, after all, he was obviously looking for somewhere else to live, Seen from that point of view, you might be right, but there are laws and customs to take into account, Oh, forget about laws and customs, Senhor Cipriano, just take what is already yours, Isn't that a bit selfish, Sometimes you have to be a bit selfish, Do you think so, I do, Well, I've really enjoyed talking to you, So have I, Senhor Cipriano, See you again sometime, Yes, see you again. With the jug clutched to her breast, Isaura Estudiosa watched from her door as the van turned around to retrace its route, she looked at the dog and at the man who was driving, the man waved good-bye with his left hand, the dog must have been thinking about home and about the mulberry tree that served as his sky.

Thus Cipriano Algor returned to the pottery much sooner than he had anticipated. The advice given by Isaura Estudiosa, or Isaura, for short, had been sensible, reasonable, and absolutely appropriate to the situation, and, if it were ever applied to the general functioning of the world, there would be no difficulty whatsoever in fitting it into the plan for an order of things that would prove little less than perfect. The truly admirable thing about it, though, was the fact that she had said it all so naturally, without even thinking, just as someone wanting to say that two and two are four doesn't waste time thinking that two and one are three, and then that three and one are four, Isaura is right, the main thing is to respect the animal's wishes and the will that transformed those wishes into action. Whoever the owner is, or, prudent correction, whoever the owner was, will have no right now to turn up here and declare, That dog is mine, when all the appearances and all the evidence show that if Found had the human gift of speech, he would have only one answer to give, Well, I don't want him as my master. Meanwhile, a thousand blessings on that broken water jug, blessings on the idea of giving the woman in black a new jug, and let us add, in anticipation of what is to come, blessings on the encounter that took place on that damp, drizzly afternoon, all dripping water, all material and spiritual discomfort, which, as we know, apart from those who have suffered a recent loss, is not the kind of weather that encourages the grief-stricken to go to a cemetery to mourn for their dead. There is no doubt about it, Found is a most favored dog, he can stay where he wants for as long as he wants. And there is another reason that only redoubles Cipriano Algor's relief and satisfaction, which is that he will not now have to knock at the door of Marçal's parents, who also live in the village and with whom he is not on the best of terms, and relations would certainly not have been helped if he had passed by their door and ignored them. Besides, he is sure that Found does not belong to them, as long as he has known them, their taste in matters canine has always inclined them to bulldogs or to some other kind of guard dog. We've had a good morning, Cipriano Algor said to the dog.

A few minutes later, they were back at the house. Once the van was parked, Found looked hard at his master, realized that, for the moment, he was relieved of his duties as navigator, and so off he went in the direction of the kennel, but with the unmistakable air of someone who has just decided that now is the moment to reconnoiter the surrounding area. Should I put him on a chain, the potter wondered anxiously, and then, when he saw what the dog was doing, sniffing around and here and there marking his territory with urine, No, I don't think I need to keep him chained up, if he had wanted to run away, he could have done so already. He went into the house and heard his daughter's voice, she was talking on the phone, Hang on, hang on, Pa's just got back. Cipriano Algor took the receiver and immediately asked, Any news. At the other end of the line, after a moment's silence, Marçal Gacho proceeded like someone who considers that this is no way to begin a conversation between two people, father-in-law and son-in-law, who have not spoken to each other for a whole week, which is why he calmly said good morning and asked how Cipriano was, to which Cipriano Algor responded with his own brusque good morning and then without a pause or without any kind of transitional phrase, I've been waiting, I've been waiting a whole week, how would you feel in my place, Sorry, but I only managed to talk to the head of the buying department this morning, Marçal explained, refraining from pointing out to his father-in-law, even indirectly, the unnecessary brusqueness of his tone, And what did he say, That they haven't come to a decision yet, but that you are not the only person affected, and that merchandise falling in and out of favor is an almost daily occurrence at the Center, that's what he said, an almost daily occurrence, And what was your impression, What was my impression, Yes, judging by his tone of voice, his way of looking at you, did you get the feeling that he was trying to be helpful, You know from your own experience that they always give the impression that their minds are on other things, Yes, you're right, And to be absolutely frank, I don't think they'll buy any more crockery from you, it's all very simple for them, either the product sells or it doesn't, they don't care about anything else, there's no halfway house for them, And what about me, what about us, is it that simple for us, is it a matter of indifference to us, is there no halfway house for us either, asked Cipriano Algor, Look, I did what I could, I am just a security guard, after all, No, you couldn't really have done much more, said the potter, and his voice faltered on that last word. Marçal Gacho felt sorry for his father-in-law when he noticed that change of tone and he tried to amend that somber prognostication, He didn't close the door entirely, he just said that they were reviewing the situation, and so we shouldn't lose hope, I'm too old for hopes, Marçal, I need certainties, immediate certainties, ones that don't pin their hopes on a tomorrow that might not even be mine, Yes, I understand, Pa, life's full of ups and downs, everything changes, but don't despair, you've got us, Marta and me, with the pottery or without it. It was easy to see where Marçal was going with this speech on family solidarity, in his view, all their problems, present or future, would be resolved on the day that the three of them moved to the Center. In different circumstances and in a different mood, Cipriano Algor would have responded sharply, but now, either because resignation had touched him with its melancholy wing, or because he had definitely not lost the dog Found, or even, who knows, because of a brief conversation between two people objectively separated by a water jug, the potter replied gently, I'll pick you up on Thursday at the usual time, and if you hear anything meanwhile, give us a call, and without leaving space for Marçal to respond, he brought the dialogue to a close, I'll pass you back to your wife. Marta exchanged a few more words with Marçal, said We'll just have to see what happens, then said good-bye until Thursday and hung up. Cipriano Algor had gone outside, he was in the pottery, sitting at one of the wheels, his head bowed. It was there that a massive heart attack had cut short the life of Justa Isasca. Marta went and sat at the other wheel and waited. After a long minute, her father looked at her, then looked away. Marta said, You didn't spend much time in the village, No, I didn't, Did you ask at all the houses to see if anyone knew the dog, if he had an owner, I asked at a few, then decided it wasn't worthwhile continuing, Why, Is this an interrogation, No, Pa, it's just me trying to take your mind off things, I hate to see you sad, I'm not sad, Well, a bit low then, I'm not low either, All right, whatever, but now tell me why you thought it wasn't worthwhile asking, I decided that if the dog did have an owner in the village and had run away, and having had the opportunity to go back, had decided not to, it was because he wanted to be free to find another owner, Seen from that point of view, you might be right, That's exactly what I said, To whom. Cipriano Algor did not answer. Then, since his daughter merely sat there calmly looking at him, he added, To that woman in the village, What woman, The one with the water jug, Oh, of course, you went to give her the water jug, That's why I put it in the van, Of course, Right, So, if I understand you correctly, she was the one who explained that it wasn't worth going looking for Found's owner, Yes, she was, She's obviously an intelligent woman, She seems to be, And she kept the water jug, Is there something wrong with that, Don't get angry, Pa, we're only talking, what on earth could be wrong about something as simple as giving someone a water jug, Exactly, anyway, we've got more important matters to deal with, and there you are trying to pretend that everything's going swimmingly, That's precisely what I want to talk to you about, Then why all this beating around the bush, Because I like talking to you as if you weren't my father, I like to pretend, if you want, that we are just two people who love each other very much, father and daughter who love each other because they are father and daughter, but who would love each other as friends even if they weren't, You'll have me crying soon, you know how treacherous tears can be at my age, You know I'd do anything to see you happy, Yet you're trying to convince me to go and live at the Center, knowing that it would be the worst thing that could possibly happen to me, Oh, I thought the worst thing that could possibly happen to you was to be separated from your daughter, That's not fair, perhaps you should apologize, You're right, it wasn't fair, forgive me. Marta got up and embraced her father, Forgive me, she said again, It doesn't matter, said the potter, if we weren't in this unfortunate situation, we wouldn't be talking like this. Marta drew her bench nearer to her father, sat down and, taking his hand, said, I had an idea while you were out with the dog, What's that, Let's just put to one side the question of the Center, that is, whether you decide to come with us or not, Agreed, It's not going to happen tomorrow or even next month, and when the time comes you can decide whether to go or whether to stay, it's your life, Thanks for the breathing space, I'm not giving you breathing space, What else have we got to deal with then, After you'd gone out, I came in here to work, I'd gone into the storeroom to have a look around and I noticed that we were very low on small flower vases, so I came in here to make a few, when suddenly, with the clay already on the wheel, I realized how absurd it was just to continue carrying blindly on, What do you mean blindly, Well, no one has ordered any flower vases, small or large, no one is waiting impatiently for me to finish them so that they can rush out and buy them, and when I say vases I could as easily say any of the other things we make, large or small, useful or useless, Yes, I understand, but, even so, we ought to be prepared, Prepared for what, For when the new orders come in, And what shall we do until that happens, what shall we do if the Center stops buying altogether, how are we going to live and on what, are we just going to wait until the mulberries ripen and Found manages to catch the odd decrepit rabbit, That won't be a problem for you and Marçal, Look, Pa, we agreed that we wouldn't talk about the Center, All right, go on, Now, just supposing that, by some miracle, the Center changes its mind, which I don't believe it will, and neither do you if you're honest, how long are we going to sit here with our arms folded or else making things for no reason and for no one, In our situation, I don't really see what else we can do, Well, I'm of a different opinion, And what different opinion is that, what marvelous idea have you come up with, That we should make other things, If the Center is going to stop buying some things, it's highly unlikely that they're going to buy anything else, They might and they might not, What are you talking about, woman, I think we should start making dolls, Dolls, exclaimed Cipriano Algor in a tone of scandalized surprise, I've never heard such a ridiculous idea, Yes, Father dear, dolls, statuettes, effigies, figurines, mannequins, knickknacks, or whatever you want to call them, but don't go telling me it's a ridiculous idea until you've seen the result, You talk as if you were sure the Center was going buy these dolls of yours, The only thing I'm sure about is that we can't just sit around here waiting for the world to fall in on us, It's already fallen in on me, Everything that falls on you, falls on me, so you help me and I'll help you, After all this time making crockery, I've probably lost my touch when it comes to modeling, The same goes for me, but if our dog got lost in order to be found, as Isaura Estudiosa so intelligently explained, who knows, we might find our lost touch, yours and mine, in the clay, It's a risky venture and it could end badly, But, as we've seen, even things that aren't risky ventures can end badly. Cipriano looked at his daughter in silence, then he picked up a piece of clay and shaped it roughly into a human figure. Where do we begin, he asked, Where you always have to begin, at the beginning, replied Marta.

Authoritarian, paralyzing, circular, occasionally elliptical stock phrases, also jocularly referred to as nuggets of wisdom, are a malignant plague, one of the very worst ever to ravage the earth. We say to the confused, Know thyself, as if knowing yourself was not the fifth and most difficult of human arithmetical operations, we say to the apathetic, Where there's a will, there's a way, as if the brute realities of the world did not amuse themselves each day by turning that phrase on its head, we say to the indecisive, Begin at the beginning, as if beginning were the clearly visible point of a loosely wound thread and all we had to do was to keep pulling until we reached the other end, and as if, between the former and the latter, we had held in our hands a smooth, continuous thread with no knots to untie, no snarls to untangle, a complete impossibility in the life of a skein, or indeed, if we may be permitted one more stock phrase, in the skein of life. Marta said to her father, Let's begin at the beginning, and it was as if all they needed to do was to sit down at the table and start making dolls with fingers grown suddenly agile and exact, having regained their former skill after a long period of inactivity. These are the delusions of the pure and the unprepared, the beginning is never the clear, precise end of a thread, the beginning is a long, painfully slow process that requires time and patience in order to find out in which direction it is heading, a process that feels its way along the path ahead like a blind man, the beginning is just the beginning, what came before is nigh on worthless. Which is why what Marta said next was less categorical, We have only three days to prepare our presentation, I think that's what businessmen and executives call it, Sorry, I don't quite follow, said her father, Today is Monday, you'll be picking Marçal up on Thursday afternoon, so that's the day when you'll have to show the head of the buying department our proposals for making the dolls, complete with drawings, models, prices, in short, everything we can think of that might persuade them to buy the dolls and help them come to a decision now rather than next year. Without noticing that he was repeating what he had already said, Cipriano Algor asked, Where do we begin, but Marta's answer this time was different, We'll have to choose half a dozen types, possibly fewer, we don't want to make things too complicated for ourselves, then work out how many dolls we can make each day, though that depends on our approach, whether we model the clay like sculptors or make identical male and female figures and then dress them according to their professions, they'll all be standing figures, of course, in my experience, they're so much easier, What do you mean by dress them, Well, dress them, by attaching to the naked figurine the clothes and accessories that characterize them and give them their individuality, I reckon that two people working like that would make faster progress, then it's just a matter of taking care with the painting, there can't be any smudges, You've obviously given this a lot of thought, said Cipriano Algor, Not really, I just thought quickly, And well, Now don't make me blush, And a lot, even though you deny it, Look, I'm blushing already, Fortunately for me, you're capable of thinking quickly, thinking a lot and thinking well all at the same time, You know what they say, naught so blind as a father's love, And what figures do you think we should make, Nothing very antiquated, a lot of professions have completely disappeared, and no one nowadays has a clue what those people did, what purpose they served, on the other hand, I don't think they should be too modern either, that's what plastic dolls are for, with their heroes, their Rambos, their astronauts, their mutants, their monsters, their superpolice and their superbandits, and, of course, their weapons, we mustn't forget their weapons, Hm, I was just thinking, because every now and then I too manage to squeeze a few ideas out of my brain, although not as good as yours, Now, now, no false modesty, it doesn't suit you, How about taking a look at the illustrated books we've got, for example, that old encyclopedia your grandfather bought, if we can find some models for the dolls in there, then we'll also have solved the problem of which drawings I should take with me to show the head of the buying department, he won't know that we've copied them and even if he did he wouldn't care, That idea would have gotten an A+ on the old scale of school marks, No, a B would do me fine, it attracts less attention, Let's get down to work then.

As you might imagine, the Algor family library is neither extensive nor of exceptional quality. You wouldn't expect great erudition in ordinary people and in a place like this, far from civilization, but even so, there are some two or three hundred books on the shelves, some old, some, the majority, middle-aged, the rest more or less recent, although only a few are brand new. The village does not have a shop that would do justice to the old and noble name of bookshop, there is only a small stationer's that will order any textbooks needed from publishers in the city, and, very rarely, some literary work that has been touted a lot on the radio or the television and whose content, style, and intentions correspond satisfactorily to the average interests of the inhabitants. Although Marçal Gacho is not himself a keen and conscientious reader, when he turns up at the pottery with a book as a gift for Marta, it must be said that he knows the difference between what is good and what is merely mediocre, although good and mediocre are such slippery terms that they always give rise to discussion and disagreement. The encyclopedia that father and daughter have just opened on the kitchen table was considered the best of its kind at the time of publication, whereas today its only use would be to find out about areas of knowledge no longer considered useful or which, at the time, were still only articulating their first, hesitant syllables. Placed in a line, one after another, the encyclopedias of today, yesterday, and the-day-before-the-day-before-yesterday represent successive images of frozen worlds, interrupted gestures, words in search of their ultimate or penultimate meaning. Encyclopedias are like immutable cycloramas, prodigious projectors whose reels have gotten stuck and which show, with a kind of maniacal fixity, a landscape which, because it is condemned to be only and for all eternity what it was, will at the same time grow older, more decrepit and more unnecessary. The encyclopedia purchased by Cipriano Algor's father is as magnificent and as useless as a line of poetry we cannot quite remember. However, let us not be too proud and ungrateful, let us remember the sensible advice of our elders who counseled us to keep what was no longer necessary because, sooner or later, although we might not think so, it could turn out to be just the thing we needed. Today, bent over the old, yellowing pages, breathing in the smell of damp, untouched by the air, unstirred by the light, and that has been contained for years in the smooth thickness of the paper, father and daughter are learning the value of that lesson, looking for what they need in something they had thought to be useless. They found along the way a member of the academy wearing a plumed bicorn hat, rapier, and lace ruffles on his shirt, they found a clown and a tightrope walker, they found a skeleton with a scythe and immediately moved on, they found a horsewoman astride a horse and an admiral without a ship, they found a bullfighter and a man in a smock, they found a boxer and his opponent, they found a carabineer and a cardinal, they found a hunter and his hound, they found a sailor on leave and a magistrate, a jester and a Roman in a toga, they found a dervish and a halberdier, they found a customs officer and a seated scribe, they found a postman and a fakir, they also found a gladiator and a hoplite, a nurse and a juggler, a lord and a minstrel, they found a fencer and an apiarist, a miner and a fisherman, a fireman and a flautist, they found two puppets, they found a boatman, they found a navvy, they found saints of both sexes, they found a demon, they found the holy trinity, they found soldiers and military men of every rank, they found a deep-sea diver and a skater, they saw a sentinel and a woodcutter, they saw a cobbler wearing glasses, they found a man playing a drum and another playing a cornet, they found an old lady in a shawl and head scarf, they found an old man smoking a pipe, they found a venus and an apollo, they found a gentleman in a top hat, they found a bishop in a miter, they found a caryatid and an Atlas, they found one lancer mounted and another on foot, they found an Arab wearing a turban, they found a Chinese mandarin, they found an aviator, they found a condottiere and a baker, they found a musketeer, they found a maid in an apron and an Eskimo, they found a bearded Assyrian, they found a pointsman, they found a gardener, they found a naked man with all his muscles exposed and a map of the nervous and circulatory systems, they also found a naked woman, although she was covering her pubis with her right hand and her breasts with her left. They found many more, but they were not suited to the ends they had in sight, either because making the figures would be too complicated in clay, or because overuse of celebrities past and present with whose portraits, accurate, plausible or imagined, the encyclopedia was filled, might be misinterpreted as a lack of respect and even give rise, in the case of famous people still alive, or of famous people now deceased but with greedy and vigilant heirs, to ruinous court cases for offence caused, moral damage and defamation of character. Who are we going to choose from this lot, then, asked Cipriano Algor, we can't possibly cope with more than three or four, you have to remember that, between now and then, while the Center is making up its mind whether to buy them, we're going to have to practice a lot if we want to deliver good-quality, presentable work, Yes, I know, Pa, but I think it would be best if we proposed six different figures, said Marta, then they'll either accept and we can divide production into two phases, in which case it will be a question of agreeing to deadlines, or, and, initially, this is much more likely, they themselves will choose two or three dolls to start with just to see if their customers would be interested and to test out their possible response, And it might go no farther than that, That's true, but I think we'll have more chance of persuading them if we show them six designs, numbers count, numbers influence people, it's a question of psychology, Psychology never was my strong point, Nor mine, but even in our ignorance we sometimes have prophetic flashes of intuition, Well, don't aim those prophetic flashes at your father's future, he has always preferred to find out each day what that day decides to bring him, good or ill, What the day brings is one thing, what we ourselves contribute to the day is quite another, The day before, Sorry, I don't know what you mean, The day before is what we bring to the day we're actually living through, life is a matter of carrying along all those days-before just as someone might carry stones, and when we can no longer cope with the load, the work is done, the last day is the only one that is not the day before another day, Now you're just trying to depress me, No, I'm not, but if I am, perhaps you're to blame for that, To blame for what, With you I always end up talking about serious things, All right, let's talk about something even more serious, let's select our dolls. Cipriano Algor is not a man much given to laughter, and even frank smiles are rare on his lips, at most one might notice a brief change in his eyes as if the gleam there had suddenly shifted slightly, sometimes one might glimpse a slight compression of the lips as if they had been forced to smile in order to stop themselves from smiling. No, Cipriano Algor is not a man much given to laughter, but, as we have just seen, today there was a smile awaiting its chance to appear. Right then, he said, I'll choose one and then you choose one, until we've got six, but remember we have to bear in mind the ease of the work and the known or presumed taste of our customers, OK, you begin, The jester, said the father, The clown, said the daughter, The nurse, said the father, The Eskimo, said the daughter, The mandarin, said the father, The naked man, said the daughter, No, you can't choose the naked man, you'll have to choose another one, the Center won't want a naked man, Why not, Well, because he's naked, The naked woman then, That's even worse, But she's covering herself up, Covering yourself up like that is worse than showing everything, How come you know so much about the subject, Because I've lived, I've looked, I've read, and I've felt, What does reading do, You can learn almost everything from reading, But I read too, So you must know something, Now I'm not so sure, You'll have to read differently then, How, The same method doesn't work for everyone, each person has to invent his or her own, whichever suits them best, some people spend their entire lives reading but never get beyond reading the words on the page, they don't understand that the words are merely stepping stones placed across a fast-flowing river, and the reason they're there is so that we can reach the farther shore, it's the other side that matters, Unless, Unless what, Unless those rivers don't have just two shores but many, unless each reader is his or her own shore, and that shore is the only shore worth reaching, Well observed, said Cipriano Algor, you have shown yet again that old people should never argue with the younger generations, we always end up losing, although we do learn a thing or two on the way, Glad to have been of help, Now let's get back to the sixth doll, It can't be the naked man, No, Or the naked woman, No, Then let's have the fakir, In general, fakirs, like scribes and potters, are sitting down, when he's standing up, a fakir is just like any other man, and sitting down, he'll be smaller than the others, In that case, what about the musketeer, The musketeer would do, but we'd have to find a solution to the problem of the sword and the feathers on his hat, we could probably manage the feathers, but the sword would have to be fixed to his leg and then it would look more like a splint, All right then, the bearded Assyrian, Suggestion accepted, let's have the bearded Assyrian, he's easy and compact, And I did consider the hunter and his hound, but the dog would cause even more difficulties than the musketeer's sword, Not to mention the shotgun, said Cipriano Algor, and speaking of dogs, I wonder what

Found is up to, we've forgotten all about him, He's probably sleeping. The potter got up and drew back the curtain, I can't see him in his kennel, he said, He'll be going about his business, fulfilling his duties as guardian of the house, keeping an eye on the neighborhood, Unless he's escaped, Stranger things have happened, but I doubt it. Anxious and fearful, Cipriano pulled open the door and almost tripped over the dog. Found was stretched out on the mat, lying diagonally across the sill, his nose pointing toward the door. When he saw his master appear, he got up and waited. Here he is, announced the potter, So I see, replied Marta from inside. Cipriano Algor was about to close the door, He's looking at me, he said, Well, he's looked at you before, But what shall I do, Either close the door and leave him outside or invite him in and then close the door, Don't be funny, I'm not being funny, you'll have to decide today whether you want Found in the house, but, you know, if he comes in now, that will be it, Old Constante used to come in whenever he wanted to, Yes, I know, but normally he preferred the independence of the kennel, whereas, unless I'm very much mistaken, this dog needs company as much as it needs food, That seems a good enough reason, said the potter. He opened the door wide and made a gesture, Come in. Without taking his eyes off his master, Found took one timid step, then, as if to indicate that he wasn't quite sure he had understood the order, he stopped. Come in, said the potter again. The dog advanced slowly and came to a halt in the middle of the kitchen. Welcome to our house, said Marta, but you had better know the house rules right away, a dog's necessities, both solid and liquid, should be taken care of outside, the same goes for food, now, during the day, you can come and go as much as you like, but at night, you go to your kennel, so as to guard the house, and I don't want you thinking I'm less well-disposed toward you than your master is, and to prove it I was the one who told him that you are a dog who needs company. During the time this lecture lasted, Found didn't take his eyes off her for a moment. He couldn't understand what Marta wanted of him, but his small dog's brain knew that in

63

order to learn, one must look and listen. He waited for a few moments after Marta had finished speaking, then he curled up in a corner of the kitchen, although he did not even have time to warm the spot up, for as soon as Cipriano Algor had sat down, Found got to his feet again and went and lay by his chair. And just so that there should be no doubts in the minds of his owners that he had a clear understanding of his duties and responsibilities, barely a quarter of an hour had passed before he got up from there and went and lay down beside Marta. A dog knows when someone needs his company.

The next three days were a time of intense activity, nervous excitement and a continual making and unmaking of things on paper and in clay. Neither of them wanted to admit that the end result of the idea, and of the work they were having to do in order to give the idea some solidity, would be a blunt refusal, with no explanation other than, The fashion for dolls like that has passed. Shipwrecked, they were rowing toward an island not knowing if it was a real island or only the ghost of an island. Marta was the better of the two at drawing and so she was the one charged with transferring to paper their six chosen types, using the classic grid method to enlarge them to the exact size the dolls would be once they had been fired, a hand span tall, not the span of her hand, which is small, but of her father's. Then came the business of coloring the drawings, this was complicated not because of any excessive care taken in the execution, but because they had to choose and combine colors which they did not know for certain would be right for the figures since the encyclopedia, illustrated in accordance with the printing technology of the time, contained minutely detailed copperplate engravings, but the only chromatic effects were apparent shades of gray achieved by printing black lines on the unvarying white of the paper. The easiest of all was, of course, the nurse. White hat, white blouse, white skirt, white shoes, all white white white, impeccably white, as if she were an angel of charity come down to earth with the mission of relieving suffering and mitigating pain until, eventually, another identi-

cally dressed angel had to be summoned urgently in order to miti-
gate and relieve her own pain and suffering. The Eskimo did not
present any great problems either, the skins he wore could be
painted half beige half gray, with a few whitish patches to imitate
the skin of a bear turned inside out, the main thing was that the Eskimo should have the face of a real Eskimo, which is what he came
into the world to be. As for the clown, the problems would be far
greater, simply because he was poor. If, instead of being the miser-
able ragamuffin he is, he were a rich clown, any bright, cheerful
color would do, with a random scattering of sequins on his conical
hat, his shirt, and his trousers. But he is a poor clown, really poor,
and wears a heterogeneous collection of rags showing neither taste
nor judgment and patched from head to toe, a waistcoat that comes
down to his knees, baggy trousers, a collar large enough to accom-
modate three necks, a bow tie that looks like a ceiling fan, a lurid
shirt, and shoes as big as barges. All of this can be painted in whatever colors one chooses, because, since he is only a poor clown, no
one is going to waste their time checking to see if the colors of this
clay creation have the decency to respect the colors the poor man
would have worn even when he was not working as a clown. The
trouble is that this jack-of-all-trades is not actually going to be
any easier to model than the hunter or the musketeer, which had
seemed so problematic at the start. Moving from the clown to the
jester will mean moving from similar to same, from alike to identical, from comparable to analogous. Though applied differently, the
colors used on one can be used on another, and a couple of changes
of costume will rapidly transform the jester into a clown and the
clown into a jester. Strictly speaking, they almost duplicate each
other as regards clothes and function, the only difference between
them, from the social point of view, is that clowns do not usually
visit the palaces of kings. The mandarin in his long gown and the
Assyrian in his tunic will require no special attention either, a few
touches to the Eskimo's eyes and he can serve as a Chinaman, and

the Assyrian's long, curly beard will make it easier to work on the lower part of the face. Marta made three series of drawings, the first totally faithful to the originals, the second stripped of all accessories, the third free of any superfluous detail. This would facilitate any examination of them by whichever Center official has the last word on the fate of the proposal, and, if the proposal is approved, it will perhaps make less likely, or so they hope, the possibility of any future complaints about a discrepancy between the drawing and the actual clay figure. Until Marta had moved on to the third series of drawings, Cipriano Algor had merely watched what was happening, frustrated because he could not help, all the more because he was aware that any intervention on his part would only slow up the work and make it more difficult. However, as soon as Marta had placed before her the piece of paper on which she would set down the last series of drawings, he rapidly gathered together the initial copies and went out to the pottery. She just had time to say, Don't get annoyed if it doesn't come out right the first time. Hour after hour, during the rest of that day and part of the following day, until it was time for him to go and fetch Marçal from the Center, the potter made, unmade and remade dolls in the form of nurses and mandarins, jesters and Assyrians, Eskimos and clowns, almost unrecognizable at the first attempt, but gradually gaining form and meaning as his fingers began to interpret for themselves and in accordance with their own laws the instructions transmitted to them by the brain. Indeed, very few people are aware that in each of our fingers, located somewhere between the first phalange, the mesophalange, and the metaphalange, there is a tiny brain. The fact is that the other organ which we call the brain, the one with which we came into the world, the one which we transport around in our head and which transports us so that we can transport it, has only ever had very general, vague, diffuse and, above all, unimaginative ideas about what the hands and fingers should do. For example, if the brain-in-our-head suddenly gets an idea for a painting, a sculpture, a piece of music or literature, or a clay figurine, it simply sends a signal to that effect and then waits to see what will happen. Having sent an order to the hands and fingers, it believes, or pretends to believe, that the task will then be completed, once the extremities of the arms have done their work. The brain has never been curious enough to ask itself why the end result of this manipulative process, which is complex even in its simplest forms, bears so little resemblance to what the brain had imagined before it issued its instructions to the hands. It should be noted that the fingers are not born with brains, these develop gradually with the passage of time and with the help of what the eyes see. The help of the eyes is important, as important as what is seen through them. That is why the fingers have always excelled at uncovering what is concealed. Anything in the brain-in-our-head that appears to have an instinctive, magical, or supernatural quality— whatever that may mean—is taught to it by the small brains in our fingers. In order for the brain-in-the-head to know what a stone is, the fingers first have to touch it, to feel its rough surface, its weight and density, to cut themselves on it. Only long afterward does the brain realize that from a fragment of that rock one could make something which the brain will call a knife or something it will call an idol. The brain-in-the-head has always lagged behind the hands, and even now, when it seems to have overtaken them, the fingers still have to summarize for it the results of their tactile investigations, the shiver that runs across the epidermis when it touches clay, the lacerating sharpness of the graver, the acid biting into the plate, the faint vibration of a piece of paper laid flat, the orography of textures, the crosshatching of fibers, the alphabet of the world in relief. And then there are colors. The truth is that the brain knows far less about colors than one might suppose. It sees more or less clearly what the eyes show it, but when it comes to converting what it has seen into knowledge, it often suffers from what one might call difficulties in orientation. Thanks to the unconscious confidence of a lifetime's experience, it unhesitatingly utters the names of the colors it calls elementary and complementary, but is immediately lost, perplexed and uncertain when it tries to formulate words that might serve as labels or explanatory markers for the things that verge on the ineffable, that border on the incommunicable, for the still nascent color which, with the eyes' often bemused approval and complicity, the hands and fingers are in the process of inventing and which will probably never even have its own name. Or perhaps it already does—a name known only to the hands, because they mixed the paint as if they were dismantling the constituent parts of a note of music, because they became smeared with the color and kept the stain deep inside the dermis, and because only with the invisible knowledge of the fingers will one ever be able to paint the infinite fabric of dreams. Trusting in what the eyes believe they have seen, the brain-in-the-head states that, depending on conditions of light and shade, on the presence or absence of a wind, on whether it is wet or dry, the beach is white or yellow or golden or gray or purple or any other shade in between, but then along come the fingers and, with a gesture of gathering in, as if harvesting a wheat field, they pluck from the ground all the colors of the world. What seemed unique was plural, what is plural will become more so. It is equally true, though, that in the exultant flash of a single tone or shade, or in its musical modulation, all the other tones and shades are also present and alive, both the tones or shades of colors that have already been named, as well as those awaiting names, just as an apparently smooth, flat surface can both conceal and display the traces of everything ever experienced in the history of the world. All archaeology of matter is an archaeology of humanity. What this clay hides and shows is the passage of a being through time and space, the marks left by fingers, the scratches left by fingernails, the ashes and the charred logs of burned-out bonfires, our bones and those of others, the endlessly bifurcating paths disappearing off into the distance and merging with each other. This grain on the surface is a memory, this depression the mark left by a recumbent body. The brain asked a question and made a request, the hand answered and acted. Marta put it another way, Now you're getting the hang of it.

I'm off to do men's work now, so this time you'll have to stay at home, Cipriano Algor told the dog, who had run after him when he saw him going over to the van. Obviously Found did not need to be told to get in, they just had to leave the van door open long enough for him to know that they would not immediately shoo him out again, but the real cause of his startled scamper toward the van, strange though this may seem, was that, in his doggy anxiety, he was afraid that they were about to leave him on his own. Marta, who had come out into the yard talking to her father and was walking with him to the van, was holding in her hand the envelope containing the drawings and the proposal, and although Found has no very clear idea what envelopes are or what purpose they serve, he knows from experience that people about to get into cars usually carry with them things which, generally speaking, they throw onto the back seat even before they themselves get in. In the light of these experiences, one can see why Found's memory might lead him to assume that Marta was going to accompany her father on this new trip in the van. Although Found has been here only a few days, he has no doubt that his owners' house is his house, but his incipient sense of property does not yet authorize him to look around him and say, All this is mine. Besides, a dog, whatever his size, breed, or character, would never dare to utter such grossly possessive words, he would say at most, All this is ours, and even then, reverting to the particular case of these potters and their property, movables and immovables, the dog Found, even in ten years' time, will be incapable of thinking of himself as the third owner. The most he might possibly achieve when he is a very old dog is a vague, obscure feeling of being part of something dangerously complex and, so to speak, full of slippery meanings, a whole made up of parts in which each individual is, simultaneously, both one of the parts and the whole of which he is a part. These challenging ideas, which the human brain is more or less capable of conceiving but not, without great difficulty, of explaining, are the daily bread of the various canine nations, both from the merely theoretical point of view and as regards their practical consequences. Don't go thinking, however, that the canine spirit is like a serene cloud floating by, a spring dawn full of gentle light, a lake in a garden with white swans swimming, were that the case, Found would not have suddenly started whimpering pitifully, What about me, he was saying, what about me. In response to the heartrending cries of this soul in torment, Cipriano Algor, weighed down as he was by the responsibility of the mission taking him to the Center, could find nothing better to say than, This time you'll have to stay at home, but what consoled the troubled creature was seeing Marta take two steps back once she had handed the envelope to her father, and thus Found realized that they were not, in fact, going to leave him all alone, for even though each part in itself constitutes the whole to which it belongs, as we hope we demonstrated above with a + b, two parts, when put together, make a very different total. Marta waved a weary good-bye to her father and went back into the house. The dog did not follow her at once, but waited until the van, having driven down the hill to the road, had disappeared behind the first house in the village. When, shortly afterward, he went into the kitchen, he saw his mistress sitting in the same chair where she had been working during the last few days. She kept wiping her eyes with her hands as if trying to rid them of some shadow or some pain. Doubtless because he was still green in years, Found had not yet had time to gain clear, definitive, formed opinions on the importance or meaning of tears in the human being, however, considering that these liquid humors are frequently manifest in the strange soup of sentiment, reason and cruelty of which the said human being is made, he thought it might not be such a very grave mistake to go over to his weeping mistress and gently place his head on her knees. An older dog and, always assuming that age carries with it a double load of guilt, a dog of an unnecessarily cynical turn of mind, would take a sardonic view of such an affectionate gesture, but this would only be because the emptiness of old age had caused him to forget that, in matters of feeling and of the heart, too much is always better than too little. Touched, Marta slowly stroked his head and, since he did not move, but remained there staring up at her, she picked up a piece of charcoal and began sketching out on a piece of paper the first lines of a drawing. At first, her tears prevented her from seeing properly, but, gradually, as her hand grew more confident, her eyes grew clearer, and the dog's head, as if emerging from the depths of a murky pool, appeared to her in all its beauty and strength, all its mystery and probing curiosity. From this moment on, Marta will love the dog Found as much as we know Cipriano already loves him.

The potter had left behind him the village and the three isolated houses that no one now will ever raise from the rubble, he is skirting the stream choked with putrefaction and will cross the abandoned fields, past the neglected wood, he has made this journey so often that he scarcely notices the surrounding desolation, but today he has two things to worry about, both of which justify his air of absorption. One of them, of course, the commercial proposition that is taking him to the Center, requires no particular mention, but the other, and there is no way of knowing how long its effects will last, is the one that most troubles his mind, the impulse, utterly unexpected and inexplicable, to pass by the street where Isaura Estudiosa lives, to find out what has happened to the water jug, to find out if subsequent use has revealed some hidden defect, if it pours well, if it keeps the water cool. Cipriano has known the woman for some time now, indeed it is highly unlikely that there is anyone in the village whom he has not met in the course of his work, and although he had never been on what you might call friendly terms with the family, he and his daughter had gone to the cemetery to attend the funeral of the late Joaquim Estudioso, which is the family name by which Isaura, who, on marrying, had moved from a village far from there, came, as is the custom in villages, to be known. Cipriano Algor can remember giving her his condolences as he left the cemetery, in the same spot where months later they would meet again to exchange impressions and promises regarding a broken water jug. She was just another widow in the village, another woman who would wear deep mourning for six months, to be followed by another mandatory six months of half-mourning, and she was one of the fortunate ones, because there was a time when deep mourning and half-mourning, each in turn, weighed upon the female body and, who knows, upon the soul too, for a whole year of days and nights, not to mention those women who, given their age, the law of custom obliged to live swathed in black until the end of their days. Cipriano Algor was wondering if, in the long interval between those two meetings in the cemetery, he had ever spoken to Isaura Estudiosa, and the answer surprised him, I've never even seen her, and it was true, except that we should not really be so very surprised by the apparent singularity of that situation, for in matters ruled by fate, it makes no difference whether you live in a city of ten million or in a village of only a few hundred inhabitants, only what has to happen happens. At this point, Cipriano Algor's thoughts tried to divert to Marta, it seemed as if he was about to blame her again for the fantasies going round and round in his head, but what prevailed were his ever-vigilant impartiality and honesty of judgment, Don't try to hide from the facts, leave your daughter out of it, she said only the words you wanted to hear, now all that matters is finding out whether you have anything more to give Isaura Estudiosa than a water jug, and, of course, to find out if she is prepared to receive

72

what you imagine you have to give her, always assuming that you do manage to imagine something. This soliloquy was brought up short by that, for the moment, insuperable obstacle, and this abrupt halt was immediately pounced upon by his second motive for concern, or, rather, three motives in one, the clay figurines, the Center, and the head of the buying department, What, I wonder, if anything, will come of all this, muttered the potter, a syntactically rather contorted sentence which, if looked at closely, could serve equally well to deck out, in the frivolous clothes of distracted, tacit complicity, the more exciting topic of Isaura Estudiosa. Too late, we are already driving through the Agricultural Belt, or Green Belt, as it continues to be called by those who simply love to disguise harsh reality with words, this slush color that covers the ground, this endless sea of plastic where the greenhouses, all cut to the same size, look like petrified icebergs, like gigantic dominoes without the spots. Inside, there is no cold, on the contrary, the men who work there suffocate in the heat, they cook in their own sweat, they faint, they are like sodden rags wrung out by violent hands. There are many ways to describe it, but the suffering is the same. Today the van is empty, Cipriano Algor no longer belongs to the guild of sellers for the irrefutable reason that people are no longer interested in buying what he produces, now he has only half a dozen drawings on the seat beside him, which is where Marta left them, and not on the back seat as the dog Found imagined, and those drawings are this journey's sole, fragile compass, fortunately he had already left home when the person who made those drawings felt, for a few moments, that all was lost. They say that landscape is a state of mind, that we see the outer landscape with our inner eye, but is that because those extraordinary inner organs of vision are unable to see these factories and these hangars, this smoke devouring the sky, this toxic dust, this never-ending mud, these layers of soot, yesterday's rubbish swept on top of the rubbish of every other day, tomorrow's rubbish swept on top of today's rubbish, here even the most contented of souls would require only the eyes in his head to make him doubt the good fortune he imagined was his.

Beyond the Industrial Belt, on the road, on the bleak plots occupied by the shacks, lies a burned-out truck. There is no sign of the merchandise it was carrying, merely a few scattered, blackened boxes bearing no clue as to contents or origin. Either the cargo went up in flames along with the truck, or they managed to unload it before the fire took hold. The surrounding area is wet, which indicates that the fire brigade must have attended the accident, but since the truck has been completely destroyed, it would seem that they arrived too late. Parked in front are two cars belonging to the traffic police, on the other side of the street is a military personnel carrier. The potter slowed down in order to get a better look at what had happened, but the policemen, brusque, blank-faced, immediately ordered him to drive on, he just had time to ask if anyone had died, but they ignored him. Drive on, drive on, they shouted, frantically waving their arms. Just then Cipriano Algor glanced to the side and noticed soldiers moving around among the shacks. Because of the speed he was traveling at he could see no more, except that they seemed to be forcing the inhabitants out of their houses. It was clear that this time the attackers had not been satisfied with merely looting. For some unknown reason, for such a thing had never happened before, they had set fire to the truck, perhaps the driver had responded with equal violence to his attackers or perhaps the organized groups from the shantytowns had decided to change their tactics, although it is hard to see what possible advantage they could hope to gain from such violent actions, which, on the contrary, will only serve to justify the equally violent actions taken by the authorities, As far as I know, thought the potter, this is the first time that the army has gone into the shantytowns, up until now, the police have always dealt with any trouble, in fact, the shantytowns relied on them, the police would arrive, sometimes ask a few questions, sometimes not, arrest a few men, and life would go on, as if nothing had happened, and sooner or later the arrested men would reappear. The potter Cipriano Algor has forgotten all about Isaura Estudiosa, the woman to whom he had given the water jug, and about the head of the Center's buying department, the man whom he will have to convince of the aesthetic appeal of the dolls, his thoughts are focused entirely on the truck so badly damaged by the flames that not a trace of its load remains, if, that is, it was carrying one. If, if. He repeated the conjunction like someone who, having tripped over a stone, turns back in order to trip over it once more, as if by striking it again and again a spark might emerge from within, but the spark seems disinclined to appear, Cipriano Algor had already spent a good three kilometers on this thought and was on the point of giving up, Isaura Estudiosa was preparing to dispute the territory with the head of the buying department, when the spark suddenly leaped up, and illumination came, the truck had not been burned by the people in the shacks, but by the police themselves, it was just an excuse to bring in the army, I'll bet my boots that's what happened, muttered the potter, and then he felt very tired, not from the mental effort, but because he had suddenly seen what the world was like, how there are many lies and no truths, well, there must be some out there, but they are continually changing, and not only does a possible truth give us insufficient time to consider its merits, we also have to check first that this possible truth is not, in fact, a probable lie. Cipriano Algor glanced at his watch, but if he was hoping to find out what time it was, this gesture was of little help, because since it had been made as an immediate consequence of the debate between the probability of lies and the possibility of truths, it was as if he had been hoping to find the answer in the position of the hands, a right angle that would mean yes, an acute angle that would place before him a prudent perhaps, an obtuse angle telling him roundly no, a straight line saying that it would be best not to think about it any more. When he glanced back at the face of the watch moments later, the hands were indicating only hours, minutes, and seconds, they had reverted to being the real, functional, obedient hands of a watch, I'm on time, he said, and it was true, he was on time, after all, we are always on time, behind time, in time, but never out of time, however often we are told that we are. He had reached the city now and was heading along the avenue that would lead him to his destination, ahead of him, traveling faster than the van, ran his thoughts, head of the buying department, head of department, head of buying, Isaura Estudiosa, poor thing, had been left behind. At the end of the avenue, on the towering gray wall blocking the road he could see an enormous white, rectangular poster on which these words were written in letters of a brilliant intense blue, LIVE IN SECURITY, LIVE AT THE CENTER. Underneath, in the right-hand corner, there is another short line, just four words, in black, which Cipriano Algor's myopic eyes cannot manage to decipher at this distance, and yet they deserve no less consideration than the big message, we could, if we wished, describe them as complementary, but never as merely superfluous, ASK FOR MORE INFORMATION was their advice. The poster appears there from time to time, repeating the same words, only the colors vary, sometimes they show images of happy families, the thirty-five-year-old husband, the thirty-three-year-old wife, an eleven-year-old son, a nine-year-old daughter, and also, but not always, a grandfather or grandmother of indefinite age, with white hair and few wrinkles, all obliged to smile and reveal their respective sets of teeth, perfect, white, gleaming. Cipriano Algor took the invitation as a bad omen, he could already hear his son-in-law announcing, for the hundredth time, that they would all go and live at the Center as soon as he got his promotion to resident guard, We'll end up on a poster like that, he thought, we've already got Marta and her husband as the couple, I would be the grandfather if they managed to persuade me, there's no grandmother, she died three years ago, and for the moment there are no grandchildren, but in their place in the photo we could put Found, a dog always looks good in advertisements featuring happy families, strange though

76

this may seem, dealing as we are with an irrational being, it confers on the people a subtle, although instantly recognizable, touch of superior humanity. Cipriano Algor turned right into a street that runs parallel with the Center, all the time thinking, no, that would be impossible, the Center doesn't take dogs or cats, at most they take caged birds, parakeets, canaries, goldfinches, waxbills, and, no doubt, aquarium fish, especially if they are of the tropical variety with too many fins, but no cats, far less dogs, that's all we need, to leave poor Found homeless again, once was enough, just then an image slips into Cipriano Algor's thoughts, the image of Isaura Estudiosa standing next to the cemetery wall, then the image of her clutching the water jug to her breast, then her waving to him from the door, but she vanished as quickly as she had appeared, for he has arrived at the entrance to the basement where one leaves one's merchandise and where the head of the buying department checks the delivery note and the invoices and decides what to take and what not to take.

Apart from the truck being unloaded, there were only two others awaiting their turn. The potter reckoned that, logically speaking, since he had not come to deliver any goods, he would not have to take his place in the line of trucks. The matter in hand was the sole responsibility of the head of the buying department and not to be dealt with by subordinate and, on principle, cautious clerks, therefore he would simply have to go up to the counter and say why he was there. He parked the van, picked up the papers, and, with what he intended to be a firm step, but in which any averagely attentive observer would have spotted the deleterious effect of unsteady legs on the body's equilibrium, he crossed the traffic lane spattered with old and more recent oil stains and approached the reception desk, where he greeted the man on duty with a polite good afternoon and asked to speak to the department head. The clerk carried off his verbal request and returned at once, He's just coming, he said. Ten minutes passed before one of the assistant heads of department appeared, not the head of department, as requested. Cipriano Algor did not like having to tell his story to someone who, generally speaking, serves no purpose other than to act as a screen for the person who is hierarchically his superior. Fortunately, from Cipriano Algor's explanation it quickly became clear to the assistant head of department that taking the matter further would only create work for him, and that, one way or another, the decision would have to be made by the person who had been appointed for that purpose and who, for that very reason, earned what he earned. The assistant head of department, as one can easily conclude from his behavior, is a social malcontent. He cut off the potter in mid-flow, snatched up the proposal and the drawings, and went away. A few minutes later, he reemerged from the door he had gone through, beckoned to Cipriano Algor to approach, we need hardly remind you that, in such situations, legs do tend to become even unsteadier, and having shown the potter in, the assistant head of department returned to his own duties. The head of the buying department was holding the proposal in his right hand, and the drawings were lined up on his desk in front of him, like cards in a game of patience. He gestured to Cipriano Algor to sit down, a stroke of good fortune that allowed the potter to stop thinking about his legs and to launch into an exposition of his subject, Good afternoon, sir, forgive me for coming and disrupting your work like this, but my daughter and I had this idea, well, to be honest, it was more her idea than mine. The head of department interrupted him, Before you go on, Senhor Algor, it is my duty to inform you that the Center has decided not to buy any more goods from your firm, I am referring to the goods you had been supplying us with until the recent suspension, which has now become definitive and irrevocable. Cipriano Algor bowed his head, he would have to watch his words, whatever happened he could not say or do anything that would put at risk a possible deal with the dolls, which is why he merely murmured, I was expecting as much, sir, but, if you'll allow me to say so, it's very hard, after all these years as a supplier, to hear such words from you, That's life, lots of things come to an end, And lots of things begin as well, Never the same ones though. The head of department paused, fiddled with the drawings as if distracted, then said, Your son-in-law came to see me, At my request, sir, at my request, just to help me out of the quandary I was in, not knowing whether to continue production, Well, now you know, Yes, sir, I do, You must also be aware that it has always been a rule at the Center, indeed a point of honor, not to tolerate pressure or interference from third parties in our commercial activities, still less from Center employees, It wasn't pressure, sir, But it was interference, In that case, I'm sorry. Another pause. How much more of this am I going to have to listen to, thought the potter in some distress. He wouldn't have to wait long to find out, the head of department was opening a register, then leafing through it, consulting one page and then another, he added up several items on a small calculator, and at last said, We have in our warehouse, with little likelihood of getting rid of them even at sale prices, even by offering them for less than cost price, a large number of articles from your pottery, articles of all kinds which are taking up valuable space, which is why I am obliged to ask you to remove them all within two weeks maximum, I was intending to have someone telephone you tomorrow and tell you, My van's only small, so heaven knows how many trips I'll have to make, Hiring a truck for the day should solve the problem, And who am I supposed to sell my crockery to now, asked the potter in despair, That is your problem, not mine, So I am at least authorized to do business with shops in the city, Our contract is canceled, so you can do business with whomever you like, If it's worth the bother, Yes, if it's worth the bother, there's a grave crisis going on out there, although, the head of department stopped speaking, gathered the drawings together, and then went through them one by one, studying them with what seemed like genuine interest, as if he were seeing them for the first time. Cipriano Algor could not ask, Although what, he had to wait, to disguise his anxiety, after all, or indeed before all, it was the head of the buying department who decided the rules of the game, and now he is playing a very unfair game, in which the cards have all been dealt to one player and in which, if necessary, the values of the cards will vary according to the whim of the person holding them, in which case the king will be worth more than the ace and less than the queen, or the jack will be worth as much as the two, and the two worth as much as the whole royal household, although it must be said, for what it's worth, that, since there are six dolls on the table, the potter has the numerical advantage, although only just. The head of the buying department again gathered up the drawings, put them absentmindedly to one side and, after another glance at the register, finished the phrase, Although, of course, leaving aside the catastrophic situation in which the traditional market finds itself, which is highly unfavorable to goods that have failed to stand the tests of time and changing tastes, the pottery will be forbidden to sell its goods elsewhere should the Center decide to commission these new proposed products, Do I understand you to mean that we will not be able to sell the dolls to other tradesmen in the city, You understand me correctly, though incompletely, Sorry, I don't quite know what you mean, Not only will you not be allowed to sell the dolls, you will not be allowed to sell any of your other products either, even if we admit the absurd hypothesis that anyone would commission them, So as soon as you accept me back as a supplier to the Center, I will be unable to supply anyone else, Exactly, though that can hardly come as a surprise, since this has always been the rule, On the other hand, sir, in the current situation, when certain products are no longer of any interest to the Center, it would seem fair to allow the supplier the freedom to find other buyers for them, We are in the world of hard commercial facts here, Senhor Algor, any theories that do not serve to consolidate those facts are irrelevant to the Center, which is not to say that we are incapable of coming up with theories of our own, and some we have even had to release, onto the market I mean, but only those that served to ratify and, if necessary, absolve those facts when they did not quite work out as planned. Cipriano Algor told himself not to rise to the bait. Falling into the temptation of having a ding-dong argument with the head of the buying department, I say one thing, you say another, I protest, you respond, was bound to end badly, you never can tell what disastrous consequences one wrongly interpreted word might have on even the most subtle and carefully honed dialectic of persuasion, as the wise old saying has it, don't quibble with the king over pears, let him eat the ripe ones and give you the green ones. The head of the buying department looked at him with a half smile and added, I don't honestly know why I'm telling you these things, To be frank, sir, I'm rather surprised too, I'm just a simple potter, the little I have to sell hardly justifies your wasting your patience on me and honoring me with your reflections, replied Cipriano Algor, and immediately bit his tongue, for he had just decided not to throw any more wood onto the fire of a conversation that was already manifestly tense, and there he was issuing another provocation, as direct as it was inopportune. Hoping to avoid the tart response he feared, he got up and said, Forgive me for taking up so much of your time, sir, I'll leave you to study the drawings further, unless, Unless what, Unless you have already come to a decision, What decision, I don't know, sir, I can't know what you're thinking, The decision not to commission the dolls, for example, asked the head of the buying department, Yes, sir, replied the potter, looking straight at him, although mentally he was accusing himself of being both stupid and imprudent, I haven't yet come to a decision, May I ask how long you will take, because, as you know, the situation we find ourselves in, I will be quick, said the head of the buying department, interrupting him, you might even hear as early as tomorrow, Tomorrow, Yes, tomorrow, I don't want you going around saying that the Center refused to give you one last chance, Might I conclude from what you are saying that the decision will be a positive one, It might be, that's all I can tell you at the moment, Thank you, sir, You have no reason to thank me as yet, No, but I'm thanking you for the hope I carry away with me now, that is already something, Never put your trust in hope, Oh, I agree, but what else can we do, we have to hold on to something in our hour of need, Good afternoon, Senhor Algor, Good afternoon, sir. The potter had his hand on the door handle, he was about to leave, but the head of the buying department had not yet finished, Sort out a plan of withdrawal for the crockery with the assistant head of department, the one who showed you in, and remember, you have only two weeks in which to remove everything, down to the last plate, Yes, sir. That expression, plan of withdrawal, does not sit well in the mouth of a civilian, it sounds more like a military operation than a routine return of goods, and if applied to the letter and to the relative positions of the Center and the pottery, either it could result in a providential tactical retreat in order to reunite scattered forces and then, at the propitious moment, that is, when approval for the dolls is given, to launch a renewed attack, or, on the contrary, it could result in the end of everything, outright defeat, a rout, a case of every man for himself. Cipriano Algor was listening to the assistant head of department telling him, without even pausing for breath or looking at him, Every day at four o'clock, and you'll have to do the work yourself or else bring help, the staff here can't be excused not even if you pay them extra, and he wondered if it was worth having to endure this humiliation, being treated like a fool, like a nobody, and having to accept that they are absolutely right, that for the Center a few rough, glazed earthenware plates or some ridiculous dolls pretending to be nurses, Eskimos, and bearded Assyrians have no importance whatsoever, none, zero, That is what we are for them, zero. He sat down at last in the van and looked at his watch, he would still have to wait nearly an hour before picking up his son-in-law, it occurred to him to go into the Center, it's been ages since he went in through the doors intended for the general public, either to look or buy, Marçal always buys anything they need because of the discounts he gets as an employee, and going into the

Center just to look around is not, if you'll forgive the apparent tautology, viewed with friendly eyes, anyone caught wandering around inside empty-handed will soon become the object of special attention from the security guards, the comical situation might even arise of his own son-in-law approaching him and saying, Pa, what are you doing here if you've no intention of buying anything, and he would reply, I'm just going to the pottery section to see if they've still got anything from the Algor Pottery on display, to find out how much they charge for that jug inlaid with little bits of marble, to say Goodness, that's a lovely jug, there aren't many craftsmen nowadays who can do really well-finished work like that, the man in charge of the section, impressed by the views of such a knowledgeable expert, might recommend the urgent purchase of another hundred such jugs, the ones inlaid with bits of marble, and then we wouldn't have to take unnecessary risks with clowns, jesters, and mandarins, when we have no idea how they'll be received. Cipriano Algor did not need to say to himself, No, I won't go, for weeks now he has been saying this to his daughter and to his son-in-law, once should be enough. He was absorbed in these pointless cogitations, his head resting on the steering wheel, when the guard who kept watch on the exit came over and said, If you've done what you came to do, please leave, this isn't a garage, you know. The potter said, I know, started the engine and left without another word. The guard noted down the number of the van on a piece of paper, he didn't need to, he's seen the van often enough since he first became a guard in the basement, but the reason he made a point of writing the number down was because he did not like that curt I know, especially when addressed to a guard, guards should be treated with respect and consideration, you don't just say I know, the old man should have said Of course, sir, nice, obedient words, suitable for all occasions, but the guard is, in fact, more disconcerted than annoyed, which is why he thought that perhaps he should not have said This isn't a garage, you know, especially not in that scornful tone, as if he were the king of the world, when he wasn't even the king of the grubby basement where he spends his days. He crossed out the number and returned to his post.

Cipriano Algor looked for a quiet street where he could pass the time until he could go and pick up his son-in-law at the entrance to the security section. He parked the van on a corner from which, three large blocks away, he could see a sliver of one of the vast Center façades, the inhabited part as it happens. With the exception of the doors that open onto the outside, there are no other openings to be seen, just impenetrable stretches of wall and it is not the vast hoardings promising security that are to blame for shutting out the light or stealing the air from those who live inside. In complete contrast to those smooth façades, this side of the building is peppered with windows, hundreds and hundreds of windows, thousands of windows, all of them closed because of the air-conditioning inside. Normally, when we do not know the exact height of a building, but want to give an approximate idea of its size, we say that it has a certain number of stories, which might be two, or five, or fifteen, or twenty, or thirty, or whatever, either fewer or more, from one to infinity. The Center building is neither that small nor that big, it makes do with the forty-eight stories visible above street level and the ten floors concealed below. And now that Cipriano Algor is parked here, let us ponder some of the numbers that will give an idea of the size of the Center, let us say that the width of the smaller façades is about one hundred and fifty meters, and the larger ones slightly more than three hundred and fifty, not taking into account, of course, the proposed extension to which we referred in detail at the beginning of this story. Proceeding a little further with our calculations and taking the average height of each story to be three meters, including the thickness of the floor separating each one, that would make, including the ten subterranean stories, a total height of one hundred and seventy-four meters. If we multiply that number by the one hundred and fifty meters in width and the three hundred and fifty meters in length, we will get, allowing, of course, for errors, omissions and sheer confusion, a volume of nine million one hundred and thirty-five thousand cubic meters, give or take a centimeter, give or take a comma or two. The Center, and there is no one who does not, with astonishment, recognize this, is really big. And that, muttered Cipriano Algor to himself, is where my dear son-in-law wants me to live, behind one of those windows that can't be opened, they say it's so as not to upset the thermal stability of the air-conditioning, but the truth is quite different, people are free to commit suicide if they choose to, but not by hurling themselves one hundred meters down into the street, such despair would attract too much attention and awaken the morbid curiosity of passersby, who would immediately want to know why. Cipriano Algor has already said, not once but many times, that he will never agree to go and live in the Center, that he will never give up the pottery that belonged to his father and to his grandfather, and even Marta herself, his only daughter, who, poor thing, will have no choice but to accompany her husband when he is promoted to resident guard, had acknowledged two or three days ago with gratifying frankness that only her father could make the final decision, without being submitted to pressure from third parties, even if they tried to justify that pressure with claims of filial love, or out of that tearful pity which old people, even when they themselves reject it, seem to arouse in the souls of well-brought-up people. I will not go, I'd rather die than go, muttered the potter, aware, however, that these words, precisely because they seem so categorical, so final, might be pretending a conviction which, deep down, he did not feel, might be disguising an inner weakness, like an as yet invisible crack in the thinnest wall of a water jug. That mention of a water jug was clearly the best possible reason for Isaura Estudiosa to return to Cipriano Algor's thoughts, and that was indeed what happened, but the route taken by that thought, or reasoning, assuming any reasoning took place and it was not just an instantaneous flash, drove him to a rather embarrassing conclusion, formulated in a dreamy murmur, That way I wouldn't have to come and live in the Center. The look of annoyance that appeared on Cipriano Algor's face as soon as he had uttered these words will not allow us to turn our backs on the fact that, despite the evident pleasure he takes in thinking about Isaura Estudiosa, he can nevertheless do nothing to prevent that apparently contradictory shift in mood. There would be little point in wasting time explaining why he likes thinking about her, there are things in life which define themselves, a particular man, a particular woman, a particular word, a particular moment, that is all we would have to say for everyone to understand what we meant, but there are other things, and it might even be the same man and the same woman, the same word and the same moment, which, viewed from a different angle, in a different light, come to signify doubts and perplexities, troubling signs, a strange presentiment, and that is why Cipriano Algor's pleasure in thinking about Isaura Estudiosa suddenly faltered, it was those words that were to blame, That way I wouldn't have to come and live in the Center, which is the same as saying, If I married her, I would have someone to look after me, a further demonstration of something that does not require demonstration, in short, the things a man finds hardest to recognize and confess are his own weaknesses. Especially when those weaknesses appear at the wrong time, like a fruit attached only tenuously to the bough because it was born too late in the season. Cipriano Algor sighed, then looked at his watch. It was time to go and pick up his son-in-law at the door of the security services department.

The dog Found did not like Marçal. There were so many things to tell, so much news, so many highs and lows in hopes and spirits, that during the journey from the Center to the pottery, it did not even occur to Cipriano Algor to mention to his son-in-law the dog's mysterious arrival or his equally unusual behavior since. Nevertheless, a love of truth, pricked on by a narrator's natural scrupulousness, will not allow to go unmentioned one brief resurfacing of that remarkable episode in the potter's faulty memory, this, however, did not get any further because Marçal, with more than justified resentment, interrupted his father-in-law's story to ask why the devil neither he nor Marta had thought to inform him of what was going on at home, the idea of the dolls, the drawings, their attempts at modeling, It's as if I don't really exist for either of you, he remarked bitterly. Caught out, Cipriano Algor mumbled some excuse citing the intensity and concentration inevitable in all artistic creation, the extreme unfriendliness with which the person who answered the phone responded to calls from the family members of guards living outside the Center, and, finally, a few decorative, half-garbled words to pad out his speech and bring it to a close. Fortunately, the sight of the burned-out truck helped divert attention from a dispute that could easily have evolved into a family quarrel, which, let it be said, it will not, although Marçal Gacho is determined to take up the matter again when he is alone with his wife in their bedroom and behind closed doors. With visible relief, Cipriano Algor left the subject of clay dolls in order to explain the suspicions that the fire had aroused in his mind, a view to which Marçal, still angry about the lack of consideration with which he had been treated, responded rather brusquely in the name of deontology, ethical awareness, and the high standard of behavior for which, by definition, the armed forces in general and the administrative and police authorities in particular have always been known. Cipriano Algor shrugged, You're just saying that because you work as a security guard at the Center, if you were a civilian like me, you would see things differently, The fact that I work as a guard at the Center doesn't make me a policeman or a soldier, retorted Marçal, No, it doesn't, but you're pretty close, on the border, Oh, I suppose now you're going to tell me that you feel ashamed to have a security guard from the Center sitting here beside you in your van, breathing the same air, The potter did not reply at once, he regretted having given in yet again to the stupid and gratuitous desire to provoke his son-in-law, Why do I do it, he asked himself, as if he didn't already know the answer, this man, this Marçal Gacho wanted to take his daughter from him, indeed he already had taken her away, irremediably and irrevocably, by marrying her, Even if, in the end, I get tired of saying no and go with them to live at the Center, he thought. Then, speaking slowly, as if he had to drag each word out one after the other, he said, I'm sorry, I didn't mean to offend you, I didn't mean to be unpleasant, but sometimes I can't help it, it just comes out, and there's no point asking me why, I wouldn't be able to give you an answer or, if I did, I'd just be telling you a pack of lies, because there are reasons, if you look you'll always find them, there's never been any shortage of reasons, even if they're not the right ones, no, it's the changing times, it's the old who age a day for every hour, it's the work which isn't what it used to be, and we, who can only be what we were, suddenly realize that we're not needed in the world, always assuming we ever were, of course, but believing that we were seemed to be enough, seemed sufficient, and that belief was, in a sense, eternal for as long as we remained alive, which is, after all, what eternity is. Marçal said nothing, he merely placed his left hand on his father-in-law's right hand, which was holding the steering wheel. Cipriano Algor swallowed hard, looked at the hand which, gently but firmly, seemed to want to protect his, looked at the oblique, jagged scar that cut across the skin from one side to the other, all that remained of a terrible burn which, by some astonishing stroke of good fortune, had not reached the veins beneath. Inexperienced and inept, Marçal had wanted to help in stoking the kiln in order to impress the girl he had been going out with for a matter of only a few weeks, perhaps to impress her father too, to show him that he was a grown man, when, in fact, he was only just out of adolescence and when the one thing in life and in the world about which he felt he knew all there was to know was that he loved the potter's daughter. No one who has at some time in their life known such certainties will have any difficulty whatsoever in imagining the feelings of enthusiasm that filled him as he dragged the logs one by one from the woodshed and then fed them into the kiln, the supreme prize for him at that moment would have been Marta's delight and surprise, her mother's benevolent smile and her father's grave, reluctant look of approval. And suddenly, though no one ever found out why, for such a thing had never happened before in the memory of potters, a flame, slender, swift and sinuous as the tongue of a snake, erupted with a roar from the mouth of the kiln and cruelly bit the hand of the boy, so near, so innocent, so unprepared. That was the origin of the Gacho family's secret antipathy for the Algor family, who had not only acted with unforgivable negligence and irresponsibility, but had also, according to the inflexible Gacho mind, flagrantly abused the feelings of an ingenuous lad by making him work for nothing. It is not only in villages far from civilization that the human cerebral appendage is capable of generating such ideas. Marta frequently dressed Marçal's hand, she frequently consoled and cooled it with her breath, and the couple were so steadfast in their desires that, after some years, they were able to get married, though this did nothing to unite the families. At the moment, their love appears to have gone to sleep, but never mind, this seems to be the natural effect of time and life's anxieties, but if ancient knowledge serves for anything, if it can still be of some use to modern ignorance, let us say, softly, so that people don't laugh at us, that while there's life, there's hope. For it is true that however thick and black the clouds over our heads, the sky above the clouds is permanently blue, but then again the rain, hail and lightning always fall downward, and indeed, when faced with such facts, it is hard to know quite what to think. Marçal has withdrawn his hand, that's how it is between men, manly displays of affection have to be quick and instantaneous, some people put this down to masculine modesty, and perhaps they're right, but it would have been much more manly, in the full sense of the word, and certainly no less masculine, if Cipriano Algor had stopped the van and embraced his son-in-law right there and then and thanked him for that gesture with the only possible words, Thank you for placing your hand on mine, that is what he should have said, instead of taking advantage of the seriousness of the moment to complain about the ultimatum imposed by the head of the buying department, Can you believe it, he gave me two weeks to take away the whole lot, Two weeks, Yes, two weeks, and with no one to help me either, I'm only sorry I can't lend a hand, Well, you can't, of course, you haven't got time and it wouldn't do your career much good to be seen working as a porter, and the worst thing is that I have no idea what to do with a load of pots that nobody wants, You might still manage to sell some, We've got more than enough at the pottery, In that case, you really have a problem, We'll see, I might just leave it here by the roadside, The police wouldn't let you, If this old crock wasn't a van but one of those dump trucks, nothing could be easier, I'd just have to push a button and, hey presto, in less than a minute, there it would all be in the gutter, You might get away with it a couple of times, but the traffic police would be bound to catch you at it in the end, Another solution would be to find a cave out in the countryside somewhere, it wouldn't have to be a very big cave, and put everything inside, can you imagine how funny it would be if, in a couple of thousand years, we were to listen in on the debates of archaeologists and anthropologists about the origin of all these earthenware plates, mugs, and dishes, and why there were so many of them and what possible use they could have been in an uninhabited place like that, It may be uninhabited now, but in a couple of thousand years it's quite possible that the city will have spread as far as here, remarked Marçal. He paused, as if the words he had just uttered required him to go back and think about them, and then, in the perplexed tone of one who, without quite understanding how, has reached a logically impeccable conclusion, he added, Or the Center. Now, knowing, as we do, that in the lives of this particular father-in-law and son-in-law the vexed question of the Center has been anything but easy, it seems odd that the security guard Marçal Gacho's unexpected allusion to the Center should have had no further consequences, that the dangerous remark, Or the Center, should not have immediately sparked off another argument that would repeat all the old misunderstandings and the usual litany of recriminations, tacit or explicit. The reason that both remained silent, always assuming that it is possible for us, observing from the outside, to uncover what, in all probability, was not even clear to them, was the fact that those words, spoken by Marçal, especially given the context in which they were pronounced, constituted a genuine novelty. Some will say that this is not the case, that, on the contrary, by admitting the possibility that the Center could, at some point in the future, as part of the process of unstoppable territorial expansion, do away with the fields that the van is now driving past, the security guard Marçal Gacho is himself underlining and secretly applauding the expansionist potential, in both space and time, of the company that pays him his modest salary. That interpretation would be perfectly valid and would settle the matter once and for all if it were not for that almost imperceptible pause, if that moment of apparent suspension of thought did not correspond, if you will permit such an audacious suggestion, with the appearance of someone quite simply capable of thinking differently. Were that the case, it is understandable that Marçal Gacho proved unable to advance along the road that opened up before him, since that road was destined for someone else. As for the potter, he has lived long enough to know that the best way of killing a rose is to force it open when it is still only the promise of a bud. He therefore stored away his son-in-law's words in his memory and pretended not to comprehend their real meaning. They did not speak again until they reached the village. As he usually did when he brought his son-in-law back from the Center, Cipriano Algor stopped at the door of Marçal's disagreeable parents, just time enough for Marçal to go in, kiss his mother and his father, if his father was at home, find out how they had been since last he saw them, and leave saying, I'll drop by tomorrow when I've got more time. In general, five minutes was more than enough for this routine of filial sentiment to be accomplished, other news and more substantial conversation would wait until the following day, sometimes over lunch, sometimes not, but almost always without Marta's presence. Today, though, five minutes was not enough, nor ten, and almost twenty minutes had passed before Marçal reappeared. He got quickly into the van and slammed the door. His face was very serious, almost somber, with an adult hardness of expression for which his young features were not prepared. You took a long time today, is anyone ill, is there some problem with the family, asked his father-in-law kindly, No, it's nothing, I'm sorry to have kept you waiting so long, You're annoyed about something, Like I said, it's nothing, don't worry. They are almost home, the van turns left in order to begin the climb up to the pottery, and as he changes gear, it occurs to Cipriano Algor that he drove past Isaura Estudiosa's house without giving her a thought, and it is then that a dog comes running down the hill, barking, Marçal's second surprise of the day, or the third, if the second was the visit to his parents. Where did that dog come from, he asked, He turned up a few days ago and we let him stay, he's a nice dog, we've called him Found, although, if you think about it, we were the ones who were found, not him. When the van reached the top of the drive and stopped, a few things happened all at once, or at minimal intervals of time, Marta came to the kitchen door, the potter and the security guard got out of the van, Found growled, Marta ran toward Marçal, Marçal ran toward Marta, the dog gave a deeper growl, husband embraced wife, wife embraced husband, then they kissed, the dog stopped growling and attacked Marçal's boot, Marçal shook his leg, the dog would not let go, Marta shouted, Found, her father shouted too, the dog released the boot and tried to grab Marçal's ankle instead, Marçal aimed a fairly gentle kick at him, Marta said, Don't hurt him, Marçal protested, He bit me, That's because he doesn't know you, Not even the dogs know me here, these terrible words left Marçal's mouth as if he had sobbed them out rather than merely spoken them, each word filled with unbearable pain and sorrow, Marta threw her arms around her husband's neck, Don't ever say that again, and of course he didn't, there are some things that are only ever said once and never again, Marta will hear those words in her head until the last day of her life, and as for Cipriano Algor, if we wanted to know what he was doing at this moment, the easiest response would be, Nothing, were it not for the revealing fact that when he heard what Marçal said, he immediately looked away, so he did do something. The dog had backed away toward the kennel, but halfway there, he stopped, turned, and stood there looking. Now and then a growl would emerge from his throat. Marta said, He doesn't know about people embracing, he must have thought you were attacking me, but Cipriano Algor, in order to clear the air, offered a more trivial suggestion, Perhaps he's just got it in for uniforms, it wouldn't be the first time. Marçal did not respond, he was caught between two feelings, regret for having spoken words that would stand for all time as a public confession of a deep-seated sorrow kept hidden until then, and an instinctive intuition that the fact of having uttered those words might mean that he was about to leave one road and follow another, even though it was still far too soon to know where it might lead him. He kissed Marta on the head and said, I'll go and change my clothes. Evening was coming on fast, in less than half an hour it would be dark. Cipriano Algor said to his daughter, I talked to the man in the buying department, Of course, what with all the fuss about the dog, I almost forgot to ask how the interview went, He said that he might be able to give me an answer tomorrow, That's quick, It's hard to believe, isn't it, and even harder to believe that the answer could well be yes, but that's what he seemed to be saying, Let's hope you're right, Alas, the only rose without thorns I know is you, What do you mean, what's all this about roses and thorns, I mean that every good piece of news is generally followed by some bad, And what's today's bad news, I've got two weeks to remove any crockery of ours that they still have in the warehouse, Well, I'll come and help you, No way, if the Center gives us the order, we'll need every spare moment we have to make the final models, create the molds, work on the modeling, do the painting, load and unload the kiln, besides, I'd like to deliver the first part of the order before we remove all our stuff from the warehouse, just in case the man changes his mind, And what are we going to do with those surplus pots, Don't worry, I've sorted that out with Marçal, I'll leave them in the countryside somewhere, in a cave, and if anyone wants them they can have them, With so much moving about, most of them will get broken anyway, Probably. The dog came over and touched Marta's hand with its nose, as if asking her to explain the new composition of the family unit, as people used to call it. Marta scolded him, Just you behave yourself from now on, and I'll tell you one thing, if it comes to a choice between my husband and you, I'll always choose my husband. The last bit of shade cast by the mulberry tree was gradually shrinking to nothing as it began to form part of the darker shade of approaching night. Cipriano Algor murmured, We'll have to be careful with Marçal, what he said just now came as a real body blow, It was a body blow and it really hurt. The light above the kitchen door came on. Marçal appeared in the doorway, he had changed into the ordinary clothes he wore around the house. The dog Found looked at him closely, and, head up, advanced a few steps toward him, then stopped expectantly. Marçal went over to him, Are we friends now, he asked. The dog's cold nose lightly brushed the scar on his left hand, We're friends. The potter said, You see, I was right, our dog Found doesn't like uniforms, Everything in life is a uniform, said Marçal, the only time our bodies are truly in civilian dress is when we're naked, but there was no bitterness in his voice now.

During supper, they talked a lot about how Marta had come up with the idea of making the dolls, as well as about the doubts, fears, and hopes that had shaken the house and the pottery during the last few days, and then, passing on to more practical matters, they calculated how much time would be needed for each phase of production, as well as the respective safety margins, which differed in both cases from those required by the products they usually made, It all depends on what quantities they order, neither too much nor too little would be best, which is a bit like asking for sun for the threshing and rain for the turnips, as people used to say in the days before plastic greenhouses, said Cipriano Algor. When they had cleared the table, Marta showed her husband the sketches she had made, the various drafts, the experiments with color, the old encyclopedia from which she had copied the models, at first sight, it looked like a very small amount of work to have provoked such large anxieties, but one must understand that in life's circumnavigations what for some is a gentle breeze, for others is a fatal storm, it all depends on the draft of the ship and on the state of its sails. In their bedroom, with the door shut, Marçal decided that there was no point asking Marta to explain why she had not told him about her idea to make the dolls, first, because that particular water had passed under the bridge several hours since, sweeping along with it all the spite and bad temper, second, because he was concerned now about something far more serious than feeling or merely imagining that he had been ignored. Something more serious and no less urgent. When a man returns to home and wife after a separation of ten days, especially a young man like Marçal, or, indeed an old man, assuming that age has not yet killed off his amatory instincts, the natural impulse is to want to give immediate satisfaction to the tremor of the senses, and to leave any talking until afterward. Women tend to think otherwise. If there is no particular pressure of time, if, on the contrary, the night is ours, or indeed the afternoon or the morning, the woman would probably prefer the act of love to be preceded by a leisurely, unhurried conversation, if possible about something other than the idée fixe that is spinning like a humming top inside the man's head. Like a deep, slowly filling water jug, the woman very gradually draws closer to the man, although it would perhaps be more accurate to say that she draws him closer to her, until the urgency of the one and the longing of the other, declared, concurrent, and unpostponable, make the unanimous water rise singing to the brim. There are exceptions, though, and one such is Marçal who, however much he would like simply to drag Marta off to bed, cannot do so until he has emptied out the heavy bag of anxieties he has been carrying, not from the Center, not from the conversation he had with his father-in-law on the way back, but from his parents' house. Nevertheless, the first word will still be spoken by Marta, The dogs may not know you, Marçal, but your wife certainly does, I really don't want to talk about that, But we should talk about the things that hurt us, It was stupid of me and unfair, Well, let's leave stupid to one side, because you're certainly not that, let's just stay with unfair, Look, I've already said that I was, But you weren't being unfair either, Don't let's complicate things, Marta, please, what's said is said, The things that seem to be over are always the things that never really are, we're the ones who have been unfair, Who's we, My father and me, especially me, my father has a married daughter and is afraid of losing her, he doesn't need any further justification, And what about you, Well, I have no excuse whatsoever, Why, Because I love you and sometimes, too often, I give the impression that I've forgotten that I do, no, sometimes I do actually forget that the person to whom I owe that love is a real person, complete in himself, not someone who should make do with some rather diffuse emotion which gradually resigns itself to its own fatal vagueness, as if that were a fate against which there were no possible appeal, That's what marriage is like, that's how people live, you just have to look at my parents, There's something else I'm guilty of too, Don't go on, please, Let me finish now, Marçal, let me finish, Please, Marta, You don't want me to go on because you know what it is I'm going to say, Please, When you said that not even the dogs know you, what you were saying to your wife was that not only does she not know you, she hasn't made the slightest effort to get to know you either, well, almost none, That's not true, you do know me, no one knows me better than you, Only enough to understand the meaning of your words, but I'm no more intelligent in that respect than my father, who cottoned on as quickly as I did, Of the two of us, you're the adult, I'm still a child, Maybe you're right, at least you seem to be saying that I'm right, yet this marvelous adult, Marçal Gacho's terribly sensible wife, was incapable of seeing, as she should have done, what it means to be a person who has the simplicity and honesty to say of himself that he is a child, Not that I'll always be a child, No, you won't, which is why, while there's still time, I'll have to do everything I can to understand you as you are and doubtless reach the conclusion that, in your case, being a child is actually just a different way of being an adult, If you carry on like this, I won't know who I am, Cipriano Algor will tell you that this is a frequent occurrence in life, You know, I think I'm beginning to get on better with your father, You cannot imagine, or perhaps you can, how happy that makes me. Marta clasped Marçal's hands and kissed them, then pressed them to her breast, Sometimes, she said, we need to return to certain ancient gestures of tenderness, How would you know, you weren't alive in the days of bowing and hand-kissing, No, but I've read about it in books, which is the same as having been there, anyway it wasn't bowing and hand-kissing I had in mind, They had different customs, different ways of feeling and communicating quite unlike our own, Strange though the comparison may sound, to me gestures are more than just gestures, they are like drawings made by one body on another body. The invitation could not have been more explicit, but Marçal pretended not to have heard, although he knew that the moment had come to draw Marta to him, to stroke her hair, slowly kiss her cheek, her eyelids, gently, as if he felt no desire at all, as if he were merely distracted, it would be a grave mistake to think that what happens on such occasions is that desire takes absolute control of the body in order to make use of it, forgive the materialistic, utilitarian simile, as if we were talking about a tool with multiple applications, as capable of smoothing as of carving, as powerful a transmitter as a receiver, as precise at counting as at measuring, as capable of going up as going down. What's wrong, asked Marta, suddenly uncertain, Nothing important, just a few niggling little problems, At work, No, What then, We have so little time together and yet they still won't leave us alone, We don't live in a bell jar, I dropped in at my parents' house, Did something happen, some complication. Marçal shook his head and went on, They started asking lots of questions about whether I had heard anything about when I might be promoted to resident guard, and I said that I hadn't, and that I didn't even have any solid proof that it would happen, You're almost sure that you will be, though, Yes, almost sure, but you know what they say, don't wash your basket out, until the last grape's in, I know, I know, so what else did they say, They kept circling around and around the subject, and I just couldn't make out what it was they were getting at, until finally, they told me their great idea, And what great idea would that be, Only that they're thinking of selling their house and coming to live with us,

With us, where, At the Center, Am I understanding you right, your parents want to come and live at the Center with us, Exactly, And what did you say, I started by pointing out that it was still a bit early to be thinking about that, but they said that selling a house wasn't something that happened overnight, that they weren't going to wait until we had moved in, you and me, and that they would start looking for a buyer, And what did you say, Well, thinking that it would settle the matter, I said that we were intending having your father to live with us when we moved, so that he wouldn't be left alone here, especially now that the pottery is going through a crisis, You told them that, Yes, but they took no notice, they practically started yelling at me and crying, well, my mother did, my father's not really the sloppy type, he just protested and waved his arms around a lot, what kind of a son am I, putting the interests of people who aren't of the same blood over the needs of my own progenitors, they actually used the word progenitors, heaven knows where they found it, that they would never have imagined that one day they would hear me saying that I was rejecting the very people to whom I owe my life, the people who brought me up and educated me, that there's certainly a deal of truth in the old saying that a son is a son until he gets him a wife, but nothing had prepared them for such indifference, anyway I wasn't to worry about them, they hadn't quite been reduced to begging in the streets, but one day I would regret what I'd done, not perhaps while they were alive, but after they were dead, which is always much worse, and they just hoped I didn't have children who would treat me as cruelly as I was treating my own parents, And that was the final word, To be honest, I don't know if it was or not, I've probably forgotten a few others, but they were all out of the same mold, You should have explained that they needn't worry, you know my father doesn't want to live at the Center, Yes, but I didn't want to tell them that, Why not, That would just encourage them to think that they're the only candidates, If they insist, you'll have no option, In that case, I won't accept the promotion, I'll just have to find some convincing excuse to give the Center, Well, I doubt you'll find one. They were sitting on the bed, almost touching, but the moment for caresses had passed, apparently as distant now as the days of hand-kissing and bowing, or even as that other moment when the man's two hands were kissed and then pressed to the woman's breast. Marçal said, I know a son shouldn't say things like this, but the fact is that I don't want to live with my parents, Why, We've never really understood each other, I've never understood them and they've never understood me, They're your parents, Yes, they're my parents, and on one particular night, they went to bed, happened to be in the mood, and I was the result, when I was little I remember hearing them say, like someone telling a funny story, that he was drunk at the time, With or without wine, that's the way we're all born, Look, I know it's unreasonable, but I hate the idea that my father was drunk when I was conceived, it's as if I were the son of another man, it's as if the man who really should have been my father couldn't be there, as if his place had been taken by another, the one who said to me today that he hoped my children would be cruel to me, That isn't quite what he said, But it's what he thought. Marta took Marçal's left hand, held it between hers, and murmured, All fathers were sons once, many sons become fathers, but some forget what they were and no one can explain to the others what they will become, That's a bit deep, Oh, I don't understand it myself really, it just came to me, pay no attention, Let's go to bed, All right. They got undressed and lay down. The moment for caresses came back into the room and apologized for having spent so much time outside, I got lost, it said, by way of an excuse, and suddenly, as sometimes happens with moments, it became eternal. A quarter of an hour later, their bodies still entwined, Marta said softly, Marçal, What is it, he asked sleepily, I'm two days late.

In the safe silence of the bedroom, between sheets rumpled by the recent amorous agitations, the man heard his wife tell him that her period was two days late, and the news seemed to him extraordinary and utterly amazing, a kind of second *fiat lux* in an age in which Latin has ceased to be used and practiced, a vernacular *surge et ambula* which has no idea where it is going and which is frightening for that very reason. Only an hour before, at most, in a moment of touching openness rare in the masculine sex, Marçal Gacho had admitted to being a child, when, quite unbeknownst to him, he had been a father in embryo for some weeks, which just goes to show that we should never be too sure about what we think we are because it could easily happen that, at that precise moment, we are, in fact, something completely different. Almost everything that Marta and Marçal said to each other that night, before falling asleep out of sheer exhaustion, is described in a thousand and one stories of couples with children, but the concrete analysis of the concrete situation in which this married couple find themselves did not leave unexamined certain questions peculiar to them, for example, Marta's diminished ability to cope with the hard physical work of the pottery, but it failed to resolve, because this was dependent on the expected promotion, whether the baby would be born before or after their move to the Center. On the first point, Marta said she was sure that her mother, the late Justa Isasca, who had worked tirelessly up until the last day of her life, would never have succumbed to the pleasures of complete idleness just because she was pregnant, I myself would be a witness to that if only I could dredge up my memories of the nine months I lived inside her, A child in the womb can't possibly know what's going on outside, replied Marçal, yawning, I suppose so, but you must at least admit that a baby would have an intimate knowledge of what's going on inside its mother's womb, it's all just a question of remembering, We don't even remember the trauma of birth, Well, that's probably when we lose the first of all our memories, Now you're just inventing things, give me a kiss. Before this delicate conversation and that kiss, Marçal had expressed a vehement wish that the move to the Center should take place before the birth, You'll have the best medical treatment and the best nursing you could possibly imagine, there's nothing like it anywhere, either near or far, as regards both medicine and surgery, How do you know if you've never been to the hospital at the Center, you've probably never even been inside it, No, but I know someone who was admitted as a patient, a superior of mine who was at death's door when he went in and came out a new man, there are people outside who try to use their influence to get admitted as patients, but the rules are very strict, To hear you talk anyone would think that no one at the Center ever dies, Of course they do, but death is less obvious somehow, That's certainly an advantage, You'll see when we go there, See what, that death is less obvious, is that what you mean, No, I wasn't talking about death, Yes, you were, Look, I'm not interested in death, I was talking about you and our child, about the hospital you'll go to, Always assuming your promotion isn't too long in coming, If they don't promote me within nine months, they never will, Give me a kiss, Mr. Security Guard, and let's go to sleep, All right, here's your kiss, but there's still one other thing we need to talk about, What's that, From now on you'll do less work in the pottery and in two or three months' time you'll stop working altogether, Do you expect my father to do everything, especially if the Center puts in an order for the dolls, Get someone in to help, You know there's no point, no one wants to work in a pottery, In your condition, What about my condition, my mother carried on working when she was pregnant with me, How do you know, Because I can remember. They both laughed, then Marta said, Let's not tell my father about this just yet, he'll be thrilled, but it's best we don't say anything to him, Why, Oh, I don't know, he's got too much on his mind as it is, The pottery, The pottery's just one thing, The Center, The Center's another thing, whether or not we'll get the order, the stock he's got to remove from the warehouse, but there are other things too, a certain water jug with a loose handle, for example, but I'll tell you about that later. Marta was the first to go to sleep. Marçal was feeling less shaken by then, he knew more or less which road he would have to take after the birth, and when, nearly half an hour later, sleep touched him with its smoky fingers, he let himself drift unresistingly off, his spirit at peace. His last conscious thought was to ask himself if Marta really had said something about the handle on a water jug, Ridiculous, I must have dreamed it, he thought. He was the one who slept the least, and he was the one to wake up first. The dawn light was sifting in through the gaps in the shutters. You're going to have a child, he said to himself, and he repeated, a child, a child, a child. Then, moved by a curiosity quite without desire, almost innocent, if innocence still exists in that place in the world we call bed, he lifted the covers and looked at Marta's body. She was turned toward him, with her knees slightly bent. The lower half of her nightshirt was caught up around her waist, her white belly was only just visible in the half-darkness and disappeared completely into the dark area of the pubis. Marçal lowered the covers and realized that the moment for caresses had not gone away, it had remained in the room all night, and there it was, waiting. Doubtless touched by the draft of cold air caused by the movement of the bedcovers, Marta sighed and changed position. Like a bird gently testing out the site for its first nest, Marçal's left hand lightly brushed her belly. Marta opened her eyes and smiled, then said jokingly, Good morning, Father-to-be, but her expression changed abruptly, she had just realized that they were not alone in the room. The moment for caresses had slipped in between them, had got in between the sheets, it could not have said precisely what it wanted, but they did exactly as it wished.

Cipriano Algor was already up and about. He had slept badly, worried about whether he would get a reply from the head of the buying department that day and what the reply would be, whether positive or negative, whether reticent or dilatory, but what prevented him from sleeping at all for some hours was an idea that sprang into his head halfway through the night and which, as is so often the case with ideas that assail us at dead of sleepless night, he found extraordinary, magnificent, and even, in the case in question, the masterstroke of a negotiating talent worthy of applause. When he woke up from the barely two hours of restless sleep that his desperate body had managed to filch from its own exhaustion, he realized that the idea was, after all, worthless, that the sensible thing would be not to feed any illusions he might have about the nature and character of the person wielding the big stick, and that any order issued by someone invested with more than the usual degree of authority should be treated as if it were an irrefutable diktat from destiny. If simplicity really is a virtue, no idea could be more virtuous than this, as you will soon see, Sir, Cipriano Algor would say to the head of the buying department, I've been pondering what you said about having two weeks to remove the stock taking up space in the warehouse, it didn't occur to me at the time, probably because of my excitement when I saw that there was a slight hope that I might be allowed to continue as a supplier to the Center, but then I started thinking about it and thinking about it, and I realized that it's difficult, if not impossible, to fulfill two obligations at once, that is, to remove the crockery and make the dolls, yes, I know you haven't yet put in a firm order for them, but just supposing that you did, it occurred to me, purely as a precaution, to suggest an alternative that would leave me free during the first week to get on with making the dolls, I would then remove half of the crockery in the second week, go back to the dolls during the third week, and remove the remaining crockery during the fourth week, I know, I know, you don't have to tell me, I'm not pretending that there isn't another option which would be to start with the crockery the first week and then alternately, in sequence, dolls, crockery, dolls, but I think, in this particular case, one should take into account the psychological factor, everyone knows how different the state of mind of the creator is from that of the destroyer, of someone who destroys, and if I could start making the dolls, that is start with creation, especially in the excellent frame of mind in which I find myself now, I would face with renewed courage the hard task of having to destroy the fruits of my own labor, because having no one to sell them to or, worse still, not even being able to give them away, is tantamount to destroying them. This speech, which, at three in the morning, appeared to its author to be possessed of an irresistible logic, seemed absurd to him in the early dawn and positively ridiculous in the revealing light of the sun. Oh, well, what will be will be, said the potter to the dog Found, the devil isn't necessarily lurking behind every door. Given the manifest difference in concepts and the different nature of their respective vocabularies, Found could not even begin to understand what his master was trying to tell him, and in a way it was just as well because an indispensable condition for passing on to the next level of understanding would be to ask him who this devil was, a figure, entity, or character who, one supposes, has been absent from the spiritual world of dogs since the beginning of time, and, as you can imagine, if he were to ask a question like that right at the beginning, the discussion would be never-ending. With the arrival of Marta and Marçal, both unusually cheerful, as if the night had rewarded them with something more than the usual alleviation of ten days' worth of accumulated desire, Cipriano Algor dismissed the last remnants of his ill humor and immediately, via mental processes, which, for those aware of the premise and the conclusion, would be easy enough to delineate, he found himself thinking about Isaura Estudiosa, about her personally, but also about her name, unable to understand why we still call her Estudiosa, if the name comes from her husband, who is dead, The first chance I get, thought the potter, I must remember to ask her what her own name is, her original family name. Absorbed in the grave decision he had just made, one of the most daring of enterprises in the very private territory of names, indeed it is not the first time that a love story, to take but one example, has begun with that fatally curious question, What's your name, Cipriano Algor did not at first notice that Marçal and the dog were fraternizing and playing like old friends who have not seen each other in ages, It was the uniform, his son-in-law was saying, and Marta was repeating, It was the uniform. The potter looked at them oddly, as if everything in the world had suddenly changed its meaning, perhaps it was because he had been thinking about Isaura more in terms of her name than as the woman she was, it really isn't that common, even when distracted, to get the two things mixed up, maybe there are some things we only begin to understand when we reach that point, Reach what point, Old age. Cipriano Algor walked over to the kiln, muttering, as if it were a senseless litany, Marta, Marçal, Isaura, Found, then in a different order, Marçal, Isaura, Found, Marta, and yet another, Isaura, Marta, Found, Marçal, and another, Found, Marçal, Marta, Isaura, finally he added his own name, Cipriano, Cipriano, Cipriano, and he repeated it until he lost count of the number of times he had said it, until a kind of vertigo whirled him outside of himself, until what he was saying became meaningless, then he pronounced the word kiln, the word woodshed, the word mud, the word mulberry, the word floor, the word lantern, the word earth, the word wood, the word door, the word bed, the word cemetery, the word handle, the word jug, the word van, the word water, the word pottery, the word grass, the word house, the word fire, the word dog, the word woman, the word man, the word, the word, and all the things in this world, those with names and those without, the known and the secret, the visible and the invisible, like a flock of birds which, grown weary of flying, descends from the clouds, all gradually took up their places, filling the gaps and reordering the senses. Cipriano Algor sat down on the old stone bench that his grandfather had placed beside the kiln and he rested his elbows on his knees and his chin on his hands, he wasn't looking at the house or at the pottery, or at the fields that stretched out beyond the road, or at the rooftops of the village to his right, he was looking at the ground scattered with tiny fragments of baked clay, at the whitish, grainy earth beneath them, at a stray ant carrying in its powerful mandibles a strand of wheat beard twice its size, at the shape of a stone from behind which the slender head of a lizard was peeping out, only to disappear at once. He had no thoughts or feelings, he was merely the largest of the bits of clay, a small dry clod that would crumble with the slightest pressure of the fingers, a strand of beard from an ear of wheat that had happened to be carried off by an ant, a stone behind which a living creature would hide from time to time, a beetle or a lizard or an illusion. Found seemed to emerge from the void, he wasn't there and then suddenly he was, he abruptly placed his paws on his master's knees, thus ruining Cipriano Algor's pose as a contemplator of the vanities of this world who is wasting time, or, as he believes, gaining time, asking questions of ants and beetles and lizards. Cipriano Algor stroked the dog's head and asked another question, What do you want, but Found did not answer, he just panted and opened his mouth, as if smiling at the inanity of the question. Just then, he heard Marçal's voice calling, Are you coming, Pa, breakfast's ready. It was the first time his son-in-law had done such a thing, something unusual must be happening in the house and in the lives of Marta and Marçal, and he could not think what it was, he imagined his daughter saying, You call him, or else, even more extraordinarily, Marçal anticipating her, I'll call him, there must be some explanation for all this. He got up from the bench, again stroked the dog's head, then off they went. Cipriano

Algor did not notice that the ant would never again travel the road that would lead it back to the anthill, it still has the strand of wheat beard firmly clenched between its mandibles, but its journey ended there, the fault of that clumsy dog Found, who doesn't look to see where he's putting his feet.

While they were eating, Marçal, as if in reply to a question, told them that he had telephoned his parents to say that an urgent job had come up and that he wouldn't be able to have lunch with them, Marta, in turn, expressed the view that they should not start transporting the crockery immediately, That way we can spend the day together, I doubt that one day out of two weeks will make a great deal of difference, Cipriano Algor said that the same thought had occurred to him, mainly because the head of the buying department might phone at any time, And I need to be here to talk to him. Marta and Marçal looked at each other doubtfully, and Marçal said cautiously, If I was in your place, and knowing as I do how the Center works, I wouldn't get my hopes up, Don't forget that he was the one who said he might give me an answer today, Even so, that might have just been talk, the sort of thing they say without really thinking about it, It's not a matter of getting my hopes up, when the power of decision lies in other people's hands, when we can do nothing to move them one way or the other, the only thing left to do is to wait. They did not have to wait long, the phone rang as Marta was clearing the table. Cipriano Algor rushed forward, grabbed the receiver with trembling hand and said, The Algor Pottery, at the other end, someone, a secretary or a telephonist, asked, Is that Senhor Cipriano Algor, Yes, speaking, One moment, please, I'll just put you through to the head of the buying department, for a long, long minute, the potter had to listen to some violin music which, with maniacal insistence, filled the waiting time, he kept looking at his daughter, but it was as if he could not see her, at his son-in-law, but it was as if he wasn't there, suddenly the music stopped, and he was through, Good morning, Senhor Algor, said the head of the buying department, Good morning, sir, I was just saying to my daughter and to my son-in-law, who's home on leave at the moment, that having promised to phone today, you were bound to do so, We have to make a fuss about the promises that are kept in order to forget about the many that are not, Very true, sir, Now, I've been looking at your proposal and I've considered the various factors, both positive and negative, Forgive me interrupting you, but did you say negative factors, Not negative in the strict sense of the word, but, rather, neutral factors that could produce a negative influence, Sorry, I'm afraid I don't quite understand what you mean, What I am referring to is the fact that your pottery has no known experience of making the products you are proposing, That's true, sir, but both my daughter and myself know how to model clay and I can say without immodesty that we are very good at it too, and the only reason we never went into such work commercially was because, right from the start, we opted for making crockery instead, Yes, I understand, but, given the current climate, it was not easy to defend the proposal, You mean, if you'll allow me the question and the interpretation, that you did defend it, Yes, I did, And the decision, The decision made was to say yes to an initial phase, Oh, thank you, sir, but I must ask you to explain what you mean by an initial phase, It means that we will place an initial, experimental order of two hundred of each of the figurines and that any future orders will obviously depend on how our customers react to the product, Sir, I don't know how to thank you, As far as the Center is concerned, Senhor Algor, the best thanks we can get are satisfied customers, if they are satisfied, that is, if they buy and keep buying, we will be satisfied too, just look what happened with your crockery, the customers lost interest in it, and since, unlike certain other products, it was deemed not to merit the trouble and expense involved in convincing the customers that they were wrong, we terminated our commercial relationship, very simple, as you see, Yes, sir, very simple, I just hope these dolls don't suffer the same fate, Oh, sooner or later they will, like everything else in life, if something no longer serves a useful purpose it will be thrown out, Including people, Exactly, including people, why, I myself will be thrown out when I'm no longer any use, You're a head of department, Yes, I am, but I'm only that to those below me, there are other judges above me, The Center isn't a court, That's where you're wrong, it is, and I know of no more implacable court, To be honest, sir, I don't know why you waste your precious time talking about these things to an insignificant potter, May I point out that you are repeating words that I myself spoke yesterday, Yes, I am, more or less, The reason is that there are some things that can only be said to those beneath one, And I'm one of those beneath you, Now I wasn't the one who put you there, but, yes, you are, At least I serve some purpose, then, but if your career progresses, as it certainly will, you will have many more people beneath you, Should that happen, Senhor Cipriano, you will become invisible to me, As you said earlier, such is life, Yes, such is life, but meanwhile, I am the person who will sign the order, Sir, I have just one more question to put to you, What's that, It's about the removal of our surplus crockery from the warehouse, That has already been decided, I gave you a deadline of two weeks, It's just that in the meantime I've had an idea, What idea is that, Since it is in our interests, ours and the Center's, to carry out the order as quickly as possible, it would be very helpful if we could alternate, Alternate, Yes, I mean spend one week removing the stock from the warehouse, the next working on the figurines, and so on, But that means you would take a month rather than two weeks to clear my warehouse, Yes, but we would gain time by getting ahead with our work, You said one week crockery and the next figurines, Yes, sir, Let's do it another way, the first week you work on the figurines, the second you remove the crockery, it's basically a question of applied psychology, creating is always so much more stimulating than destroying, You're very kind, sir, I would never have dreamed of asking for so much, Oh, I'm not kind, I'm just practical, said the head of the buying department sharply, Perhaps kindness is a question of practice, muttered Cipriano Algor, Could you say that again, I didn't quite catch it, Oh, it doesn't matter, sir, it wasn't important, But say it again anyway, I said that perhaps kindness is a question of practice, That's the opinion of a potter, Yes, sir, but not all potters would share it, Potters are dying out, Senhor Algor, And so are opinions like mine. The head of the buying department did not respond immediately, he must have been considering whether it was worth amusing himself further with this kind of cat-and-mouse game, but his position on the Center's organization chart reminded him that the whole definition and maintenance of hierarchical configurations is based on their being scrupulously respected and never contravened or transgressed, and, of course, the inevitable result of being too free and easy with one's inferiors or subalterns is to undermine respect and to encourage license, or, to put it more explicitly and unambiguously, it all ends in insubordination, indiscipline and anarchy. Marta, who for some moments had been vainly trying to attract her father's attention, so absorbed was he in this verbal dispute, had finally scribbled down two questions in large letters on a piece of paper and placed it under his nose, Which ones, How many. When he read them, Cipriano Algor raised his unoccupied hand to his head, there was no excuse for his distraction, a lot of talk for talk's sake, a lot of argument and counterargument, and yet he had only found out part of what he really needed to know, and then only because the head of the buying department had told him, that is, that they would be placing an order for two hundred of each of the figurines. The silence did not last as long as it no doubt seems, but it must be remembered that in one moment of silence, even briefer than this one, many things can happen, and when, as in the present case, it is necessary to enumerate them, describe them and explain them in order fully to understand the meaning of all these things both jointly and individually, someone immediately jumps in to say that it's impossible, that you can't fit the whole world in the eye of a needle, when the truth is that the whole universe, even two universes, would fit easily. However, using a circumspect tone, so as not to awaken the sleeping dragon too abruptly, it is now time for Senhor Algor to mutter, Er, sir, time too for the head of the buying department to draw to a close a conversation which tomorrow, for the reasons given above, he may perhaps regret and may even wish had never happened, Right, then, we're agreed, you can start work, the requisition will be sent off today, and, finally, it is time for Cipriano Algor to say that there is still one detail to resolve, And what detail is that, Which ones, sir, Which ones of what, you mentioned one detail, not several, Which of the figurines will you be ordering, that's what I need to know, All of them, replied the head of the buying department, All of them, repeated Cipriano Algor, astonished, but the other man did not hear him, he had hung up. Stunned, the potter looked at his daughter, then at his son-in-law, Well, I never expected that, I heard what I heard and I don't believe it, he said they're placing an order for two hundred of each of the figurines, All six, asked Marta, Well, I think so, that's what he said, all of them. Marta ran to her father and hugged him hard, not saying a word, Marçal also went over to his father-in-law, Some days everything seems to go wrong, but then there are other days that bring only good news. Had Cipriano Algor been paying slightly more attention to what was being said, had he not been so distracted by the joyful prospect of guaranteed work, he would certainly have wanted to know what other good news that day had brought. Besides, the pact of silence that the two parents-to-be had agreed to a few hours before was almost broken right there and then, as Marta realized when she found her lips forming the words, Pa, I think I'm pregnant, however, she managed to bite them back. Marçal, steadfast in keeping his part of the bargain, did not notice, nor did Cipriano, entirely innocent of suspicion. The truth is that such a revelation would be given only to someone who could not only read lips, a relatively common skill, but could also predict what they were going to say when the mouth was just about to open. This magical gift is as rare as that other gift mentioned elsewhere, that of being able to see into bodies through the skin that encloses them. However, we will immediately have to abandon the seductive profundity of both subjects, so rich in juicy reflections, to listen to what Marta has just said, Pa, do the sums, six times two hundred is one thousand two hundred, we're going to have to deliver one thousand two hundred figurines, it's a lot of work for two people, especially with so little time in which to do it. The other good news of the day, the likelihood of a child for Marçal and Marta, which they felt to be certain, paled into insignificance beside that enormous number, it became a simple everyday possibility, the chance or intentional result of a man and a woman having come together in sexual union, by what we call natural methods and without taking any precautions. The security guard Marçal Gacho said, half serious, half joking, I can see that from now on I will vanish from the landscape, I hope, at least, that you don't forget I exist, You've never existed so much as now, said Marta, and Cipriano Algor stopped thinking for a moment about the one thousand two hundred figurines to wonder to himself what she meant.

So the people who live at the Center do die after all, said Cipriano Algor as he went into the house with the dog following behind him, having dropped off his son-in-law at work, I shouldn't think anyone ever doubted it, replied Marta, everyone knows they've got their own cemetery in there, You can't see the cemetery from the road, but you can see the smoke, What smoke, The smoke from the crematorium, There isn't a crematorium in the Center, There wasn't, but there is now, Who told you, Marçal did, when we were driving down the avenue, I saw the smoke rising up from the roof, it's something they've been discussing, apparently, and now it's happened, according to Marçal they were beginning to run out of space, What I find odd is the smoke, I'd have thought that modern technology would have done away with that, They might be experimenting and burning other things, old things that have gone out of fashion, like our plates, Forget about the plates, we've got lots of work to do, Well, I came home as quickly as I could, I dropped Marçal at his work and drove straight back, said Cipriano Algor. He omitted the little detour that had allowed him to go past Isaura Estudiosa's house and did not realize that his words sounded like an excuse, or else he did realize, but was unable to avoid it. It's true that he had lacked the courage to stop the van and go and knock on the door of the widow of Joaquim Estudioso, but that was not the only reason why, to use a somewhat blunt expression, he lost his nerve, what he feared above all was finding himself standing like a fool in front of the woman and having nothing to say, and, in desperation, asking her about the water jug. One important doubt will remain forever unresolved, that is, had Cipriano Algor spoken for, say, two minutes with Isaura Estudiosa, would he have come into the house talking about death, smoke, and crematoria, or, on the contrary, would the pleasures of a doorstep conversation have brought a more pleasing subject to mind, for example, the return of the swallows and the abundance of flowers already blooming in the fields. Marta placed on the kitchen table the six designs from the last preparatory phase, in the order that they had chosen them, the jester, the clown, the nurse, the Eskimo, the mandarin, and the bearded Assyrian, identical to those sent to be judged by the head of the buying department, apart from one or two tiny differences of detail, which were not enough to consider them as different versions of the proposed figurines. Marta drew up a chair for her father, while she remained standing. He was resting his hands on the tabletop, looking at the drawings one by one, then he said, It's a shame we haven't got drawings of them in profile too, Why, To give us a clearer indication of how to make them, My idea, remember, was to make them all naked and then paint the clothes on afterward, But I don't honestly think that's a viable solution, Why not, You're forgetting that there are one thousand two hundred of them, Yes, I know there are one thousand two hundred of them, Well, modeling one thousand two hundred naked figurines and then putting clothes on each of them, one by one, would just be doing the same thing twice, it would double the workload, You're right, of course, it was stupid of me not to have thought of that, Well, if it comes to it, I was as stupid as you were, we thought the Center would choose at most three or four figurines, and it never occurred to either of us that the first order would be so large, So there's only one way of working, said Marta, Exactly, We model the six figurines that we will use for the molds, fire them, make the wooden mold frames, decide if we're going to work using casting slip or press molding, Well, I don't think we're experienced enough to use casting slip, knowing the theory of it simply isn't enough, we've always done press molding before, said Cipriano Algor, Fine, then that's what we'll continue to do, As for the mold frames, we can get a carpenter to make them, But first I've got to draw the profiles, said Marta, as well as the backs of the figurines, of course, You'll have to make it up, That won't be difficult, just a few simple lines to show the basic shape. They were two peaceful generals studying the operations map, drawing up strategy and tactics, calculating the costs, assessing the sacrifices to be made. The enemies to beat are these six dolls, half-serious, half-grotesque, made out of painted paper, they will have to be forced into surrender using the weapons of clay and water, wood and plaster, paints and fire, not to mention the tireless stroking of hands, for it is not only love that requires both stroking and hands. That was when Cipriano Algor said, There's one thing we must consider, we should have only two mold pieces, any more will just complicate matters further, Two would be enough I reckon, the dolls are very simple, just front and back and there you are, I daren't even think about the difficulties we would have had if we'd tried making the halberdier or the fencer, the navvy or the flautist, or the lancer on horseback, or the musketeer with his plumed hat, said Marta, Or the skeleton with wings and a scythe, or the holy trinity, said Cipriano Algor, Did it have wings, Which do you mean, The skeleton, Yes, it did, although Lord knows why they depict death with wings when death is everywhere, even in the Center, as I saw this morning, Does it date back to your youth that saying about how if you talk about a boat, it's because you want to embark, commented Marta, No, it's not, it's from the days of your great-grandfather, who never even saw the sea, and if his grandson keeps talking about boats, it's in order to remind himself that he doesn't want to set sail quite yet, Truce, Pa, Why, I see no white flag, Here it is, said Marta, giving him a kiss. Cipriano Algor gathered together the drawings, the battle plan had been drawn up, all that was needed now was to blow the bugle and give the order to attack, Forward, prepare for battle, but at the last moment he saw that a nail was missing from the shoe of a horse belonging to the general staff, the fate of the war might well depend on that horse, that horseshoe and that nail, everyone knows that a lame horse can carry no messages, or, if it does, it risks losing them along the way, There's one other thing, the last I hope, said Cipriano Algor, Now what, The molds, We've already discussed the molds, We've only discussed the matrixes, the wooden mold frames, which we'll keep, but what about the actual molds we'll use, we can't make two hundred figurines from just one mold, it wouldn't last very long, we'd start off with a clean-shaven clown and end up with a bearded nurse. Marta had looked away when she heard his first words, she felt the blood rushing to her face and she could do nothing to force it back down into the protective thickness of veins and arteries where shame and embarrassment go disguised as nonchalance and candor, the fault lay with that word, matrix, and the other words that spring from it, mater, maternity, maternal, the fault lay with her silence, Let's not say anything to my father just yet, she had said, and now she could not keep silent, it's true that being two days late, or even three if we count today, is nothing for most women, but she had always been exact, mathematical, very, very regular, a biological pendulum, so to speak, and had there been the slightest doubt in her mind she would not have immediately told Marçal, but what should she do now, her father is waiting for a reply, her father is looking at her, bemused, she hadn't even laughed at his joke about the bearded nurse, she simply hadn't heard it, Why are you blushing, and she cannot possibly tell him that it's not true, that she isn't blushing, in a little while she will be able to say so, because she will suddenly grow pale, there is no defense against this telltale blood and its two opposing ways of pointing the finger, Pa, I think I'm pregnant, she said and lowered her eyes. Cipriano Algor's eyebrows suddenly shot up, the expression on his face changed from puzzlement to surprised perplexity to confusion, then he seemed to be looking for the most appropriate words in the circumstances, but could find only these, Why are you telling me now, why are you telling me like this, obviously she can't say, Oh, I suddenly remembered, there's been quite enough pretense already, It was because you used the word matrix, Did I really use that word, Yes, when you were talking about the molds, You're right, I did. The dialogue was sliding rapidly into absurdity, into comedy, Marta felt a mad desire to laugh, but then suddenly her eyes filled with tears, the color returned to her face, it is not uncommon for such opposing, contrary emotions to manifest themselves in such similar ways, I think I am, Pa, I think I'm pregnant, But you're not certain yet, Yes, I am, Why did you say that you only thought you were pregnant, then, Oh, I don't know, anxiety, nerves, it's the first time it's happened to me, Presumably Marçal knows, Yes, I told him when he came home, So that's why you both seemed so different yesterday morning, Don't be silly, that's just your imagination, we were the same as we always are, And I suppose you think your mother and I were the same as we always were when we found out about you, No, of course not, forgive me. The question that Marta could see coming from the very beginning of that conversation finally arrived, So why didn't you tell me before, We've got quite enough to worry about, Pa, Do you see me looking worried now that I know, asked Cipriano Algor, Well, you don't look exactly happy, remarked Marta, trying to change the way the conversation was going, I'm happy inside, very happy, but you surely don't expect me to break into a dance, it's not really my style, Oh, Pa, I'm sorry, I've hurt you, Yes, you have, if I hadn't used that word matrix, how much longer would I have remained in ignorance of the fact that my daughter is pregnant, how much longer would I have looked at you without knowing that, Pa, please, Probably until it began to show, until you started to feel sick, then I would be the one asking are-you-ill-your-stomach's-all-distended, and you would say don't-be-silly-Pa-I'm-pregnant-and-I-forgot-to-tell-you, Pa, please, said Marta, crying now, today shouldn't be a day for tears, You're right, I'm being selfish, It's not that, No, I am being

118

selfish, but I just can't understand why you didn't tell me, you mentioned worries, well, my worries are exactly the same as yours, the pottery, the pots, the dolls, the future, if you share one thing, you share them all. Marta quickly wiped away her tears with her hands, There was a reason, but it was just some childish idea of mine, imagining feelings that probably don't even exist, and if they do exist, I shouldn't be sticking my nose in where it doesn't belong, What are you talking about, what do you mean, asked Cipriano Algor, but his tone of voice had changed, that allusion to vague feelings whose existence seemed doubtful one minute and perfectly believable the next, had troubled him, I'm talking about Isaura Estudiosa, said Marta as if she were forcing herself to plunge into a bath of cold water, What, exclaimed her father, It's just that if you were interested in her, as it seems to me sometimes you are, I thought that perhaps coming to you and telling you that you're about to have a grandchild, look, I know it's silly, but I couldn't help it, Couldn't help what, Oh, I don't know, it might make you realize, perhaps make you think that, That I'm being imbecilic, ridiculous, Those are your words, not mine, Put another way, there's the old widower out preening himself and making sheep's eyes at the young widow woman, and along comes the old boy's daughter and tells him he's going to be a grandfather, which is tantamount to saying your time is up and all you can look forward to now is taking your little grandchild out for walks and giving thanks to heaven that you've lived so long, Oh, Pa, You will have great difficulty in convincing me that this wasn't precisely the sort of thinking that lay behind your decision to keep silent about something you should have told me about immediately, I'm so sorry, murmured Marta, giving up, and this time there was no holding back her tears. Her father slowly stroked her hair and said, It's all right, time is a master of ceremonies who always ends up putting us in our rightful place, we advance, stop, and retreat according to his orders, our mistake lies in imagining that we can catch him out. Marta took his hand, which he was about to withdraw, and kissed it, pressing it hard against her lips, I'm sorry, I'm sorry, she said again. Cipriano Algor tried to console her, but the words that came out, It's all right, nothing's that important, were probably not the best suited to the purpose. He went out into the yard with a vague sense that he had been unfair to his daughter, but, more than that, he was aware that he had just said about himself what until today he had refused to admit, that his time as a man had reached its end, that during the last few days a woman called Isaura Estudiosa had been merely a fantasy in his head, an illusion gladly accepted, a last invention by the mind for the consolation of his sad flesh, a trick played on him by the fading evening light, an ephemeral breeze that passed and left no trace, a tiny drop of rain that fell and soon evaporated. The dog Found noticed that once again his master was not in the best of moods, even yesterday, when he had gone to see him at the kiln, he had been surprised by the absent look on his face, that of someone who enjoys thinking about things that are hard to understand. He touched his master's hand with his cold, damp nose, someone really should have taught this primitive animal to proffer one of his front paws as all dogs trained in the social graces end up doing perfectly naturally, moreover, there is no other way of preventing the master's beloved hand from abruptly fleeing that contact, proof, if it were needed, that not all has been resolved in the relationship between human persons and canine persons, perhaps because that dampness and coldness awakens old fears in the most ancient part of our brain, the slow, viscous caress of some giant slug, the chill, undulating touch of a serpent, the glacial breath of a cave inhabited by beings from another world. So much so that Cipriano Algor really does withdraw his hand, although the fact that he immediately strokes Found's head, clearly by way of an apology, must be interpreted as a sign that one day he might react differently, always supposing, of course, that their shared life together lasts long enough for what currently manifests itself as instinctive repugnance to become mere habit.

The dog Found cannot understand these subtleties, the use he makes of his nose is natural, it comes to him from nature, and is therefore more healthily authentic than the way humans shake each other's hands, however cordial that may seem to our eyes and touch. What the dog Found wants to know is where his master will go when he finally emerges from the state of distracted immobility in which he sees him now. In order to communicate to him that he is awaiting a decision, he again touches him with his nose, and when Cipriano Algor immediately headed off toward the kiln, Found's animal mind, which, regardless of what others may say, is the most logical of all the minds to be found in the world, led him to conclude that in the lives of humans once is never enough. While Cipriano Algor sat down heavily on the stone bench, the dog devoted himself to sniffing the large pebble from beneath which the lizard had appeared, but his master's evident concerns weighed more in his mind than the seductions of what would doubtless prove to be a futile hunt, and so it was not long before he had lain down in front of him, prepared for an interesting conversation. The first words that the potter said, So that's that, then, a precise, laconic sentence with no ifs, ands, or buts, did not seem to promise any further developments, however, in these cases, the best thing a dog can do is to remain silent until the silence of his master grows weary, dogs know that human nature is, by definition, a talkative one, imprudent, indiscreet, gossipy, incapable of closing its mouth and keeping it closed. Indeed, we can never imagine the abyssal depths of introspection reached by such an animal when it looks at us, we think he is doing simply that, looking, and we do not realize that he only appears to be looking at us, when the truth is that, having seen us, he moves on, leaving us to flounder like idiots on the surface of ourselves, spattering the world with pointless and fallacious explanations. The silence of the dog and the famous silence of the universe to which we made theological reference elsewhere, an apparently impossible comparison given the vast differences in material and objective size, are, in fact, absolutely equal in density and specific weight to two tears, the difference lying only in the pain that made them form, overflow, and fall. So that's that, then, said Cipriano Algor again, and Found did not even blink, knowing perfectly well that what was being referred to was not the supply of plates to the Center, that's ancient history now, no, there's a woman involved in all this, and it can only be that same Isaura Estudiosa whom he had seen from inside the van when his master delivered the water jug, a woman with a pretty face and a pretty figure, although we must point out that this is not an opinion formulated by Found, concepts like ugly and pretty do not exist for him, the canons of beauty are human ideas, Even if you were the ugliest of men, the dog Found would say of his master were he able to speak, your ugliness would have no meaning for me, I would only find you odd if you acquired a different smell or stroked my head in a different way. The trouble with digressions is the ease with which the digressor can become distracted by diversions, making him lose the thread of words and events, as has just happened to Found, who caught only the second half of the following words spoken by Cipriano Algor, which is why, as you will notice, they do not start with a capital letter, that's it, I won't go running after her any more, said the potter, obviously he wasn't referring to the above-mentioned capital letter, since he doesn't use them when he speaks, but to the woman called Isaura Estudiosa, with whom, from then on, he vowed to have no more dealings, I've been behaving like a stupid child, from now on, I won't go running after her any more, that was the entire sentence, but the dog Found, although not doubting for a moment the little he had heard, could not help noticing that the melancholy look on his master's face openly contradicted the resolution expressed by his words, although we know that Cipriano Algor's decision is final, Cipriano Algor will not go looking for Isaura Estudiosa, Cipriano Algor is grateful to his daughter for having made him see the light of reason, Cipriano Algor is a grown man, grown up but not yet grown old, not one of those silly adolescents who, because they are at the age of unthinking enthusiasms, spend their time chasing fantasies, will-o'-the-wisps, and imaginings, and they don't give up on them until both their head and the feelings they thought they had collide with the wall of impossibilities. Cipriano Algor got up from the stone bench, he seemed to find it hard to lift his own body, which is not surprising, for the weight of what a man feels is not always the same as the weight registered on the scales, sometimes it's more, sometimes it's less. Cipriano Algor is about to go into the house, but contrary to what was said earlier, he will not thank his daughter for having made him see the light of reason, that is too much to ask of a man who has just given up a dream, modest though it was, a mere widow woman, he will say instead that he is going to order the mold frames from the carpenter, not because that is the most urgent task, but in order to gain a bit of time, when it comes to deadlines, carpenters and tailors can never be relied on, at least that is how it was in the old world, although, what with ready-to-wear and do-it-yourself, the world has changed a lot. Are you still angry with me, asked Marta, I wasn't angry, just a bit disappointed, but it's not a subject we want to go on talking about ad infinitum, you and Marçal are going to have a child, I'm going to have a grandchild, and it will all be for the best, with everything in its place, it was time to put an end to fantasies, when I come back, we'll sit down and plan our work, we've got to make the most of this coming week, next week I'll be busy transporting the crockery from the warehouse, at least for most of the day, Take the van, said Marta, there's no point wearing yourself out, It's not worth it, the carpenter doesn't live far away. Cipriano Algor called to the dog, Come on, and Found followed him, He might bump into her, he was thinking. Dogs are like that, they sometimes decide to do their owners' thinking for them.

The very genuine motives for complaint that Cipriano Algor has about the Center's pitiless commercial policy, largely presented in this story from the point of view of frank class solidarity without, or so we believe, ever departing from the most rigorous impartiality, cannot disguise the fact, though we run the risk here of stirring up the slumbering bonfire of the historically difficult relationship between capital and work, cannot, as we were saying, disguise the fact that Cipriano Algor bears some of the blame for this himself, the main reason, ingenuous and innocent enough, but also, as so often with the ingenuous and the innocent, the malignant root of all the other reasons, was his assumption that certain tastes and needs common to his founding grandfather's contemporaries vis-à-vis ceramics would remain unchanged per omnia saecula saeculorum or, at least, for the rest of his life, which, when you think about it, comes to the same thing. We have seen the very traditional way in which the clay here is kneaded, we have seen the rustic, almost primitive wheels they use, we have seen that the kiln outside shows traces of an antiquity unforgivable in this modern age, which, for all its scandalous defects and prejudices, has had the goodness to allow a pottery like this to coexist with a Center like that, at least until now. Cipriano Algor complains and complains, but he does not seem to understand that kneaded clay is no longer stored like this, that it will not be long before the basic ceramics industries of today turn into laboratories with employees in white coats taking notes and with immaculate robots doing all the work. This pottery, for example, is crying out for hygrometers to measure the atmospheric humidity and the appropriate electronic mechanisms for keeping it constant and correcting it whenever it gets too high or too low, there is no place now for working things out by eye or by touch, by feel or by smell, according to the retrograde technological procedures of Cipriano Algor, who has just said to his daughter as if it were the most natural thing in the world, The clay's fine, just the right degree of wetness and plasticity, nice and easy to work, now, we ask ourselves, how can he be so sure of what he's saying when all he has done is to place his hand on the clay, if all he has done is to pinch the clay between his thumb, forefinger, and middle finger, as if, with eyes closed, depending entirely on the interrogative sense of touch, he were appreciating, not a homogeneous mixture of red clay, kaolin, silica, and water, but the warp and weft of silk. It is likely, as we have recently had occasion to observe and to propose for consideration, that it is not he, but his fingers who know. At any rate, Cipriano Algor's verdict must be in accordance with the physical reality of the clay because Marta, who is much younger and much more modern, much more in tune with the age we live in, and, as we know, no fool when it comes to making pots, passed without comment to another matter, asking her father, Do you think there's enough here to make one thousand two hundred figurines, Yes, I think so, but I'll try to beef it up a bit. They moved into the part of the pottery where they kept the colors and other finishes, recorded what was there and made a note of what was not, We're going to need more colors than this, said Marta, the dolls have to be attractive to the eye, And we'll need plaster for the molds and ceramic soap and oil for the paints, added Cipriano Algor, we'd better get everything we need now, so that we won't have to stop work in order to go and buy things later. Suddenly Marta looked very thoughtful, What's wrong, asked her father, We've got a really serious problem, What's that, We'd decided to use press molding, Right, But we haven't discussed the making of the figurines themselves, we can't possibly make one thousand two hundred figurines using press molding, the molds wouldn't take it and we wouldn't be able to work quickly enough, it would be like trying to empty the sea with a bucket, You're right, Which means that we're going to have to resort to slip casting, We don't have much experience with that, but we're not too old to learn, That isn't the worst of it, Pa, What is then, Well, I remember reading, I'm sure we've got the book in the house somewhere, that to do slip casting, it's best not to use a clay that contains kaolin, and ours does, at least thirty percent, My brain clearly isn't what it was, why didn't I think of that, It's not your fault, we're not used to working with casting slip, Yes, I know, but you learn that in pottery kindergarten, it's absolutely basic to the craft. They looked at each other in bewilderment, they were not father and daughter, not future grandfather and future mother, they were just two potters confronted by the enormous and risky task of having to extract the kaolin from the worked clay and then making it less heavy by introducing some lighter clay. In fact, such an alchemical operation is simply impossible. What shall we do, asked Marta, let's look at the book, perhaps, No, it's not worth it, you can't remove kaolin from clay or neutralize it, it doesn't even make sense, how could you remove or neutralize kaolin I ask myself, the only solution is to prepare more clay with the right components, There isn't time, Pa, No, you're right, there isn't. They left the pottery, two dejected figures whom Found did not even attempt to approach, and now they were sitting in the kitchen, looking at the drawings that were looking back at them, and they could see no way of getting over this sticking point, they knew from experience that heavy clays tend to shrink too much, to crack and become distorted, they are too plastic, soft, pliable, but they did not know how this would affect the casting slip nor what negative consequences this might have for the finished work. Marta looked for and found the book, there it said that to prepare the slip, it was not enough to dissolve the clay in water, you had to use deflocculants, such as sodium silicate, or soda ash, or potassium silicate, or even caustic soda if it wasn't such dangerous stuff to handle, ceramics is the art in which it is truly impossible to separate chemistry from its physical and dynamic effects, but what the book doesn't say is what will happen to my dolls if I make them with the only clay I've got, and about which there is nothing I can do, the other problem is quantity, if there were only a few of them, we would use press molding, but one thousand two hundred, good grief. If I understand it correctly, said Cipriano Algor, the most important things to bear in mind with casting slip are density and viscosity, Yes, it explains that here, said Marta, Read it, then, The ideal density is one point seven, in other words, one liter of slip should weigh one thousand seven hundred grams, if you don't have a suitable densimeter and you want to know the density of the slip, use a test tube and a pair of scales, minus the weight of the test tube of course, And what about viscosity, To measure viscosity, use a viscosimeter, of which there are various types, each of them giving readings drawn from scales based on different criteria, It's not much help that book, Yes, it is, pay attention, All right, One of the most frequently used is the torsion viscosimeter which gives a reading in degrees Gallenkamp, Who was he, It doesn't say, Read on, According to that scale, the ideal viscosity is between two hundred and sixty and three hundred and sixty degrees, Can't you find anything in there I can understand, asked Cipriano Algor, Coming up now, said Marta, and she read, In our case we will use a traditional method, which, though empirical and imprecise, can, with practice, give an approximate measurement, Which method is that, Plunge your hand deep into the casting slip, then take it out and let the slip run off your open hand, if it forms a membrane between the fingers like a duck's webbed foot then the viscosity is right, Like a duck's webbed foot, Yes, like a duck's foot. Marta put the book down and said, We're not much farther forward, Yes, we are, now we know that we won't be able to work without deflocculants and that until we have duck's feet we won't have any usable casting slip, Well, I'm glad you're in a good mood, Moods are like the tides, they come in and they go out, mine has just come in, we'll see how long it lasts, It has to last, this house is in your hands, The house is, yes, but not life, Has the tide gone out already, asked Marta, It's hesitant, vacillating, not quite sure whether it's high tide or low tide, Then stay with me, because I'm in a fluctuating mood, as if I wasn't quite sure that I am what I think I am, Sometimes I think we might be better off not knowing who we are, said Cipriano Algor, Like Found, Yes, I imagine that a dog knows less about himself than he does about his master, he can't even recognize himself in a mirror, Perhaps a dog's mirror is his master, perhaps that's the only mirror in which he can recognize himself, suggested Marta, It's a nice idea, You see, even wrong ideas can be nice, If the pottery goes under, we can always breed dogs, There are no dogs at the Center, Poor Center, not even dogs want to live there, It's the Center that doesn't want the dogs, Well, that problem is of interest solely to those who live there, said Cipriano Algor in an angry tone of voice. Marta did not respond, realizing that anything she said might give rise to another argument. As she reordered the somewhat dog-eared drawings yet again, she thought, If Marçal comes home tomorrow and says that he's been made a resident guard, that we have to move, then what we're doing now makes no sense, whether Pa comes with us or not, one way or another the pottery will be condemned, even if he insists on staying, he can't work on his own and he knows that. What thoughts Cipriano Algor had meanwhile remain a mystery, and it's hardly worth inventing some which might not coincide with any real and actual thoughts he had, however, always supposing that words were not given to man in order to conceal his thoughts, it would be permissible for us to conclude from what the potter said after a long silence, There's nothing wrong with having illusions, what's wrong is deluding yourself, that he had probably been thinking the same as his daughter and that, logically speaking, they would both have reached the same conclusions. Anyway, said Cipriano Algor, without realizing, or perhaps only realizing at the very moment in which he spoke it, what sibylline subtleties it contained, anyway, a moored boat goes nowhere, whatever happens tomorrow, we've got to work today, there's no way of knowing if the tree you plant will also turn out to be the tree you hang yourself from, In an oil slick like that our boat will never get anywhere, said Marta, but you're quite right, time isn't out there waiting for us, we have to start work, my first task is to draw the side views and back views of the figures and color them in, I should finish them by tonight if no one disturbs me, We're not expecting any visitors, said Cipriano Algor, and I'll make the lunch, It's just a matter of heating it up, so all you have to do is make a salad, said Marta. She went off to get the drawing paper, watercolors, paint pots, and brushes and an old rag to dry them on, placed everything neatly and methodically on the table, sat down, and picked up the drawing of the bearded Assyrian, I'll start with this one, she said, Simplify as much as possible so that we won't have any problems with bits sticking or catching when the mold is removed, two molds will be enough, a third one would be beyond us, All right, I won't forget. Cipriano Algor remained for a few minutes watching his daughter draw, then he went outside to the pottery. He was going to grapple with the clay, to lift the weights and barbells involved in learning something anew, to rediscover a lost dexterity and to make a few experimental figures that are clearly not jesters or clowns, Eskimos or nurses, nor Assyrians or mandarins, figures that anyone, man or woman, young or old, could look at and say, They look just like me. And perhaps one of those people, woman or man, old or young, out of the pleasure or possible vanity of taking home with them that extraordinarily faithful representation of the image they have of themselves, will come to the pottery and ask Cipriano Algor how much that figurine over there costs, and Cipriano Algor will tell them that it's not for sale, and the person will ask why, and he will reply, Because it's me. It was late afternoon, almost dusk, when Marta came into the pottery and said, I've finished, I've left them to dry on the kitchen table. Then, noticing the work her father had been doing, two unfinished standing figures about two spans high, one male, the other female, both naked, and one of whom has a bit of wire sticking out of one shoulder, she said, Not bad, Pa, not bad, but don't forget that our figurines won't need to be so big, we were thinking of a height of about one span, They should be a bit bigger than that, I think, then they'll stand out more on the shelves in the Center, and we have to take into account shrinkage inside the kiln when they lose the last bit of moisture, besides, I was just experimenting, No, I think they're good, I really do, and they're not like anything else I've ever seen, although the woman does remind me of someone, Make up your mind, said Cipriano Algor, first you say they're nothing like anything you've ever seen and then you say the woman reminds you of someone, It's a kind of dual impression, of strangeness and familiarity, Perhaps I won't have to breed dogs after all, perhaps I can take up sculpture, which is, so I hear, one of the more lucrative arts, An exemplary family of artists, commented Marta with a half-ironic smile, Fortunately, we've got Marçal, so all is not lost, replied Cipriano Algor, but he did not smile.

This was the first day of creation. On the second day, the potter went into town to buy plaster for the molds, as well as the soda ash he had decided to use as a deflocculant, colors, a few plastic buckets, new wooden and wire spatulas, paddles and drill bits. The question of colors had been the subject of lively debate during and after supper on that first day, the point of controversy being whether the figurines should be placed in the kiln after being painted or if, on the contrary, they should be painted after firing and then not refired. If they chose one way, the paints had to be of one kind, and if they chose the other way, the paints had to be of another, so the decision had to be made at once, it could not be left until the last minute, when they were sitting poised with brush in hand, It's a question of aesthetics, said Marta, It's a question of time, said Cipriano Algor, and confidence, Painting them before firing will give them a glossier, higher-quality finish, she insisted, But if we paint them afterward, we avoid any unpleasant surprises, the color we use is the one that will remain, we won't be dependent on the effect on the pigments of firing, because you know how temperamental the kiln can be. Cipriano Algor's view prevailed, the colors to be bought would, therefore, be those known in the specialist market as china paints, quick-drying and easy to apply, with a great variety of colors, and, as for a dilutant, which is essential because the paint itself is normally far too thick, if you don't want to use a synthetic dilutant, ordinary lamp oil will do. Marta opened the art book again, looked for the chapter on cold painting and read, To be applied to pieces that have already been fired, the piece should be sanded down with fine sandpaper so as to eliminate any rough edges or other defects in the finish, rendering the surface more uniform and allowing the paint to adhere more easily in areas where the piece may have been overfired, Sanding down one thousand two hundred figurines is going to take forever, Once this has been done, Marta read on, you must remove any trace of dust produced by sanding, using a compressor, We haven't got a compressor, said Cipriano Algor, Another preferable albeit slower method is to use a stiff brush, The old ways have their advantages, Not always, Marta corrected him, and went on, As happens with nearly all such colors, china paints do not remain homogeneous in the can for very long, which is why it is essential to stir well before applying, That's elementary, everyone knows that, skip to the next bit, The colors can be applied directly to the piece, but they adhere better if you begin by applying an undercoat, usually matte white, We hadn't thought of that, It's difficult to think of things you don't know about, I disagree, I think we think about things precisely because we don't know about them, Leave that enthralling idea for another time and just listen, I am listening, The undercoat can be applied with a brush, but in order to achieve a smooth coat, there is some advantage in using a spray gun, We haven't got one, Or else dipping, That's the classic way of doing it, so let's use dipping, The whole process will be carried out cold, Good, Once painted and dried, the piece should not and cannot be subject to any further firing, That's what I was telling you, it saves time, It gives some other recommendations too, but the most important is that you must let the first color dry completely before applying the next, unless you want to achieve a layered or fused effect, We don't want effects or transparencies, we want speed, this isn't oil painting, Anyway, the mandarin's costume will need more careful treatment, said Marta, remember the design itself calls for great diversity and richness of color, We'll simplify it. Those words closed the debate, but the debate continued in Cipriano Algor's mind as he was making his purchases, for, at the last moment, he bought a spray gun. Given the size of the figurines, there's no point in applying a thick undercoat, he explained to his daughter, I think the gun will work best, just give the figurine a quick spray and there you are, We'll need masks, said Marta, Masks are expensive, we haven't got money to spend on luxuries, It's not a luxury, it's a precaution, we're going to be breathing in a cloud of paint, That's easily solved, How, I'll do the work outside in the open air, the weather looks set fair, Why did you say I'll do it rather than we'll do it, asked Marta, Because you're pregnant and I'm not, as far as I know, Your good humor's returned, Pa, Oh, I do my best, and I realize that there are some things that are slipping away from me and others that are threatening to do so, I just have to work out which of them it's worth struggling to hold on to and which I should just let slip away painlessly, Or painfully, The worst pain, my dear, isn't the pain you feel at the time, it's the pain you feel later on when there's nothing you can do about it, They say that time heals all wounds, But we never live long enough to test that theory, said Cipriano Algor, and at that precise moment he realized that he was working at the very wheel over which his wife had collapsed when she suffered her fatal heart attack. Then, obliged to do so by his own moral honesty, he asked himself if the pain of which he had spoken also included that death, or if it was true that, in that particular case, time had carried out its work as master healer, or if the pain invoked was not, after all, about death, but about life, about lives, yours, mine, ours, whoever's. Cipriano Algor was working on the figure of the nurse, Marta was busy with the clown, but neither of them felt satisfied with their successive attempts, perhaps because copying is, in the end, more difficult than creating freely, at least that might be the view of Cipriano Algor, who had conceived those two figures, male and female, with such passion and spontaneity, and which are over there, wrapped in damp cloths so that they do not dry out and allow the spirit that keeps them erect, static, and yet alive to crack. Marta and Cipriano Algor have their work cut out for them, part of the clay they are using now comes from other figures they had to discard and reknead, so it is with all things in this world, words, for example, which are not things, which merely designate things as best they can, and in doing so shape them, even if employed with exemplary correctness, always assuming that this could happen, words are used millions of times and rejected as many times again, and then we, tails between our legs, like the dog Found when he shrinks with shame, must humbly go in search of them again, like the pounded clay that they are, kneaded and chewed, swallowed down and regurgitated, the eternal return really does exist, but not in that form, in this. The clown Marta has made might be usable, the jester too bears some resemblance to a real jester, but the nurse, who had seemed so simple, so straightforward, so clear-cut, refuses to allow her breasts to emerge from beneath the clay, as if she too were wrapped in a damp cloth and was keeping a tight grip on the corners. Only when the first week of creation was nearly over, when Cipriano Algor was about to move into the first week of destruction, picking up the crockery from the Center warehouse and getting rid of it somewhere like so much useless rubbish, did the fingers of the two potters, simultaneously free and disciplined, finally begin to invent and forge the straight path that will lead them to the right shape, the precise line, the harmonious whole. Moments never arrive either late or early, they merely arrive at the right time for them, not for us, there is no need to feel grateful when what they propose happens to coincide with what we need. On the half day during which her father will be carrying out the absurd task of unloading as useless trash the very objects he had loaded onto the van as being surplus to requirements, Marta will be alone in the pottery with her half dozen figurines almost finished, busy now with sharpening up any blurred angles and in rounding out any curves unwittingly lost in the modeling process, evening out the height, strengthening the bases, working out for each of the statues the optimum seams for the two molds. The mold frames have not yet been delivered by the carpenter, the plaster is waiting inside great sacks made of thick impermeable paper, but the time to multiply is approaching.

When Cipriano Algor returned home on the first day of the week of destruction, more incensed at the indignity of it all than exhausted by the effort involved, he recounted to his daughter the absurd adventure of a man traipsing around the countryside in search of some deserted place where he could unload the useless crocks he was carrying, as if it were his own excrement, Caught with my trousers down, he was saying, that's what I felt like on the two occasions when people came to ask me what I was doing there, on private property, with a van overflowing with pots and plates, I had to make up some feeble excuse about trying to get to a road farther along and thinking that this was the best route to take, I'm terribly sorry, and by the way, if there's anything in the van you'd like, I'll be happy to give it to you, one of them was very rude and said that, in his house, even the animals wouldn't eat their food off rubbish like that, but the other one took a fancy to a casserole dish and carried it off, So where did you leave the stuff in the end, Near the river, Where, Well, I'd thought a natural cave would be the best bet, but even then there was always the chance that the things would be on full view to anyone passing by and that they would immediately recognize the product and the maker, and we've suffered enough embarrassments and humiliations as it is, I don't feel particularly embarrassed or humiliated, Perhaps you would if you had been in my place from the beginning, Yes, you're probably right, so did you manage to find somewhere, The ideal hollow, Is there such a thing as the ideal hollow, asked Marta, That depends on what you want to put inside it, but imagine in this case a large, more or less circular hollow with trees and bushes growing in it, about nine feet deep and with an easy slope down into it, which, seen from the outside, looks like a green island in the middle of the countryside, in the winter it fills up with water, in fact, there's still some water in the bottom now, It's about a hundred yards from the river edge, said Marta, Oh, so you know it, said her father, Yes, I discovered it when I was ten years old, and it really was the ideal hollow, whenever I went down into it, I felt as if I were going through a door into another world, Yes, I used to go down there too when I was about that age, And my grandfather when he was that age, And my grandfather too, Everything is lost in the end, Pa, for years the hollow was just a hollow, as well as a magic door for a few imaginative children, and now, it'll get filled up with debris and it will be neither one thing nor the other, There aren't that many pots and plates and the brambles will soon grow over them, no one will even notice, So you left it all there, did you, Yes, I did, At least it's near the village, one day, one of the children here, if, that is, they still visit the ideal hollow, will turn up at home with a cracked plate, they'll ask him where he found it and, before you know it, everyone will be rushing over there to take their pick of the very things that, right now, nobody wants, It wouldn't surprise me in the least, that's the way people are. Cipriano Algor finished the cup of coffee that his daughter had placed before him when he got home and asked, Any sign of the carpenter, No, Right, I'd better go over there and chivy him along, Yes, I think you'd better. The potter got up, I'm going to have a wash, he said, then took a few short steps and stopped, What's this, he asked, What, This, he was pointing at a plate covered with an embroidered napkin, It's a cake, You made a cake, No, I didn't make it, someone brought it over, it's a present, Who from, Guess, I'm not in the mood for guessing games, But this one's really easy. Cipriano Algor shrugged as if to say that he wasn't interested and said again that he was going to have a wash, but he did not move, he did not take the step that would carry him out of the kitchen, a debate was going on inside his head between two potters, one was arguing that it was our duty to behave naturally under all circumstances, that if someone is kind enough to bring us a cake covered with an embroidered napkin, it is only right and proper to ask whom one should thank for this unexpected generosity, and if, in reply, we are told to guess, it would look most suspicious if we pretended not to hear, these little games played in families and in society are not of great importance, no one is going to draw hasty conclusions if we guess correctly, mainly because the number of people who might give us a cake is never going to be that large, indeed often there might be only one, that, at least, is what one of the potters was saying, but the other replied that he was not prepared to play the part of fall guy in some silly circus game of riddles, that it was precisely because he did know the name of the person who had brought the cake that he would not say it, and also because the worst thing about conclusions, at least in some cases, is not that they might occasionally be hasty, but that they are precisely that, conclusions. So, you don't want to guess, then, insisted Marta, smiling, and Cipriano Algor, slightly annoyed with his daughter and very annoyed with himself, but aware that the only way out of the hole he had dug for himself was to admit defeat and turn back, abruptly said a name, though wrapping it up in words, It was the widow, our neighbor, Isaura Estudiosa, as a thank-you for the water jug. Marta shook her head slowly, Her name isn't Isaura Estudiosa, she said, it's Isaura Madruga, Ah, I see, said Cipriano Algor, thinking that now there would be no

need to ask Isaura, So what's your maiden name, but then he immediately reminded himself that, while sitting on the stone bench beside the kiln, with the dog Found as witness, he had decided to
declare null and void all the words that had been exchanged and all
the incidents that had occurred between him and the widow Estudiosa, let us not forget that the words pronounced were So that's
that, then, one does not bring an episode in one's sentimental life to
such a peremptory close only to unsay what you have said two days
later. The immediate effect of these reflections was for Cipriano
Algor to adopt such a convincingly nonchalant, superior air that he
was able to remove the napkin without a tremor and say, It looks
good. It was at that moment that Marta thought fit to add, In a way
it's a good-bye present. The hand was slowly lowered, delicately re-
placing the napkin on top of the cake like a circular crown, Good-
bye, Marta heard him ask, Yes, if she doesn't manage to find any
work here, Work, You keep repeating what I've just said, Pa, No, I
don't, I'm not some kind of echo and I don't keep repeating everything you've said. Marta ignored this answer, We had a cup of coffee, and I wanted to cut a slice of the cake, but she wouldn't let me,
she was here for over an hour, we chatted, she told me a bit about
her life, the story of her marriage, how they never got a chance to
find out whether theirs was a happy marriage or whether the happiness was just beginning to fade, those were her words, not mine,
anyway, if she can't find any work, she's going back to where she
came from and where she still has family, There's no work for anyone around here, said Cipriano Algor gloomily, That's what she
thinks too, that's why the cake is like the first half of a good-bye,
Well, I hope I'm not here when the second half arrives, Why, asked
Marta. Cipriano Algor did not answer. He left the kitchen and entered his bedroom, undressed rapidly, glanced at what the wardrobe
mirror revealed to him of his body and went into the bathroom. A
little salt water mingled with the fresh water falling from the shower.

With remarkable and reassuring unanimity, the dictionaries all define ridiculous as meaning anything deserving of mockery or laughter, anything that merits scorn, seems ludicrous or lends itself to comedy. For dictionaries, the particular circumstance does not appear to exist, although when they have to explain what it is, they describe it simply as a state or quality that accompanies a fact, which, in parenthesis, clearly warns us not to separate the facts from their circumstances and not to judge the former without first considering the latter. Yet could there be anything more profoundly ridiculous than Cipriano Algor wearing himself out trudging down the slope into the hollow, carrying the unwanted crockery in his arms, instead of hurling it willy-nilly down from above, transforming it instantly into mere crocks as he scornfully referred to it when describing to his daughter the various stages of the whole traumatic journey. The ridiculous, however, knows no limits. If one day, as Marta imagined, a boy from the village were to retrieve a cracked plate from the rubble and take it home with him, we can be sure that the unfortunate defect had either occurred in the warehouse itself or been caused, given the inevitable clashing of pots and plates, by the uneven road surface during the trip from the Center to the hollow. We have only to observe the care with which Cipriano Algor goes down the slope, the trouble he takes in placing the various bits of pottery on the ground, in keeping like with like, fitting one inside the other when he can and when it seems advisable, it is enough to see this laughable scene with our own eyes for us to state categorically that not a single plate was broken, that not a single cup lost its handle and not a single teapot was deprived of its spout. The regular lines of piled-up pottery fill one chosen corner of the hollow, they encircle the trunks of the trees, snake about among the low vegetation as if it had been written in some great book that they should remain like that until the end of time and until the unlikely resurrection of their remains. Some will say that Cipriano Algor's behavior is utterly ridiculous, but even here we must not forget the crucial importance of point of view, we are referring this time to Marçal Gacho, who, home once more for his day off, and fulfilling what might normally be understood as elementary duties of family solidarity, not only helped his father-in-law to unload the pottery, but also, without any show of puzzlement or bemused perplexity, without asking any questions direct or indirect, without a single ironic or pitying glance, calmly followed his example, even, on his own initiative, steadying some perilously swaying stack, neatening a ragged line, and reducing the height of any piles that have grown excessively tall. It would therefore be only natural, should Marta ever repeat the unfortunate pejorative term which she used in conversation with her father, that her own husband, with the irrefutable authority of one who has seen something with his own eyes, would correct her, It isn't debris. And if she, whom we have come to know as someone who requires clear explanations of all things, were to insist that it was indeed debris, which is the name that has always been used to designate detritus and other useless matter used to fill up holes, apart, of course, from human remains, which are called something else entirely, Marçal would doubtless say to her in his grave voice, It isn't debris, I was there. Nor, he would add, should the question arise, is it ridiculous.

Awaiting them when they got home were two novelties, each important in its own way. The carpenter had finally delivered the mold frames, and Marta had read in her book that when filling with casting slip, one could only sensibly expect one mold to yield forty satisfactory copies, That means, said Cipriano Algor, that we will need at least thirty molds, five for every two hundred figurines, which means a lot of work before and a lot of work afterward, and, given our lack of experience, we can't be sure that the molds will work perfectly anyway, When do you reckon you'll have finished removing all the crockery from the Center warehouse, asked Marta, I shouldn't think I'll need the whole of the second week, just two or three days might be enough, This is the second week, said Marçal, Yes, the second week of the four weeks, but the first week of ferrying the crockery back and forth, the third week will be the second week of actual production, explained Marta, With all these different weeks, I'm not surprised you and your father are a bit disoriented, We each have our own reasons for being disoriented, I, for example, am pregnant and haven't quite got used to the idea, And your father, He can speak for himself if he wants to, The only disorientation I'm suffering from is having to make one thousand two hundred clay dolls without the faintest idea whether or not I'll be able to do it, said Cipriano Algor. They were standing in the pottery, where, lined up on the work surface, were the six figurines, looking exactly and dramatically what they were, six insignificant objects, some more grotesque than others because of what they represented, but all identical in their poignant futility. Marta had removed the damp cloths wrapped about them so that her husband could see the dolls, but she almost regretted it, for it was as if those obtuse idols had not deserved all the work that had gone into creating them, the repeated making and unmaking, the trying and failing, the experimenting and adjusting, it is not only great works of art that are born out of suffering and doubt, even a simple clay body and a few simple clay limbs sometimes refuse to surrender to the fingers modeling them, to the eyes interrogating them, to the will calling them into being. Any other time and I would have asked for some leave so that I could help you out, said Marçal. Although that sentence was apparently complete, it contained problematic implications which did not need to be articulated in order for Cipriano Algor to understand them. What Marçal had wanted to say and what, without actually doing so, he had in fact said, was that, since he was awaiting a more or less definite promotion to the rank of resident guard, his superiors would not be very pleased with him if he went off on holiday at that precise moment, as if public notification of his rise on the career ladder were a banal episode of little importance. That was the most obvious and probably the least problematic of whatever other implications there might be. The heart of the matter, which Marçal's words unwittingly concealed, was a sense of continuing concern about the future of the pottery, about the work carried out there and the people who did the work and who, for better or worse, had, until then, made a living from it. Those six figurines were like six ironic, insistent question marks, each of them asking Cipriano Algor if he was still confident that he had the necessary strength, and for how long, dear sir, to run the pottery alone when his daughter and son-in-law went to live at the Center, if he was naive enough to think that he could fulfill with satisfactory regularity the ensuing orders, always assuming there were any more orders, and, indeed, if he was foolish enough to imagine that from now on his relationship with the Center and with the head of the buying department, both commercial and personal, would be one long honeymoon, or, as the Eskimo was asking with discomfiting acuity and bitter skepticism, Do you really think they are always going to want me. It was at this point that Cipriano Algor remembered Isaura Madruga, he thought that she could help him in the work at the pottery, sit beside him in the van on his trips to the Center, he thought of her in diverse and ever more intimate and soothing situations, having lunch at the same table, chatting on the stone bench, giving Found his food, picking the fruit from the mulberry tree, lighting the lamp above the door, drawing back the sheets on the bed, these thoughts were doubtless too many and too adventurous for someone who had not even wanted to try a slice of cake. Marçal's words did not, of course, require an answer, they merely verified a fact obvious to all, it was just as if he had said, I would like to help you, but I can't, nevertheless, Cipriano Algor thought he should give expression to some of the thoughts that had filled the silence following Marçal's words, not the intimate thoughts, which he keeps locked up in the strongbox of his pathetic old man's pride, but those which, in one way or another, whether they want to admit it or not, are common to those living in the house, and which can be summed up in little more than half a dozen words, I wonder what tomorrow holds for us. He said, It's as if we were walking in the dark, with each step we take, we could as easily go forward as fall flat on our face, we'll soon be worrying about what awaits us once the first order goes on sale, we'll start calculating how long they'll want to keep us on, a long time, a short time, no time at all, it will be like plucking the petals off a daisy to see what answer we get, Not unlike life really, remarked Marta, Yes, except that what would once have been a process of years will now take weeks or days, the future suddenly seems very short, in fact, I think I've said as much before. Cipriano Algor paused, then added with a shrug, Which just proves that it must be true, There are only two ways ahead, said Marta, resolute and impatient, we either continue working as we have up until now, without thinking about anything except how to make a good job of what we're doing, or else we give up, tell the Center that we can't complete the order and wait, Wait for what, asked Marçal, For you to be promoted and for us to move to the Center, and for my father to decide once and for all if he wants to stay or to go with us, what we can't do is carry on in this will-we-won't-we situation that has been going on for weeks now, In other words, said Cipriano Algor, if Dad would only die, we could get on with the soup, I'll forgive you for what you've just said, replied Marta, because I know what's going on inside your mind, Don't fall out about it, please, begged Marçal, I get quite enough of that from my own family, Calm down, don't worry, said Cipriano Algor, although it might look like it to some people, your wife and I never really fall out, No, although there are times when I feel like hitting you, threatened Marta, smiling, and it will only get worse you know, people have told me that pregnant women often suffer sudden mood changes, they have caprices, fads, tantrums, crying attacks, and violent rages, so prepare yourselves for what is to come, For my part, I'm resigned to it, said Marçal, then addressing Cipriano Algor, What about you, Pa, Oh, I've been resigned to it for years, ever since she was born, At last, all power to the woman, tremble, O men, tremble and be afraid, exclaimed Marta. This time the potter did not adopt his daughter's jovial tone of voice, instead he spoke calmly and seriously as if he were picking up one by one words that had been set down in the place where they had been thought and left to ripen, no, these words had not been thought and left to ripen, they emerged at that moment from his mind like roots suddenly rising to the surface of the soil, Work will proceed normally, he said, I will fulfill our commitments as best I can, without protest or complaint, and when Marçal receives his promotion then I will consider the situation, You'll consider the situation, asked Marta, what does that mean, Since it will be impossible to keep the pottery going, I will close it and cease being one of the Center's suppliers, Fine, and what will you live on then, where, how, with whom, insisted Marta, I will go and live with my daughter and my son-in-law at the Center, that is, if they still want me to. This unexpectedly clear statement from Cipriano Algor elicited very different responses from his daughter and from his son-in-law. Marçal exclaimed, At last, and he went over and embraced his father-in-law, You've no idea how pleased I am, it's been like a doubt gnawing away at me. Marta looked at her father skeptically at first, like someone who cannot quite believe what they are hearing, but gradually her face lit up with understanding, it was her memory hard at work reminding her of certain popular sayings, certain snippets from the classics, certain old saws, it did not, it is true, recall everything there was to recall, for example, burn your boats, burn your bridges, make a clean break, cut the Gordian knot, cut loose, cut and run, in for a penny, in for a pound, a dying man needs no advice, cut your losses, sour grapes, a bird in the hand is worth two in the bush, all these and many more, and all meaning more or less the same thing, I don't want what I can't have, and what I can't have I don't want. Marta went over to her father and stroked his face with a long, tender, almost maternal caress, It will be better this way, if that's what you really want, she murmured, and she gave no other sign of contentment than the little conveyed by those few, plain words, but she was sure that her father would understand that this was not out of indifference but out of respect. Cipriano Algor placed his hands on his daughter's shoulders, then drew her to him, kissed her on the forehead and, in a low voice, said the words she wanted to hear or to read in his eyes, Thank you. Marçal did not ask Thank you for what, he had long ago learned that the territory in which this father and daughter moved was not just peculiar to that family, it was in some way sacred and inaccessible. It was not jealousy he felt, merely the melancholy of one who knows himself to be definitively excluded not, however, from that territory, which could never be his, but from another in which, if they were ever there or if he could ever be there with them, he would at last find and recognize his own father and his own mother. He realized, without much surprise, that now that his father-in-law had decided to go and live at the Center with them, the idea of his parents selling their house in the village in order to do the same would inevitably be set aside, however hard that might be for them and however much they protested, first, because one of the Center's inflexible rules, determined and imposed by the actual structure of the living quarters, is not to admit large families, and second, because since the two families have never got on well, one can easily imagine the hell their lives would become if they were all crammed together in a small space. Despite certain situations and certain outbursts that might lead one to conclude the opposite, Marçal does not deserve to be considered a bad son, it is not his fault alone that his feelings and desires do not accord with those of his family, and yet, providing still further proof that the human soul is a poisoned well of contradictions, he is glad not to have to live in the same house as those who brought him into being. Now that Marta is pregnant, let us hope that mysterious Fate does not confirm in her and in him those ancient dictums, Like breeds like and Do as you would be done by. It is true, however, that one way or another, by a kind of infallible tropism, filial nature drives children to find substitute parents when, for good motives or bad, for reasons fair or unfair, they cannot, will not or are unable to recognize themselves in their own parents. Indeed, for all its defects, life loves balance, if it was up to life every cloud would have a silver lining, every concavity would have its convexity, there would be no farewell without an arrival, and word, gesture and glance would behave like inseparable triplets who always say the same thing in all circumstances. By routes whose detailed description we do not feel fitted or able to carry out, but of whose existence and intrinsic communicative value we are absolutely convinced, it was precisely the above-mentioned cluster of observations that planted an idea in Marçal Gacho's head, an idea that was immediately transmitted to his father-in-law with due filial enthusiasm, We could transport what's left of the crockery in the warehouse in one load, he announced, You don't even know how much is left, there are a good few vanloads yet, objected Cipriano Algor, I'm not talking about vans, I mean that an ordinary truck would be enough to carry all of it in one load, And where are we going to find this precious truck, asked Marta, We'll hire one, That would cost me money I could ill afford, said the potter, but hope made his voice tremble, It would just take one day's work, if we pooled our money, ours and yours, I'm sure we could do it, and besides, with me working as a security guard at the Center, we might get a discount, it's worth a try, With just me doing all the loading and unloading I don't think I could manage, my arms and legs are killing me as it is, You won't be alone, I'll go with you, said Marçal,

No, they might recognize you and that could look bad, Oh, I don't think there's much danger of that, I've only ever been to the buying department once, and in dark glasses and a beret, I could be anyone, It's a good idea, very good, said Marta, then we could get straight on with the work of making the dolls, That's what I thought, said Marçal, Me too, admitted Cipriano Algor. They stood looking at each other, silent and smiling, until the potter asked, When shall we do it, Tomorrow if you like, replied Marçal, we can use my free time, we won't get another chance for another ten days and then it will be too late, Tomorrow, repeated Cipriano Algor, that would mean we could set to work properly immediately afterward, Exactly, said Marçal, and gain nearly two weeks, You've given me new heart, said the potter, then he asked, How shall we do it, I don't think there are any trucks for hire in the village, We'll hire one in the city, we'll set off first thing tomorrow so that we have time to find someone who'll give us a good price, Look, I know that's the best plan, said Marta, but I really think you should have lunch with your parents, you didn't go last time you were home and they're bound to be put out. Marçal bristled, I don't feel like it, and besides, he turned to his father-in-law and asked, What time do you have to be at the warehouse, At four, You see, there isn't time to have lunch with my parents, drive all the way to the city, hire a truck and be at the warehouse to pick up the crockery, Tell them you've got to have lunch really early, There still won't be time, and anyway I don't want to, I'll go next time I'm home, At least phone your mother, All right, I'll phone her, but don't be surprised if she asks me again when we're moving. Cipriano Algor had left his daughter and son-in-law to discuss the momentous question of the Gacho family lunch and had gone over to where the six dolls stood on the worktable. He very carefully removed the damp cloths and studied the figures closely, one by one, they just needed a little retouching on their heads and faces, parts of the body which, on such small figurines, little more than a span high, would inevitably be affected by the pressure of the cloths, Marta will be in charge of restoring them to new, then they will remain uncovered in order to dry off before being placed in the kiln. A shudder of pleasure ran through Cipriano Algor's aching body, he felt as if he were about to begin the most difficult and delicate task of his life as a potter, the potentially hazardous firing of an object of enormous aesthetic value modeled by a great artist who did not mind lowering himself to work in the precarious conditions of this humble place, and who, and we are speaking now of both object and artist, could not possibly accept the ruinous consequences that would result from a variation in heat of just one degree in either direction. What this is really about, without making a great drama out of it, is placing half a dozen insignificant figurines in the kiln and firing them in order to produce two hundred equally insignificant copies from each one, some say that our fate is already planned for us when we are born, but what is clear is that only a few come into this world to make clay adams and eves or to multiply loaves and fishes. Marta and Marçal had left the pottery, she in order to make the supper and he to deepen his incipient relationship with the dog Found, who, although reluctant to accept without protest a uniform in the family, does seem prepared to adopt a position of tacit acquiescence as long as the said uniform is replaced, on arrival, by some type of civil garment, whether ancient or modern, new or old, clean or dirty, Found really doesn't mind. Cipriano Algor is now alone in the pottery. He absentmindedly tested the solidity of one of the mold frames, quite unnecessarily moved a bag of plaster and, as if his steps had been guided not by will but by chance, found himself standing before the two figures he had modeled, the man and the woman. In a matter of seconds, the man had been transformed into a shapeless ball of clay. The woman might have survived if the question Marta would be sure to ask him the following morning had not rung in his ears, Why, why the man and not the woman, why only one and not both of them. The woman's clay soon joined that of the man, they are once more one clay.

The first act of the play is over, the scenery has been removed, the actors are resting from their exertions in the final climactic scene. Not a single piece of pottery made by the Algor family remains in the Center's warehouses, apart from a scattering of red dust on the shelves, it is always as well to recall that the cohesive nature of matter is not eternal, if the continual rubbing of time's invisible fingers can so easily destroy marble and granite, what will it not do to mere clay of precarious composition and doubtless the product of somewhat hit-and-miss firing. Marçal Gacho went unrecognized in the buying department thanks to the beret and dark glasses he was wearing, not to mention his unshaven face, which he had deliberately left unshaven in order to make his protective disguise still more effective, since among the various distinguishing characteristics of a Center security guard is a perfect, closely shaven chin. The assistant head of department was, however, puzzled by the suddenly improved mode of transport, a logical feeling for a person who had more than once allowed himself an ironic smile at the sight of Cipriano Algor's ancient van, but what was surprising, to say the least, was the barely contained irritation evident in his eyes and in his face when Cipriano Algor informed him that he had come to take away the rest of the crockery, All of it, the man asked, All of it, replied the potter, I've brought a truck and someone to help me. If this demonstrably ill-natured assistant head of department were to have any kind of future in the story we have been following, we would probably eventually get around to asking him to explain what lay behind his feelings on that occasion, that is, to explain the underlying reason for his clearly illogical annoyance, which he either made no attempt to hide or else was simply incapable of doing so. He would doubtless try to fob us off by saying, for example, that he had grown used to Cipriano Algor's daily visits and, although he could not in all honesty say that they were friends, he had grown rather fond of him, especially given the poor man's distinctly inauspicious professional situation. A barefaced lie, of course, since if we go beyond merely uncovering the depths and excavate the even lower depths, we will see that his sense of exasperation betrayed his frustration at losing that most perverse of pleasures, that of gloating over other people's misfortunes even when one stands to gain nothing from them oneself. On the pretext that the work would take too long and that they would get in the way of other suppliers unloading their goods, the ghastly man even tried to stop them loading the truck, but Cipriano Algor, as the eloquent phrase has it, dug his heels in, and asked who then would pay for the hire of the truck if they had to turn back, he demanded to be given the complaints book, and his final, desperate gambit was to say that he would not leave until he had spoken to the head of the buying department. Any book on elementary applied psychology, in the chapter on behavior, will tell you that nasty people are often cowards, and so we should not be too surprised that the assistant head of department's fear of being overruled in public by his hierarchical superior produced an instantaneous change of attitude. He made some rude comment to cover up his feelings of humiliation, then disappeared into the back of the warehouse and remained there until the truck, fully loaded up, had left the basement. Neither Cipriano Algor nor Marçal Gacho sang a victory song, either literally or figuratively, they were too tired to waste what was left of their breath on trills and congratulations, the older man merely said, He'll make our lives a misery when we deliver the other merchandise, he'll examine the dolls with a magnifying glass and reject them by the dozen, and the younger man said that, yes, he might, but it was by no means certain, and, besides, it was the head of the buying department who was in charge, at least we've solved one problem, Pa, and we'll deal with the next one when it arises, that's how life should be, when one person loses heart, the other must have heart and courage enough for both. They had parked the van on a nearby street corner, and it would stay there until they returned from unloading the last bits of crockery in the hollow near the river, then they would return the truck to the garage and, finally, as dusk was falling, they would arrive home, exhausted, more dead than alive, one because he had grown too used to walking the smooth corridors of the Center and had thus lost the healthy habit of physical effort, the other because of the all too familiar disadvantages of age. The dog Found will come down the road to meet them, leaping and barking the way dogs do, and Marta will be waiting at the door. She will ask, So, is it all taken care of then, and they will say, yes, it's all taken care of, and then all three of them are bound to think or feel, always assuming that there is some imbalance or contradiction between feeling and thinking, that the part that has just finished is the same part that is now impatient to begin, that the first, second, and third acts, whether in the theater or in life, are always part of one play. It is true that some of the props have been removed from the stage, but the clay from which the new props will be made is the same as yesterday's clay, and the actors, when they wake tomorrow from their sleep in the wings, will place their right foot in front of the mark made by their left foot, then place the left foot in front of the right, and, do what they will, they will not depart from that path. Despite Marçal's exhaustion, he and Marta will repeat, as if it were the first time, the gestures, movements, groans, and sighs of love. And the words too. Cipriano Algor will sleep dreamlessly in his bed. Tomorrow morning, as usual, he will take his son-in-law to work. Perhaps, on the way back, he will have a look at the hollow by the river, for no particular reason, not even out of curiosity, he knows exactly what is there, but despite that, he might nevertheless walk to the edge of the hollow and, if he does, he will look down and wonder if he should cut a few more branches in order to camouflage the pots and plates more effectively, it is as if he did not want anyone to know about them, as if he wanted the pots to stay there, hidden, stored away, until the day when they are needed again, ah, how difficult it is to separate ourselves from what we have made, be it reality or a dream, even if we have actually destroyed it with our own hands.

I'm going to clean out the kiln, said Cipriano Algor when he got home. The dog Found's previous experiences made him think that his master was about to sit down again on the bench of meditations, the poor man's mind must still be clouded with conflicts, his life turned upside down, and it is on just such occasions that dogs are most needed, when they sit before us with the infallible question in their eyes, Do you need help, and although, at first glance, it might seem beyond the ken of an animal like that to offer a remedy for pain, anxiety and other human afflictions, perhaps it is only because we are incapable of perceiving what lies beyond our humanity, as if other afflictions in the world only have a tangible reality if they can be measured by our standards or, put more simply, as if only what is human existed. Cipriano Algor did not sit down on the stone bench, he walked straight past it, then, having drawn back, one after the other, the three great bronze bolts installed at different heights, at the top, in the middle and at the bottom, he opened the kiln door, which creaked gravely on its hinges. After the first few days of sensorial investigations, which had satisfied his immediate curiosity as a newcomer, the dog Found had shown no further interest in the kiln. It was a brick structure, old and crudely built, with a high, narrow door, it was a building with no known use and where no one lived, with three things on the top like chimneys, but which were obviously not chimneys, since the provoking smell of food had never once issued forth from them. And now the door had unexpectedly opened and his master had gone inside as nonchalantly as if he were entering his house, just like the other house over there. On principle and as a precautionary measure, a dog should always bark at any surprises life throws at him, because he has no way of knowing beforehand if the good surprises could turn bad or the bad cease to be what they were, therefore Found barked and barked, first out of concern when his master appeared to vanish into the shadowy depths of the kiln, then out of joy to see him emerge whole and with a changed look on his face, these are the small miracles of love, for caring about what you do also deserves that name. When Cipriano Algor went back into the kiln, this time wielding a broom, Found was not in the least concerned, for, when you think about it, a master is in some ways like the sun and the moon, we must be patient when he disappears and wait for time to pass, a dog, of course, will be unable to say whether a long time or a short time has passed, for he cannot distinguish between such periods as an hour and a week, between a month and a year, for such an animal there is only absence and presence. During the cleaning of the kiln, Found made no attempt to go in, he moved to one side to avoid the shower of small fragments of fired clay and shards from broken pots expelled by the broom, and lay down, his head between his paws. He seemed absorbed, half-asleep, but even a person inexperienced in canine ways would know, if only from the furtive manner in which the dog occasionally opened and closed his eyes, that the dog Found was simply waiting. Once the task of cleaning was done, Cipriano Algor left the kiln and went over to the pottery. As long as he remained in view, the dog did not move, then he slowly got up, advanced with outstretched neck toward the kiln door and looked in. It was a strange, empty house with a vaulted ceiling, utterly devoid of furniture or decoration and lined with off-white slabs, but what most impressed Found's nose was the extreme dryness of the air inside, as well as the pungency of the one perceptible smell, the final smell of an infinite process of calcination, and do not be surprised by that flagrant and conscious contradiction between final and infinite, for we are dealing here not with human sensations, but with what it was humanly practicable for us to imagine a dog might have felt on entering an empty kiln for the first time. Contrary to what one would naturally expect, Found did not mark the new place with urine. It is true that he began to do as instinct ordered him, it is true that he did threateningly raise one leg, but he controlled himself and stopped at the very last moment, perhaps terrified by the surrounding mineral silence, by the rough construction of the place, by the whitish, phantasmagorical color of walls and floor, perhaps, more simply, it was because he thought his master might react violently if the kingdom, throne and dossal of the fire, the crucible in which the ordinary clay dreams of being turned into a diamond, were found to be sullied by urine. With the hairs along his back bristling, with his tail between his legs, as if he had been spurned and driven far away, the dog Found left the kiln. He could not see either of his owners, the house and the countryside looked utterly empty, and the mulberry tree, though this was doubtless merely the effect of the sun's angle of incidence, seemed to cast a strange shadow that lay on the ground as if it had been cast by an entirely different tree. Contrary to the general view, dogs, however well cared for and however kindly treated, do not have an easy life, first, because they have not as yet reached a satisfactory understanding of the world into which they were born, and, second, because that difficulty is continually exacerbated by the contradictory and unstable behavior of the human beings with whom they share, if we may put it like that, house, food, and occasionally bed. His master has disappeared, his mistress is nowhere to be seen, so the dog Found vents his melancholy and his full bladder on the stone bench whose only use is as a place of meditation. It was then that Cipriano Algor and Marta emerged from the pottery. Found ran to meet them, it is at moments like this that he has the feeling that he is finally going to understand everything, that feeling did not last, however, it never does, his master bawled at him, Get out of here, his mistress, alarmed, shouted, Down, boy, there really is no fathoming these people, only afterward will the dog Found notice that each of his owners is carrying some clay figures balanced on small planks, three apiece and three on each plank, you can imagine how disastrous it would have been if they hadn't reined in his enthusiasm in time. The funambulists move toward the long drying shelves which, for weeks now, have been empty of plates, mugs, cups, saucers, bowls, jugs, jars, pitchers, pots, and other ornaments for house and garden. These six dolls, which are going to dry in the open air, protected by the shade of the mulberry tree, but touched occasionally by the sun that slips in and out between the leaves, are the advance guard of a new occupation, that of hundreds of identical figures whose serried ranks will fill the long shelves, one thousand two hundred figurines, six times two hundred according to their earlier calculations, but the calculations were wrong, the joy of victory is not always a good counselor, these potters, despite their three generations of experience, seem to have forgotten that, since even scissors can eat the cloth they cut, it is vital to allow some margin for losses, a piece can fall or break, can become distorted, can contract too much or too little, can crack under heat because it was poorly made, can emerge badly fired because of the faulty circulation of hot air, and to all of this, which is directly related to the physical contingencies of a craft that has much to do with alchemy, that, as we know, is not an exact science, to all of this, as we were saying, must be added the rigorous examination to which, as is only to be expected, the Center, not to mention that assistant head of department who seems to have it in for them, will subject each of the dolls. Cipriano Algor only thought of these two threats, one definite and one potential, when he was sweeping out the kiln, that's the good thing about the association of ideas, they draw each other out, one after the other, the skill lies in not losing the thread, in understanding that a shard of pottery on the ground is not only what it is at present, it is also what it was in the past when it was something else, as well as what it might become in the future.

It is said that a long time ago a god decided to make a man out of the clay from the earth that he had previously created, and then, in order that the man should have breath and life, he blew into his nostrils. The whisper put around by certain stubborn, negative spirits, when they do not dare to say so out loud, is that after this supreme act of creation, the god never again practiced the arts of pottery, a roundabout way of denouncing him for, quite simply, having downed tools. Given its evident importance, this is too serious a matter to be treated in simplistic terms, it requires thought, complete impartiality and a great deal of objectivity. It is a historical fact that from that memorable day onward, the work of modeling clay ceased to be the exclusive attribute of the creator and passed to the incipient skills of his creatures, who, needless to say, are not equipped with sufficient life-giving puff. As a result, fire was given responsibility for all the subsidiary operations that can, through color, sheen or even sound, endow whatever emerges from the kilns with a reasonable semblance of life. However, this would be to judge by appearances. Fire can do a great deal, as no one can deny, but it cannot do everything, it has serious limitations and even some grave defects, for example, a form of insatiable bulimia which causes it to devour and reduce to ashes everything it finds in its path. Returning, however, to the matter in hand, to the pottery and its workings, we all know that if you put wet clay in a kiln it will have exploded in less time than it takes to say so. Fire lays down one irrevocable condition if we want it to do what we expect of it, the clay must be as dry as possible when it is placed in the kiln. And this is where we humbly return to that business about breathing into nostrils, and here we will have to recognize how very unjust and imprudent we were to take up and adopt as our own the heretical idea that the said god coldly turned his back on his own work. Yes, it is true, that no one ever saw him again, but he left us what was perhaps the best part of himself, the breath, the puff of air, the breeze, the soft wind, the zephyr, the very things that are now gently entering the nostrils of the six clay dolls that Cipriano Algor and his daughter have, with great care, just placed on one of the drying shelves. That god, a writer as well as a potter, knew how to write straight on crooked lines, for, not being here himself to do the blowing, he has sent someone to do the job for him, so that the still fragile life of these clay figures will not be extinguished tomorrow in the blind and brutal embrace of the fire. When we say tomorrow, that is, of course, just a manner of speaking, because if it is true that, in the beginning, one puff of air was enough for the clay of the man to gain breath and life, many more will be necessary before the jesters, clowns, bearded Assyrians, mandarins, Eskimos, and nurses, those who are here now and those who will later form serried ranks on these same shelves, gradually lose, by evaporation, the water without which they would never have become what they are, and can thus go safely into the kiln in order to be transformed into what they will be. The dog Found had got up on his hind legs and rested his paws on the edge of the shelf to get a closer view of the six idols lined up in front of him. He sniffed once, twice, and immediately lost interest, but not quickly enough to avoid the sharp, painful slap his master dealt him on the head nor the repetition of the harsh words he had heard before, Get out of here, how could he explain that he wasn't going to harm any of the figurines, he just wanted to have a closer look and to sniff them, it was unfair of you to hit me for such a minor offense, anyone would think you didn't know that dogs do not have only eyes with which to investigate the outside world, our nose is like an extra eye, it sees what it smells, at least this time, though, she didn't shout, Down, boy, fortunately, there's always someone capable of understanding the motives of others, even those who, dumb by nature or lacking vocabulary, do not know how or do not have words enough to explain themselves, You didn't have to hit him, Pa, he was just curious, said Marta. It is likely that Cipriano Algor himself had not wanted to hurt the dog, he just acted out of instinct, which, contrary to what most people think, we human beings have still not lost and are not about to lose either. It lives side by side with the intelligence, but is infinitely faster, which is why the poor thing is so often made fun of and frequently spurned, that was what happened in this case, the potter reacted out of the fear of seeing something over which he had labored destroyed, exactly as a lioness would react at seeing her cub in danger. Not all creators neglect their creations, be they cubs or clay figurines, not all of them go away and leave in their place an inconstant zephyr that only blows now and then, as if we had no need to grow and go into the kiln to find out who we are. Cipriano Algor called the dog, Come here, Found, come here, there really is no understanding either of these creatures, they lash out and immediately stroke the creature they hit, if you hit them, they immediately kiss the hand that did the hitting, maybe this is just a consequence of the problems we have been encountering since the very beginning of time in our attempts to understand each other, we dogs and we humans. Found has already forgotten the blow he was dealt, but his master has not, his master remembers, he will forget tomorrow or in an hour's time, but for the moment he cannot forget, in these cases memory is like the instantaneous touch of the sun on the retina that burns the surface, a tiny, unimportant thing, but bothersome while it lasts, the best thing would be to call the dog over and say, Found, come here, and Found will go, he always does, and he licks the hand that strokes him because that is the way dogs kiss, soon the burn will vanish, sight will return to normal, and it will be as if nothing had happened.

Cipriano Algor went to check how much wood they had and realized that it wasn't enough. For years he had cherished the idea that the time would come when the old wood-burning kiln would be demolished and in its place would rise a new kiln, a modern, gas-fired one, capable of reaching extremely high temperatures very fast and of producing excellent results. Inside himself, though, he knew that this would never happen, first, because it would require a lot of money, more than he would ever have, but also for other less materialistic reasons, such as knowing beforehand that it would sadden him to destroy what his grandfather had built and what his father had later perfected, if he did, it would be as if he were, quite literally, wiping them from the face of the earth, for the kiln sits precisely on the face of the earth. He had another reason, less easy to own up to, which he could dispatch in three words, I'm too old, but which, objectively, implied the use of pyrometers, pipes, security pilot lights, burners, in short, new techniques and new problems. There was, therefore, no alternative but to continue fueling the old kiln in the old way, with wood and wood and more wood, perhaps that is the hardest part of working with clay. Just like the stokers on steam trains, who used to spend all their time shoveling coal into the furnace, the potter, at least this one, Cipriano Algor, who cannot afford to pay an assistant, spends hour upon wearisome hour feeding this archaic fuel into the kiln, twigs that the fire enfolds and devours in an instant, branches that the flame gradually nibbles and licks into embers, it is best when fed with pinecones and sawdust, which burn more slowly and produce more heat. Cipriano Algor will get supplies from the surrounding area, order a few cartloads of wood from foresters and farmers, buy a few sacks of sawdust from sawmills and carpenter's workshops in the Industrial Belt, preferably from hardwoods like oak, walnut, and chestnut, and he will do all this alone, it does not even occur to him to ask his daughter to come with him and help him load the sacks onto the van, especially now that she's pregnant, he will take Found with him, just to show that they're friends again, which seems to indicate that the burn in Cipriano Algor's memory has not yet fully healed. The wood in the shed will be more than enough for firing the six figures to be used as molds, but Cipriano Algor hesitates, he finds absurd, crazy, unforgivably wasteful, the huge disproportion between the means to be used and the ends to be achieved, in other words, in order to fire the ridiculously small number of six dolls, he will have to use the kiln as if it were packed to the roof. He said as much to Marta, who agreed and half an hour later came up with a solution, The book explains how to solve the problem, it even gives a helpful drawing. It is quite possible that, when he was starting out as a potter, Marta's great-grandfather, who lived in the olden days, might once have used the process of pit firing, which was antiquated even then, but the installation of the first kiln must have gradually dispensed with that rustic practice and, in a way, consigned it to oblivion, for it was not passed on to Cipriano Algor's father. Fortunately, there are books. We can leave them on a shelf or in a trunk, abandon them to the dust and the moths, dump them in dark cellars, we may not even lay eyes on them or touch them for years and years, but they don't mind, they wait quietly, closed in upon themselves so that none of their contents are lost, for the moment that always arrives, the day when we ask ourselves, I wonder where that book about firing clay has got to, and the book, summoned at last, appears, it's here in Marta's hands while her father, beside the kiln, is digging a small hole about half a meter deep and half a meter wide, that is all the space the dolls need, then he arranges on the bottom a layer of small branches and sets light to them, the flames rise and caress the walls, getting rid of any surface moisture, then the fire will die down and all that will remain are the hot ashes and a few small embers, and it is on these that Marta, having passed the book, open at the relevant page, to her father, very carefully places, one by one, the six test pieces, the mandarin, the Eskimo, the bearded Assyrian, the clown, the jester, and the nurse, inside the pit, the hot air still shimmers, it touches the gray epidermises and the dense interiors of the bodies, from which almost all the water has already evaporated thanks to the effects of the light wind and the breeze, and now, over the mouth of the pit, for lack of a proper grille especially made for the purpose, Cipriano Algor is placing, not too close together, not too far apart, as the book tells him, some narrow iron bars, through which will fall the embers from the fire that the potter had already begun to kindle. So happy were they to have found that invaluable book, neither father nor daughter had noticed that the near-twilight hour at which they had started work would mean that they would have to keep feeding the fire throughout the night, until the embers had filled the hole completely and the firing was over. Cipriano Algor said to his daughter, You go to bed and I'll stay and watch the fire, and she said, I wouldn't miss this for all the gold in the world. They sat down on the stone bench to watch the flames, from time to time, Cipriano Algor gets up and puts on more wood, smallish branches so that the embers will fall between the bars, when it was time for supper, Marta went into the house to prepare a light meal, which they ate afterward in the light that flickered on the side kiln wall as if the kiln too were burning inside. The dog Found shared what there was to eat, then lay down at Marta's feet, staring into the flames, he had been near other fires in his time, but none like this, well, that is probably not quite what he meant, fires, large and small, are all very similar, burning wood, sparks, charred logs, and ashes, what Found was thinking was that he had never been as he was now, lying at the feet of two people upon whom he had bestowed forever his doggy love, next to a stone bench suited for serious meditations, as he himself, from then on and from direct personal experience, will be able to attest. Filling half a cubic meter with embers takes some time, especially if the wood, as in this case, is not completely dry, and the proof of this is that you can see the last drops of sap sizzling at the ends of the logs that have not yet caught fire. It would be interesting, were it possible, to look inside, to see if the embers have already reached the dolls' waists, but all one can do is to imagine what it must be like inside the pit, vibrant and glowing with the light from the many brief flames that consume the small pieces of incandescent wood as they fall. As the night grew colder, Marta went into the house to fetch a blanket which they, father and daughter, wrapped about their shoulders to keep warm. They did not need anything in front, what was happening now was what used to happen when, in times past, we would go over to the fireside to warm ourselves on winter nights, our backs freezing while our faces, hands and legs were scalding hot. Especially our legs because they were nearest to the fire. Tomorrow the hard work begins, said Cipriano Algor, I'll help, said Marta, Oh, you'll help, all right, you've no alternative, although I don't like it, But I've always helped, Yes, but now you're pregnant, Only a month, if that, it doesn't make any difference yet, I feel absolutely fine, What worries me is that we might not be able to see this through to the end, We'll manage, If only we could find someone to help us, You yourself said that no one wants to work in potteries any more, besides, we'd just waste our time teaching whoever came and for very negligible gains, Right, agreed Cipriano Algor, suddenly distracted. He had just remembered that Isaura Estudiosa, or Isaura Madruga, as she seemed to call herself now, was looking for work, and that if she didn't find anything she would leave the village, but this thought barely troubled him, indeed he did not even want to imagine that Madruga woman working at the pottery, with her hands in the clay, the only talent she had shown for the job so far was the way she had clasped a water jug to her breast, but that's no help when what you've got to do is manufacture figurines, not just clasp them to you. Anyone can do that, he thought, although he wasn't entirely sure that this was true. Marta said, What we could do is get someone in to take care of the household chores, leaving me free to work in the pottery, We can't afford a maid or a domestic or a char or whatever they're called, said Cipriano Algor sharply, It could be someone who needs something to do and who doesn't mind not earning very much for a while, insisted Marta. Her father impatiently removed the blanket from his shoulders as if he were too hot, If you're thinking what I think you're thinking, we'd better stop this conversation right now, What we don't know is whether it only entered your mind because I thought of it, said Marta, or if you had already thought of it when it entered mine, Please, don't play with words, you're very good at it and I'm not, it's certainly not a talent you inherited from me, There must be some part of us which is all our own work, but anyway, what you call playing with words is just a way of making them more visible, Well, you can cover those particular words up again, because I'm not interested. Marta replaced the blanket, draping it over her father's shoulders again, They're already covered up, she said, and if ever anyone uncovers them again, I can guarantee that it won't be me. Cipriano Algor pushed the blanket off again, I'm not cold, he said, and went to put more wood on the fire. Marta was touched by the meticulous way in which he placed the new logs on the burning embers, careful and precise, like someone who, in order to drive out troubling thoughts, gives all his attention to some unimportant detail. I shouldn't have brought the matter up again, she said to herself, especially not now when he's said that he'll come with us to the Center, besides, if they did get on well enough to want to live together, we would be faced by a difficult, not to say, impossible problem, it's one thing going to the Center with your daughter and son-in-law, it's quite another taking your wife, we wouldn't be one family, we'd be two, I'm sure they wouldn't take us then, Marçal told me that the apartments are tiny, so they would have to stay here and live on, what exactly, two people who hardly know each other, how long would their understanding last, I'm not so much playing with words as playing with the feelings of other people, with the feelings of my own father, what right have I, what right have you, Marta, just put yourself in his place, you can't, of course, well, then, if you can't, just be quiet, they say each person is an island, but it's not true, each person is a silence, yes, that's it, a silence, each of us with our own silence, each of us with the silence that is us. Cipriano Algor came back to the stone bench, and he himself wrapped the blanket around his shoulders even though his clothes were still warm from the fire, Marta snuggled up to him, Pa, she said, Pa, What, Oh, nothing, just ignore me. It was gone one o'clock when the pit began to fill up. We can go in now, said Cipriano Algor, in the morning, when they've cooled off, we can remove the figurines and see how they've turned out. The dog Found accompanied them to the door of the house. Then he went back to the fire and lay down. Beneath the fine layer of ashes, the embers still glowed, giving off a tenuous light. It was only when the embers had burned out completely that Found closed his eyes to go to sleep.

Cipriano Algor dreamed that he was inside his new kiln. He felt happy because he had managed to persuade his daughter and his son-in-law that the sudden increase in activity at the pottery called for radical changes in the way they made the pots and a rapid updating of the means and methods of production, beginning with the urgent replacement of the old kiln, an archaic remnant of a way of life that would not even merit preservation as a ruin in an open-air museum. Let us jettison any feelings of nostalgia which will only hinder and hold us back, Cipriano had said with unusual vehemence, progress moves implacably forward, and we have no option but to keep pace with it, and woe to those who, fearful of future upheavals, are left sitting by the roadside weeping for a past that was no better than the present. These words emerged from his mouth so complete, perfect, and polished that it convinced the two reluctant young people. Besides, it must be said that the technological differences between the new kiln and the old were nothing out of the ordinary, everything that had been in the first kiln in antiquated mode was present, in updated form, in the second kiln, the only really striking differences were the sheer size, with twice the capacity of the old kiln, and, although perhaps less noticeable, the slightly abnormal proportions inside the kiln between height, length, and breadth. Given that all this was happening in a dream, however, the latter point is not so very odd. What is odd, regardless of the liberties and excesses that the logic of dreams may allow the dreamer, is the presence of a stone bench, identical to the bench of meditations, of which Cipriano Algor can see only the back, because, most un-usually, the bench is turned to face the rear wall and is positioned barely five spans away from it. The builders probably put it here to sit on during their lunch break, then forgot to take it with them, thought Cipriano Algor, but he knew this couldn't be true, builders, and this is borne out by historical fact, always prefer to have their lunch outside, even when working in the desert, and especially when they're in a pleasant rural setting like this, with the drying shelves set out beneath the mulberry tree and a lovely midday breeze blowing. Well, wherever you came from, you'll have to join the other one outside, said Cipriano Algor, the problem is how to shift you, you're too heavy to carry and if I tried to drag you out, it would ruin the floor, I can't understand why they put you inside the kiln in the first place and in that position too, anyone sitting there would have their nose almost pressed against the wall. To prove to himself that he was right, Cipriano Algor slipped carefully in-between one end of the bench and the relevant bit of wall and sat down. He had to admit that his nose did not, in fact, run the slight-est risk of being grazed by one of the refractory bricks, and that his knees, even though they were further forward, were also safe from any unpleasant abrasions. However, he could, without the slightest effort, touch the wall with his hand. Just as Cipriano Algor's fingers were about to touch it, a voice from outside said, I wouldn't bother lighting the kiln if I were you, my friend. This unexpected advice came from Marçal, and it was his shadow that was cast briefly on the back wall only to disappear immediately. Cipriano Algor thought it rude and disrespectful of his son-in-law to speak to him like that, He's never usually that familiar with me, he thought. He started to turn around and ask why it wasn't worth lighting the kiln and why he should suddenly start being so familiar with him, but he could not turn his head, this often happens in dreams, we want to run and our legs won't respond, it's usually the legs, but this time it was his neck that refused to turn. The shadow had gone, so he couldn't ask it any questions, in the vain and irrational hope that a shadow might have a tongue to articulate an answer, but the harmonics of the words Marçal had spoken continued to reverberate between the ceiling and the floor, between one wall and another wall. Before the vibrations had completely died away and before the scattered substance of the broken silence had had time to reconstitute itself, Cipriano Algor wanted to know for what mysterious reason he should not light the kiln, if that really was what his son-in-law's voice had said, for now it seemed to him that he had said something else even more enigmatic, It's not worth sacrificing yourself, Pa, as if Marçal thought that his father-in-law, whom, it would seem, he had not, in fact, treated with disrespectful familiarity, had decided to try out the powers of the fire on his own body before delivering up to them the work made by his hands. He's mad, the potter muttered to himself, my son-in-law would have to be completely crazy to think such a thing, the reason I came into the kiln was because, but the sentence remained incomplete because Cipriano Algor did not know why he was there, which is hardly surprising, if the same thing happens often enough when we're awake, not knowing why we are doing this or that or why we did something else, what can we expect when we are asleep and dreaming. Cipriano Algor thought that the best and easiest solution would be to get up from the stone bench and go outside and ask his son-in-law what the hell he was talking about, but his body felt like a lead weight, or not even that, because no lead weight could possibly be so heavy that it could never be lifted, he was, in fact, tied to the back of the bench, tied without ropes or chains, but tied nevertheless. He again attempted to turn his head, but his neck would not obey him, I'm like a stone statue sitting on a stone bench looking at a stone wall, he thought, although he knew that this was not strictly true, the wall, as his eyes, those of a man who knew about matters mineral, could see, had not been built of stone but of refractory bricks. Just then Marçal's shadow again appeared on the wall, I've brought you the good news we've been expecting for so long, said his voice, I've finally been promoted to resident guard, so there's no point in continuing production, we'll tell the Center we've closed the pottery, they'll understand, it had to happen sooner or later, so you might as well come out of there, the truck's here to take all the furniture away, it was a complete waste of money buying this kiln. Cipriano Algor opened his mouth to reply, but the shadow had already gone, what the potter wanted to say was that the difference between the word of a craftsman and a divine commandment was that the latter had had to be written down, with the disastrous consequences with which we are all familiar, anyway, if he was in such a hurry he could just bugger off, a rather vulgar expression that contradicted the solemn declaration he himself had made not many days since, when he had promised his daughter and his son-in-law that he would go and live with them if Marçal was promoted, since if both of them moved to the Center, he could not possibly continue to work in the pottery. Cipriano Algor was just rebuking himself for having promised to do something that his honor would never allow him to go through with when a new shadow appeared on the wall. In the feeble light that can squeeze in through the door of a kiln this size, it is very easy to confuse two human shadows, but the potter knew at once whose shadow it was, neither the shadow, which was darker, nor the voice, which was deeper, belonged to his son-in-law, Senhor Cipriano Algor, I have come to tell you that we have just canceled our order for the clay figurines, said the head of the buying department, I don't know and I don't want to know why you're in there, if you fancied yourself as some romantic hero waiting for the wall to reveal the secrets of life to you, that strikes me as plain ridiculous, but if you were intending to go further than that, if your intention was to perform some act of self-immolation, you should know right now that the Center takes no responsibility for your death, that's all we need, getting blamed for the suicides of incompetents who go bust because of their own failure to understand the dictates of the market. Cipriano Algor did not turn his head toward the door, although he was certain that now he would be able to do so, he knew that the dream had ended, that nothing would prevent his getting up from the stone bench whenever he wanted to, only one thing still troubled him, doubtless absurd, doubtless foolish, but understandable if we bear in mind the perplexed state in which he was left by the dream of having to go and live in the very Center that had just spurned his work, and what troubled him, we will get there, don't worry, we haven't forgotten, has to do with the stone bench. Cipriano Algor is asking himself if he has taken a stone bench to bed with him or if he will wake up covered with dew on that other stone bench, the bench of meditations, that is what human dreams are like, sometimes they attach themselves to real things and transform them into visions, at others they make delirium play hide-and-seek with reality, which is why we so often say that we don't know where we are, our dream pulling at us from one side, reality pushing us from the other, the truth is that straight lines exist only in geometry and even then they are only an abstraction. Cipriano Algor opened his eyes. I'm in bed, he thought, relieved, and at that moment he realized that his memory of the dream was about to flee, that he would only manage to hold on to bits of it, and he did not know whether he should rejoice over the little that remained or regret the much that was lost, this is something else that often happens after we have dreamed. It was still dark, but the first changes in the sky, presaging the dawn, would soon be revealed. Cipriano Algor did not go back to sleep. He thought a lot of things, he thought that his work had become totally pointless, that his existence had ceased to have any real or even halfway acceptable justification, I'm just an impediment, he muttered, and, at that moment, a fragment of his dream appeared to him with absolute clarity as if it had been cut out and stuck on a wall, it was the head of the buying department saying to him, If your intention is to perform some act of self-immolation, good luck to you, I warn you, though, that it is not one of the Center's eccentricities, if it had any, to send representatives and floral tributes to the funerals of our ex-suppliers. Cipriano Algor had dropped off for a few seconds, and it should be said, before anyone points out to us the apparent contradiction, that dropping off for a few seconds is not the same as falling asleep, the potter merely dreamed briefly about the dream he had had, and, if the words spoken by the head of the buying department did not come out exactly the same as they did the first time, this was for the simple reason that it is not only when we are awake that the words we say depend on the mood of the moment. That unpleasant and quite uncalled-for reference to a possible act of self-immolation did, however, manage to draw Cipriano Algor's thoughts back to the clay figurines left to be fired in the pit, and then, by paths and alleyways in the brain that it would be impossible for us to reconstruct and describe with sufficient precision, to a sudden recognition of the advantages of the hollow figurine over the solid figurine, both as regards the amount of time spent and the quantity of clay used. The frequent reluctance of obvious truths to reveal themselves without first playing hard to get really ought to be the object of deep analysis by experts, who must be out there somewhere, on the different, but certainly not opposing, natures of the visible and the invisible, in the sense of finding out if, in the innermost part of what is revealed to us, there exists, as there are strong motives to suspect, some chemical or physical quality with a perverse tendency toward negation or extinction, a threatening slide in the direction of zero, an obsessive dream of the void. Be that as it may, Cipriano Algor is pleased with himself. Only a few minutes ago he had considered himself an impediment to his daughter and son-in-law, a hindrance, an obstacle, a complete waste of space, a catchall term to describe something that is no longer useful, and yet he had been capable of producing an idea whose intrinsic goodness is already proven by the fact that others have not only thought of it before, but have frequently put it into action. It is not always possible to have original ideas, it is enough to have ideas that are at least practicable. Cipriano Algor would like to go on luxuriating in the tranquillity of his bed, to take advantage of that delicious morning sleep, which, perhaps because we are vaguely aware of it, is always the most restoring, but the excitement provoked by the idea he has just had, the thought of the figurines under the doubtless still-warm ashes, and, let's be honest, the rather rash statement given earlier that he had not gone back to sleep, all of this made him push back the covers and slip out of bed as lightly and nimbly as he used to in his salad days. He got dressed noiselessly, left the room carrying his boots in his hand and tiptoed into the kitchen. He did not want to wake his daughter, but he did, unless, of course, she was already awake and busily patching together fragments of her own dreams or had ears pricked for the secret work that life, second by second, was carpentering together inside her womb. Her voice rang out light and clear in the silence of the house, Pa, where are you off to so early, I can't sleep, so I'm going to see how the firing went, but you stay where you are, don't get up. Marta said only, All right, knowing him, it was not difficult to imagine that he would want to be alone during the serious business of removing the ashes and the figurines from the pit, just as a child, in the silent depths of night, trembling with fear and excitement, feels his way down the dark corridor to find out what long-imagined toys and presents have been placed in his stocking. Cipriano Algor put on his shoes, opened the kitchen door and went out. The dense foliage of the mulberry tree still had a firm grip on night, it would not let it leave just yet, the first dawn twilight would linger for at least another half an hour. He glanced at the kennel, then looked around him, surprised not to see the dog. He gave a low whistle, but there was still no sign of Found. The potter went from perplexed surprise to outright concern, I can't believe he's just gone, he muttered. He could call out the dog's name, but he did not want to alarm his daughter. He'll be out there somewhere, on the trail of some nocturnal creature, he said to reassure himself, but the truth is that, as he crossed the yard in the direction of the kiln, he was thinking more about Found than about his precious clay figurines. He was only a few steps away from the pit when he saw the dog appear from beneath the stone bench, You gave me quite a fright, you rascal, why didn't you come when I called you, he scolded him, but Found said nothing, he was busily stretching, getting his muscles back into their appointed places, first stretching his front paws, lowering his head and spine, then carrying out what one can only assume to be, to his way of thinking, a vital exercise of adjustment and rebalancing, lowering and stretching his hindquarters as if he wanted to detach himself from his legs entirely. Everyone tells us that animals stopped talking a long long time ago, however, no one has yet been able to prove that they have not continued to make secret use of thought. In the case of this dog Found, for example, despite the faint light that is only gradually beginning to fall from the skies, you can see from his face what he's thinking, neither more nor less than Ask a silly question and you'll get a silly answer, which means in his language that Cipriano Algor, with his long, albeit not very varied experience of life, should not need to have the duties of a dog explained to him, we all know that human sentinels will only keep watch properly if they are given a definite order to do so, whereas dogs, and this dog in particular, do not wait for someone to tell them, Stay there and watch the fire, we can be sure that, until the coals have burned right down, they will simply remain on watch, eyes open. However, in all fairness to human thought, its famous slowness does not always prevent it from reaching the correct conclusions, as has just happened inside Cipriano Algor's head, a light suddenly came on, allowing him to read and then pronounce out loud the words of recognition that Found so richly deserved, So while I was tucked up asleep in my warm sheets, you were out here on guard, it doesn't matter that your vigilance would not have helped the firing one iota, it's the gesture that counts. When Cipriano Algor had finished praising him, Found ran off to cock his leg and relieve his bladder, then he returned, wagging his tail, and lay down a short distance from the pit, ready to watch the removal of the figurines from the fire. At that moment, the light in the kitchen went on, Marta had gotten up. The potter turned his head, he wasn't clear in his mind whether he wanted to be alone or whether he wanted his daughter to come and keep him company, but he found out a minute later, when he realized that she had decided to allow him to play the principal role to the very last. The frontier of the morning was slowly moving westward, rather like the lip of a luminous vault pushing in front of it the dark cupola of night. A sudden low breeze whipped up, like a dust storm, the ashes on the surface of the pit. Cipriano Algor knelt down, removed the iron bars and, using the same small spade with which he had dug the pit, he began to remove the ashes, along with small bits of as yet unburned coal. The white, almost weightless particles stuck to his fingers, some, even lighter, were sucked in on his breath or went up his nose and made him snort, the way Found sometimes does. As the spade reached farther into the pit, the ashes became hotter, but not enough to burn him, they were merely warm, like human skin, and just as smooth and soft. Cipriano Algor put the spade down and plunged his two hands into the ashes. He touched the thin and unmistakable roughness of the fired clay. Then, as if he were helping at a birth, he grasped between thumb, forefinger, and middle finger the still buried head of a figurine and pulled it out. It happened to be the nurse. He brushed the ashes from her body and blew on her face, as if he were endowing her with some kind of life, giving to her the breath of his own lungs, the beating of his own heart. Then, one by one, the remaining figurines, the bearded Assyrian, the mandarin, the jester, the Eskimo, and the clown were taken out of the pit and placed beside the nurse, more or less clean of ashes, but without the extra benefit of that vital breath. No one was there to ask the potter about that difference in treatment, apparently determined by the difference in sex, unless that demiurgic intervention occurred simply because the nurse was the first to emerge from the hole, it was ever thus, since the world began, creators tire of their creation as soon as it ceases to be a novelty. Remembering, however, the difficulties that Cipriano Algor had had to grapple with when shaping the nurse's bust, it would not be too bold to suggest that the real reason for that breath is to be found, in however obscure and imprecise a form, in the immense effort it took to achieve what the very ductility of the clay denied him. Who knows. Cipriano Algor refilled the hole with the earth that rightfully belonged to it, pressed it down well so that not so much as a handful was lost, and with three figurines in each hand, he went back to the house. Curious, his head up, Found bounded along beside him. The shade of the mulberry tree had bidden farewell to the night, the sky was beginning to open up into the first blue of morning, the sun would soon appear above a horizon that could not be seen from there.

How did they turn out, asked Marta when her father came in, All right, I think, but we need to wash off any ash still clinging to them. Marta poured some water into a small earthenware basin, Wash them in here, she said. The first to enter the water and, whether by chance or coincidence, also the first to leave the ashes, this nurse may have her reasons to complain in the future, but she won't be able to complain about any lack of attention. How's this one, asked Marta, unaware of the debate on gender that has been going on, All right, said her father again tersely. It was indeed all right, evenly fired, a lovely red color, with no imperfections, not even the tiniest crack, and the other figurines were all equally perfect, apart from the bearded Assyrian, who had a black stain on his back, the fortunately limited effect of incipient carbonization caused by an unwanted indraft of air. It doesn't matter, it won't affect it, said Marta, and now will you please sit down and rest while I prepare your breakfast, that body of yours has been up since before dawn, Yes, I woke up and couldn't back get to sleep again, The figurines could have waited for daylight, But I couldn't, As the saying goes, a worried man can't sleep, Or else he sleeps, but dreams all

172

night about his problems, Is that why you woke up so early, so as not to dream, asked Marta, Some dreams are best escaped from quickly, Was that what happened last night, Yes, it was, Do you want to talk about it, There's no point, In this house, the problems of one have always been the problems of all, But not dreams, Unless they're dreams about problems, Honestly, there's no arguing with you, In that case, don't waste any more time and tell me, All right, I dreamed that Marçal had been promoted and that the order had been canceled, They're not likely to cancel the order, That's what I think too, but anxieties get tangled up together like cherries, one gets caught on another and, in two shakes, the basket's full, as for Marçal's promotion, we know that could happen any day now, That's true, The dream was a warning to work fast, Dreams don't act as warnings, Unless the person who dreamed them feels that he has been warned, You've woken up in a very aphoristic mood this morning, dear father, Every age has its defects, and that's the defect that has been afflicting me of late, Oh, I don't mind, I like your aphorisms, I'm learning from them, Even when I'm just playing with words, like now, asked Cipriano Algor, Yes, I think words were born to play with each other, they don't know how to do anything else, and contrary to what people may say, there are no such things as empty words, Now who's being aphoristic, It runs in the family. Marta put the breakfast on the table, coffee, milk, scrambled eggs, toast, butter, and some fruit. She sat down opposite her father to watch him eat. What about you, asked Cipriano Algor, I'm not hungry, she said, That's a bad sign in your state, They say that lack of appetite is quite common in pregnant women, But you need to eat well, logically speaking, you should be eating for two, Or for three, if I'm carrying twins, No, I'm being serious, Don't worry, soon I'll start getting morning sickness and other such delights. There was a silence. The dog curled up under the table, feigning indifference to the smell of food, when what he really feels is resignation, knowing, as he does, that his turn won't come for a few hours yet. Are you going to start work now, asked Marta, As soon as I finish eating, replied Cipriano Algor. Another silence. Pa, said Marta, what if Marçal phoned today to say that he'd been promoted, Have you any reason to think he will, No, it's just a hypothesis, All right, let's imagine that the phone is ringing right now and you get up to answer it, and it's Marçal telling us he's been promoted to resident guard, What would you do then, Pa, I would finish my breakfast, take the figurines over to the pottery, and start making the molds, As if nothing had happened, As if nothing had happened, Do you think that's a sensible decision, don't you think it would be more logical to stop making them and simply turn the page, My dear daughter, folly and illogicality may be a duty to the young, but the old have a perfectly respectable right to them too, Thanks, I'll make a note of the part that concerns me, Even if you and Marçal have to move to the Center first, I'll stay here until I've finished the order, then I'll come and join you as I promised, That's mad, Pa, Mad, foolish, illogical, you don't have a very high opinion of me, It's mad wanting to do this work alone, how do you think I would feel knowing what's going on here, And how do you think I would feel if I abandoned the work halfway through, you don't seem to understand that, at my age, I don't have that many things to hold on to, You've got me, you'll have your grandchild, Sorry, but that's not enough, It will have to be enough when you come and live with us, Yes, I suppose it will, but at least I will have completed my last job, Don't be so melodramatic, Pa, who knows when your last job will be. Cipriano Algor got up from the table. Have you suddenly lost your appetite, asked his daughter, seeing that there was still food left on the plate, I find it hard to swallow, my throat feels tight, It's nerves, Yes, it must be. The dog had got up too, ready to follow his master. Ah, said Cipriano Algor, I forgot to mention that Found spent the night under the stone bench keeping a watch on the fire, So one can learn from dogs too, Yes, what one learns above all is not to discuss what has to be done, simple instinct has its advantages, Are you saying that it's instinct that is telling you to finish the job, that in human beings, or at least in some, there is a behavioral factor similar to instinct, asked Marta, All I know is that reason would have only one piece of advice for me, What's that, Not to be so stupid, the world won't end if I don't finish the figurines, Well, yes, what importance can a few clay figurines have to the world, You wouldn't be so offhand about it if instead of figurines we were talking about ninth or fifth symphonies, unfortunately, my dear, your father was not born a musician, If you really thought I was being offhand, I'm sorry, No, of course I didn't, forgive me. Cipriano Algor was about to leave the kitchen, but he paused for a moment at the door, Anyway, reason is capable of coming up with some useful ideas too, when I woke up in the early hours, it occurred to me that it would save a lot of time and material if we made the figurines hollow, they dry and fire much more quickly and we'll save on clay, Well, long live reason, But then again, you see, birds know to make their nests hollow, but they don't go around boasting about it.

From that day on, Cipriano Algor interrupted his work in the pottery only to eat and to sleep. His lack of experience of the necessary techniques meant that he mistook the proportions of plaster and water needed for making the mold piece, made everything worse by getting the wrong quantities of clay, water, and deflocculant to make a balanced mixture for the casting slip, and then poured the resulting mixture in far too quickly, thus creating air bubbles inside the mold. The first three days were spent making and unmaking, despairing over his mistakes, cursing his own clumsiness and trembling with joy whenever some delicate operation turned out well. Marta offered to help, but he asked her, please, to leave him in peace, a turn of phrase that bore very little resemblance to the reality inside the old workshop, what with plasters that hardened too soon and water added too late, what with clay that wasn't dry enough and slips that were too thick to be sieved, it would have been far nearer the truth if he had said, Just leave me in peace to wage my own war. On the morning of the fourth day, as if the mischievous, slippery goblins, which were the various materials he was using, had repented of their cruel treatment of this unexpected beginner in the new art, Cipriano Algor began to find softnesses where before he had found only harshness, docilities that filled him with gratitude and secrets that willingly unveiled themselves to him. Every five minutes, he consulted the manual, all sticky and marked with fingerprints, which he kept open on the worktop, sometimes he misunderstood what he had read, at others, a sudden intuition would illuminate a whole page, it would be no exaggeration to say that Cipriano Algor's mood swung between lacerating misery and utter bliss. He got up at first light, bolted his breakfast and then stayed in the pottery until lunchtime, after lunch, he worked all afternoon and into the evening, with only a brief interval for supper, whose frugality owed nothing to the previous meals. His daughter protested, You'll get ill working so hard and eating so little, I'm fine, he said, I've never felt better in my life. This was both true and untrue. At night, when he finally went to bed, having washed away the smells of his labors and the dirt from his work, his joints creaked and his whole body ached. I can't do as much as I used to, he said to himself, but deep down in his consciousness, a voice which was also his disagreed, You've never been able to do as much, Cipriano, you've never been able to do as much. He slept as one imagines a stone must sleep, without dreaming, without stirring, almost it seemed without breathing, laying on the world the whole weight of his infinite weariness. Sometimes, like an anxious mother, unwittingly anticipating future broken nights, Marta would get up and look in to see how her father was. She went silently into his room, walked slowly to the bed, bent over him slightly to listen, then left with her worries unassuaged. That big man, with his white hair and battered face, her father, was also a son, anyone who refuses to understand this knows little of life, the webs that weave around human relationships in general and family relationships in particular, especially close family relationships, are more complex than they seem at first sight, we talk about parents and children, and think we know perfectly well what we mean, and we do not ask ourselves about the profound reasons for the affection that lies therein or indeed the indifference or the hatred. Marta leaves his room and is thinking, He's sleeping, and those words apparently do no more than express the verifiable truth, and yet those eleven letters, those three syllables were capable of translating all the love that a human heart can hold at any one moment. It is worth saying, for the enlightenment of the innocent, that in matters of sentiment, the more grandiloquent the feeling the less true.

The fourth day happened to be the day on which he had to go to the Center to fetch Marçal for his day off, which we would call weekly if it were not, as we know, decimal, that is, every ten days. Marta told her father that she would go, so that he wouldn't have to interrupt his work, but Cipriano Algor said no, what an idea, There are fewer robberies on the road, it's true, but there's always a risk, If there's a risk for me, then there's a risk for you too, In the first place, I'm a man, in the second place, I'm not pregnant, Respectable reasons which do you credit, There's a third reason too, the most important, And what's that, I wouldn't be able to do any work until you got back, so it won't make any difference if I go, besides the journey will help to clear my head, which certainly needs an airing, all I can think about are molds, mold pieces, and slips, It would help to clear my head too, so why don't we both go and pick Marçal up, and Found can stay here to guard the castle, If that's what you want, Don't be silly, I was just kidding, you usually go and fetch Marçal and I usually stay at home, so long live usually, No, seriously, we can both go, No, seriously, you go. They both smiled, and the debate on the central question, that is, the objective and subjective reasons we usually do what we do, was postponed. That afternoon, at the appointed hour, and still in his work clothes so as not to waste time, Cipriano Algor set off. As he was leaving the village, he realized that he had not turned his head when he went past the street where Isaura Madruga lives, and when we say turned his head, that could be in either direction, because in recent days, Cipriano Algor had sometimes turned to see if he could spot her, and sometimes turned away so that he would not see her. It occurred to him to wonder what interpretation to put on that troubling indifference, but a stone in the middle of the road distracted him and the moment was gone. The journey to the city passed without incident, he was delayed only once by a police block that was stopping every other car to check the drivers' documents. While he was waiting for them to return his documents, Cipriano Algor had time to notice that the boundary of the shantytown seemed to have shifted closer to the road, Any day now and they'll push it back again, he thought.

Marçal was there waiting for him. Sorry I'm late, said his father-in-law, I didn't leave the house early enough, and then the police wanted to have a nose through my papers, How's Marta, asked Marçal, I didn't manage to phone yesterday, She's fine, I think, but you should ask her yourself really, she's not eating much, no appetite, but she says that's normal in pregnant women, and maybe it is, I don't know much about these things, but if I were you, I wouldn't be too sure, Right, I'll talk to her, don't worry, maybe it's because she's just in the very early stages of pregnancy, We men haven't a clue really, confronted by these things, we're like lost children, you should take her to the doctor. Marçal did not reply. His father-in-law fell silent. They were both probably thinking the same thing, that she would get the best possible treatment at the hospital in the Center, at least that's what people say, although, as the wife of an employee, being resident in the Center isn't a necessary condition for receiving decent treatment. After a moment, Cipriano Algor said, I can bring Marta in any time you want. They had left the city and so could drive more quickly. Marçal asked, How's the work going, We're still only at the beginning really, we've fired the figurines we made, and now I'm tackling the molds, How's that going, We fool ourselves, we think that clay is just clay, that if you can do one thing with it, you can do anything, and then you realize that it simply isn't true, that we have to relearn everything from scratch. He paused, then added, But I feel happy, it's a bit like trying to be born again, well, not quite, Tomorrow I'll give you a hand, said Marçal, I know next to nothing about making pottery, but I'm sure I can be of some help, You need to spend time with your wife, go for a walk somewhere, No, tomorrow we'll be having lunch with my parents, they still don't know about Marta being pregnant, it'll start to show soon, and you can imagine what they'd say then, And quite right too, I mean, be fair, said Cipriano Algor. Another silence. Nice weather, remarked Marçal, Let's hope it lasts another two or three weeks, said his father-in-law, the dolls need to be as dry as possible before we put them in the kiln. Another silence, longer this time. The police block had been removed, and the road was free. Twice Cipriano Algor was about to speak, the third time he did, Any news about your promotion, he asked, No, not yet, replied Marçal, Do you think they've changed their minds, No, there are various procedures that have to be gone through, the bureaucracy in the Center is as nit-picking as anywhere else, With police patrols checking driving licenses, insurance policies, and health certificates, Yes, that's about the size of it, We don't seem to know how else to do things, Perhaps there isn't another way, Or perhaps it's too late to find another way. They did not speak again until they reached the village. Marçal asked his father-in-law to stop at the door to his parents' house, I won't be a minute, I just want to tell them that we'll be coming to lunch tomorrow. It was, indeed, not a long wait, but, again, Marçal seemed unhappy when he got back in the van. What was it this time, asked Cipriano Algor, Oh, I don't know, nothing seems to go right between me and my parents, Don't exaggerate, man, family life was never what you might call a bed of roses, we have good times and bad times, and we're extremely lucky if most of the time it's just so-so, Well, I went in, and my mother was there alone, my father hasn't got back yet, and I said what I had to say and then, to jolly things along a bit, I put on a sort of half-solemn, half-happy face and said that I had a big surprise for them tomorrow, And, guess what my mother's response was, My prophetic gifts don't stretch that far, She asked if the big surprise was them coming to live with me at the Center, And what did you say, I said it wasn't worth saving the secret until tomorrow, I have to tell you, I said, that Marta is pregnant, we're going to have a baby, She was pleased, of course, Oh, yes, she couldn't stop hugging me and kissing me, So what are you complaining about, It's just that with them there's always some dark cloud looming in the sky, at the moment, it's their obsession with wanting to go and live at the Center, You know I don't mind giving up my place to them, No, that's out of the question, and it's not that I'm exchanging my parents for my father-in-law, it's just that they have each other, but you'd be left on your own, Well, I wouldn't be the only person in the world to live on his own, As far as Marta is concerned, I can guarantee that you would, Oh dear, I don't know what to say, Some things are just the way they are and need no explanation. Faced by such a categorical display of basic wisdom, the potter again found himself lost for words. Another contributory factor to this sudden silence might be that, at that precise moment, they just happened to be passing Isaura Madruga's street, and, unlike on the outward journey, Cipriano Algor's consciousness was unable to remain indifferent. When they reached the pottery, Marçal had the unexpected pleasure of being greeted by Found as if he were wearing not the intimidating uniform of a Center security guard, but the plainest and most pacific of clothes. The young man's sensitive soul, still smarting from the unfortunate conversation with his mother, was so moved by the animal's effusions that he embraced him as if he were the person he loved most in the world. These are exceptional moments, needless to say, the person Marçal loves most in the world is his wife, and she is waiting beside him, smiling sweetly, for her turn to be embraced, but just as there are times when all it takes for us to dissolve into tears is for someone to place a hand on our shoulder, so the disinterested joy of a dog can reconcile us for one brief minute to the pains, sorrows, and disappointments of this world. Given that Found knows little of human emotions, be they positive or negative, but of whose existence there is ample proof, and given that Marçal knows still less about canine emotions, about which there are few certainties and a myriad of doubts, someone will one day have to explain to us the reasons, apparently perfectly comprehensible to both parties involved, why these two should be locked in an embrace when they do not even belong to the same species. Since the making of molds was such a novelty, Cipriano Algor could not really avoid showing his son-in-law what he had been up to for the past few days, but his pride, which had already led him to refuse his daughter's help, trembled at the thought that Marçal might notice some mistake, some botched repair, or any of the other innumerable signs that provided such clear evidence of the mental agonies he had suffered within those four walls. Although Marçal was far too preoccupied with Marta to pay much attention to clay, sodium silicate, plaster of Paris, mold frames, and molds, the potter decided not to work after supper and to spend the evening with them, thus affording him the opportunity to discourse with a degree of theoretical exactitude on a subject whose practical pitfalls and disastrous consequences he knew better than anyone. Marçal warned Marta that they would be having lunch with his parents the next day, but he did not even mention the painful conversation he had had with his mother, which made his father-in-law think that this was a subject that had moved into the private domain, a problem to be analyzed in the privacy of the bedroom, not to be picked over and analyzed in a three-way conversation, unless, of course, with praiseworthy prudence, Marçal merely wanted to avoid falling yet again into a debate on the thorny topic of moving to the Center, we have seen far too often how it begins and have seen far too often where it usually ends.

The following morning, Cipriano Algor was already at work when Marçal came into the pottery, Good morning, he said, your apprentice reporting for duty. Marta came with him, but she did not offer to help with the work, even though she was sure that this time her father would not send her away. The pottery was like a battle-field on which, for four consecutive days, one person had been battling with himself and with everything around him. I'm afraid it's a bit untidy in here, Cipriano Algor said apologetically, it's not like it used to be when we made pots and plates, we had a system then, an established routine, It's just a matter of time, said Marta, with time, hands and objects become used to each other, and when they do, the objects don't get in the way and neither do the hands, In the evening, I feel so tired that my arms grow heavy just thinking about imposing some order on this chaos, Well, if I wasn't banned from coming in here, I'd be delighted to take on the task, I didn't ban you, protested her father, Not in so many words, no, It's just that I don't want you wearing yourself out, when it's time to do the painting, that will be different, you can work sitting down, you won't have to make much physical effort, Then you'll probably tell me that the smell of the paints could damage the baby, There really is no talking to this woman, Cipriano Algor said to Marçal, in feigned desperation, You've known her longer than I have, so be patient, but, you know, the place certainly could do with a thorough cleaning and a proper tidying, May I have an idea, asked Marta, would you gentlemen allow me to have an idea, You've already had the idea and you'll burst if you don't let it out, muttered her father, What is it, asked Marçal, The clay is resting this morning, so let's get this place shipshape again, and since my beloved father doesn't want me to wear myself out working, I'll just give the orders. Cipriano Algor and Marçal looked at each other to see who would speak first, and since neither one could bring himself to take the lead, they said in unison, All right. Before it was time for Marçal and Marta to go off to lunch, the pottery and everything in it was as clean and tidy as one could expect in a workplace in which mud is the basic ingredient for the product being made. Indeed, whether we mix water and clay, or water and plaster, or water and cement, we can cudgel our brains for as long as we like to come up with a name that is less vulgar, less prosaic, less common, but always, sooner or later, we come back to that word, the word that says all there is to say, mud. Many of the best-known gods chose mud as the material for their creations, but it is hard to know now if that preference represents a point in mud's favor or a point against.

Marta left her father's lunch ready for him, You just have to heat it up, she said as she left with Marçal. The feeble noise of the van's engine faded and then rapidly disappeared altogether, silence filled the house and the pottery, for just over an hour Cipriano Algor will be completely alone. Now fully recovered from the nervous excitement of recent days, he soon became aware that his stomach was showing signs of dissatisfaction. First, he gave Found his food, then he went into the kitchen, removed the lid from the pan and sniffed the contents. It smelled good and it was still hot. There was no reason to wait. When he had finished eating and was seated once more in his easy chair, he felt at peace. It is a well-known fact that spiritual contentment is not entirely unrelated to having a well-fed body, however, the reason why Cipriano Algor was, at that moment, feeling at peace, the reason why his whole being was filled by a near ecstasy of joy, had nothing to do with the material fact of having eaten. What also contributed to that happy state of mind were, in order of importance, the undeniable advances he had made in mastering the techniques of molds, the hope that from now on the problems would be largely over or at least prove to be less intractable, the harmonious relationship between Marta and Marçal, which, as people say, was there for anyone with eyes to see, and finally, though less important, the thorough cleaning and tidying they had given the pottery. Cipriano Algor's eyelids slowly closed, lifted once, then again, this time with more difficulty, and the third time was a feeble attempt lacking all conviction. With soul and stomach in this state of plenitude, Cipriano Algor let himself slip into sleep. Outside, in the shade of the mulberry tree, Found was sleeping too. They could have stayed like that until Marçal and Marta got back, but suddenly the dog barked. The tone was neither threatening nor frightened, it was merely a conventional warning, a who-goes-there performed purely out of duty, Although I know the person who has just arrived, I have to bark because that is what is expected of me. However it was not Found's cheerful barking that woke Cipriano

Algor, but a voice, the voice of a woman who was standing outside calling, Marta, and then asking, Marta, are you there. The potter did not rise from the chair, he merely sat up, as if preparing for flight. The dog was no longer barking. The kitchen door stood open, the woman was approaching, getting closer all the time, at any moment she would appear in the room, if this new encounter is not the result of mere chance, a mere coincidence, if it was foreseen and set down in the book of destinies, not even an earthquake will stop it in its tracks. Found came in first, wagging his tail, followed by Isaura Madruga. Oh, she said, surprised. It was not easy for Cipriano Algor to get up, the low chair and the fact that his legs had suddenly turned to water were to blame for the pathetic figure he knew he must be cutting. He said, Good afternoon. She said, Good afternoon, I mean, good morning, I'm not quite sure what time it is. He said, It's gone midday. She said, Oh, I thought it was earlier. He said, Marta isn't here, but do come in. She said, I don't want to bother you, I'll come back some other time, it's nothing urgent. He said, She and Marçal have gone to have lunch with his parents, she won't be long. She said, I just came to tell Marta that I've found a job. He said, Where. She said, Here in the village fortunately. He said, What sort of job is it. She said, In a shop, behind the counter, it could be worse. He said, Do you like that kind of work. She said, Well, we can't always do what we want to do in life, and for me, the main thing was being able to stay here, to this Cipriano Algor did not respond, he said nothing, confused by the questions which, almost without thinking, had issued from his mouth, it's obvious to anyone that if someone asks a question it's because he wants to know the answer, and there must be some reason why he wants to know, now the principal question that Cipriano Algor has to make sense of among his tangled feelings is the reason for those questions which, taken literally, and it's hard to see how else to take them, reveal an interest in the life and future of this woman that goes far beyond what one would normally expect in a good neighbor, an interest, moreover, as we know very well, that stands in complete and irreconcilable contradiction to the decisions and ideas which, throughout these pages, Cipriano Algor himself has made and formulated in relation to Isaura, who was Estudiosa but is now Madruga. The problem is a serious one requiring long, uninterrupted consideration, but the orderly logic and discipline of the story, which can, on occasions, be violated and, when appropriate, should be, will not permit us to leave Isaura Madruga and Cipriano Algor in this distressing situation any longer, standing there facing each other, silent and constrained, with the dog looking at them, unable to understand what is going on, with the clock on the wall that must be asking itself, as it tick-tocks on, what these two people want with time if they don't make some use of it. Something must be done. Yes, something, but not just anything. We could and should violate the orderly logic and discipline of the story, but we must never ever violate what constitutes the exclusive and essential character of a person, that is, his personality, his way of being, his own, unmistakable nature. A character can be full of contradictions, but never incoherent, and if we insist on this point it is because, contrary to what dictionaries may say, incoherence and contradiction are not synonymous. A person or character contradicts himself within the bounds of his own inner coherence, whereas incoherence, which, far more than contradiction, is a constant behavioral characteristic, resists contradiction, eliminates it, cannot stand to live with it. From this point of view, and at the risk of falling into the paralyzing webs of paradox, we should not exclude the hypothesis that contradiction is, in fact, one of the most coherent contraries of incoherence. Oh dear, these speculations, perhaps not entirely without interest for those who do not content themselves with the apparent and accepted nature of concepts, have diverted us still further from the difficult situation in which we left Cipriano Algor and Isaura Madruga, alone with each other, while Found, realizing that nothing much was going to happen there, had decided to leave and return to the shade of the mulberry tree to continue his interrupted sleep. It is time, therefore, to find a solution to this inadmissible state of affairs, for example, by having Isaura Madruga, who, being a woman, is the more resolute of the two, say a few words just to see what happens, these will do as well as any others, Well, I'll be off then, often that's all that's needed, it's enough just to break the silence, moving the body slightly as if about to leave, and in this case, at least, it proved to be a sovereign remedy, although, unfortunately for the potter Cipriano Algor, the only thing that occurred to him to ask was a question which, later on, will cause him to strike his head with the palm of his hand, we can each judge for ourselves if he was right, So, what news of our water jug, he asked, is it still doing a good job. Cipriano Algor will later strike his head as a punishment for what he considers an unforgivable gaffe, but we hope that later, when his self-punishing fury has passed, he will remember that Isaura Madruga did not unleash an offensive guffaw of mocking laughter, she did not give a sarcastic titter, she did not even smile the slightly ironic smile that the situation seemed to call for, on the contrary, she looked very serious and folded her arms over her chest as if she were still embracing the water jug, which Cipriano Algor, without noticing the slip, had called ours, perhaps later that night, when sleep will not come, this word will question him as to his intentions when he said it, if the water jug was ours simply because one day it had passed from his hand to hers and because he was referring to that moment, or ours because it was ours, plain and simple, just ours, ours as in belonging to us, ours full stop. Cipriano Algor will not reply, he will merely mutter as he has before, How stupid, but he will do so automatically and, indeed, vehemently, though without any real conviction. Only when Isaura Madruga had left with a murmured, See you again, then, only when she had gone out through that door like a subtle shadow, only when Found, having accompanied her to the top of the slope that leads to the road, had come into the kitchen with a patently interrogative look about him, head cocked, tail wagging, ears up, did Cipriano Algor realize that she had not said a word in response to his question, not a yes or a no, just that gesture of embracing her own body, perhaps in order to find herself inside it, perhaps to defend it or to defend herself from it. Cipriano Algor looked around him perplexed, as if lost, the palms of his hands were sweating, his heart was pounding, with the anxiety of someone who has just escaped a danger the gravity of which he has not yet fully grasped. And that was the first time that he struck his head with the palm of his hand.

When Marta and Marçal returned from lunch, they found him in the pottery, pouring liquid plaster into a mold, Did you manage all right without us, asked Marta, I didn't pine away if that's what you mean, I gave the dog his food, had lunch, had a rest, and here I am again, and how did things go at your parents' house, Oh, the usual, said Marçal, I'd already told them about Marta, so there wasn't any great fuss, just the hugs and kisses you'd expect on these occasions, and we didn't talk about the other matter, Just as well, said Cipriano Algor, continuing to pour the liquid plaster into the mold. His hands were trembling slightly. I'll come and help you, I'll just go and change my clothes, said Marçal. Marta did not leave with her husband. A minute later, Cipriano Algor, without looking at her, asked, Do you want something, No, I don't want anything, I was just watching you work. Another minute passed, and this time it was Marta's turn to ask, Are you feeling all right, Of course I am, You seem odd, different, That's just your eyes, Generally speaking, my eyes and I agree, You're very lucky, then, I never know who I agree with, replied her father brusquely. Marçal would soon be back. Marta asked again, Did anything happen while we were out. Her father put the bucket down on the ground, wiped his hands on a cloth and, looking straight at his daughter, replied, Isaura was here, Isaura Estudiosa or Madruga, or whatever her name is, she wanted to talk to you, You mean Isaura came here, That's what I just said, isn't it, We don't all have your analytical powers, and may one ask what she wanted, To tell you that she'd found a job, Where, Here, Oh, I am glad, very glad, I'll pop around and see her in a while. Cipriano Algor had started work on another mold, Pa, Marta began, but he stopped her, If it's about that same subject, please don't go on, I've given you the message I had to pass on and there's nothing more to be said, Seeds get buried too, but end up springing into life, oh, sorry, is that the same subject. Cipriano Algor did not respond. Between his daughter's departure and his son-in-law's return he again struck his head with his open palm.

W e have already mentioned the fact that many anthropogenic myths made use of clay in the creation of man, and anyone moderately interested in the subject can find out more in know-it-all almanacs and know-it-almost-all encyclopedias. Generally speaking, this is not the case with the followers of different religions, since it is through the organs of the church to which they belong that they receive this and other information of equal or similar importance. There is, however, one case, at least one, in which the clay had to be fired in the kiln for the work to be considered finished. And then only after various attempts. This singular creator, whose name we forget, probably did not know about or else did not have sufficient confidence in the thaumaturgic efficacy of blowing air into the nostrils as another creator did before or would do later, indeed, as Cipriano Algor did in our own time, although with the very modest intention of cleaning the ashes from the face of the nurse. To return to the creator who had to fire his man in the kiln, we give below a description of events, and there you will see that the failed attempts referred to above were a result of the said creator's lack of knowledge as regards the correct firing temperatures. He started out by making a human figure out of clay, whether male or female is of no importance, placed it in the kiln and lit the fire. After what seemed to him the right length of time, he took the figure out and, oh dear, his heart sank. The figure had come out pitch black, nothing like his idea of how a man should look. However, perhaps because he was only in the early stages of this venture, he could not face destroying the failed product of his own ineptitude. He gave him life, apparently by flicking him on the head, and sent him away. He made another figure, placed it in the kiln, and this time took great care to keep the fire low. He succeeded in this, but the temperature was too low this time, for the figure turned out whiter than the very whitest of white things. It still wasn't what he wanted. Despite this new failure, though, he did not lose patience, he must have thought kindly, Poor thing, it's not his fault, and so he gave him life too and sent him off. So there was already a black man and a white man in the world, but the left-handed creator had still not achieved the creature he had hoped for. He set to work again, and another human figure took up his place in the kiln, the problem, even without a pyrometer, should be easier to solve now, that is, the secret was to heat the kiln not too much and not too little, neither too hot nor too cold, and by that rule of thumb, things should finally work out. They did not. The new figure was not black, but neither was it white, it was, oh heavens, yellow. Anyone else would perhaps have given up, would have hurriedly despatched a flood to finish off the black man and the white man, and broken the yellow man's neck, indeed, one might even think this the logical conclusion of the thought that went through the creator's mind in the form of a question, If I myself don't know how to make a proper man, how will I ever be able to call him to account for his mistakes. For a few days, our amateur potter could not get up the courage to go back into the pottery, but then, as they say, the creative bug bit him again and, after a few hours, the fourth figure was ready to go into the kiln. Assuming that there was at the time another creator above this creator, it is very likely that the lesser sent up to the greater a prayer, an entreaty, a supplication, or some such thing, Please, don't let me make a mess of it. Finally, with anxious hands, he placed the clay figure in the kiln, then he carefully chose and weighed what seemed to him the correct amount of firewood, eliminated any that was too green or too dry, removed one piece that was burning badly and clumsily, added another that produced a cheerful flame, calculated approximately the time and intensity of the heat, and, repeating that plea, Please, don't let me make a mess of it, he put a match to the fuel. We modern-day human beings, who have experienced so many moments of anxiety, taking a difficult exam, being stood up by a lover, waiting for a child to come home, not getting a job, can imagine what this creator must have gone through as he waited for the result of his fourth attempt, the sweat which, but for the proximity of the kiln, would doubtless have been ice-cold, the fingernails bitten down to the quick, every minute that passed taking with it ten years of life, for the first time in the history of various creations of the universe, the creator himself felt the torments that await us in eternal life, because it is eternal, not because it is life. But it was worth it. When our creator opened the door of the kiln and saw what was inside, he fell to his knees, amazed. This time the man was not black or white or yellow, he was red, yes, as red as the red of sunrises and sunsets, as red as the molten lava from volcanoes, as red as the fire that had made him red, as red as the blood that was already flowing in his veins, for with this human figure, because he was the one the creator had wanted to create, there was no need to give him a flick on the head, he merely had to say, Come, and the figure stepped out of the kiln of its own accord. Anyone who does not know what happened in later ages will say that, despite all the errors and anxieties or, given the instructive, educational nature of the experiment, precisely because of them, the story had a happy ending. As with all things in this world, and doubtless in all other worlds too, that judgment will depend on the point of view of the observer. Those whom the creator rejected, those whom, albeit with praiseworthy benevolence, he sent away, that is, those with black, white, and yellow skins, grew in number and multiplied, they cover, so to speak, the whole globe, while those with red skins, those who cost the creator so much effort and for whom he suffered such pain and anxiety, they are now the impotent proof of how a triumph can, in time, become the disappointing prelude to a defeat. The fourth and last attempt by the first creator of men to place his creatures in a kiln, the one that apparently brought him a definitive victory, turned out to be a rout. Cipriano Algor, an assiduous reader of know-it-all or know-it-almost-all almanacs and encyclopedias, had read this story when he was a boy and, though he had forgotten many things in his life, for some reason he had not forgotten this. It was a legend that came from the American Indians, the so-called redskins, to be exact, by which the distant creators of the myth must have set out to prove the superiority of their race over all others, including those of whose actual existence they knew nothing at the time. This last point is bound to provoke the objection, the vain and futile argument that, since they had no knowledge of other races, they could not possibly have imagined them white or black or yellow or, even, iridescent. A great mistake. Anyone putting forward such an argument would only be demonstrating their ignorance of the fact that we are dealing here with a people who are potters, as well as hunters, who, in the difficult work of transforming clay into a dish or an idol, would have learned that all kinds of things can happen inside a kiln, the disastrous and the glorious, the perfect and the botched, the sublime and the grotesque. How often, over and over, generation after generation, they must have removed from the kiln pieces that were distorted, cracked, scorched, unbaked, or half-baked, all of them useless. Indeed, there is not much difference between what happens inside a kiln and what happens inside a bread oven. Bread dough is just a different sort of clay, made from flour, yeast, and water, and just like clay, it can emerge from the oven undercooked or burned. There may not be much difference inside, Cipriano Algor admitted, but once out of the oven, I can tell you that I would give anything to be a baker.

The days and nights passed, as did the afternoons and the mornings. According to books and to life, the labors of men have always taken longer and been more backbreaking than those of the gods, the creator of the redskins is a case in point, for he, after all, made only four human images, and yet that minuscule result, which had little success among its intended public, merited an entry in the history set down in almanacs, while Cipriano Algor, for whom there will be no reward in the form of a printed note on his life and works, will have to wrest from the clay, in this first phase alone, one hundred and fifty times more than that, six hundred figurines with different origins, characteristics, and social backgrounds, three of them, the jester, the clown, and the nurse, are more easily definable by the jobs they do, which is not the case with the mandarin and with the bearded Assyrian, about whom, despite the reasonable amount of information drawn from the encyclopedia, it was not possible to discover exactly what they did in life. As for the Eskimo, one assumes that he will continue to hunt and fish. The truth is that Cipriano Algor does not much care any more. When he starts removing the figurines from the molds, identical in size, the differences in clothing attenuated by their uniform color, he will have to make a real effort not to confuse them and mix them up. He will be so immersed in the work, that he will sometimes forget that the molds have a limited life, that they can only be used about forty times, after which the shapes begin to blur, to lose vigor and clarity, as if the figurine were gradually growing weary of existence, as if it were being drawn back to an original state of nakedness, not just its human nakedness, but to the absolute nakedness of clay before it had begun to be clothed in the first physical expression of an idea. At first, in order not to waste time, he had simply thrown the rejected figurines into a corner, but then, out of a strange and inexplicable feeling of pity and guilt, he had gathered them up, most of them misshapen and confused by the fall and by the shock, and placed them carefully on a shelf in the pottery. He could have reused them in order to give them a second chance of life, he could have pitilessly flattened them as he had those two figures of a man and a woman that he had made at the beginning, the clay is still there, dry,

cracked, shapeless, and yet instead he rescued the malformed creatures from the rubbish, protected them, sheltered them, as if he
loved his successes less than he did these mistakes that he had not
proved skillful enough to avoid. He will not fire these figurines, it
would be a waste of firewood, but he will leave them there until the
clay cracks and crumbles, until fragments break off and fall away,
and, if there is time, until the dust from them is transformed back
into resurrected clay. Marta will ask him, What are those rejects
doing there, to which he will simply reply, I like them, but he will
not, like Marta, call them rejects, for to do so would be to drive
them from the world for which they had been born, to deny them as
his own work and thus condemn them to a final, definitive orphan-
hood. The dozens of finished figurines that are transferred every
day to the drying shelves, outside, in the shade of the mulberry tree,
are also his work, and very tiring work they are, but these are so
many and so difficult to tell apart that the only care and attention
they require is to ensure that they do not suffer any last-minute in-
juries. He and Marta had no option but to tie Found up to stop him
jumping onto the shelves, where he would doubtless commit the
worst depredations ever seen in pottery's turbulent history, which,
as we know, is prodigal in shards and undesirable amalgamations.
Remember that when the first six figurines, the others, the proto-
types, were placed here to dry, and Found wanted to find out, by direct contact, what they were, Cipriano Algor's instantaneous shout
and slap had been enough for Found's hunting instinct, further
aroused by the objects' insolent immobility, to withdraw without
causing any damage, but it would, of course, be unreasonable to expect such an animal to resist, unmoved, the provoking sight of a
horde of clowns and mandarins, of jesters and nurses, of Eskimos
and bearded Assyrians, all thinly disguised as redskins. He was deprived of liberty for only an hour. Impressed by the hurt, almost
wounded look on Found's face as he submitted to his punishment,
Marta suggested to her father that education must have some uses,

even when it comes to dogs, It's just a matter of adapting the methods, she declared, And how are you going to do that, The first thing we'll have to do is to untie him, And then, If he tries to get onto the shelves, then we tie him up again, And then, We untie him and tie him up again as many times as it takes for him to learn, It might work, but don't go deluding yourself that he really has learned the lesson, because obviously he won't dare go near the shelves with you there, but, when he's alone, with no one watching him, I fear that none of your educational methods will be enough to discipline the instincts of the jackal grandfather inside Found's head, Surely Found's jackal grandfather wouldn't even give the figurines a sniff, he would just walk straight past and go off in search of something he could actually eat, All right, I just want you to be aware what would happen if the dog did get onto the shelves, imagine the amount of work we'd lose, It might be a lot, it might be a little, we'll see, but if it does happen, I undertake to remake any figurines that get damaged, that's probably the only way I'll be able to convince you to let me help you, Let's not get into that, you just carry on with your pedagogical experiments. Marta left the pottery and, without a word, she removed the lead from the dog's collar. She took a few steps toward the house, then stopped as if she had just thought of something. The dog looked at her and lay down. Marta advanced a few more steps, stopped again, and then went straight into the kitchen, leaving the door open. The dog did not move. Marta closed the door. The dog waited for a moment, then got up and slowly went over to the shelves. Marta did not open the door. The dog looked back at the house, hesitated, looked again, then placed his paws on the shelf where the bearded Assyrians were drying. Marta opened the door and came out. The dog quickly removed his paws and stood there waiting. He had no reason to run away, his conscience told him that he had done nothing wrong. Marta grabbed his collar and, again without saying a word, tethered him with the lead. Then she went back into the kitchen and shut the door. She reckoned that the dog would think about what had happened, well, think or do whatever he would normally do in such a situation. After two minutes, she released him again, it was best not to give the animal time to forget, the relationship between cause and effect had to be fixed in his memory. This time the dog waited longer before putting his paws on the shelf, but he did so nonetheless, though perhaps with slightly less conviction than before. Shortly afterward he was again tethered. After the fourth time, he began to show signs of understanding what was expected of him, but he kept putting his paws on the shelf, as if to make absolutely certain that this was precisely what he should not do. During all this tying and untying, Marta did not say a word, she went in and out of the kitchen, closed and opened the door, and to every movement by the dog, which was always the same, she responded with her own movement, which was also always the same, in a chain of successive and reciprocal actions that would end only when one of them, by making a different movement, broke the sequence. The eighth time that Marta closed the kitchen door behind her, Found again went over to the shelves, but once there, he did not raise his paws as if he wanted to touch the bearded Assyrians, he stood there looking at the house, waiting, as if he were daring his mistress to be bolder than he was, as if he were asking her, What answer have you got to this brilliant move of mine, which will give me victory and which will defeat you. Pleased with herself, Marta murmured, I've won, I knew I would. She went out to the dog, stroked his head and said gently, Good dog, nice dog, her father had come to the door of the pottery to witness the happy result, Fine, now we just have to find out if it sticks, Bet you anything you like that he never again tries to get up on the shelves, said Marta. Very few human words ever enter a dog's own vocabulary of snarls and barks, and, for that reason alone, because he did not understand them, Found did not protest at his owners' irresponsible display of smug satisfaction, because anyone with any knowledge of these matters and able to make an impartial evaluation of what had happened would say that the winner of this battle was not Marta, the owner, however convinced she might be of that, but the dog, although it must be said that people who judge only by appearances would say exactly the opposite. Let everyone, then, boast about the victory they imagine to be theirs, even the bearded Assyrian and his colleagues, now safe from attack. As for Found, we cannot resign ourselves to leaving him with an unwarranted reputation as a loser. The ultimate proof that victory was his is the fact that, from that day forth, he became the most vigilant of guards ever to watch over clay figurines. You should have heard him barking to alert his owners when an unexpected gust of wind blew over half a dozen nurses.

The first kiln-load contained three hundred figurines, or, rather, three hundred and fifty, allowing for likely breakages. They were all that would fit. This happened to coincide with Marçal's day of rest, and so for Marçal it proved instead to be a day of hard work. Patient and willing, he helped his father-in-law to arrange the dolls on the shelves inside and he took charge of feeding the fire, which is a job only for the robust, as much because of the physical effort of carrying the wood to the furnace and stoking the fire as because of the long hours involved, for an old kiln like this, rudimentary in the light of the latest technology, takes a considerable time to reach the optimum temperature for firing, and once it does, that temperature has to be kept as stable as possible. Marçal will work into the night, until his father-in-law, once he has completed a task in the pottery that he had insisted on finishing, can take over from him. Marta took her father's supper out to him and then brought Marçal his and, sitting on the bench that had served as the bench of meditations, she ate her supper with him. Neither of them had much appetite, though for different reasons. You're not eating, you must be exhausted, she said, Yes, I am a little, I'm not very fit, so it takes more out of me, he said, It was my idea to make these figurines, Yes, I know, It was my idea, but for the last few days I've been tormented by a kind of remorse, I keep asking myself if it was worth our while to start making them, if it isn't all just pathetically futile, At the moment, the most important thing for your father is the work that he's doing, regardless of whether or not it's of any use, if you took away the work from him, whatever that work was, then in a way you'd be taking away his reason for living, and if you said to him that what he's doing is pointless, even if the evidence was staring him in the face, he probably wouldn't believe you, because he simply couldn't, The Center stopped buying our crockery and he managed to withstand the shock, Only because you immediately came up with the idea of making these dolls, Yes, but I have a feeling that the bad days are just about to begin, even worse than these, My promotion to resident guard, which shouldn't be long in coming now, will be a bad day for your father, He said he'd come and live with us at the Center, He did, but he said it in the same way that we all say that one day we're going to die, there's a part of our mind that refuses to accept what it knows is the fate of all living creatures and pretends that it has nothing to do with it, that's how it is with your father, he says he'll come and live with us, but, deep down, he doesn't really believe it, As if he were waiting for some last-minute diversion that will take him off along another road, He should know by now that as far as the Center's concerned there's only one road, the one that goes from the Center to the Center, I work there and I know what I'm talking about, A lot of people say that life at the Center is one nonstop miracle. Marçal did not reply at once. He gave a piece of meat to the dog, who had been waiting patiently for a few leftovers to come his way, and only then did he reply, Yes, much as, at this hour of the night, that piece of meat I gave to Found must have seemed like a miracle to him. He stroked the animal's back, twice, three times, the first out of simple, normal affection, the other two times with anxious insistence, as if there were some urgent need to comfort him, when he was the one who needed calming down in order to drive away the idea that had just resurfaced from its hiding place in his memory, The Center doesn't allow dogs. It's true, they don't allow dogs in the Center, or cats, only caged birds and aquarium fish, and even those are becoming rare, ever since they invented virtual aquariums, without fish that smell of fish or water that you have to change. Fifty examples of ten different species swim gracefully about inside, and, in order for them not to die, they have to be cared for and fed as if they were living creatures, the water quality has to be checked, and, so that it's not all hard work, not only can one decorate the bottom of the aquarium with various types of rocks and plants, but the happy owner of this marvel will have at his disposal a range of sounds that will allow him, while he watches these gutless, boneless fish, to surround himself with such diverse ambient sounds as a Caribbean beach, a tropical jungle, or a storm at sea. They don't want dogs at the Center, Marçal thought again, and he noticed that his worry was gradually driving out the other worry, Should I talk to her about this or shouldn't I, he began to think that he should, then he thought it would be better to leave it until later, when he would have to talk about it, when there would be no other option. He decided to say nothing, but, true to the inconstant fluctuations of the will inside the virtual aquarium of the mind, less than a minute later he was saying to Marta, It's just occurred to me that we're not going to be able to take Found with us to the Center, they don't allow dogs, it's going to be a real problem, poor thing, having to abandon him like that, Perhaps there's a solution, said Marta, You've obviously already thought about it, said Marçal, surprised, Yes, I have, a long time ago, So what's your solution, It occurred to me that Isaura wouldn't mind looking after Found, in fact, I think she'd really like that, and besides they already know each other, Isaura, Yes, you remember, Isaura of the water jug, the one who brought us the cake, the one who came here to talk to me the last time we went to have lunch with your parents, Seems like a good idea to me, Yes, I think it would be best for Found, But will your father agree, Half of him will protest and say, certainly not, a single woman isn't good company for a dog, I should imagine he's quite capable of inventing some such theory of disaffinities, and that there must be other people who wouldn't mind taking him in, but we also know that the other half of him will hope against hope that the first half doesn't win, How are the lovebirds, asked Marçal, Poor Isaura, poor Pa, Why do you say poor Isaura, poor Pa, Because it's obvious that she loves him, but she can't get over the barrier he's built around himself, And what about him, Oh, with him it's that old story about the two halves again, one half probably thinks of nothing else, And the other, The other half is sixty-four years old, the other half is afraid, People are so complicated, That's true, but if we were simple we wouldn't be people. Found was no longer there, he had suddenly realized that there was no one to keep the older master company, alone in the pottery and laboring over the second batch of three hundred figurines for the first delivery of six hundred, a dog sees these things and they create an enormous feeling of confusion in him, he sees them but cannot understand them, all that work, all that effort, all that sweat, and I am not referring now to the amount of money that will be earned, it will not be much, it will only be so-so, it certainly won't be a lot, as Marta said a while ago, isn't all of this just pathetically futile. As has been seen before, and has been confirmed now, thanks to the long, deep conversation between Marta and Marçal, the stone bench fully merits the grave and ponderous name we gave to it, that of the bench of meditations, but needs must, and it is time once more to attend to the kiln, to feed more firewood into the mouth of the furnace, carefully though, Marçal, don't forget that tiredness slows down one's defensive reflexes, increases the time they take to respond, we don't want a repeat of what happened on that other ill-fated day, when the snake of howling fire leaped out at you and marked your left hand forever. That is also, more or less, what Marta said, I'm going to wash the dishes and then go to bed, take care, Marçal.

The following morning, very early as usual, Cipriano Algor drove Marçal back to the Center in the van. He had said to Marçal as they left the house, I don't know how to thank you for all your help, and Marçal had replied, I did my best, I just hope it all continues to go smoothly, Oh, I'm sure that the next lot of figurines will prove less problematic, I've worked out a few shortcuts to simplify the work, that's the great thing about gaining more experience, I reckon the next three hundred figurines could be on the drying shelves in a week, Well, you can certainly count on my help again if they're ready to go into the kiln in ten days' time when I have my next leave, Thanks, do you know something, if it wasn't for this wretched crisis over the pottery, you and I could have made a good team, you could stop being a guard at the Center and devote yourself to the pottery, Possibly, but it's a bit late for that, besides, if we had done that, we would both be without a job, But I've still got a job, Yes, of course you have. Later on, once they were on the road into the city, and after a long silence, Cipriano Algor said, I've had an idea and I'd like to know what you think of it, What is it, Well, I'm thinking of taking those first three hundred figurines to the Center as soon as they've been painted, that way the Center would see that we were serious about the work and they could put them on sale earlier than expected, which would be good for them and even better for us, we wouldn't have to wait so long for the results, and if everything goes as we hope it does, we could take the next stage a bit more easily and not have to do things in quite such a rush, what do you think, Seems like a good idea to me, said Marçal, and it occurred to him that he had said the same thing about Marta's idea of leaving the dog to be looked after by the woman with the water jug, After I drop you off, I'm going to have a word with the head of the buying department, I'm sure he'll agree, said Cipriano Algor, Let's hope so, said Marçal, and again he was aware of repeating words he had used only a short time before, this happens all the time with words, we repeat them constantly, but, quite why we don't know, we seem more aware of it some times than others. When they were entering the city, Marçal asked, Who's going to paint the dolls, Well, Marta insists that she wants to paint them, she says I can't be saying mass and ringing the bell at the same time, she didn't put it quite like that, but that's what she meant, But, Pa, paints contain poisons, Yes, I know, And in Marta's condition it doesn't seem right, I'll do the undercoat and I'll use a spray gun, I know it sprays the paint into the air, but it's much quicker, And then, Then we have to apply the paint with a brush, which is quite safe, You should at least have bought a mask, It was too expensive, muttered Cipriano Algor, as if ashamed of his own words, If we could get enough money together to hire the truck to transport the rest of the pottery from the Center, surely we could afford a mask, We didn't think of that, said Cipriano Algor, then contritely corrected himself, Or, rather, I didn't think of that. They were on the avenue now that led in a straight line to the Center, and although it was still a long way off, they could already make out the words on the giant hoarding, YOU'RE OUR BEST CUSTOMER, BUT, PLEASE, DON'T TELL YOUR NEIGHBOR. Cipriano Algor made no comment, but Marçal echoed his thoughts, They're having fun at our expense. When the van drew up opposite the door of the security department, Marçal said, Drop by here again when you've spoken to the head of the buying department, I'm going to see if I can get hold of a mask, Like I said, I don't really need it for me, and Marta will only be painting with brushes, You know her as well as I do, you'll get distracted for a while in the pottery and, by then, it'll be too late, Look, I don't know how long I'll be at the buying department, shall I ask for you here, or should I come and find you, No, don't do that, it's not worth it, I'll leave the mask with my colleague at the door, All right, See you in ten days' time, then, Fine, Take care of Marta for me, Pa, Don't worry, I will, you don't love her any more than I do, you know, I don't know if you love her more or less than I do, I just love her differently, Marçal, What, Give me a hug. When Marçal got out of the van, his eyes were wet with tears. This time, Cipriano Algor did not thump his head with the palm of his hand, he just said to himself with a sad half-smile, See what a man's reduced to, asking for a hug like a love-starved child. He started the van, drove around the block, which was bigger now because of the new extension to the Center, Soon no one will even remember what used to be here, he thought. Fifteen minutes later, he was driving down the ramp into the basement, feeling as strange as if he were returning to the place after a long absence, even though he could see no changes that could objectively justify that feeling of strangeness. After telling the guard that he had come to get some information and not in order to unload, he parked the van at the side. There was already a long line of trucks waiting, and some of the trucks were enormous. It would be another two hours before the reception desk for merchandise opened. Cipriano Algor settled back in his seat and tried to sleep. His last glance through the kiln peephole, before driving into town, had shown that the firing process had finished, now they just had to leave the kiln to cool down, unhurriedly, slowly, like someone walking at their own pace. In order to go to sleep, he started counting dolls as if he were counting sheep, he began with the jesters and counted all of them, then he moved on to the clowns and managed to count every one of them too, fifty of those, fifty of these, he wasn't interested in the spares, the ones that were there just in case any of the others were damaged, then he tried to move on to the Eskimos, but for some reason the nurses got in the way, and during the battle he had to wage to drive them off, he fell asleep. It was not the first time that he had completed his morning sleep in the basement of the Center, it was not the first time that he had been wakened by the sound of engines roaring into life, amplified and multiplied by the echo. He got down from his van and went over to the reception desk, explained who he was and that he had come to sort something out, to talk, if possible, to the boss, It's an important matter, he added. The clerk he spoke to looked at him doubtfully, it was perfectly obvious that neither the matter nor the person standing before him could possibly be important, emerging as they had from a wretched little van with the word Pottery on the side, which is why he said that the boss was busy, He's in a meeting, he said, he would be busy all morning, what exactly did he want. The potter explained what he had to explain, and, in order to impress the clerk, he made sure to mention the telephone conversation he had had with the head of the buying department, and, in the end, the other man said, I'll just go and ask the assistant head of department. Cipriano Algor feared that this would be the wretch who had given him such a hard time before, but the assistant head of department who came out to see him was polite and attentive, and he agreed that it was an excellent idea, Yes, a very good idea indeed, it's good for you and even better for us, while you're producing the next batch of three hundred figurines and preparing for the production of the next six hundred, whether you do it in two stages, as now, or in one, we will be able to observe how the buying public responds, their reactions to the new product, their explicit and implicit responses, it will even give us time to have some questionnaires drawn up to look at two main aspects, first, the situation prior to purchase, that is, customer interest or appetite, whether there is a spontaneous, genuine desire for the product, second, the situation after use, that is the degree of pleasure obtained, the object's perceived usefulness, the sense of pride in ownership, both from the personal point of view and from the group point of view, be it family, professional or whatever, the really important thing for us is to ascertain if the use value, a fluctuating, unstable, highly subjective element, is too far below or too far above the exchange value, And when that happens, what do you do, asked Cipriano Algor simply in order to say something, and the assistant head of department replied in patronizing tones, My dear sir, surely you're not expecting me to reveal to you, here and now, the secret of the bee, But I've always understood that the secret of the bee doesn't actually exist, that it's a mystification, a false mystery, an unfinished fable, a tale that might have been but wasn't, Yes, you're quite right, the secret of the bee doesn't exist, but we know what it is. Cipriano Algor recoiled as if he had been the victim of an unexpected attack. The assistant head of department smiled and insisted politely that it was a good idea, a really excellent idea, that he would await the first delivery and then they would get back in touch. Feeling intimidated and filled with a sense of foreboding, Cipriano Algor got into his van and left the basement. The man's last words kept going around and around in his head, The secret of the bee doesn't exist, but we know what it is, we know what it is, we know what it is. He had seen the mask fall and realized that behind it lay another identical mask, and he knew that the masks beneath would also be identical to those that had fallen, it's true that the secret of the bee does not exist, but they know what it is. He could not speak of his disquiet to Marta and Marçal because they would not understand, and they would not understand because they had not been there with him, on that side of the counter, listening to the assistant head of department explaining the difference between exchange value and use value, perhaps the secret of the bee consists precisely in provoking in the customer sufficient stimuli and desires so that the use value gradually rises in their estimation, a stage followed shortly afterward by a rise in the exchange value, imposed on the buyer by the wily producer who gradually and subtly undermines the buyer's inner defenses, which are the result of his awareness of his own personality, the same defenses that once, if an unsullied once ever really existed, gave him, however precariously, at least some chance of resistance and self-control. Cipriano Algor is entirely to blame for this laborious and confused explanation, because, despite being what he is, a simple potter with no diploma in sociology and no studies in economics, he nevertheless dared, inside his rustic head, to pursue an idea, only to be forced to recognize, due to the lack of a suitable vocabulary and to a grave and evident lack of precision in the terms he had to use, that he was unable to transpose that idea into a sufficiently scientific language that would perhaps allow us, finally, to understand what he had tried to say in his own language. Cipriano Algor will always remember this moment of bafflement with life and his blundering attempt to understand it, when, having gone one day to the buying department at the Center to ask the simplest of questions, he returned with the most complex and obscure of replies, so dark and obscure that nothing could be more natural than that he should lose himself in the labyrinth of his own brain. At least he tried. To his credit, Cipriano Algor will always be able to say that he did everything that a potter could do to try to untangle the hidden meaning behind the sibylline words spoken by the smiling assistant head of department, and although it was clear to him that he had failed, at least he had made it absolutely clear to anyone following behind that the particular road he had taken led nowhere. These are matters for people who know, thought Cipriano Algor, unable to silence his inner disquiet. And, or so say we, other people have done far less and made much more fuss about it.

The package Marçal had left with the guard at the door contained two masks, not one. Just in case the air-purifying system in one of them goes wrong, said the note. And again that plea, Please look after Marta for me. It was almost lunchtime. A wasted morning, thought Cipriano Algor, remembering the molds, the clay waiting for him, the cooling kiln, the rows of dolls inside. Then, halfway down the avenue, with his back to the Center where the phrase You're our best customer, but don't tell your neighbor set out with ironic impudence the relational diagram that defined the city's unconscious complicity with the conscious deception that was manipulating and absorbing it, it occurred to Cipriano Algor that not only had the morning been wasted, but the assistant head of department's obscene phrase had done away with what remained of the reality of the world in which he had learned how to live and in which he had grown used to living, from now on everything would be little more than appearance, illusion, absence of meaning, questions with no answers. I might as well just drive the van into a wall, he thought. He wondered why he didn't do so and why he probably never would, then he listed his reasons. Although inappropriate in the context of his analysis, after all, being alive is, at least in principle, the main reason why people kill themselves, the first of Cipriano Algor's strong reasons for not doing so was the fact of being alive, this was immediately followed by his daughter Marta, and close behind, so intimately bound up with her father's life that it was as if he had thought of both simultaneously, came the pottery, the kiln and, of course, his son-in-law Marçal, who is such a good lad and really does love Marta, and Found, although it may strike many people as scandalous to say so, and, objectively speaking, it is inexplicable that even a dog can bind someone to life, and then, and then, then what, Cipriano Algor could find no other reasons, and yet he had a feeling that there was another reason, what could it be, then suddenly, with no warning, memory threw in his face the name and features of his late wife, the name and features of Justa Isasca, because, if Cipriano Algor was looking for reasons not to crash the van into a wall and if he had already found enough of them in number and substance, namely, himself, Marta, the pottery, the kiln, Marçal, the dog Found, and even the mulberry tree, which we forgot to mention earlier, it was absurd that the last of those reasons, that unexpected reason, whose existence he had queasily glimpsed like a shadow or a mirage, should be someone who was no longer of this world, it's true that she isn't just anyone, she is, after all, the woman he married and worked with, the mother of his daughter, but, even so, however much dialectical talent you add to the pot, it will be hard to sustain that the memory of a dead person can be reason enough for a living person to want to go on living. A lover of proverbs, adages, maxims, and other popular sayings, one of those rare eccentrics who imagines he knows more than he was taught, would say that there's something so fishy going on here, you can even see the fish's tail. With apologies for the inappropriate and disrespectful nature of the comparison, we would say that, in the case in question, the fish's tail is the late Justa Isasca, and that in order to find the rest of the fish, all one has to do is to grab the tail. Cipriano

Algor will not do so. However, when he reaches the village, he will leave the van at the cemetery gate, for the first time since that other day, and walk over to his wife's grave. He will spend a few minutes there thinking, perhaps to say thank you, perhaps to ask, Why did you suddenly reappear, perhaps to hear someone else ask him, Why did you suddenly reappear, then he will glance up as if looking for someone. In this heat, at lunchtime, that's highly unlikely.

The first fifty to emerge from the kiln were the Eskimos, which were nearest to hand, right inside the door. This was, in Marta's immediate view, a fortunate coincidence, Just to get used to the technique we couldn't have a better start, they're easy to paint, in fact, only the nurses, who are all dressed in white, will be easier. When the figurines had cooled completely, they took them over to the drying shelves, where Cipriano Algor, armed with a spray gun and protected by the filter of his face mask, methodically covered them with the matte white of the undercoat. He grumbled to himself that it wasn't worth having that thing covering his mouth and nose, I'd just need to make sure I had the wind behind me, and the paint would be carried away from me, it wouldn't even touch me, but then he thought that he was being unfair and ungrateful, especially considering that, with the good weather they've been having, there could be days when there wasn't any breeze at all. When he had finished his part of the work, Cipriano Algor helped his daughter to set out the paints, the jar of oil, the brushes, the colored drawings on which she had based the dolls, he brought her the bench she would be sitting on, but as soon as he saw her make the first brushstroke, he said, This isn't going to work, if you have the figurines in a row like that, you're going to have to keep moving the bench along and it'll be too tiring, and Marçal said, What did Marçal say, asked Marta, That you should be very careful not to wear yourself out, What I find really tiring is having to hear the same advice over and over, It's for your own good, Look, if I put a dozen figurines in front of me, like that, they're all within easy reach and I'll only have to move the bench four times, besides it does me good to move around a bit, and now that I've explained to you how this assembly line in reverse is going to work, I would remind you that there is nothing more off-putting to someone working than the presence of those who are not, which, in this instance, seems to be you, Right, I'll remember to say the same to you when I'm working, You already have, worse than that, you sent me away, All right, I'm going, there's obviously no talking to you today, Just two things before you go, first, if there's anyone you can talk to, it's me, And second, Give me a kiss. Yesterday it was Cipriano Algor who had asked his son-in-law for a hug, now it's Marta asking her father for a kiss, something is happening to this family, any moment now there'll be comets appearing in the sky, aurora borealises, and witches on broomsticks, Found will sit howling all night at the moon, even when there is no moon, and from one moment to the next the mulberry tree will turn barren. Unless, of course, this is just the result of overly impressionable sensibilities, Marta because she is pregnant, Marçal because Marta is pregnant, Cipriano Algor for all the reasons we already know and some that only he knows. Anyway, father kissed daughter, daughter kissed father, and they made a bit of a fuss of Found too when he tried to join in, so he will have no reason for complaint either. And that, as they say, is that. Cipriano Algor went into the pottery to start making the molds for the next three hundred figurines, and Marta, in the shade of the mulberry tree, beneath the conscientious eye of Found, who had resumed his responsibilities as guard, prepared herself to start painting the Eskimos. Alas, she could not, she had forgotten that first she had to sand them down, remove any sharp edges, any irregularities or imperfections in the finish, then clean off the dust, and, since misfortunes never come singly and since one omission usually reminds you of another, she would not be able to paint them as she had at first thought, moving seamlessly from one color to the next, until the last brush stroke. She remembered the page in the manual where it explicitly stated that only when one color has completely dried should you apply the next, Now I really could do with an assembly line, she said, with the figurines passing before me, once to receive the blue, then the yellow, then the violet, then the black and the red and the green and the white, and, of course, for the final blessing, the one that carries within it all the colors of the rainbow, May God make you good, for I have done what I could, and it won't be so much because of any additional goodness that God, as subject as any ordinary mortal to lapses and oversights, may contribute to crown my efforts, but because of a humble awareness that the reason we didn't do any better was simply because we couldn't. Arguing with what must be has always been a waste of time, as far as what must be is concerned, arguments are more or less random groups of words waiting to be placed in a syntactical order that will give them a sense they themselves are not entirely sure that they have. Marta left Found to keep an eye on the dolls and, declining all further debates with the inevitable, she went into the kitchen to get the only bit of fine sandpaper in the house, This won't last long, she thought, I'll have to buy some more. If she had looked round the door of the pottery, she would have seen that things were not going well in there either. Cipriano Algor had boasted to Marçal that he had invented a few shortcuts to speed up the work, which, from, shall we say, a global perspective, was true, but speed had soon proved itself to be incompatible with perfection, and produced a far larger number of defective dolls than had been the case with the first batch. When Marta went back to her work, the first spoiled figurines had already been placed on the shelf, but Cipriano Algor, having calculated time gained and figurines lost, decided not to give up his fecund, but, on the other hand, neither reprehensible nor ever fully explained shortcuts. And so the days passed. The Eskimos were followed by the clowns, then came the nurses, then the mandarins and the bearded Assyrians, and finally the jesters, who had been placed along the back wall of the kiln. On the second day, Marta had gone down to the village to buy two dozen sheets of sandpaper. This was the shop where Isaura had just started work, as Marta already knew, having visited Isaura after the latter's troubling encounter, emotionally speaking, of course, with Marta's father. These two women do not see each other very often, but there are plenty of reasons for them to become great friends. Discreetly, so that her words did not reach the ears of the owner of the shop, Marta asked Isaura if she was settling into the job, and Isaura said yes, she was, I'll get used to it, she said. She spoke without any show of pleasure, but firmly, as if she wanted to make it clear that pleasure had nothing to do with it, that it had been will, and will alone, that had made her accept the job. Marta remembered the words that Isaura had spoken some time ago, Any job will do, as long as I can go on living here. In the question that Isaura asked next, while she was rolling up the sheets of sandpaper, loosely, as prescribed, Marta heard an echo, distorted but still recognizable, of those words, And how's everyone at home, Oh, tired, working very hard, but pretty well really, Marçal, poor thing, had to stoke the kiln on his day off, his back is probably killing him now. The sheets of sandpaper had been rolled up. While she was taking the money and returning the change, Isaura, without looking up, asked, And how's your father. Marta could say only that her father was fine, an anxious thought had just flashed through her mind, What will this woman do with her life when we leave. Isaura said good-bye, she had to serve another customer, Give him my regards, she said, and if, at that moment, Marta had asked her, What will you do with your life when we leave, she would perhaps have replied as calmly as she had before, I'll get used to it. Yes, we often hear it said, or we say it ourselves, I'll get used to it, we say or they say, with what seems to be genuine acceptance, because there really isn't any other way, at least none has yet been discovered, of expressing in as dignified a way as possible our sense of resignation, what no one asks is at what cost do we get used to things. Marta left the shop almost in tears. With a kind of desperate remorse, as if she were accusing herself of having deceived Isaura, she was thinking, She has no idea, she doesn't even know that we're about to leave.

Twice they forgot to give the dog his food. Recollecting his days as an indigent, when hope for the morrow was all the food he had after many hours spent with his stomach longing for sustenance, Found did not complain, instead, neglecting his duties as guard dog, he simply lay down beside the kennel, for it is ancient knowledge that a prone body can withstand hunger far longer, waiting patiently until one of his owners struck his or her head and exclaimed, Oh, damn, we've forgotten about the dog. It is hardly surprising, since, during that time, they had almost forgotten about themselves. But it was thanks to that total absorption in their respective tasks and to the hours stolen from their sleep, even though Cipriano Algor kept telling Marta, You must rest, you must rest, it was thanks to that parallel effort that, when the time came for Cipriano Algor to go and pick up his son-in-law from the Center again, the three hundred figurines that had emerged from the kiln were sanded, brushed, painted, and dried, every single one of them, and that the other three hundred, erect and impeccable in their raw clay, with no visible defects, were also, with the help of the heat and the breeze, perfectly dry and ready to be fired. The pottery seemed to be resting after a great labor, the silence had lain down to sleep. In the shade of the mulberry tree, father and daughter looked at the six hundred figurines lined up on the shelves and it seemed to them that they had done an excellent job. Cipriano Algor said, I won't work in the pottery tomorrow, that way Marçal won't have to deal with the kiln all alone, and Marta said, I think we should rest for a few days before we launch into the second batch, and Cipriano Algor said, What about three days, and Marta replied, It's better than nothing, and Cipriano Algor asked, How are you feeling, and Marta said, Tired, but well, and Cipriano Algor said, I feel great, and Marta said, That must be what we call the reward of a job well done. Although it might not seem like it, there was no irony in these words, only a weariness that could be described as infinite if such a description were not a manifestly wild exaggeration. Whatever it was, it was not so much the physical tiredness, but having to stand helplessly by, unable to do anything, watching her father's bitter disappointment and ill-concealed sadness, his ups and downs, his pathetic attempts to appear confident and authoritative, the obsessive, categorical restating of his doubts as if, by doing so, he could remove them from his head. And then there was that woman, Isaura, Isaura Madruga, she of the water jug, to whom she had replied only, He's fine, to the question Isaura had murmured, eyes lowered, while she was counting out the change, And how's your father when what she should have done was to take her by the arm, march her to the pottery where her father was working and say, Here he is, and then close the door and leave them inside until words came to their rescue, because silences, poor things, are just that, silences, everyone knows how often even apparently eloquent silences have given rise to mistaken interpretations, with serious and sometimes fatal consequences. We're too fearful, too cowardly to risk doing something like that, thought Marta, looking at her father, who seemed to have fallen asleep, we are too caught in the net of so-called proprieties, in the web of what is proper and improper, if anyone found out I had done it, they would immediately come to me and say that throwing a woman at a man like that, because that's the expression they would use, shows a complete lack of respect for another person's identity, that it was an act of irresponsible imprudence, after all, who knows what might happen to them in the future, people's happiness is not something that we can build today with any certainty that it will still be there tomorrow, later on, we might meet one disunited half of the couple we had united and risk hearing them say, It was all your fault. Marta did not want to give in to that common-sense argument, the logical and skeptical result of many hard battles with life, It's ridiculous to throw away the present just because you're afraid there might not be a future, she said to herself, adding, Besides, not everything will necessarily happen tomorrow, some things will happen only the day after tomorrow, What did you say, asked her father abruptly, Nothing, she said, I've just been sitting here quietly so as not to wake you, But I wasn't asleep, Well, I thought you were, You said that there are some things that will happen only the day after tomorrow, How odd, did I really say that, asked Marta, Yes, I wasn't dreaming it, Then I must have dreamed it, I must have fallen asleep and then immediately woken up again, that's what dreams are like, you can make neither head nor tail of them, not because they don't have a head and a tail, but because the head and the tail aren't where you expect them to be, which is why dreams are so hard to interpret. Cipriano Algor got up, It's nearly time to go and pick up Marçal, but I was just thinking that perhaps it would be a good idea to go a bit earlier and drop in at the buying department to tell them that the first three hundred are ready and to agree on a delivery date, That seems like a good idea, said Marta. Cipriano Algor went to change his clothes, put on a clean shirt and some different shoes, and in less than ten minutes he was getting into the van, See you later, he said, See you later, Pa, go carefully, And come back even more carefully of course, Of course, because then there will be two of you, You see what I mean, there's no arguing with you, you have an answer for everything. Found came over to ask his master if this time he could go with him, but Cipriano Algor said no, be patient, cities are not the best places for dogs.

The journey, one of many, would have been of no consequence were it not for the potter's uneasy feeling that something bad was about to happen. He suddenly remembered what he had heard his daughter say, Some things will happen only the day after tomorrow, a few random words, with no apparent rhyme or reason, which she had been unable or unwilling to explain, I doubt very much she was sleeping, but I can't understand why she should have said she was dreaming, he thought, and then, as a continuance of the remembered phrase, he allowed his mind to follow the same road, and the phrase began to ring in his head like an obsessive litany, Some things will happen only the day after tomorrow, some things will happen only tomorrow, some things will happen today, then he took up the sequence again and reversed it, Some things will happen today, some things will happen only tomorrow, some things will happen only the day after tomorrow, and he repeated and repeated it so many times that the meaning of tomorrow and the day after to-morrow finally lost all sound and sense, and all that remained in his head, like a danger light flashing on and off, Happen today, happen today, today, today, today, Today what, he asked himself abruptly, trying to shake off the absurd feeling of apprehension that made his hands shake as they gripped the steering wheel, I'm driving into town to pick up Marçal, I'm going to the buying department to tell them that the first batch is ready to be delivered, everything I'm doing is perfectly normal and ordinary and logical, I have no reason to be worried, and I'm driving carefully, there's not much traffic, the hijackings have stopped, at least I haven't heard about any, therefore, nothing out of the usual monotonous routine is going to happen to me, the same steps, the same words, the same gestures, the recep-tion desk, the smiling assistant head of department or the rude one, or even the head of the buying department himself if he isn't in a meeting and takes it into his head to see me, then the van door opening, Marçal getting in, Afternoon, Pa, Good afternoon, Marçal, how was work this week, I don't know if you can really call ten days a week, but I don't know what else to call it, Oh, pretty much as usual, he'll say, We've finished the first batch of figurines, and I've arranged a delivery time with the buying department, I'll say, How's Marta, he'll ask, Oh, tired, but otherwise fine, I'll say, words we are constantly using, it wouldn't surprise me in the least if, as we were passing from this world to the next, we didn't dredge up the strength to respond to someone who had the imbecilic idea to ask how we were, Oh, dying, but otherwise fine, is what we would say. In order to shake off the company of the ominous thoughts that persist in bothering him, Cipriano Algor tried to look at the landscape outside, he did so out of sheer desperation because he knew perfectly well that he would find no solace in the depressing sight of plastic greenhouses stretching out on either side, as far as the horizon, which he could see even more clearly from the top of the small hill the van was climbing. And this is what they call the Green Belt, he thought, this desolation, this gloomy encampment, this flock of grubby blocks of ice that melt those who work inside them into pools of sweat, for a lot of people these greenhouses are machines, machines for making vegetables, nothing could be easier, it's like a recipe, mix all the ingredients together, set the thermostat and the hygrometer, press a button, and shortly afterward up pops a lettuce. Cipriano Algor's displeasure does not blind him to the fact that thanks to these greenhouses, he can have vegetables on his plate all year round, what he can't bear is that they should have chosen the name Green Belt for a place where that color is nowhere to be seen, apart from the few weeds that manage to spring up outside the greenhouses. Would you be any happier if the plastic sheeting were green, was the blunt question asked by the thought process that toils away on the lower landing of the brain, a restless thought process that is never satisfied with what was thought or decided by that on the upper landing, but Cipriano Algor preferred not to respond to that highly pertinent question, he pretended that he hadn't heard, perhaps because of the somewhat impertinent tone that all pertinent questions automatically adopt, simply because they have been asked, and however hard they try to disguise themselves. The Industrial Belt, which more and more resembles a continually expanding tubular construction, a network of pipes designed by an eccentric and built by a maniac, did not improve his mood, but at least his agitated, confused presentiment was now merely muttering quietly to itself. He noticed that the visible boundary of the shantytowns was now much closer to the road, like an army of ants that resumes its march after the rain has stopped, he gave a resigned shrug as he thought that soon the attacks on trucks would be bound to start again, and then, making a heroic effort to drive away the shadow sitting beside him, he joined the city's disorderly traffic. It was early yet to pick up Marçal, he had plenty of time to go to the buying department. He did not ask to speak to the head of the buying department, he knew very well that the matter which brought him there was merely an excuse to remind them of his existence, a visiting card so that they would not forget him or the fact that about thirty kilometers away a kiln was diligently firing clay, a woman was painting, and her father was making molds, and that all had their eyes fixed on the Center, and don't go telling me that kilns don't have eyes, because they do, if they didn't, they wouldn't know what they were doing, so they do have eyes, it's just that they're not like our eyes. He was greeted by the nice, smiling assistant head of department who had dealt with him on the previous occasion, So what brings you here today, he asked, The three hundred figurines are ready, and I just came to find out when you would like me to bring them in, Whenever you want, tomorrow if you like, Ah, I don't know that I can tomorrow, my son-in-law will be home on leave and he'll be helping me put the other three hundred in the kiln, The day after tomorrow, then, as soon as you can, though, because I've had an idea that I want to put into practice right away, To do with my figurines you mean, Exactly, do you remember that I mentioned drawing up a questionnaire, I do, yes, the one comparing the situation before buying and the situation afterward, Congratulations, you've got a good memory, Not bad for a man my age, Well, that idea, which we have used in a number of cases with excellent results, will consist in distributing a certain number of figurines to a fixed number of potential buyers, based on an as yet undefined social and cultural universe, to test their opinion of the product, obviously I'm simplifying matters, the way we ask our questions is, as you can imagine, much more complicated than that, To be honest,

I've no experience in the area, sir, I've never asked the questions or been asked, Well, I'm even thinking of using your initial batch of three hundred in the questionnaire, I select fifty customers, provide each of them with a complete set of six figurines, gratis, and in a matter of days I will know their views, Gratis, said Cipriano Algor, does that mean you're not going to pay us, My dear sir, of course we'll pay you, the experiment is made at our expense, we will make sure any costs are covered, we would not want to do anything that might harm you. The relief felt by Cipriano Algor assuaged for a moment the question that had irrupted into his mind, that is, What will happen if the result of the questionnaire is negative, if the majority of the customers, or all of them, give the same definitive answer to all the questions, No, I'm not interested. He heard himself saying, Thank you, not just out of politeness, but out of fairness too, it isn't every day that someone comes along and soothes us with the benign information that they do not wish to do anything to harm us. Unease had begun gnawing at his stomach again, but now he was the one who would not let the question leave his mouth, he would depart as if he were carrying in his pocket a sealed letter to be opened only once he was on the high seas and in which his fate had been recorded, plotted, written, today, tomorrow, the day after tomorrow. The assistant head of department had asked, And what brings you here today, then he had said, Tomorrow if you like, and had concluded, The day after tomorrow then, it's true that this is quite simply the nature of words, they come and go, and go, and come, and come, and go, but why were these waiting for me here, why did they leave the house with me and stay with me during the whole journey, not tomorrow, not the day after tomorrow, but today, right now. Suddenly, Cipriano Algor hated the man standing before him, this nice, genial, almost affectionate assistant head of department, with whom the other day he had been able to discuss practicalities on equal terms, apart, of course, from the obvious distances and differences in age and social class, neither of which, or so it had seemed then, had been an impediment to a relationship founded on mutual respect. If someone sticks a knife in your guts, they should at least have the moral decency to wear a face in keeping with that murderous act, a face that oozes hatred and ferocity, a face that speaks of wild rage or even of inhuman coldness, but please, dear God, don't let them smile while they are tearing out your innards, don't let them despise you that much, don't let them feed you with false hopes, saying, for example, Don't worry, it's nothing, a couple of stitches and you'll be as good as new, or else, I sincerely hope that the results of the questionnaire prove favorable, believe me, few things would give me greater satisfaction. Cipriano Algor made a vague movement with his head, a gesture that could as easily have meant yes as no, which might indeed have meant nothing, then he said, I have to go and pick up my son-in-law.

He left the basement, drove around the Center and parked his car where he could see the entrance to the security department. Marçal took longer than usual to come out and he seemed nervous as he got into the van, Afternoon, Pa, he said, and Cipriano Algor said, Good afternoon, how was work this week, Oh, pretty much as usual, replied Marçal and Cipriano Algor said, We've finished the first batch of figurines, and I've arranged a delivery time with the buying department, How's Marta, Tired, but otherwise fine. They did not speak again until they were out of the city. And it was only as they were passing the shantytown that Marçal said, Pa, I've just been told that I've got my promotion, from today I'm a resident guard. Cipriano Algor turned to his son-in-law and looked at him as if he were seeing him for the first time, today, not the day after tomorrow, not tomorrow, today, his presentiment had been right. Today, what, he asked himself, the threat hidden in the questions on the questionnaire, or this threat now, which has been coming for so long. It has been known, albeit more often in storybooks than in real life, that a sudden surprise can, for a matter of moments, render the surprised person speechless, but a half-surprise that has remained silent, perhaps pretending, perhaps wanting to be mistaken for a complete surprise, does not, in principle, merit such a reaction. Only in principle, mind you. We have always known that the man driving this van has never doubted for a moment that the dreaded news would arrive one day, but it is understandable that today, caught between two fires, he was suddenly incapable of deciding which one to put out first. Let us reveal, then, right away, even though we risk disrupting the regular order of events, that, over the next few days, Cipriano Algor will not say a word either to his son-in-law or to his daughter about the disquieting conversation he had with the assistant head of the buying department. He will talk about it eventually, but only much later, when everything is lost. Now all he says to his son-in-law is, Congratulations, you must be really pleased, banal, almost neutral words that should not have taken so long to show themselves, and Marçal will not say thank you, just as he will not confirm that he is as pleased as his father-in-law believes him to be, or a little less, or a little more, what he says is as serious as an outstretched hand, It isn't good news for you. Cipriano Algor understood what he meant, glanced at him with a half-smile that seemed to mock his own resigned attitude, and said, Not even the best news is good for everyone, You'll see, everything will work out fine, said Marçal, Don't worry, it was all decided on the day I told you that I would go and live with you at the Center, I gave my word and I won't go back on it, Living at the Center isn't like being sent into exile, Yes, but I have no way of knowing what it will be like and I'll only find out when I get there, you already know it, but I've never heard from your mouth a single explanation, story, or description that has ever really brought home to me the nature of what you so confidently declare not to be a place of exile, You've been to the Center, Not very often and only in passing, as a customer who knew what he wanted, Well, the best way to explain the Center is to think of it as a city within a city, Hm, I don't know if that would be the best explanation, because it still doesn't help me to understand what is inside the Center, There are all the things you would expect to find in any city, shops, people walking around, buying things, talking, eating, having fun, working, You mean just like in the backward little place where we live now, More or less, it's just a question of size, The truth can't be that simple, There must be some simple truths, Possibly, but I don't think they're inside the Center. There was a pause, then Cipriano Algor said, Talking about size, it's odd, you know, but whenever I look at the Center from the outside, I have the feeling that it's bigger than the city itself, I mean, the Center is inside the city, but it's bigger than the city, which means that the part is bigger than the whole, it's probably just because it's taller than the buildings around it, taller than any building in the city, probably because, right from the start, it has been swallowing up streets, squares, whole districts. Marçal did not reply at first, his father-in-law had just given almost visual expression to the vague feeling of disorientation that overwhelmed him whenever he returned to the Center after his days off, especially when he was on night patrol, and all the lights were dimmed and he walked along the deserted galleries, went up and down in the elevators, as if he were keeping watch over nothing in order to ensure that it continued to be nothing. Inside an empty cathedral, if we raise our eyes to the roof, to the highest part of the building, we have the impression that it is higher than the sky is when we stand in a field and look up. After a silence, Marçal said, I think I know what you mean, and left it at that, he did not want to encourage in his father-in-law's mind a train of thought that might lead him to shut himself up behind a desperate new line of resistance. But Cipriano Algor's preoccupations had gone off in another direction, When are you moving, As soon as possible, I've already seen the apartment they've set aside for me, it's smaller than our house, but that's understandable, however big the Center is, the space they've got isn't infinite, and so it has to be rationed out, Do you think we'll all fit in, asked the potter, hoping that his son-in-law did not notice the tone of melancholy irony that had slipped into his words at the last moment, We'll fit, don't worry, the apartment is plenty big enough for a family like ours, replied Marçal, we won't have to take it in turns to sleep or anything. Cipriano Algor thought, Now I've annoyed him, I shouldn't have asked that question. They did not speak again until they got home. Marta showed no emotion when she heard the news. When you know something is going to happen, in a way it's almost as if it had happened already, expectation does more than simply cancel out surprise, it dulls feelings and trivializes them, everything that one desired or feared has already been experienced while one was desiring it or fearing it. It was during supper that Marçal gave an important bit of news that he had forgotten about, something that irritated Marta intensely, You mean that we can't take any of our own things with us, You can take some things, ornaments, for example, but not furniture or crockery or glasses or cutlery or towels or curtains or bed linen, the apartment has all those things already, So we won't really be moving then, at least not what is usually meant by moving, said Cipriano Algor, The people will be moving, So we'll have to leave this house with everything in it, said Marta, There's no other option. Marta thought for a bit, then had to accept the inevitable, I'll come back now and then to open the windows and air the rooms, a house that stays all shut up is like a plant you forget to water, it dies, dries up, shrivels. When they had finished eating, and before Marta had cleared the table, Cipriano Algor said, I've been thinking. Daughter and son-in-law exchanged glances, as if transmitting words of alarm to each other, You never know what he'll come out with when he's been thinking. My first idea, the potter went on, was that Marçal should help me tomorrow with the kiln, May I remind you that we agreed to take three days off, said Marta, Your time off begins tomorrow, And yours, Mine won't be long in coming, it'll just have to wait a while, So that was your first idea, what about your second and your third, asked Marta, We'll sort out the kiln first thing in the morning, the figurines that are still to be fired I mean, but we won't light the kiln, I'll do that later, then you'll help me load the van with the finished figurines and while I take them to the Center, you two can stay here without a father or a father-in-law sticking his nose in where it isn't wanted, Is that what you agreed with the buying department, to deliver the dolls tomorrow, asked Marçal, that wasn't the impression I got, I thought we'd take them with us later, when all three of us go there, It's better this way, said Cipriano Algor, we gain time, You gain it in one way, but you lose it in another, the other dolls will be delayed, Not by much, I'll light the kiln as soon as I get back from the Center, who knows it might be the last time, What do you mean, we've still got six hundred dolls to make, said Marta, Hm, I'm not so sure, Why, Well, the move to start with, the Center is not the sort of place prepared to wait until the father-in-law of resident guard Marçal Gacho has completed an order, although it has to be said that, given time, always supposing there is time, I could finish it on my own, and second, Second what, asked Marçal, In life there is always something that comes after what appears first, sometimes we think we know what it is, but we'd prefer to ignore it, at other times we can't even imagine what it might be, but we know it's there, Please, stop talking like an oracle, said Marta, All right, the oracle is silent, let's just stick with what came first, what I was trying to say was that if the move has to be made soon, there won't be time to resolve the problem of the remaining six hundred figurines, It would just be a matter of talking to the Center, said Marta, addressing her husband, three or four more weeks won't make much difference, talk to them, after all, they took long enough to decide on your promotion, so they can help us out now, besides they'd be helping themselves because then they'd get the full order, No, I can't talk to them, there's no point, said Marçal, we have exactly ten days to make the move, not an hour more, that's the regulations, by the time I have my next day off I'll have to have moved into the apartment, You could spend it here instead, said Cipriano Algor, at your house in the country, It would look bad, being promoted to resident guard and then spending my first leave away from the Center, Ten days isn't much time, said Marta, It would be if we had to take the furniture and everything, but the only things we really have to move are ourselves and the clothes that we wear, and they could be in the apartment in less than an hour if necessary, In that case, what shall we do about the rest of the order, asked Marta, The Center knows, the Center will tell us when the time is right, said the potter. Helped by her husband, Marta cleared the table, then went to the door to shake the crumbs off the tablecloth, she stood there for a moment looking out, and when she came back, she said, There's one matter still to be resolved and which cannot be left to the last moment, What's that, asked Marçal, The dog, she said, You mean Found, said Cipriano Algor, and Marta went on, Since we're not the sort to kill him or to abandon him, we'll have to find a home for him, entrust him to someone else to look after, You see they don't allow animals, Marçal explained, looking at his father-in-law, Not even a tortoise, not even a canary, not even a sweet little dove, Cipriano Algor wanted to know, You seem to have suddenly lost interest in the fate of the dog, said Marta, Of Found, Of Found, of the dog, it's the same thing, what matters is that we decide what to do with him, I've got one suggestion, So have I, Cipriano Algor broke in, and immediately got up and went to his room. He reappeared after a few minutes, walked through the kitchen without saying a word and left. He called the dog, Come on, he said, we're going for a walk. He went down the slope with him, turned left at the road, away from the village, and strode out into the countryside. Found did not leave his master's heels, he must have been remembering his unhappy times as a wanderer, when he was driven from farms and even denied the means to slake his thirst. Although he is not a fearful dog, although he is not afraid of the dark, he would much prefer to be lying down in his kennel right now, or, better still, curled up in the kitchen at the feet of one of those three people, he does not say this out of indifference, as if it didn't matter, because he would keep the other two within sight and smell, and because he could change places whenever he wanted without spoiling the harmony and happiness of the moment. It was not a long walk. The stone on which Cipriano Algor has just sat down will serve as his bench of meditations, that was why he left the house, if he had gone to the real bench, his daughter would have seen him from the kitchen door and it would not have been long before she came out to ask him if he was all right, such acts of consideration are gratefully received, but human nature is so strangely made that even the most sincere and spontaneous gestures of the heart can occasionally prove importunate. It is not worth describing what Cipriano Algor thought about because he had thought about it on other occasions and we have supplied more than enough information on the subject already. The only new thing here is that he allowed a few painful tears to run down his cheeks, tears that had been dammed up for a long, long time, always just about to be shed, but, as it turned out, they were being reserved for this sad hour, for this moonless night, for this solitude that has not yet resigned itself to being solitude. What was truly not a novelty, because it had happened before in the history of fables and in the history of the marvels of the canine race, was that Found went over to Cipriano Algor to lick his tears, a gesture of supreme consolation which, however touching it might seem to us, capable of touching hearts normally not given to displays of emotion, should not make us forget the crude reality that the salty taste of tears is greatly appreciated by most dogs. One thing, however, does not detract from the other, were we to ask Found if it was because of the salt that he licked Cipriano Algor's face, he would probably have replied that we do not deserve the bread that we eat, that we are incapable of seeing beyond the end of our own nose. There they stayed for more than two hours, the dog and his owner, each one immersed in his own thoughts, with no tears now for one to cry and the other to dry, waiting perhaps for the world to turn and to restore everything to its proper place, even those things which, up until now, had not found a place.

The following morning, as agreed, Cipriano Algor took the finished figurines to the Center. The others were already in the
kiln, awaiting their turn. Cipriano Algor had gotten up early, while
his daughter and son-in-law were still asleep, and when Marçal and
Marta finally lurched into wakefulness and appeared at the kitchen
door, most of the work had been done. They had breakfast together, making the usual polite noises, would you like more coffee,
can you pass me the bread, there's jam if you'd like it, then Marçal
went and helped his father-in-law complete the work and began the
delicate task of placing the three hundred figurines in the boxes they
used to use for transporting the crockery. Marta told her father that
she would go with Marçal to his parents' house, they had to tell
them about the imminent move, let's see how they react, but, whatever happened, they would not stay there for lunch, We'll probably
be here when you get back from the Center, she concluded. Cipriano said that he would take Found with him, and Marta asked if he
had been thinking of someone in the city when he said last night
that he had a possible solution for the problem of the dog, and he
said no, but it was worth thinking about, that way Found would at
least be nearby, and they could see him whenever they wanted.
Marta remarked that, to her certain knowledge, her father had no
close friends in the city, not people trustworthy enough to merit,
and she used the word merit deliberately, being given charge of a
creature whom they, as a family, considered to be as worthy of respect as a person. Cipriano Algor replied that he did not recall ever

having said that he had close friends in the city, and that the reason he was taking the dog with him was to distract himself from unwanted thoughts. Marta said that if he had such thoughts then he should share them with his daughter, who was there with him now, to which Cipriano Algor replied that talking to her about any thoughts he had would be a waste of time, because she was as familiar with them as he was himself, not word for word, of course, as if captured on tape, but she knew the underlying essence, and then she said that, in her humble opinion, the reality was quite different, she knew nothing about the underlying essence of his thoughts and, besides, many of the words he uttered were merely smoke screens, which, in a way, is hardly surprising, since words are often used for precisely that purpose, but it's worse still when the words remain unspoken and become a thick wall of silence, because, when confronted by such a wall, it's very hard to know what to do, Last night I sat up here waiting for you, Marçal went to bed after an hour, but I waited and waited, while you, my dear father, were off heaven knows where walking the dog, We went into the countryside somewhere, Ah, yes, the countryside, there's nothing nicer than going for a walk in the countryside at night, when you can't even see where you're putting your feet, You should have gone to bed, That's what I did in the end, before I turned into a statue, So that's all right then, there's nothing more to be said, No, it's not all right, Why not, Because you robbed me of what I most wanted at that moment, And what was that, To see you come back, that's all, just to see you come back, One day you'll understand, Well, I certainly hope so, but no more words, please, I'm sick of words. Marta's eyes shone with tears, Take no notice, she said, it seems that when we fragile women are pregnant, we don't know how else to behave, we experience everything too intensely. Marçal called from the yard to say that he had finished loading and that his father-in-law could leave whenever he wanted, Cipriano Algor left the house, got into the van, and called to Found. The dog, who had never even imagined the possibility of such good fortune, leaped up beside his master and sat there, smiling, his mouth open and his tongue lolling, thrilled at the prospect of the journey about to begin, in this, as in so many other things, human beings are very like dogs, they pin all their hopes on what might appear around the corner, and then say, oh, well, we'll see what happens next. When the van disappeared behind the first houses, Marçal asked, Did you have a fight, Oh, it's the usual problem, if we don't talk, we're unhappy, if we do talk, we disagree, We have to be patient, it doesn't take twenty-twenty vision to see that your father feels as if he were living on an island that is getting smaller with each day that passes, one piece gone, then another piece, right now, he's just driven off to take the figurines to the Center, then he'll come back home and light the kiln, but he's doing all these things as if he didn't quite know why any more, as if he wished some insurmountable object would place itself in his path so that he could at last say, that's it, it's over, Yes, I think you're probably right, Well, I don't know if I'm right or not, I'm just trying to put myself in his position, in a week's time everything we can see around us now will lose much of its meaning, the house will still be ours, but we won't live in it, the kiln won't deserve the name of kiln if someone doesn't call it that every day, the mulberry tree will still produce its mulberries, but there will be no one to come and pick them, I wasn't born and brought up under this roof, but even for me it's not going to be easy to leave all this, so for your father, We'll often come back, Yes, to our house in the country, as he ironically referred to it, Is there any other solution, asked Marta, you could stop being a guard and come and work with us in the pottery, making pottery that no one wants or figurines that no one is going to want for very long, The way things are, there's only one solution for me, to be a resident guard at the Center, You've got what you wanted, That was when I thought it was what I wanted, And now, Recently I've learned from your father something I didn't know before, you may not have noticed, but it is my duty to warn you that the man you are married to is much older than he seems, That's not news to me, I've had the privilege of witnessing the aging process, said Marta, smiling. But then her face grew grave, It's true, though, my heart aches at the thought of having to leave all this. They were sitting together under the mulberry tree on one of the drying shelves, opposite them was the house with the pottery beside it, if they turned their heads slightly, they could see the open door of the kiln through the foliage, it's a lovely sunny morning, but cool, perhaps the weather is changing. They felt good, despite their sadness, they felt almost happy, in that melancholy way in which happiness sometimes chooses to manifest itself, but suddenly Marçal got up from the drying shelf and cried, Oh, no, I'd forgotten, my parents, we have to go and talk to my parents, I'll bet you anything you like that they'll start going on and on about how they should be the ones to come with us to the Center and not your father, They probably won't if I'm there, it's a question of politeness, of good taste, Well, I certainly hope so, I certainly hope you're right.

She wasn't. When Cipriano Algor, on his return from taking the figurines to the Center, was driving through the village toward the house, he saw his daughter and son-in-law walking along ahead of him. Marçal had his arm around her shoulders as if to console her. Cipriano Algor stopped the van, Get in, he said, and he did not send Found to the back seat because he knew that they would want to be together. Marta was trying to brush away her tears, and Marçal was saying, Don't get upset, you know what they're like, if I'd known how they would react, I wouldn't have taken you with me, What happened, asked Cipriano Algor, The same thing as happened the other day, they want to go and live at the Center, they deserve it more than other people, it's time they had a chance to enjoy life, it didn't matter to them that Marta was there, they made the most terrible scene, and I apologize on their behalf. This time Cipriano Algor did not repeat his offer to give up his place, that would be like rubbing salt in the wound, he merely asked, And how did it end, Oh,

I told them that the apartment I've been given is basically meant for a couple with one child, and allows for, at most, one other family member to live there, but only if we make the spare room, which was originally intended to provide some storage space, into a bedroom, but that it's much too small for two people, And what did they say, They wanted to know what would happen if we had more children, and I told them the truth, that, in that case, the Center would move us to a bigger apartment, and they asked why they couldn't do that now, bearing in mind that the resident guard's own parents also wanted to live there, And what did you say, I told them that the request hadn't been made early enough, that there are rules and deadlines and regulations to meet, but that perhaps, later on, we might be able to review the situation, You managed to convince them, then, I doubt it, but it cheered them up a bit to think that they might be able to move to the Center one day, Until the next time, Oh, yes, because they wouldn't just let it go at that, they said that it wasn't their fault that the matter hadn't been dealt with earlier, Your parents are no fools, Especially my mother, because she's much keener on the idea than he is, she's always been a pretty tough nut to crack. Marta had stopped crying, And how do you feel, the question came from Cipriano Algor, Humiliated and ashamed, humiliated at having to be present during an argument that was aimed directly at me, but in which I was unable to intervene, and ashamed too, Why, Because whether we like it or not, they have as much right as we do, and we're the ones who are bending the rules so that they can't move to the Center, We're not, I am, broke in Marçal, I'm the one who doesn't want to live with my parents, you and your father have nothing to do with it, But we're accomplices in an injustice, Look, I know that to an outsider my attitude must seem reprehensible, but it was a decision I made freely and consciously in order to avoid an even worse situation, I don't want to live with my parents and I certainly don't want my wife and child to have to put up with them, love unites, but it doesn't unite everyone, and it could be that the reasons why some want union might be the very reasons why others want disunion, And how can you be so sure that our reasons will incline toward union rather than disunion, asked Cipriano Algor, There is only one reason I'm glad not to be your son, said Marçal, Let me guess, It's not that difficult, Because if you were, you wouldn't be married to Marta, Exactly, you guessed. They both laughed. And Marta said, I hope by this stage my child has taken the wise decision to be born a girl, Why, asked Marçal, Because her poor mother won't be strong enough to bear alone and unsupported the terrible smugness of her father and her grandfather. They laughed again, fortunately, Marçal's parents were not around at the time, they might think that the Algor family was laughing at their expense, hoodwinking their son into laughing at those who gave him life. They had left the last houses in the village behind them now. Found barked out of sheer contentment to see appearing at the top of the hill the roof of the pottery, the mulberry tree, and the upper part of one of the side walls of the kiln. Those who know about such things say that travel is of vital importance in shaping the mind, but one does not need to be an intellectual luminary to know that minds, however well-traveled, need to come back home now and then because only there can they achieve and maintain a reasonably satisfactory sense of themselves. Marta said, Here we are talking about family incompatibilities, about shame, humiliation, vanity, monotony, and mean little ambitions, and we haven't given a thought to this poor animal, who has no idea that in ten days' time he will no longer be with us. I have, said Marçal. Cipriano Algor said nothing. He took his right hand off the steering wheel and, as he would to a child, he ran his hand over the dog's head. When the van stopped by the woodshed, Marta was the first to get out, I'm going to make lunch, she said. Found did not wait for the door on his side to be opened, he slipped between the two front seats, leaped over Marçal's legs and shot off in the direction of the kiln, his startled bladder suddenly demanding urgent satisfaction. Marçal said, Now that we're alone, tell me how the delivery went, As it usually does, I handed in the advice notes, unloaded the boxes, which they then counted, the man who served me examined the figurines one by one, and they were all fine, none of them was broken and there were no scratches on the paint, you did a really excellent job of packing them, And that's all, Why do you ask, Ever since yesterday, I've had the feeling that you were hiding something, But I told you what happened, I didn't hide anything, No, I don't mean about the delivery you've just made, it's a feeling I've had ever since you picked me up at the Center, What do you mean, To be honest, I'm not sure, I was waiting for you to explain, for example, the enigmatic remarks you made over supper last night. Cipriano Algor remained silent, drumming his fingers on the steering wheel, as if he were deciding, depending on whether the last drumbeat was even or odd, what answer to give. In the end, he said, Come with me. He got out of the van and, followed by Marçal, walked over to the kiln. He had already placed his hand on one of the door handles, but he stopped for a moment and said, Don't say a word to Marta about what you are about to hear, I promise, Not a single word, Fine, I've said I promise. Cipriano Algor opened the kiln door. The bright light of day abruptly revealed the figurines lined up in groups, blinded first by the darkness and now by the light. Cipriano Algor said, It's possible, indeed very probable, that these three hundred figurines will never leave here, But why, asked Marçal, The buying department decided to draw up a questionnaire to evaluate the level of interest among customers, that's what the figurines I took in today will be used for, A questionnaire about a few clay figurines, said Marçal, That's what one of the assistant heads of department told me, The one who was rude to you, No, another one, who seems terribly nice and friendly, and who always speaks to you as if he had your best interests at heart. Marçal thought for a moment and said, Not that it makes much difference, not that it really matters to us now, because in ten days' time we'll be living in the Center, Do you really think it doesn't make much difference, that it doesn't matter to us, asked his father-in-law, If the result of the questionnaire is positive, there will still be time to finish the figurines and deliver them, as for the rest of the order, that will automatically be canceled by the irrefutable fact that the pottery will have ceased to operate, And if the result is negative, Well, in a way, that would be better still, because it would save both of you, you and Marta, the labor of firing the figurines and painting them. Cipriano Algor slowly closed the kiln door and said, You're forgetting certain doubtless insignificant aspects, What, You're forgetting the slap in the face of having the fruits of your labor rejected, you're forgetting that if it wasn't for the fact that these tragic events coincided with our move to the Center, we would be in the same situation we found ourselves in when they stopped buying the crockery, only without the absurd hope that a few ridiculous figurines could save our lives, We have to live with what is, not with what could be or might have been, That's a wonderfully accepting philosophy, Well, I'm sorry I can't come up with anything better, No, I can't either, but I was born with a mind that suffers from the incurable disease of worrying precisely about what could be or might have been, And what good has all that worrying done you, asked Marçal, You're quite right, none at all, as you said, we have to live with what is, not with fantasies about what might have been, if only. Relieved now of that physiological urgency and having hared about to stretch his legs, Found came over, tail wagging, his usual way of showing contentment and cordiality, but which, in this instance, given the proximity of lunch, signaled another urgent bodily need. Cipriano Algor stroked him, gently twisting his ear, We have to wait until Marta calls us, my lad, it doesn't look good if the dog of the house eats before his owners, we have to respect the hierarchy, he said. Then, to Marçal, as if the idea had just occurred to him at that moment, I'll fire the kiln today, You said you'd only do it tomorrow, when you got back from the Center, Well, I've changed my mind, it will be a way of occupying my time while you two have a rest or, if you'd rather, take the van and go for a drive, once we've moved, you probably won't want to leave the new apartment for a while, especially not to come out here, Whether or not we come out here and when is something we'll have to sort out later, but do you really think I'm the sort of man who could go off for a ride with Marta and leave you here all alone stoking the furnace with wood, Why, I can manage on my own, Of course you can, but if you don't mind, I would like to play an active role in this last lighting of the kiln, if it is the last time, All right, if that's what you want, we'll start after lunch, Fine, But remember, please, not a word about the questionnaire, Don't worry. With the dog at their heels, they walked toward the house and were only a few yards away when Marta appeared at the kitchen door, I was just about to call you, she said, lunch is ready, I'll give the dog his food first, the journey will have given him an appetite, said her father, His food's over there, Marta said. Cipriano Algor picked up the pan and said, Come on, Found, it's just as well you're not a person, if you were, you would have begun to feel suspicious of all the care and attention we've been lavishing on you lately. Found's bowl was, as it always was, beside the kennel and that was where Cipriano Algor headed. He emptied the contents of the pan into the bowl and stood for a moment, watching the dog eat. In the kitchen, Marçal was saying, We're going to light the kiln after lunch, Today, asked Marta, surprised, Your father doesn't want to leave it until tomorrow, There's no hurry, we were going to have three days off, He doubtless has his reasons, And, as usual, only he knows what those reasons are. Marçal thought it best not to respond, the mouth is an organ that is all the more trustworthy the more silent it is. Shortly afterward, Cipriano Algor came into the kitchen. The food was on the table, Marta was serving it out. In a moment, her father will say, We're lighting the kiln today, and Marta will reply, I know, Marçal told me.

It has already been said, in these or other words, that all the days gone by were once the eves of days to come and all future days will in turn be the eves of other future days. To become an eve, if only for an hour, is the impossible desire of every yesterday that has been and gone and of every today that is happening right now. No day has ever managed to be the eve of another day for as long as it had hoped. Only yesterday, Cipriano Algor and Marçal Gacho were busily stoking the furnace with wood, and anyone walking by, and not knowing the full facts, could easily have thought, judging himself to be right, There they are again, they'll spend their whole life doing that, and now there they are in the van with the word Pottery written on both sides, on their way to the city and the Center, and Marta is with them, sitting beside the driver, who this time is her husband. Cipriano Algor is alone on the back seat, Found is not there, he stayed behind to guard the house. It's morning, but very early, the sun is not yet up, the Green Belt will appear soon, then it will be the Industrial Belt, then the shantytowns, then the no-man's-land, then the buildings being constructed on the periphery, and at last the city, the broad avenue, and finally the Center. Any road you take leads to the Center. None of the passengers in the van will speak during the journey. Although usually so loquacious, it seems now that they have nothing to say to one another. However, it is easy to understand that it might not be worth speaking, wasting time and saliva on articulating speeches, phrases, words, and syllables when what one of them is thinking is already being thought by the others. If Marçal, for example, were to say, Let's go to the Center to see the apartment where we'll be living, Marta will say, How odd, that's exactly what I was thinking, and though Cipriano Algor might demur, Well, I wasn't, I was thinking that I won't come in, that I'll just wait outside for you, even so, however peremptory his words may sound, we shouldn't pay too much attention, Cipriano Algor is sixty-four, he is past the age of childish sulking and has some way to go before he reaches the elderly equivalent. What Cipriano Algor really thinks is that he has no alternative but to go in with his daughter and his son-in-law and to respond as cheerfully as he can to their remarks, to give his opinion when asked, in short, as they used to say in old novels and dramas, to drain the cup of sorrow to the dregs. At that early hour, Marçal found a parking space only a couple of hundred yards from the Center, it will be different when they are actually living there, resident guards have a right to six square meters of space in the parking lot inside. We're here, Marçal said unnecessarily, when he put on the hand brake. The Center was not visible from there, but it appeared before them as soon as they turned the corner of the street where they had left the van. As chance would have it, this was the side, part, face, end, or extremity reserved for residents. It was not a new sight for any of them, but there is a great difference between looking for looking's sake and looking while someone is saying to us, Two of those windows are ours, Only two, asked Marta, We can't complain, some apartments have only one, said Marçal, not to mention the ones that have only windows with a view of the inside, The inside of what, The inside of the Center, of course, Do you mean there are apartments with windows that overlook the inside of the Center itself, Lots of people actually prefer them, they find the view from there much more pleasant, varied, and interesting, whereas from the other side you have just a view over the same rooftops and the same sky, Even so, someone living in one of those apartments would be able to see only the floor of the Center that coincides with the floor they live on, remarked Cipriano Algor, less out of any genuine interest than to show that he hadn't completely withdrawn from the conversation, The height from floor to ceiling on the commercial floors is vast, so it's all very spacious and airy, apparently people never tire of the spectacle, especially older people, But I've never noticed any windows, Marta said abruptly, in order to stall the comment her father was bound to make on what might constitute suitable distractions for the elderly, The décor disguises them. They continued walking along the main façade of the building to the door reserved for security staff, Cipriano Algor remained two reluctant steps behind, as if he were being pulled along by an invisible thread. I feel nervous, said Marta softly so that her father would not hear, You'll see, everything will be easier once we've settled in, it's just a question of getting used to it, said Marçal equally softly. A little farther on, in a normal tone of voice, Marta asked, What floor is our apartment on, The thirty-fourth, That's awfully high, There are another fourteen floors above us, A bird in a cage hung outside a window could easily imagine it was free, You can't open the windows, Why not, Because of the air-conditioning, Of course. They had reached the door. Marçal went in, greeted the two guards on duty, said in passing, This is my wife and my father-in-law, and opened the inner door that led into the building. They entered an elevator, We'll have to pick up the key, said Marçal. They got out on the second floor, walked down a long, narrow corridor of gray walls with doors at regular intervals on either side. Marçal opened one door, This is my section, he said. He greeted his colleagues who were on his shift and made the same introductions, This is my wife and my father-in-law, then added, We've come to see the apartment. He went over to a locker bearing his name, opened it, took out a bunch of keys, and said to Marta, Here they are. They entered another elevator. There are two speeds, explained Marçal, we'll go slowly to start with, He pressed the relevant button, then button number twenty, Let's go to the twentieth floor first so that you have time to appreciate the view, he said. The part of the elevator that looked out over the Center was entirely made of glass. It traveled slowly past the different floors, revealing a succession of arcades, shops, fancy staircases, escalators, meeting points, cafés, restaurants, terraces with tables and chairs, cinemas and theaters, discotheques, enormous television screens, endless numbers of ornaments, electronic games, balloons, fountains and other water features, platforms, hanging gardens, posters, pennants, advertising billboards, mannequins, changing rooms, the façade of a church, the entrance to the beach, a bingo hall, a casino, a tennis court, a gymnasium, a roller coaster, a zoo, a racetrack for electric cars, a cyclorama, a cascade, all waiting, all in silence, and more shops and more arcades and more mannequins and more hanging gardens and things for which people probably didn't even know the names, as if they were ascending into paradise. And is this speed used only so that people can enjoy the view, asked Cipriano Algor, No, at this speed the elevators are used as an extra security aid, said Marçal, Isn't there enough security what with the guards, the detectors, the video cameras, and all the other snooping devices, Cipriano Algor asked. Tens of thousands of people pass through here every day, it's important to maintain security, replied Marçal, his face tense and with a touch of annoyance in his voice, Pa, said Marta, stop tormenting him, please, Don't worry, said Marçal, we understand each other, even when we appear not to. The elevator continued to rise slowly. The floors are still only minimally lit, there are few people around, just the occasional worker who has got up early out of either necessity or habit, it will be at least an hour before the doors are opened to the public. The people who live and work in the Center don't need to rush, those who have to leave the Center don't go through the commercial and leisure areas, they go straight from their apartments down to the underground garages. When the elevator stopped, Marçal pressed the fast button and within a matter of seconds, they were on the thirty-fourth floor. While they were walking along the corridor that led to the residential part, Marçal explained that there were elevators exclusively for the use of residents and that he had used the other one today only because of having to pick up the keys first. From now on, we keep the keys, they're ours, he said. Contrary to what Marta and her father had expected, there was not just one corridor separating the blocks of apartments with a view onto the outside world from those with a view inside. There were, in fact, two corridors and, between them, another block of apartments, but this was twice the width of the others, which, put plainly, means that the inhabited part of the Center is made up of four vertical, parallel sequences of apartments, arranged like cells in a storage battery or honeycombs in a beehive, the interiors joined back to back, the exteriors joined to the central structure by the corridors. Marta said, These people never see the light of day when they're at home, Neither do the people who have apartments with a view onto the inside of the Center, replied Marçal, But as you said, at least they can find some distraction watching the view and the people moving about, while the others are practically enclosed, it can't be easy to live in an apartment with no natural light, breathing canned air all day, Well, you know, there are plenty of people who prefer it like that, they find the apartments more comfortable, better equipped, just to give you a few examples, they all have ultraviolet machines, atmospheric regenerators, and thermostats that can regulate temperature and humidity so accurately that it's possible to keep the humidity and temperature in the apartment constant day and night, all year round, Am I glad we didn't get one of those, I don't think I could stand living there for very long, said Marta, We resident guards have to make do with an ordinary apartment with windows, Well, I would never have imagined that being the father-in-law of a resident guard at the Center would prove to be the best fortune and the greatest privilege that life would offer me, said Cipriano Algor. The apartments were numbered like hotel rooms, the only distinguishing feature being the introduction of a hyphen between the floor number and the number of the door. Marçal put the key in the lock, opened the door and stood aside, After you, he said loudly, pretending an enthusiasm he did not feel, this is our new home. They were neither happy nor excited by the novelty. Marta stood poised on the threshold, then took a few uncertain steps inside and looked around. Marçal and her father hung back. After a few moments of hesitation, as if she did not quite know what she should do, she headed alone for the nearest door, peered in and went inside. And that was her first encounter with the new apartment, passing swiftly from the bedroom to the kitchen, from the kitchen to the bathroom, from the living room that would also serve as a dining room to the small room intended for her father, There's nowhere for the baby, she thought, and then, While it's young, it can sleep with us, then we'll have to see, they'll probably give us a bigger place. She went back to the hall, where Marçal and Cipriano Algor were waiting for her. Have you been up here before, she asked her husband, Yes, What did you think, Well, as you'll have seen for yourself, the furniture is new, everything's new, as I told you, And what do you think, Pa, I can't give an opinion on something I haven't seen, Well, come in, then, I'll be your guide. She was noticeably tense and nervous, so different from her usual self that she announced each room as if she were singing its praises, This is the master bedroom, this is the kitchen, this is the bathroom, this is the living room that will also serve as our dining room, this is the spacious and comfortable room in which my dear father will sleep and enjoy a well-earned rest, there doesn't seem to be anywhere to put our child when she's older, but I'm sure we'll find a solution. Don't you like the apartment, asked Marçal, It's going to be our new home, so there's no point in discussing whether I like it a lot or a little or not at all, like someone pulling petals off a daisy. Marçal turned to his father-in-law for help, saying nothing, merely fixing him with his gaze, It's not at all bad really, said Cipriano Algor, everything's nice and new, the furniture's made of excellent wood, obviously it isn't going to be like our furniture, but that's how people want things nowadays, in light colors, not like the stuff we've got at home, which looks as if it had been baked in the kiln, as for the rest, we'll get used to it, you always do. Marta was frowning as she listened to her father's little speech, then she made an attempt at a smile and set off around the apartment again, this time opening and closing drawers and cupboards, checking the contents. Marçal shot his father-in-law a look of gratitude, then glanced at his watch and said, It's nearly time for me to start work. Marta said from another room, I won't be long, I'm just coming, that's the advantage of these small apartments, you cautiously let out a deeply felt sigh and immediately someone at the other end of the apartment says accusingly, You sighed, now don't deny it. And some people complain about the guards, the cameras, the detectors, and all those other snooping devices. The visit to the apartment was over, and judging by the difference between how they looked when they had gone in and how they looked now that they were leaving, without, of course, claiming to be able to lay bare the secrets of people's hearts, it appeared to have been worthwhile. They went straight down from the thirty-fourth floor to the ground floor because Marta and her father still did not have the necessary documents to prove that they were residents, and Marçal had to accompany them to the exit. After walking only a few steps as the elevator doors closed behind them, Cipriano Algor said, What an odd sensation, it feels as if the ground was vibrating beneath my feet. He stopped, listened and added, And I think I can hear something that sounds like excavators at work, They are excavators, said Marçal, quickening his pace, they work nonstop on six-hour shifts, they're quite a few feet beneath the surface, Some sort of construction work, I suppose, said Cipriano Algor, Yes, apparently they're going to install some new cold-storage units, and possibly something else, perhaps more garages, they're always building something here, the Center grows every day without your even noticing it, if not outward, upward, if not upward, downward, In a while, when everything starts up again, you probably won't even notice the noise of the excavators, Marta said, What with the music, the sales announcements over the loudspeakers, the general buzz of conversation, and the escalators going endlessly up and down, you won't even notice they're there. They had reached the door. Marçal said that he would phone later if there was any news, but that, in the meantime, it would make sense to start preparing things for the move, making sure to take only what was absolutely essential, Now that you've seen the amount of space we've got to play with, you can appreciate that there isn't much room to spare. They were outside on the walk, they were about to say good-bye, but Marta said, In a way, it's not like moving at all, our pottery home is still ours, we can hardly bring anything from there, it's more as if we were taking off one set of clothes and putting on another, a sort of masked ball, Yes, said her father, it is a bit like that, but, contrary to what people have generally believed and unthinkingly affirmed, the cowl really does make the monk and clothes do make the man, you might not notice at first, but it's only a matter of time. Good-bye, said Marçal, giving his wife a kiss, you can spend the whole journey home philosophizing, so make the most of it. Marta and her father walked back to where they had parked the van. On the Center façade, above their heads, a gigantic new poster proclaimed, WE WOULD SELL YOU EVERYTHING YOU NEED, BUT WE WOULD PREFER YOU TO NEED WHAT WE HAVE TO SELL.

On the drive back home, or as Marta called it, in order to differentiate it from their new home, their pottery home, father and daughter, despite Marçal's half-mocking, half-affectionate remarks, spoke little, very little, although the simplest examination of the multiple probabilities arising from the situation would suggest that they had much to think about. To leap ahead, by bold suppositions, or by dangerous deductions, or, worse still, by ill-considered guesswork, to what their thoughts were would not, in principle, if we consider how promptly and impudently the heart's secrets are often violated in stories of this kind, would not, as we were saying, be an impossible task, but, since those thoughts will, sooner or later, be expressed in actions, or in words that lead to actions, it seems to us preferable to move on and wait quietly for the actions and words to make those thoughts manifest. We do not have to wait long for the first one. Neither father nor daughter spoke during lunch, which must mean that new thoughts were being added to those of the journey, then suddenly she decided to break the silence, That was an excellent idea of yours to take three days off, and quite apart from being very welcome, it was, at the time, perfectly justifiable, but Marçal's promotion has changed the situation completely, do you realize we have only just over a week to organize the move and to paint the three hundred figurines that are fired and ready in the kiln, we have an obligation to deliver those three hundred at least, Yes, I've been thinking about the figurines too, but have reached exactly the opposite conclusion, What do you mean, The Center already has an advance guard of three hundred figurines, which should be enough for now, clay figurines are not like computer games or magnetic bracelets, people aren't pushing and shoving and screaming I want my Eskimo, I want my bearded Assyrian, I want my nurse, No, I'm sure the Center's customers aren't going to come to blows over the mandarin or the jester or the clown, but that doesn't mean we shouldn't finish the job, Of course not, but it just seems to me that there's no point in rushing, Let me remind you again that we have only a week in which to do everything, I haven't forgotten, So, So, as you yourself said when we left the Center, it's not really as if we were moving at all, our pottery home, as you now call it, will still be here, Look, Pa, I know what a lover of enigmas you are, I'm not a lover of enigmas at all, I always like things to be clear, All right, you don't love enigmas, but you are enigmatic, and I would be very grateful if you could tell me where all this is leading, It's leading to precisely where we are now, where we will be for another week and, I hope, for many weeks afterward, Don't make me lose my patience, please, Same here, look, it's as simple as two plus two makes four, In your head, two plus two always makes five or three or anything but four, You'll be sorry you asked, I doubt it, All right, imagine that we don't paint the figurines, that we move to the Center and leave them in the kiln just as they are now, OK, I've imagined that, Living at the Center, as Marçal explained very clearly, is not like living in exile, people aren't imprisoned there, they're free to leave whenever they want, to spend all day in the city or the countryside and go back at night. Cipriano Algor paused to study his daughter, knowing that soon he would see the dawning of understanding on her face. And so it was. Marta said, smiling, All right, I was wrong, even in your head two plus two can occasionally make four, Didn't I tell you it was easy, We'll come and finish the work when we need to, and that way we won't have to cancel the order for the six hundred figurines still to come, it's just a matter of agreeing on deadlines with the Center that will suit both sides, Exactly. The daughter applauded her father, her father thanked her for her applause. And you know, said Marta, suddenly filled with enthusiasm by the ocean of positive possibilities that had opened up before her, if the Center really likes the figurines, we could go on making them and we wouldn't have to close the pottery, Exactly, And not just figurines either, we might have another idea they'd like to take up, or we could add other figures to the six we've got already, Precisely. While father and daughter savored these pleasant prospects, which demonstrated yet again that the devil is not always lurking behind every door, let us take advantage of this pause to examine the real value or real meaning of the thoughts of both father and daughter, of those two thoughts which, after that long, long silence, finally found expression. Let us say at once, however, that it will not be possible to reach a conclusion, even a provisional one, as all conclusions are, if we do not start with an initial premise that will doubtless prove shocking to decent, nicely brought up souls, but which is nonetheless true, the premise that, in many cases, the thought actually expressed was, so to speak, dragged into the front line by another thought that preferred not to reveal itself just yet. It is easy enough to see that some of Cipriano Algor's strange behavior is motivated by his own tormenting concerns about the results of the questionnaire, and that his aim in reminding his daughter that, even once they have moved to the Center, they can still come and work in the pottery, was simply to dissuade her from painting the figurines, so that, should a command arrive tomorrow or later on from the smiling assistant head of department or from his immediate superior canceling the order, she would not have to suffer the pain of leaving her work unfinished or, if finished, redundant. Much more surprising is Marta's behavior, that impulsive and in some ways unnaturally joyful reaction to the doubtful possibility of coming back to the pottery and keeping it going, unless, of course, one could establish a link between that behavior and the thought that originated it, a thought that has been tenaciously pursuing her ever since she entered the apartment at the

Center and which she swore to herself never to confess to anyone, not even to her father, even though he is there by her side, nor, can you imagine it, to her own husband, even though she loves him very much. What went through Marta's head and put down roots there the moment she crossed the threshold of her new home, in that lofty thirty-fourth floor with its pale furniture and two vertiginous windows that she had not even had the courage to approach, was that she would not be able to stand living there for the rest of her life, with no other identity than that of being the wife of resident guard Marçal Gacho, with no other future than that of the daughter growing inside her. Or the son. She thought about this all the way back to the pottery, she continued to think about it as she was preparing lunch, she was still thinking about it when, not feeling in the least bit hungry, she kept pushing the food on her plate around with her fork, and she was still thinking when she said to her father that, before they moved to the Center, they had a strict obligation to finish the figurines that were still waiting in the kiln. Finishing them meant painting them, and painting was her job, if she could just have three or four days to spend sitting under the mulberry tree with Found lying by her side, his mouth open in a broad grin, his tongue lolling. This was all she asked, like the last desperate wish of a condemned man, and suddenly, with a few simple words, her father had opened up the door to freedom, she would, after all, be able to leave the Center whenever she wanted, unlock the door to her house with the key to her house, find all the things she had left behind in their accustomed places, go into the pottery to see if the clay was the right consistency, then sit down at the wheel and surrender her hands to the cool clay, only now did she understand that she loved these places the way a tree, if it could, would love the roots that feed it and hold it erect in the air. Cipriano Algor was looking at his daughter, reading her face as if it were the page of an open book, and his heart ached because of the entirely false hopes he would have been nurturing in her if the results of the questionnaire turned out to be so negative that the buying department at the Center decided to abandon the figurines once and for all. Marta had got up from her chair and come over to give him a kiss and a hug, What will she feel in a few days' time, thought Cipriano Algor, reciprocating her affection, but the words he spoke were quite different, they were the usual words, As our grandparents more or less believed, while there's life, we're guaranteed hope. The resigned tone in which he said this would perhaps have given Marta pause for thought had she been less absorbed in her own happy expectations. Let's enjoy our three days off in peace, said Cipriano Algor, we certainly deserve them, and, after all, we're not stealing them from anyone, then we'll start getting ready for the move, You set the example, then, and go and have a nap, said Marta, you spent the whole of yesterday working the kiln and today you had to get up early, now even for a father like mine, stamina has its limits, as for the move, don't worry about that, that's a matter for the mistress of the house. Cipriano Algor went to his bedroom, got undressed with the weary gestures born of a tiredness that was not purely physical and lay down on the bed with a deep sigh. He did not stay there long. He propped himself up on the pillow and looked around him as if this was the first time he had ever come into this room and as if, for some obscure reason, he had to fix it in his memory, as if this was also the last time that he would come here and as if he wanted his memory to serve some purpose other than merely one day recalling for him that stain on the wall, that line of light on the floor, that photograph of a woman on the chest of drawers. Outside, Found barked as if he had heard a stranger coming up the drive, but then he fell silent, he was probably just responding in somewhat desultory fashion to the barking of a distant dog, or else simply wanted to make his presence felt, he must sense that something is going on that he cannot understand. Cipriano Algor closed his eyes in order to summon up sleep, but his eyes preferred not to. There is nothing as sad, nothing as unutterably sad, as an old man crying.

The news arrived the next day. The weather had changed, there was an occasional heavy downpour that flooded the whole yard in minutes and drummed on the mulberry tree's crisp leaves like ten thousand drumsticks. Marta had been making a list of the things they should take with them to the apartment, always keenly aware at every moment of the two contradictory impulses battling inside her, one telling her the most perfect of truths, that is, that a move would not be a move if nothing was moved, the other advising her simply to leave everything as it was, Especially, it said, since you'll often be back here to work and to breathe the country air. As for Cipriano Algor, with the intention of clearing his head of the web of anxieties that made him keep looking at his watch again and again throughout the day, he had busied himself sweeping out and cleaning the pottery from top to bottom, once more refusing Marta's offer of help, I'd only have to answer to Marçal later on, he said. Found had just been sent back to his kennel after having covered the kitchen floor with the mud clinging to his feet after his first sally forth since the rain had cleared. The rain would never be heavy enough to flood the kennel, but, just in case, his master had placed four bricks underneath it, transforming an ordinary, modern-day canine refuge into a prehistoric stilt house. He was engaged in this when the phone rang. Marta answered and, at first, when she heard the voice say, It's the Center here, she thought it was Marçal, that they were about to put him through to her, but those were not the words that followed, The head of the buying department would like to speak to Senhor Cipriano Algor. Generally speaking, a secretary knows what her boss is going to say when he asks her to get him a particular number, but an actual telephone operator knows nothing at all, which is why she has the neutral, indifferent voice of someone who is no longer of this world, but let us do her the justice of thinking that she might occasionally have shed sorrowful tears if she could have guessed what would happen after uttering the mechanical words, You're through. Marta began by imagining that the head of the buying department was phoning to express his annoyance at the delay in delivering the missing three hundred figurines, or even, who knows, the six hundred that they had not even started yet, and when, having told the telephone operator, Just a moment, please, she ran out to call to her father in the pottery, she did so thinking that she would have a quick critical word with him about his mistaken decision not to get on with the work as soon as the first series of figurines was finished. Any recriminatory words, however, remained stuck fast to her tongue when she saw the agitated look on her father's face as he heard her say, It's the head of the buying department, he wants to talk to you. Cipriano Algor thought it best not to run, it should be enough that he managed to walk with a firm step to the bar where he would be sentenced. He picked up the receiver that his daughter had left on the table. Hello, Cipriano Algor speaking, and the telephone operator said, I'm just connecting you, there was a silence, a slight buzzing, a crackle, and the loud, sonorous voice of the head of the buying department boomed out at the other end, Good afternoon, Senhor Cipriano Algor, Good afternoon, sir, Now I imagine you know why I'm ringing today, You imagine correctly, sir, please go on, I have before me the results and conclusions of the questionnaire on your products which one of my assistants, with my approval, decided to carry out, And what were the results, sir, asked Cipriano Algor, I regret to inform you that they were not as good as we had hoped, If that's the case, then no one can regret it more than I do, Your participation in the life of our Center is, I'm afraid, over, New things begin every day, but sooner or later, they all end, Wouldn't you like me to read out the results, I'm more interested in the conclusions and I know what those are already, the Center won't be buying any more of our figurines. Marta, who had been listening with ever-increasing concern to her father's words, raised her hands to her mouth as if to suppress a cry. Cipriano Algor gestured to her to remain calm, at the same time responding to a question from the head of the buying department,

Yes, I understand your desire to clarify any doubts in my mind, and I agree that presenting conclusions without first explaining the reasons that led to them might be seen as a rather clumsy way of disguising an arbitrary decision, which would never, of course, be the case with the Center, So glad you agree with me, It would be hard not to, sir, Right, then, these are the results, Go on, The statistical population of customers who were to be sent the questionnaire was defined at the start by the exclusion of all those people who by virtue of age, social class, education, and culture, as well as by their known buying habits, were predictably and radically averse to acquiring articles of this type, it is important that you should know that we took that decision, Senhor Algor, in order not to prejudice you from the outset, Thank you very much, sir, Let me give you an example, if we had selected fifty modern young people, fifty ordinary young men and women, you can be sure, Senhor Algor, that none of them would want to take home one of your figurines, or if they did, it would only be in order to use them as target practice, I understand, We chose twenty-five people of each sex, with average jobs and salaries, people from modest family backgrounds, who still had traditional tastes and in whose houses the rustic nature of the product would not look too out of place, And even then, Yes, Senhor Algor, even then the results were bad, Oh, well, Twenty men and ten women said that they did not like clay figurines, four women said that they might buy them if they were bigger, three that they might buy them if they were smaller, of the five remaining men, four said that they were too old to be playing with dolls and the other man was outraged that three of the figurines represented foreigners, exotic ones to boot, and as for the eight remaining women, two said they were allergic to clay, four said that such objects had bad associations for them, and only the last two replied thanking us very much for the opportunity to decorate their house with such lovely statuettes entirely free of charge, it has to be said that both were elderly people living alone. Well, I'd like to have their

names and addresses so that I could write and thank them, said
Cipriano Algor, Ah, I'm afraid I'm not authorized to reveal any personal data about those questioned, it's a strict condition of any such
research to respect the anonymity of respondents, Perhaps you
could tell me, though, if those people live in the Center, Who do
you mean, all of them, asked the head of the buying department,
No, sir, just the two who were kind enough to like our figurines,
said Cipriano Algor, Since that hardly constitutes factual information, I don't think I would be betraying the deontology of the questionnaires if I were to tell you that those two women both live
outside the Center, in the city, Thank you for that information, sir,
Was it any help, Alas, no, sir, Then why did you want to know, Because I might have had the opportunity of meeting them and thanking them personally, but since they live in the city, it would be well
nigh impossible, And if they lived here, When, at the beginning of
this conversation, you said that my participation in the life of the
Center had reached an end, I almost interrupted you, Why, Because,
contrary to what you think, despite the fact that you want nothing
more to do with the pots, plates, or figurines made by this pottery,
my life will continue to be linked to the Center, I don't understand,
please be good enough to explain yourself more clearly, In five or six
days' time I will be living there, my son-in-law was promoted to the
position of resident guard and I'll be going to live there with my
daughter and with him, Well, I'm glad to hear it and please accept
my congratulations, you are a lucky man after all, you certainly can't
complain, just when you thought you'd lost everything, it turns out
you've won, Oh, I'm not complaining, sir, Perhaps we would be justified in proclaiming that the Center writes straight on crooked
lines, and what it takes away with one hand, it gives with the other,
If I remember rightly, that business about crooked lines and writing
straight used to be said about God, remarked Cipriano Algor, Nowadays, it comes to pretty much the same thing, I would not be exag-
gerating if I were to say that the Center, as the perfect distributor of

material and spiritual goods, has, out of sheer necessity, generated from and within itself something that almost partakes of the divine, although I realize that this may offend certain of the more sensitive orthodoxies, Do you distribute spiritual goods as well, sir, Oh, yes, and you cannot imagine the extent to which the Center's detractors, although these are becoming fewer and less combative all the time, are completely blind to the spiritual side of our activities, when the truth is that, thanks to these activities, life has taken on new meaning for millions and millions of people who before were unhappy, frustrated and helpless, and believe me, whether you like it or not, that was not the work of vile matter but of sublime spirit, Yes, I'm sure, Anyway, I just want to say, Senhor Algor, that I have found in you someone to whom, even in difficult situations like the present one, it has always been a pleasure to talk about this and other serious matters, matters in which I take a particular interest because of the transcendent dimension which, in some way, they add to my work, and I hope that, after your imminent move to the Center, we will be able to meet again and continue this exchange of ideas, So do I, sir, Good-bye, Good-bye. Cipriano Algor replaced the receiver on its rest and looked at his daughter. Marta was sitting down with her hands in her lap, as if in response to a sudden need to protect the incipient and still barely perceptible roundness of her belly. Are they not going to buy from us any more, she asked, No, they did a survey of their customers and the results were negative, So they won't be buying the three hundred figurines that are in the kiln, No. Marta got up and went over to the kitchen door, she looked out at the teeming rain and, turning her head slightly, she asked, Haven't you anything to say to me, Yes, said her father, Go on then, I'm all ears. Cipriano Algor joined her at the door and, leaning against the doorjamb, took a deep breath and began, This hasn't come as a surprise, I knew this might happen, one of the assistant heads of department told me that they were going to carry out a survey to find out how their customers felt about the figurines, although the idea almost certainly came from the department head, So I've been deceived these past three days, deceived by you, my own father, dreaming about a pottery in full production, imagining us leaving the Center early in the morning, arriving here and rolling up our sleeves, breathing in the smell of the clay, working beside you, having Marçal with me on his days off, It was just that I didn't want you to suffer, But now I'm suffering twice, your good intentions didn't save me from any suffering at all, Forgive me, And please don't waste your time asking my forgiveness, because you know perfectly well that I'll always forgive you, whatever you do, If the decision had gone the other way, if the Center had decided to buy the figurines, you would never have known anything about the danger we had been in, Now it's no longer a danger, it's a reality, We've still got the house, we can come here whenever we like, Yes, we have the house, a house with a view of the cemetery, What cemetery, The pottery, the kiln, the drying shelves, the woodshed, what was and is no more, could there be a bigger cemetery than that, asked Marta, on the brink of tears. Her father placed one hand on her shoulder, Don't cry, I realize now that it was a mistake not to have told you what was going on. Marta did not reply, she reminded herself that she had no right to criticize her father, for she too had a secret that she was keeping from her husband and which she would never tell him, How are you going to manage to live in that apartment now, with all hope gone, she was asking herself. Found had left the kennel, plump drops of water fell on him from the mulberry tree, but he did not dare to venture farther. His paws were muddy, his fur dripping, and he was sure that he would not be well received. And yet he it was that they were talking about at the kitchen door. When she saw him appear there and stop to look at them, Marta had asked, What are we going to do with that dog. Calmly, as if discussing a subject they had talked about thousands of times before and which it was hardly worth mentioning again, her father replied, I'll ask Isaura Madruga if she'll have him, Am I hearing right, can you repeat that, please, did you really say that you were going to ask Isaura Madruga if she'll have Found, You heard me perfectly, that was exactly what I said, You mean Isaura Madruga, If you keep this up, I'll say Yes, Isaura Madruga and you'll say You mean Isaura Madruga and we'll spend the rest of the afternoon going back and forth, It's just such a surprise, It can't be that much of a surprise, she's the person you had in mind too, It isn't the person that's the surprise, the surprising thing for me is that you should have had the same idea, There isn't another person in the village, possibly in the whole world, that I would leave Found with, I'd rather kill him first. Expectantly, slowly wagging his tail, the dog was still watching from afar. Cipriano Algor crouched down and called, Found, come here. The dog began to shake himself, spraying water everywhere, as if he could only go to his master once he was decent and presentable, then he made a quick dash and, an instant later, he had his great head pressed against Cipriano Algor's chest, so hard it was as if he were trying to burrow inside. That was when Marta asked her father, Just so that everything is perfect, which doesn't only mean having Found in your arms, tell me if you told Marçal about the survey, Yes, I did, He didn't say anything to me, For the same reason that I didn't tell you. At this point in the dialogue, you might be expecting Marta to respond, Honestly, Pa, fancy telling him and leaving me in the dark, that is how people normally react, no one likes to be left out or to have their right to information and knowledge thwarted, however, every now and then, one still comes across the occasional rare exception in this dull world of repetitions, as the Orphic, Pythagorean, Stoic, and Neoplatonic sages might have called it had they not preferred, with poetic inspiration, to give it the prettier and more sonorous name of the eternal return. Marta did not protest, she did not make a scene, she merely said, I would have been angry with you if you hadn't told Marçal. Detaching himself from the dog and sending him back to his kennel, Cipriano Algor said, At least I manage to get things right sometimes. They stood watching the endless rain, listening to the mulberry tree's monologue, and then Marta asked, What can we do about those figurines in the kiln, and her father replied, Nothing. Terse and to the point, the word left no room for doubt, Cipriano Algor did not proffer instead one of those vulgar, everyday phrases which, in their attempt to declare themselves to be definitively negative, happily carry within them two negatives, which, according to the expert opinion of grammarians, should turn them into a positive affirmation, as if one such phrase, for example, We can't do nothing, were going to all the trouble of denying itself in order to end up meaning that we can do something.

Marçal phoned after supper, I'm speaking from our new home, he said, I left the security staff dorm today and tonight I'll be sleeping in our own bed, Good, you must be pleased, Yes, and I have some news to give you too, So have we, said Marta, Which shall we begin with, mine or yours, he asked, It would be best to begin with the bad news and leave the good news, if there is any, to last, My news is neither good nor bad, it's just news, Then I'll begin with ours, this afternoon the Center told us that they won't be buying the figurines, they carried out a survey and the result was negative. There was a silence at the other end. Marta waited. Then Marçal said, I knew about the survey, Yes, I know you knew, Pa told me, And I was afraid that would be the result, Your fears were confirmed, Are you annoyed with me for not telling you what was going on, No, I'm not angry with you or with him, that's how things are, we have to do our best to understand and accept it, what I found most difficult was having to give up the hope that, even once we were living in the Center, we would still be able to come and work in the pottery, That wasn't a possibility I had ever considered, It wasn't an idea that I thought up either, it emerged in conversation with Pa, But he couldn't be sure that the figurines would be accepted, Like you, he wanted to save me any pain, and the result of that deceit was that I've been happy as a lark these last few days, which, I suppose, is better than nothing, but there's no point crying over the spilt milk that has been the cause of so many tears in this world, tell me your news, They've given me three days' leave for the move, that's including my normal day off, which this time happens to fall on a Monday, so I'll leave here on Friday afternoon, in a taxi, it's not worth your father's coming to pick me up, we'll get everything ready on Saturday, and on Sunday morning, we'll set sail, Hm, I've already put to one side everything we need to take with us, said Marta rather distractedly. There was another silence. Aren't you happy, asked Marçal, Yes, I am, really I am, replied Marta. Then she said again, I am happy, really I am. Outside, the dog Found barked, some shadow in the dark night must have moved.

The van had been loaded, the windows and doors of the pottery and the house had been closed, all they had to do now, as Marçal had said a few days before, was to set sail. Strained and tense, looking suddenly much older, Cipriano Algor called the dog. Despite the anxious tone that any attentive ear would have picked up, his master's voice raised Found's spirits. He had spent the morning running about, perplexed and uneasy, sniffing the suitcases and packages that were brought out of the house, he had barked loudly in order to attract their attention, and his instincts had not misled him, something singular and out of the ordinary had been happening lately, and now the time had come when luck or fate or chance or the unstable nature of human desires and constraints were about to reach a decision on what was to become of him. He had lain down by the kennel, his head resting on his paws, waiting. When his master said, Found, come here, he thought he was being summoned in order to get into the van as had happened on other occasions, a sign that nothing had really changed in his life, that today would be the same as yesterday, which is the constant dream of all dogs. He thought it odd that they should put the lead on him, which they did not usually do when they went traveling, and this sense of oddness only increased and changed into confusion when his mistress and his younger master stroked his head, at the same time murmuring incomprehensible words among which the sound of his own name kept being repeated in the most disquieting fashion, not that they were saying anything very bad, We'll come and see you soon. A gentle tug on the leash told him that he should follow his master, the situation had suddenly become clear, the van was for his mistress and his other master, he would be going for a walk with the older master. Having to wear a leash still struck him as odd, but it nevertheless seemed a relatively minor detail. Once they reached the countryside, his master would let him off the leash so he could race off after whatever living creature happened to appear, even if it was only a lizard. It's a cool morning, the sky is cloudy, but there's no sign of rain. When they reached the road, instead of turning left toward the open countryside, as he expected, his master turned right, which meant that they would be going into the village. Three times during the walk, Found had to stop suddenly. Cipriano Algor was doing what most of us would do in similar circumstances, when we engage in a futile discussion with our inner selves as to whether we do or do not want what it has become clear that we do in fact want, we begin a sentence and fail to finish it, we stop suddenly, then tear along as if we had to save our own father from the gallows, then we stop again, even the most patient and devoted of dogs will end up wondering if he wouldn't be better off with a more decisive master. He cannot know how firm his master's resolve is. Cipriano Algor has already reached Isaura Madruga's door, he holds out his hand as if to knock on the door, hesitates, and again holds out his hand, at that moment, the door opens as if it had been expecting him, which wasn't, in fact, the case, Isaura Madruga had heard the bell and come to see who it was. Good morning, Senhora Isaura, said the potter, Good morning, Senhor Algor, Forgive me for troubling you at home, but there's something I'd like to discuss with you, I have a great favor to ask of you, Come in, We can talk out here, there's no need for us to come inside, No, please, don't stand on ceremony, come in, Can the dog come too, asked Cipriano Algor, he's got muddy feet, Oh, Found is like one of the family, we're old friends. The door closed, the darkness in the small sitting room closed around them. Isaura indicated a chair and sat down herself. I have a feeling that you know what I've come about, said the potter, as he made the dog lie down at his feet, That's possible, Perhaps my daughter has already spoken to you, About what, About Found, No, we've never spoken about Found, at least, not in the way you mean, What way, In the sense of having spoken specifically about Found, we've often talked about him, of course, but never had a real chat about him in particular. Cipriano Algor looked down, I've come to ask you if you would look after Found in my absence, Are you going away, asked Isaura, Yes, today, and obviously we can't take the dog with us, the Center doesn't allow pets, I'll look after him, Yes, I know you'll look after him as if he was your own, I'll look after him better than if he was my own, because he's yours. Without thinking, perhaps just to ease his nerves, Cipriano Algor had removed the dog's leash. I think I owe you an apology, he said, Why, Because I haven't always treated you with the politeness you deserve, My memory remembers other things, the afternoon when I met you at the cemetery, the conversation we had about the jug handle that had come off, your coming to my house to bring me a new water jug, Yes, but it was afterward that I behaved badly, rudely, and on more than one occasion too, It doesn't matter, It does, The proof that it doesn't matter is that you're here now, But I'm just about to cease being here, Yes, just about to cease being here. Dark clouds must have covered the sky, the darkness inside the house grew still denser, the natural thing would have been for Isaura to get up now from her chair and turn on the light. She did not do so, though not out of indifference or for some other subterranean reason, but simply because she had not noticed that she could barely see Cipriano Algor's face opposite her, just within reach of her arm if she were to lean slightly forward. The pitcher is still all right then, keeping the water nice and fresh, asked Cipriano Algor, As it did from the start, replied Isaura, and it was at that moment that she realized how dark the room was, I should turn on the light, she said to herself, but she did not get up. No one had ever told her that the fates of many people in the world have been changed radically by that simple gesture of turning a light on or off, whether it be an old-fashioned lantern, or a candle, or an oil lamp, or a modern electric lightbulb, it's true that she thought she should get up, this was what common sense was telling her, but her body would not move, it refused to obey the order from her brain. This was the darkness that Cipriano Algor had needed in order finally to declare himself, I love you, Isaura, and she replied in what seemed wounded tones, And you leave it until the day you're going away to tell me, It would have been pointless telling you before, well, as pointless as it is for me to be telling you now, But you have told me, It was my last chance, take it as a farewell, Why, Because I have nothing else to offer you, I'm a species on the verge of extinction, I have no future, I haven't even got a present, We do have a present, this moment, this room, your daughter and son-in-law waiting to carry you off, this dog lying at your feet, But not this woman, You haven't asked, I don't want to ask, Why not, Like I said, because I have nothing to offer you, If what you told me just now was truly felt and meant, you have love to offer, Love isn't a house, it isn't clothes or food, But food, clothes, and a house are not in themselves love, Please, let's not play with words, a man isn't going to ask a woman to marry him if he has no way of earning a living, Is that how it is with you, asked Isaura, You know it is, the pottery has closed and I don't know how to do anything else, So you're going to live off your son-in-law, What other option do I have, You could live off what your wife earned, How long would love last in those circumstances, asked Cipriano Algor, But I didn't work when I was married, I lived off my husband's earnings, No one could disapprove of that, that's normal, but put a man in that situation and see what happens, Would love necessarily have to die because of that, asked Isaura, does love die for such trivial reasons, I'm not in a position to answer that, I've no experience. Found got discreetly to his feet, in his opinion, this courtesy visit was going on far too long, he wanted to go back to the kennel, to the mulberry tree, to the bench of meditations. Cipriano Algor said, I have to go, they're waiting for me, So this is good-bye, then, said Isaura, We'll come back now and then, to see how Found is, to see if the house is still standing, it's not good-bye forever. He put the dog on the leash again and placed the leash in Isaura's hands, Here you are, he's only a dog, but. We will never know what ontological ideas Cipriano Algor was about to develop after that conjunction left hanging in the air, because his right hand, the one holding the leash, got lost or else allowed itself to be found in the hands of Isaura Madruga, the woman he had not wanted to include in his present and who, nevertheless, was saying to him now, I love you, Cipriano, you know that. The leash slipped to the floor, and Found, suddenly free again, wandered off to sniff the baseboard, and when, shortly afterward, he turned his head, he realized that the visit had changed direction, there was nothing courteous about that embrace, those kisses, that irregular breathing, nor the words which, for very different reasons, were begun but never completed. Cipriano Algor and Isaura had got to their feet, she was crying with laughter and grief, he was stammering, I'll come back, I'll come back, it really is a shame that the street door is not suddenly flung wide open so that the neighbors can see for themselves and spread the word that the widow Estudioso and the old potter love each other with a true and finally declared love. In a voice that had almost recovered its normal tone, Cipriano Algor said again, I'll come back, I'll come back, there must be some solution for us, The only solution is for you to stay, said Isaura, You know I can't, We'll be here waiting for you, Found and me. The dog could not understand why the woman was holding his leash, since all three of them were moving toward the door, a sure sign that he and his master were finally leaving, he could not understand why the leash had still not been passed back to the hand of the person who had the right to put it on him. Panic began to rise from his guts to his throat, but at the same time, his legs were trembling with excitement at the plan that instinct had just outlined to him, to lunge forward when the door was opened and then triumphantly wait outside for his master to come for him. The door only opened after more embraces and more kisses, more murmured words, however, the woman was still holding him firmly, saying, Stay, stay, as is the way with speech, the same verb that had proved incapable of preventing Cipriano Algor from leaving was the very verb that would not now allow Found to escape. The door closed, separating the dog from his master, but, as is the way with feelings, the pain of abandonment experienced by one could not, at least at that moment, expect to find sympathy or understanding in the tormented happiness of the other. It will not be long before we find out more about Found's life in his new home, whether it was easy or difficult to adapt to his new mistress, if the kindness and limitless affection she showered on him were enough to make him forget the sadness of being unjustly abandoned. Right now we have to follow Cipriano Algor, just follow him, trot along behind him, accompany his somnambular footsteps. As for imagining how one person can possibly contain such opposing feelings as, in the case we have been looking at, the most profound of joys and the most painful of griefs, and then going on to discover or to create the single word by which the particular feeling born of that conjunction would come to be designated, this is a task that many have undertaken in the past, but all abandoned the attempt knowing that, as is the case with a constantly shifting horizon, they would never even reach the threshold of the door to those ineffabilities longing for expression. Human vocabulary is still not capable, and probably never will be, of knowing, recognizing, and communicating everything that can be humanly experienced and felt. Some say that the main cause of this very serious difficulty lies in the fact that human beings are basically made of clay, which, as the encyclopedias helpfully explain, is a detrital sedimentary rock made up of tiny mineral fragments measuring one two hundred and fifty-sixths of a millimeter. Until now, despite long linguistic study, no one has managed to come up with a name for this.

Meanwhile, Cipriano Algor had reached the end of the street, turned off into the road that divided the village in two and, neither walking nor dawdling, neither running nor flying, as if he were dreaming that he was trying to break free from himself, but kept stumbling over his own body, he reached the top of the slope where the van was waiting with his son-in-law and his daughter. Before, the sky had seemed set fair, but now a hesitant, indolent rain had begun to fall, it might not perhaps last very long, but it greatly exacerbated the melancholy of these people who were only the turn of a wheel away from leaving much-loved places, even Marçal felt his stomach tighten uneasily. Cipriano Algor got into the van, sat down next to the driver, in the place that had been left for him, and said, Let's go. He would not say another word until they reached the Center, until they got into the service elevator that carried them and their suitcases and packages up to the thirty-fourth floor, until they opened the door of the apartment, until Marçal exclaimed, Here we are, only then did he open his mouth to utter a few organized sounds, albeit nothing very original, he merely repeated his son-in-law's words, with a small rhetorical addition, Yes, here we are. Marta and Marçal had also said very little during the journey. The only words worthy of recording in this story, and only superficially, purely incidentally, because they have to do with people about whom we have only heard, were those they exchanged when the van was going past the house of Marçal's parents, Did you tell them we were leaving, asked Marta, Yes, the day before yesterday, when I came back from the Center, I just popped in, the taxi was waiting, Don't you want to stop, she asked again, No, I'm tired of arguments, fed up to the back teeth, Even so, Remember the way they behaved when we both went to see them, you surely don't want a repeat performance, said Marçal, It's a shame, though, they are your parents after all, It's a funny expression that, What, After all, That's what people say, Yes, I know, but words which, at first sight, seem to be mere adornment and could, in every sense of the word, easily be discarded, become frightening once you start to think about them and realize what they imply, After all, Marta had said, which is another disguised way of saying what else can we do, what do you expect, that's the way things are, or, put more bluntly, resign yourself, We have to live with the parents we've got, said Marçal, Not forgetting that someone will have to live with the parents we will become, concluded Marta. It was then that Marçal glanced to his right and said, smiling, Needless to say, this conversation about warring parents and children does not apply to you, but Cipriano Algor did not respond, he merely nodded vaguely. Sitting behind her husband, Marta could just see her father's profile. I wonder what happened with Isaura, she thought, he obviously didn't just go there, leave Found and come back, judging by the delay, they must have said something to each other, what I wouldn't give to know what he's thinking, his face looks quite serene, but at the same time it's the face of someone who isn't quite in control, someone who has escaped a great danger and is surprised to find himself still alive. She would know much more if she could see her father from the front, then she might perhaps say, I recognize those tears that never fall but are absorbed back into the eyes, I recognize that joyful pain, that painful happiness, that being and not being, that having and not having, that wanting and not being able to act. But it was early days yet for Cipriano Algor to answer her. They had left the village, left behind them the three ruined houses, now they were crossing the bridge over the stream with its dark, evil-smelling waters. Over there, in the middle of the countryside, in the clump of trees hidden by brambles, is where the archaeological treasure from Cipriano Algor's pottery is hidden. Anyone would think that ten thousand years had passed since the last remains of an ancient civilization were dumped there.

When, on the morning after his day off, Marçal left the thirty-fourth floor in order to go to work as a fully fledged resident guard, the apartment was clean, tidy, and orderly, with the things brought from the other house in their proper places, and all that was necessary now was for the inhabitants willingly to take up their rightful places among them. It won't be easy, a person is not like a thing that you put down in one place and leave, a person moves, thinks, asks questions, doubts, investigates, probes, and while it is true that, out of the long habit of resignation, he sooner or later ends up looking as if he has submitted to the objects, don't go thinking that this apparent submission is necessarily permanent. The first problem to be resolved by the new inhabitants, with the exception of Marçal Gacho, who will continue with his familiar, routine work of watching over the security of the people and property institutionally or incidentally associated with the Center, the first problem, we were saying, will be to find a satisfactory answer to the question, And now what am I going to do. Marta is in charge of running the household, when her time comes, she will have a child to bring up, and that will be more than enough to keep her occupied for many hours of the day and for some hours of the night. However, because people are, as pointed out above, subject to both action and thought, we should not be surprised if she should ask herself, in the middle of a task that has already taken up an hour and could well take up another two, And now what am I going to do. In any case, it is Cipriano Algor who is confronted by the worst possible situation, that of looking at his hands and knowing that they are useless, of looking at the clock and knowing that the next hour will be the same as this, of thinking about tomorrow and knowing that it will be as empty as today. Cipriano Algor is no adolescent, he cannot spend the whole day lying on the bed that barely fits into his tiny bedroom, thinking about Isaura Madruga, repeating the words that they said to each other, reliving, if one can give such an ambitious name to the memory's insubstantial operations, their shared kisses and embraces. Some will think that the best medicine for Cipriano Algor's ills would be for him to go down to the garage right now, get into the van and drive off to see Isaura Madruga, who, back in the village, will more than likely be going through the same anxieties of body and soul, and for a man in his position, for whom life holds no more industrial and artistic triumphs of primary or secondary importance, having a woman whom he loves and who has already told him that she reciprocates his love, is the most sublime of blessings and the greatest good fortune. They obviously don't know Cipriano Algor. He has already told us that a man should not ask a woman to marry him if he lacks the means to guarantee his own living, and he would say to us now that he is not someone to take advantage of favorable circumstances and to behave as if he had a right to the resulting satisfactions, however justified by the qualities and virtues that adorn him, by the mere fact of being a man and of having made a particular woman the focus of his male attentions and desires. In other words, put more frankly and directly, what Cipriano Algor is not prepared to do, even though he will pay for it with the bitter pain of solitude, is to see himself playing the part of the fellow who periodically visits his mistress and returns from there with, as his only sentimental souvenirs, an evening or night spent agitating his body and shaking up his senses, then planting an absentminded kiss on a face now bereft of makeup, and in the case in point, patting the head of a canine, See you again soon, Found. Cipriano Algor, therefore, has two ways of escaping the prison which the apartment has, in his eyes, suddenly become, apart from the short-lived and merely palliative act of going over to the window now and then and looking out at the sky through the glass. His first recourse is the city, that is, Cipriano Algor, who has always lived in the insignificant village which we know only slightly and who knows only that part of the city he used to see en route to the Center, will now be able to spend his time strolling, ambling, and airing his feathers, a figurative caricature of an expression that must date from the days in which noblemen and gentlemen of the court wore feathers in their hats and would sally forth to air both hats and feathers. He also has at his disposal the city's public parks and gardens where elderly men tend to gather in the afternoons, men who have the face and typical gestures of the retired and the unemployed, which are two ways of saying the same thing. He could join them and become friends with them, and enthusiastically play cards until dusk, until it is no longer possible for their myopic eyes to tell whether the spots on the cards are red or black. He will demand vengeance if he loses and encourage it in others if he wins, the rules of the park are simple and easy to learn. The second recourse, needless to say, is the Center in which he lives. Naturally, he knows it already from before, but not as well as he knows the city, because, on his few visits to the Center, always with his daughter, just to do a bit of shopping, he could never quite remember how he got where. Now, in a way, the Center is all his, it has been handed to him on a plate of sound and light, he can wander about in it as much as he likes, enjoy the easy-listening music and the inviting voices. If, when they came to visit the apartment for the first time, they had used the elevator on the other side, they would have been able to see, during the slow ride upward, as well as the new arcades, shops, escalators, meeting points, cafés, and restaurants, many other equally interesting and varied installations, for example, a carousel of horses, a carousel of space rockets, a center for toddlers, a center for the Third Age, a tunnel of love, a suspension bridge, a ghost train, an astrologer's tent, a betting shop, a rifle range, a golf course, a luxury hospital, another slightly less luxurious hospital, a bowling alley, a billiard hall, a battery of table football games, a giant map, a secret door, another door with a notice on it saying experience natural sensations, rain, wind, and snow on demand, a wall of china, a taj mahal, an egyptian pyramid, a temple of karnak, a real aqueduct, a mafra monastery, a clerics' tower, a fjord, a summer sky with fluffy white clouds, a lake, a real palm tree, the skeleton of a tyrannosaurus, another one apparently alive, himalayas complete with everest, an amazon river complete with indians, a stone raft, a corcovado christ, a trojan horse, an electric chair, a firing squad, an angel playing a trumpet, a communications satellite, a comet, a galaxy, a large dwarf, a small giant, a list of prodigies so long that not even eighty years of leisure time would be enough to take them all in, even if you had been born in the Center and had never left it for the outside world.

Cipriano Algor, having excluded, as entirely inadequate, staring out at the city and its rooftops through the apartment windows, having eliminated the parks and gardens because he has not yet reached the state of mind that could be classified as mute despair or utter tedium, and having set aside, for the potent reasons explained above, the tempting but problematic visits to Isaura Madruga for sentimental and physical relief, found that all that was left to him, if he did not want to spend the rest of his life yawning and, figuratively speaking, banging his head against the walls of his inner prison, was to throw himself into the discovery and methodical investigation of the marvelous island on which he had been cast up after the shipwreck. Every morning, therefore, after breakfast, Cipriano Algor tosses his daughter a hurried See you later, and sets off, like someone on his way to work, sometimes going up to the top floor, at others going down to the ground floor, using the elevators, now at maximum speed, now at minimum speed, according to his observational needs, walking down corridors and passageways, crossing large halls, skirting vast, complex conglomerations of shop windows, displays, showrooms, and showcases containing everything that could possibly exist to be eaten and drunk or worn on the body or the feet, to pamper hair and skin, nails and body hair, both above and below, to hang around the neck, to dangle from ears, to slip onto fingers, to jingle on wrists, to do and to undo, to sew and to sow, to draw and to erase, to increase and to diminish, to gain weight with and to lose weight, to stretch and to shrink, to fill up and to empty, and to say all this is to say nothing, since for this, too, it would require more than eighty years of leisure time to read and analyze the fifty-five fifteen-hundred-page volumes that constitute the Center's commercial catalogue. Obviously, Cipriano Algor is not much

interested in the goods on display, after all, making purchases is neither his responsibility nor his concern, that is the business of the
wage earner, i.e. his son-in-law, and of the person who then manages, administers and uses the money, i.e., his daughter. He is the
one who walks around with his hands in his pockets, stopping here
and there, occasionally asking a guard the way, although never
Marçal, even if he happens to bump into him, so as not to reveal their
family ties, and, above all, making the most of that most precious
and enviable of the many advantages of living at the Center, that is,
being able to enjoy for free or at much reduced prices the multiple
attractions at the disposal of customers. We have already given two
sober and condensed accounts of these, the first about what could
be seen from the elevator on this side, the second about what could
be seen from the elevator on the other side, however, out of a desire
for objectivity and informational rigor, we should point out that,
in both cases, we never went beyond the thirty-fourth floor. Above
this, as you will recall, sits a universe of another fourteen floors.
Dealing as we are here with a person of a reasonably inquisitive turn
of mind, we hardly need say that Cipriano Algor's first investigative
steps led him to the mysterious secret door, which, however, had to
remain mysterious because, despite insistent ringing at the doorbell
and a few raps on the door, no one emerged from inside to ask him
what he wanted. He did, however, have to give a full and prompt explanation to a guard who, attracted by the noise or, more likely,
guided by the images on the closed circuit television, came over to
ask who he was and what he was doing there. Cipriano Algor explained that he lived on the thirty-fourth floor and that he just happened to be passing and his interest had been aroused by the sign on
the door, Simple curiosity, sir, the simple curiosity of someone who
has nothing else to do. The guard asked him for his official identity
card and the card that proved he was a resident, compared his face
with the photos on both, examined the fingerprints on both documents through a magnifying glass, and, finally, took a print of that

same finger, which Cipriano Algor, after due instruction, pressed against what was presumably the scanner of a portable computer that the guard removed from a bag he wore slung across his shoulder, at the same time saying, Don't worry, it's just a formality, but take my advice, don't come here again, it could get you into trouble, being curious once is enough, besides, there's nothing secret behind that door, there was once, but not now, In that case, why don't they remove the sign, asked Cipriano Algor, It acts as a lure so that we can find out who are the inquisitive ones living in the Center. The guard waited until Cipriano Algor had moved a few meters off, then followed him until he met a colleague and, in order to avoid being recognized, he passed the duty of surveillance on to him, What did he do, asked Marçal Gacho, pretending unconcern, He was knocking at the secret door, That's hardly a serious offense, it happens several times a day, said Marçal, relieved, Yes, but people have to learn not to be curious, to walk on by, not to stick their nose in where it isn't wanted, it's just a question of time and training, Or force, said Marçal, Apart from certain very extreme cases, force is no longer necessary, I could have taken him in for interrogation, but I just gave him some good advice, used a bit of psychology, Right, I'd better go after him, then, said Marçal, I wouldn't want him to give me the slip, If you notice anything suspicious, tell me so that I can add it to the report and then we can both sign it. The other guard left, and Marçal continued to follow at a distance as his father-in-law explored two floors above, then he let him go. He wondered what would be the best thing to do, to talk to him and tell him to take care when wandering around the Center, or simply to pretend that he knew nothing about this very minor incident and to pray that nothing more serious happened. He chose the latter option, but when Cipriano Algor laughingly told him about it over supper, he had no alternative but to assume the role of mentor and ask him to behave in a way that would not attract the attention of guards or nonguards, If you're going to live here, that's the only correct way to proceed. Then Cipriano Algor took a piece of paper out of his pocket, I copied down these phrases from some posters, he said, I hope I didn't attract the attention of some spy or observer, So do I, said Marçal grumpily, Is it regarded as suspicious to copy down phrases that are on display for customers to read, asked Cipriano Algor, Reading them is normal, copying them down isn't, and anything that isn't normal is, at the very least, suspected of being abnormal. Marta, who, until then, had taken no part in the conversation, said to her father, Read them out to us. Cipriano Algor smoothed the paper out on the table and began to read, Be bold, dream. He looked at his daughter and at his son-in-law, and since they seemed disinclined to comment, he went on, Experience the thrill of dreaming, that's just a variant on the first one, and here are the others, one, Get operational, two, the south seas within your grasp without even leaving home, three, this isn't your last chance, but it's the best you'll get, four, we think about you all the time, now it's time for you to think about us, five, bring your friends, as long as they buy something, six, with us, you will never want to be anything else, seven, you're our best customer, only don't tell your neighbor, That's the one they had up on the façade outside, said Marçal, Well, now it's inside, the customers must have liked it, replied his father-in-law. What else did you find on this dangerous exploratory expedition of yours, asked Marta, You'll fall asleep if I tell you, All right, then, send me to sleep, The thing I liked best, began Cipriano Algor, were the natural sensations, What's that, Just imagine this, All right, I'll try, You go into a reception area, you buy your ticket, I had to pay only ten percent of the normal price because they gave me a discount of forty-five percent for being a resident and the same discount for being over sixty, It looks like you get a pretty good deal if you're over sixty, said Marta, Oh, yes, the older you are, the more you earn, and you die rich, And then what happened, asked Marçal impatiently, Have you never been in there, asked his father-in-law, somewhat surprised, No, I knew it existed, but I've never been inside, never had the time, Well, you've no idea what you've missed, If you don't tell us, I'm off to bed, threatened Marta, All right, after you've paid and they've furnished you with a raincoat, a hat, Wellingtons, and an umbrella, all in bright colors, you can get them in black too, but it costs more, you're ushered into a changing room where a voice from a loudspeaker tells you to put on the boots, the raincoat, and the hat, and then you go into a kind of corridor where they line you up in fours, but with enough space between you so that you can move freely, there were about thirty of us, for some, like me, it was the first time, others, it seemed to me, went there now and then, and at least five of them were old hands, I even heard one of them say This is like a drug, you try it once and you're hooked. And then what happened, asked Marta, Then it began to rain, just a few drops at first, then a bit harder, we all opened our umbrellas, and the voice over the loudspeaker gave us the order to advance, and it was just indescribable, you would have to have been there, the rain started falling in torrents, then suddenly there's a gale blowing, one gust, then another, umbrellas turn inside out, hats fly off heads, the women are screaming so as not to laugh, the men are laughing so as not to scream, and the wind gets stronger, it's like a typhoon now, the people slither around, fall over, get up, fall over again, the rain has become a deluge, it takes us a good ten minutes to cover, oh, about twenty-five or thirty meters, And then what, asked Marta, yawning, Then we turned around, and immediately snow started falling, just a few scattered flakes at first like threads of cotton, then it got thicker and thicker, it was falling ahead of us like a curtain through which we could barely see our colleagues, some still had their umbrellas up, which only made matters worse, finally we got back to the changing room and there was the most splendid sun shining, A sun in the changing room, said Marçal doubtfully, Well, it wasn't a changing room any more, by then, it was more like a meadow, And these were the natural sensations, asked Marta, Yes, But that's nothing you can't see every day outside, That was precisely what I said when we were giving back the equipment, but I should have kept my mouth shut, Why, One of the old hands looked at me scornfully and said I feel sorry for you, you just don't understand, do you. Helped by her husband, Marta started clearing the table. Tomorrow or the day after, I'm going to the beach, announced Cipriano Algor, Now I have been there once, said Marçal, And what's it like, Very hot and tropical, and the water is warm, And the sand, There is no sand, there's a plastic floor which, from a distance, looks real, And presumably there aren't any waves either, Ah, that's where you're wrong, there's a machine inside that produces a wave motion just like the sea, No, It's true, The things people think up, Yes, I know, said Marçal, it's a bit sad really. Cipriano Algor got to his feet, wandered about, asked to borrow a book from his daughter and then, as he was going into his bedroom, he said, I went downstairs again, the floor doesn't vibrate any more and you can't hear the diggers now, and Marçal replied, They must have finished the work.

Marta had suggested to her husband that they should use his first day off since moving to the Center to go and fetch a few things from their other home that, according to her, they needed, Normally when you move, you take all your possessions with you, but that wasn't the case with us, besides, I'm sure we'll go there on other occasions, and it would be rather nice, we could spend the night in our own bed and come back the following morning, like you used to do. Marçal said that he didn't think it was a good idea to create a situation in which they ended up not knowing where they really lived, Your father seems to want to give us the impression that he's having a wonderful time discovering the secrets of the Center, but I know him, behind that mask, his brain is still working away, He hasn't said a single word to me about what happened at Isaura's house, he's just clammed up, and that's not like him, one way or another, however angrily or reluctantly, he always ends up telling me everything, I think that if we went back to the house now it might help him, he'd obviously want to go and see how Found is, and he'd have another chance to talk to Isaura, All right, if that's what you want, we'll go, but remember what I said, we either live here or we live at the pottery, trying to live in two places as if they were one will be like living nowhere at all, Perhaps that's how it will be for us, What do you mean, Like living nowhere, Everyone needs a home, and we're no exception, The home we had was taken from us, It's still ours, But not like it was, This is our home now. Marta looked around her and said, I don't think it will ever really be our home.

Marçal shrugged, these Algors were difficult people to understand, but, then again, he wouldn't change them for the world. Shall we tell your father, he said, Only at the last moment, so that he doesn't have too long to brood over it and end up poisoning his blood.

Cipriano Algor never knew that his daughter and his son-in-law had plans for him. Marçal Gacho's day off was canceled, and the same happened with his colleagues on the same shift. In absolute confidence, the resident guards, because they were considered the most trustworthy, were told that the work on building the new cold-storage units on floor zero five had uncovered something that would require long and careful examination, For the moment, access is limited, said the captain of the security guards, in a few days' time, a team will be working down there made up of various specialists, geologists, archaeologists, sociologists, anthropologists, forensic experts, and PR people, someone told me there would even be a couple of philosophers too, though don't ask me why. He paused, scanned the faces of the twenty men lined up before him and went on, You are forbidden to speak to anyone at all about what I have just told you or about anything you might find out in the future, and when I say anyone at all, I mean anyone, wife, children, parents, I require absolute secrecy from you, do you understand, Yes, sir, chorused the men, Good, the entrance to the cave, I forgot to mention that it's a cave, will be under constant guard day and night, in four-hour shifts, this chart shows you who's on duty when, it's five o'clock now, and we start at six. One of the men raised his hand, he wanted to know, if at all possible, when the cave had been found and who had been guarding it since, We will only have responsibility for security from six o'clock onward, he said, so presumably we can't be held responsible for any slipups that happened before that, The entrance to the cave was discovered this morning when the earth was being shifted manually, work was stopped immediately and the administration informed, since then, three engineers from the construction department have been there all the time, Is there something inside the cave, another guard asked, Yes, said the captain, you will have a chance to see what it is with your own eyes, Is it dangerous, should we be armed, asked the same guard, As far as we know, there is no danger, however, as a precaution, you should not touch anything or go too close, we don't know what the consequences of any contact might be, For us or for whatever is in there, asked Marçal, For you and for them, So there is more than one of them in the cave, then, Yes, said the captain, and the expression on his face changed. Then, as if making an effort to pull himself together, he went on, Now if there are no further questions, these are your instructions, first, as for whether you should go armed or not, I think it will be enough if you carry your truncheons with you, not because I think you'll need them, but just so that you feel more confident, the truncheon is like a vital piece of clothing, a uniformed guard feels naked without it, second, anyone not on guard duty should dress in plainclothes and patrol the various floors listening for any conversations that have or seem to have some bearing on the cave, and should that happen, although this is highly unlikely, the central service should be informed immediately and we will take the necessary steps. The captain paused again and concluded, That's all you need to know, just remember your orders, absolute secrecy, it's your career that's on the line here. The guards went over to look at the duty roster, Marçal saw that he would be on the ninth shift, so he would be on duty between two and six o'clock on the morning of the day after next. Down below, thirty or forty meters underground, you would not notice the difference between night and day, there would be nothing but darkness pierced by the crude beams from floodlights and arc lights. As the elevator was carrying him up to the thirty-fourth floor, he was thinking about what he could tell Marta without compromising himself too much, the prohibition seemed to him absurd, a person has not so much a right but an obligation to confide in his family, but this was purely theoretical, for whichever way he looked at it, he would have no option but to do as he was told, orders are orders. His father-in-law was not at home, he was doubtless off on one of his inquisitive-child jaunts, in search of the meanings of things and quite astute enough to find them out however hidden they were. He told Marta that his duties had changed temporarily, he was to wear plainclothes, although it wouldn't be permanent, just for a few days. Marta asked why and he said that he wasn't authorized to say, that it was confidential, I gave my word of honor, he said by way of justification, and that wasn't exactly true, the captain had not asked them to do so, such formulas belong to other times and to other mores, but sometimes we find ourselves saying them without thinking, the same thing happens with our memory, which always has more to offer us than the little we ask of it. Marta did not reply, she opened the wardrobe and removed one of Marçal's two suits from its hanger, Will this do, she said, That will be fine, said Marçal, glad that they were in agreement on this important point. He thought it best to warn her about what else was involved, to sort the matter out once and for all, if he were in his colleague's shoes, he would be going on duty very shortly and he would have to tell Marta right there and then, I'm on duty from six until ten, don't ask me any questions, it's a secret, that's all he has to say, he just has to change the hours and the day, I'm on duty the day after tomorrow, from two until six in the morning, don't ask me any questions, it's a secret. Marta looked at him, intrigued, But the Center's closed then, Well, I won't be in the Center exactly, You'll be outside, then, No, inside, but not in the Center, I don't understand, Look, I'd prefer it if you didn't ask me any questions, All I'm saying is that I can't understand how something can happen inside and outside at the same time, It's in the excavations they're doing for the new cold-storage units, but I won't say any more, Have they struck oil or found a diamond mine or the stone that marks the belly button of the world, asked Marta, I don't know what they've found, And when will you know, When I go on guard duty, Or when you ask your colleagues who have been on duty before you, We were forbidden to talk to each other about it, said Marçal, looking away because these words could not strictly be described as true, they were, rather, a partial version of the captain's orders and recommendations, freely adapted to suit his current rhetorical difficulties, It's obviously a great mystery, said Marta, Yes, so it seems, agreed Marçal, taking exaggerated care over getting just the right amount of shirt cuff to appear beneath the sleeves of his jacket. In plainclothes he looked older than he really was. Will you be here for supper, asked Marta, I haven't been told otherwise, but, if I can't make it, I'll phone. He left before his wife could come up with any more questions, relieved to have escaped her insistent curiosity, but sad too because the conversation, on his part, had not been exactly a model of honesty, No, I was just being loyal, he protested to himself, I told her right away that it was a secret. Despite the vehemence and good sense of this protest, Marçal remained unconvinced. When, more than an hour later, Cipriano Algor returned home, barely recovered from the terrors of the ghost train, Marta asked him, Did you see Marçal, No, I didn't, Well, even if you had, you probably wouldn't have recognized him, Why, He came home to change his clothes, now he's a plainclothes security guard, That's new, Those were his orders, Being a plainclothes guard isn't guarding, it's spying, declared her father. Marta told him what she knew, which was almost nothing, but it was enough to quell Cipriano Algor's interest in the amazon river complete with indians where he had been intending to go the next day, That's odd, but you know, right from the start, I've had the feeling that something was going to happen here, What do you mean, right from the start, asked Marta, The floor trembling and vibrating, the noise of excavators, do you remember, when we first came to see the apartment, We would be in a real state if we had presentiments every time we heard an excavator at work, like the sewing machine noise we used to think we could hear in the kitchen wall and which Mama used to say was a sign that some poor seamstress had been condemned for the sin of having worked on a Sunday, But this time I've been proved right, Yes, so it seems, said Marta, repeating her husband's words, We'll see what he has to say when he comes back, said Cipriano Algor. They learned nothing more. Marçal clung to the answers he had given before, repeating them over and over, and he finally resolved to put an end to the matter, If you were to press me, I would be the first to find the order ridiculous, but that was the order I was given, so there's nothing more to be said about it, At least tell us why you suddenly had to start patrolling in plainclothes, asked his father-in-law, We don't patrol, we just keep an eye on security in the Center, All right, whatever, Look, I've nothing more to add, so please don't ask, said Marçal angrily. He glanced at his wife as if wanting to know why she said nothing, why she didn't defend him, and she said, Marçal is right, Pa, don't go on at him, and addressing Marçal and at the same time planting a kiss on his head, Forgive us, we Algors can be terrible bullies. After supper, they watched a television program broadcast on the Center's own channel, exclusively for residents, then they went to their rooms. With the lights out, Marta apologized again, Marçal gave her a kiss and the only reason he did not continue with a second and a third kiss was that he realized just in time that, if he carried on like that, he would end up telling her everything. Cipriano Algor, meanwhile, was sitting on his bed, with the light on, he had thought and thought again, only to conclude that he had to find out what was going on in the depths of the Center, and that, if there was another secret door down there, they would at least not be able to tell him that there was nothing on the other side. There was no point in cross-questioning Marçal again, besides, it was unfair to the poor boy, if he had orders not to say anything and he was carrying them out, he should be congratulated, not submitted to the various shameless forms of emotional blackmail at which families excel, I'm your father-in-law, you're my son-in-law, tell me everything, Marta was right, he thought, we Algors are bullies. Tomorrow he would leave the river amazon complete with indians to its own devices and devote himself to walking through the whole Center, from end to end, listening to people's conversations. In essence, a secret is rather like the combination to a safe, although we don't know what it is, we know that it is made up of six digits, that one or more of them might even be repeated, and that however numerous the possible sequences, they are not infinite. As with all things in life, it is just a question of time and patience, a word here, another word there, an insinuating remark, an exchange of glances, a sudden silence, small disparate cracks that start opening up in the wall, the art of sleuthing lies in knowing how to bring them all together, how to eliminate the rough edges separating them, there will always come a moment when we must ask ourselves if the dream, the ambition, the secret hope of all secrets is, in fact, the possibility, however vague, however remote, of ceasing to be a secret. Cipriano Algor got undressed, turned out the light, thought that he was in for a sleepless night, but after only five minutes, was sleeping such a dense, opaque sleep that not even Isaura Madruga could have managed to peer around the last door as it closed upon him.

When Cipriano Algor left his room, later than usual, his son-in-law had already gone off to work. Still half-asleep, he said good morning to his daughter, sat down to eat his breakfast, and at that moment, the phone rang. Marta went to answer it and came right back, It's for you. Cipriano Algor's heart skipped a beat, For me, who would want to speak to me, he asked, already convinced that his daughter would reply, It's Isaura, but instead what she said was, It's the buying department, one of the assistant heads of department. Caught between disappointment that the call was not from the person he would have liked it to be from and relief at not having to explain to his daughter this sudden intimacy with Isaura, although it might easily have been something to do with Found, that he was pining for example, Cipriano Algor went to the phone, gave his name and, shortly afterward, the nice assistant head of department was saying at the other end of the line, I was most surprised to learn that you had come to live at the Center, as you see, the devil isn't necessarily lurking behind every door, it's an old saying, but much truer than you might think, Quite right, said Cipriano Algor, The reason I'm calling is to ask if you could drop by this afternoon so that we can pay you for the figurines, What figurines, The three hundred that you gave us for the survey, But none of them were sold, so there's nothing to pay, My dear sir, said the assistant head of department in an unexpectedly severe tone, please allow us to be the judges of that, but anyway, you should know that even when payment represents a loss of more than one hundred percent, as in this case, the Center always pays its debts, it's a matter of ethics, now that you're living among us you will doubtless come to understand this better, Fine, but what I can't understand is how you can possibly make a loss of more than one hundred percent, It's precisely because people fail to take such things into consideration that whole families fall into ruin, If only I had known that earlier, Now listen, first, we're going to pay the exact value of the figurines that you invoiced us for, not a penny less, Right, I'm with you so far, Second, we will obviously also have to pay for the survey, that is, the materials used, the people who analyzed the data, and the time it took, now, when you think that those materials, those people, and that time could have been employed on more profitable tasks, you don't have to be gifted with great intelligence to reach the conclusion that we did in fact suffer a loss of over one hundred percent, when you take into account what we did not sell and what we spent on concluding that we should not sell, Well, I'm sorry the Center lost money because of me, It's an occupational hazard, sometimes you lose, sometimes you win, but it wasn't a matter of any great consequence, it was a very minor deal, Of course, I too, said Cipriano Algor, could invoke my own ethical scruples and refuse to be paid for work that people declined to buy, but the fact is that I could do with the money, That's a very good reason, the best possible reason, All right,

I'll drop by this afternoon, then, You don't need to ask for me, just go straight to the till, since this is the last commercial transaction we will have with your now extinct company, we want you to have the best possible memories of us, Thank you, Enjoy the rest of your life, you're certainly in the right place to do so, Exactly what I've been thinking myself, sir, Take advantage of the tide of fate, That's precisely what I'm doing. Cipriano Algor put down the phone, They're going to pay us for the figurines, he said, so we won't have lost out entirely. Marta gave a nod which could have meant anything, resignation, disagreement, indifference, and went back into the kitchen. Aren't you feeling well, asked her father, standing at the door, Oh, I'm just a bit tired, it must be the pregnancy, You seem a bit down, distracted, you should get out more, go for a walk, What, like you, you mean, Yes, like me, Are you really interested in all that stuff out there, asked Marta, now think twice before you answer, Once is quite enough, no, it doesn't interest me in the least, I'm just pretending, To yourself, of course, You're old enough to know that there is no other way of pretending, although it might not seem like it, we are only ever pretending to ourselves, never to other people, Well, I'm pleased to hear you say that, Why, Because it confirms what I've been thinking about you with regard to Isaura Madruga, The situation has changed, Even better, If the occasion arises, I'll tell you, but, for the moment, I'm like Marçal, a closed mouth.

Cipriano Algor's auricular expedition achieved nothing, afterward, over lunch, by some kind of tacit accord, none of the three dared touch on the awkward subject of the excavations and what might have been uncovered. Father-in-law and son-in-law left at the same time, Marçal to resume his work of listening and spying, which would no doubt prove as fruitless as it had that morning for both of them, and Cipriano Algor to find out, for the first time, how to get from inside the Center to the buying department. He realized that his resident's badge, complete with photo and fingerprint, would allow him a certain ease of movement when the guard responded to his request for directions as if it were the most natural thing in the world, Keep straight on down this corridor and, when you reach the end, you just have to follow the signs, you can't miss it, he said. He was on the ground floor, at some point in the journey he would have to go down to the basement where, in happier times, although this is probably not a view shared by the nice assistant head of department, he used to go to unload his plates and his mugs. An arrow and an escalator told him where to go. I'm going down, he thought. I'm going down, I'm going down, he repeated, and then, How stupid, of course I'm going down, that's what stairs are for except when they're for going up, with stairs, those that don't go down, go up, and those that don't go up, go down. He seemed to have reached an unanswerable conclusion, of the sort for which there is no possible logical rebuttal, but suddenly, with the brilliance and instantaneity of a lightning flash, another thought crossed his mind, Go down, yes, down there. Yes, go down there. Cipriano Algor has just decided to try to join Marçal tonight when he is on guard duty, between two and six in the morning, if you remember. Good sense and prudence, which always have something to say in such situations, had already asked him how, without knowing the way, he thought he would reach such a recondite place, and he replied that while the combinations and compositions of chance are indeed many, they are not infinite, and that it is always better to take a risk and climb the fig tree in order to pick the fig than to lie down in the shade of the tree and wait for the fig to fall into your mouth. The Cipriano Algor who presented himself at the till of the buying department, having first gotten lost twice, despite the help of all those arrows and signs, was not the man we thought we knew. His hands were trembling badly, not because of the petty thrill of receiving for his work money he had not been expecting, but because the orders and directions sent by his brain, occupied now with matters of more transcendent importance, were arriving at their respective terminals in incoherent, confused, and contradictory form. When he returned to the commercial part of the Center, he seemed slightly calmer, all his agitation had disappeared inside him. Freed now from having to worry about hands, the brain was busily planning ruses, tricks, ploys, stratagems, dodges, and subterfuges, it even went so far as to consider the possibility of resorting to telekinesis to whisk the impatient body it was having such difficulty controlling from the thirty-fourth floor down to the mysterious excavations.

Although he still had long hours of waiting ahead of him, Cipriano Algor decided to go back to the apartment. He tried to give his daughter the money he had received, but she said, No, you keep it, I don't need it, and then she said, Would you like a cup of coffee, Yes, that's a good idea. The coffee was made, poured into a cup and drunk, everything indicates that, for now, there will be no further words between them, it seems, as Cipriano Algor has sometimes thought, although we failed to record these thoughts at the time, that the apartment in which they are now living has the malign gift of silencing its inhabitants. Meanwhile, Cipriano Algor's brain, now that it has had to abandon the idea of telekinesis, lacking as it does the necessary training, has a burning need for a particular bit of information without which his plan for a nighttime raid will, to put it bluntly, go down the tubes. That is why he throws out the question, while apparently distractedly stirring the little coffee that remains in the bottom of his cup, Do you happen to know how far down the excavation is, Why do you want to know, Just curious, that's all, Marçal never said. Cipriano Algor concealed his frustration as best he could and said he was going to have a nap. He spent all afternoon in his room and only came out when his daughter called him for supper, Marçal was already sitting at the table. As had happened at lunch, no one mentioned the excavation until after supper, and it was only when Marta said to her husband, You should try to rest until it's time for you to go down there, otherwise you won't get any sleep at all, and he said, It's too early, I'm not sleepy, that Cipriano Algor, grabbing this unexpected opportunity, repeated his question,

How far down is the excavation, Why do you want to know, Just to get an idea, out of curiosity really. Marçal hesitated before replying, but it seemed to him that the information did not fall into the strictly confidential category, Access is from floor zero five, he said at last, Oh, I thought the diggers had been working deeper down than that, It's still fifteen or twenty meters below ground, said Marçal, Yes, you're right, that is pretty deep. They did not mention the subject again. Marçal did not appear annoyed by the brief conversation, on the contrary, one might almost say that he was somewhat relieved to have been able to speak a little about the matter that was clearly preoccupying him, but without touching on any dangerous or secret matters. Marçal is no more fearful than the average person, but he is not at all looking forward to the prospect of spending four hours down in a hole, in utter silence, knowing what lies behind him. We weren't trained for these situations, one of his colleagues had said to him, let's hope those specialists the captain talked about arrive soon, so that we don't have to do this any more, Were you afraid, asked Marçal, Well, no, I don't know that I was afraid, but I warn you now that you're going to feel all the time as if someone behind you was about to put their hand on your shoulder, Worse things could happen, That depends on the hand, to be honest, I spent the whole four hours fighting off a desperate urge to run away, to escape, to get out of there, Forewarned is forearmed, at least I know what to expect, No, you don't, you just think you do, and you're wrong, his colleague said. Now it is half past one in the morning, Marçal is saying good-bye to Marta with a kiss, she says, Don't hang around when you come off duty, No, I'll come straight back and I promise that tomorrow I'll tell you everything. Marta went with him to the door, they kissed again, then she came back in, tidied up a few things and returned to bed. She wasn't sleepy. She told herself that there was nothing to worry about, that other guards had already been on duty down there and survived, how often the most trifling of incidents have formed the bases for terrible mysteries, as if they were some hydra-headed monster, and yet, when looked at closely, they were just smoke, air, illusion, the desire to believe in the unbelievable. The minutes passed and sleep was still a long way off, Marta had just said to herself that she might as well turn on the light and read a book when she thought she heard her father's bedroom door opening. Since he was not in the habit of getting up during the night, she listened carefully, he probably needed to go to the bathroom, but the footsteps she heard shortly afterward, cautious but audible, were in the small entrance hall. Perhaps he's going to the kitchen to get a drink of water, she thought. At the unmistakable sound of the door latch, however, she sprang to her feet. She pulled on her dressing gown and left her room. Her father had his hand on the door handle. Where are you off to at this hour, Marta asked, Oh, just out, said Cipriano Algor, You can go where you like, I mean, you're old enough to do as you please, but you can't just go off without a word, as if there was no one else living here, Look, I can't hang around here wasting time, Why, are you afraid you might get there after six, asked Marta, If you already know where I'm going then you don't need any explanations, You should at least consider the problems you might be creating for your son-in-law, As you yourself said, I'm old enough to do as I please, and Marçal can't be held responsible for my actions, His bosses may think otherwise, No one will see me, and if someone does order me away, I'll just tell them that I walk in my sleep, This is no time for jokes, All right, I'll be serious, And I should think so, Something is going on down there that I need to know about, Whatever it is can't stay a secret forever, and Marçal said that he'd tell us all about it when he finishes his shift, That's fine, but a description isn't enough for me, I want to see it with my own eyes, In that case, just go then and don't torture me any more, said Marta, crying. Her father went over to her, put his arm around her shoulders and gave her a hug, Please, don't cry, he said, do you know what the worst thing is, the fact that we haven't been the same since we moved here. He gave her a kiss, then left, slowly closing the door behind him. Marta went to get a blanket and a book, sat down on one of the small sofas in the living room and covered her knees. She did not know how long she would have to wait.

Cipriano Algor's plan could not have been simpler. He would go down in a service elevator as far as floor zero five and then abandon himself to fate and to chance. Battles have been won with fewer weapons, he thought. Then, in order to be totally impartial, he added, and many more have been lost. He had noticed that the service elevators, probably because they were intended exclusively for transporting materials, were not fitted with closed-circuit cameras, at least none that he could see, and if there were any of those tiny camouflaged ones, the guards on duty would probably be concentrating their attention on the outer doors and on the floors containing the shops and the attractions. If he was wrong, he would soon find out. In the first place, assuming that the residential floors above ground level formed a block with the ten underground floors, it would be best if he used the service elevator that was nearest the inner façade in order not to waste time looking for a way through the thousands of containers that he imagined would be kept belowground, especially on zero five, the particular floor that interested him. Nevertheless, he was not that surprised when he found a large open space, clear of all merchandise, which was obviously intended to facilitate access to the excavation. One section of a supporting wall, between two pillars, had been demolished, and it was through there that one entered. Cipriano Algor looked at his watch, it was two forty-five. Despite the dim lighting on that floor, there was no way of telling if there was any light inside the excavation itself to alleviate the blackness of the great maw about to swallow him. I should have brought a flashlight, he thought. Then he remembered having read once that the best thing to do when entering a dark place, if you wanted to be able to make out what was inside as soon as you got in there, was to close your eyes before going in and open them afterward. Yes, he thought, that's what I should do, close my eyes and plummet down into the center of the earth. He did not plummet anywhere. To his left, almost at floor level, was a tenuous glow which, once he had advanced a few more steps, gradually revealed itself as a line of lights. They illuminated a dirt ramp that led down to a landing from which another downward ramp emerged. The silence was so thick, so dense that Cipriano Algor could hear his own heart beating. Here we go, he thought, poor Marçal is going to get the fright of his life. He began walking down the ramp, he reached the first landing, went down the next ramp to another landing and stopped. In front of him two spotlights, one on either side, so that the light would not fall directly into the interior, revealed the oblong shape of the cave entrance. On some cleared ground to the right stood two small diggers. Marçal was sitting on a low bench, beside him was a table on which stood a flashlight. He had not yet seen his father-in-law. Cipriano Algor emerged from the half-darkness of the final landing and said out loud, Don't be frightened, it's me. Marçal leaped to his feet, what else would he do, he that would have replied nonchalantly, Hi, fancy seeing you here, let him cast the first stone. It was only when his father-in-law was standing right in front of him that Marçal, still with some difficulty, managed to say, What are you doing here, what kind of stupid idea was it coming down here, and yet, contrary to the demands of logic, there was no anger in his voice, what there was, apart from the natural relief of someone who has just realized that he is not being threatened by some malign spirit, was a kind of shamefaced satisfaction, something like an intense feeling of gratitude to which he might even admit one day. What are you doing here, he said again, I just came to have a look, said Cipriano Algor, And I suppose it didn't occur to you to think of the trouble I might get into if anyone found out, it didn't occur to you that it might cost me my job, Just tell them that your father-in-law is a complete idiot, an irresponsible fool who should be locked up in a lunatic asylum in a straitjacket, Oh, yes, that would really help. Cipriano Algor looked over at the cave and said, Have you seen what's inside, Yes, said Marçal, What is it, Go and see for yourself, here's the flashlight if you need it, Come with me, No, I went alone too, Is there some path marked out, a passageway, No, you just have to keep left all the way and never lose contact with the wall, you'll find what you're looking for at the end. Cipriano Algor switched on the flashlight and set off. I forgot to close my eyes, he thought. The indirect light from the spotlights allowed him to see only about three or four meters in front of him, beyond that it was as black as the inside of someone's body. There was a fairly gentle, albeit uneven slope. Very cautiously, touching the wall with his left hand, Cipriano Algor began to descend. At one point, he thought he could see something to his right that appeared to be a platform and a wall. He said to himself that on his way back, he would find out what it was, It's probably some structure to shore up the earth, and then he continued on down. He had the impression that he had already come some distance, perhaps thirty or forty meters. He looked back at the mouth of the cave. Lit only by the spotlights, it looked a long way off, I haven't really come very far, he thought, I'm just getting disoriented. He noticed that panic had started to grate insidiously on his nerves, and he had thought he was so brave, so much better than Marçal, and now he was almost ready to turn tail and stumble his way back up to the top. He leaned against the wall and took a deep breath, I'd rather die first, he said, and started walking again. Suddenly, the wall appeared in front of him, as if it had turned back on itself to form a right angle. He had reached the end of the cave. He shone the beam downward to see if he was on firm ground, took two steps and was just taking a third when his right knee struck something hard, and he cried out. The shock made the flashlight flicker, and, for a moment, there appeared before his eyes what seemed to be a stone bench, and, the following moment, a row of vague shapes appeared and disappeared. A violent tremor ran through Cipriano Algor's limbs, his courage faltered like a piece of fraying rope, but inside him he heard a voice calling him to order, Remember, you'd rather die first. The tremulous light from the torch swept slowly over the white stone, caught some bits of dark cloth, then moved upward to reveal a human body sitting there. Beside it, covered in the same dark fabric, were five other bodies, all sitting as erect as if a metal spike had been put through their skulls to keep them fixed to the stone. The smooth rear wall of the cave was about ten spans away from their hollow eye sockets, in which the eyeballs had been reduced to mere grains of dust. What is this, murmured Cipriano Algor, what nightmare is this, who were these people. He went closer, shone the flashlight beam on the dark, parched heads, this is a man, this is a woman, another man, another woman and another man and another woman, three men and three women, he saw the remnants of the ropes that had been used to keep their necks from moving, then he shone the light lower down, identical ropes were around their legs. Then slowly, very slowly, like a light in no hurry to show itself, but which had come in order to reveal the truth of things, even those hidden in the darkest and most hidden crannies, Cipriano Algor saw himself going into the kiln again, he saw the stone bench that the builders had left there and he sat down on it, he heard Marçal's voice, although the words were different now, they call and call again, anxiously, from afar, Pa, can you hear me, say something. The voice echoes around the inside of the cave, the echoes bounce off the walls, they multiply, if Marçal doesn't keep quiet for a moment, we won't be able to hear Cipriano Algor's voice, sounding as distant as if it too were an echo, I'm fine, don't worry, I won't be long. His fear had vanished. The flashlight once more caressed the wretched faces, the skin-and-bone hands folded on the knees, and, more than that, it guided Cipriano Algor's own hand when it touched, with a respect that would have been religious had it not been merely human, the dry forehead of the first woman. There was nothing more to do there, Cipriano Algor had understood. Like the circular route of a calvary, which will always find a calvary ahead, the climb back up was slow and painful. Marçal had come down to meet him, he held out his hand to help him, and when they emerged from the darkness into the light, they had their arms around each other, though they could not have said for how long they had been like that. Drained of all his strength, Cipriano Algor flopped down on the bench, rested his head on the table and, noiselessly, his shoulders almost imperceptibly shaking, he began to cry. It's all right, Pa, I cried too, said Marçal. A little while later, more or less recovered, Cipriano Algor looked at his son-in-law in silence, as if at that moment he had no better way of telling him how fond he was of him, then he asked, Do you know what that is, Yes, I remember reading something about it once, replied Marçal, And do you know that, since that's what it is, what we saw there has no reality, cannot be real, Yes, I do, And yet I touched the forehead of one of those women with my own hand, it wasn't an illusion, it wasn't a dream, if I went back there now, I would find the same three men and the same three women, the same cords binding them, the same stone bench, the same wall in front of them, If they can't be those other people, since they never existed, who are they, asked Marçal, I don't know, but after seeing them, I started thinking that perhaps what really doesn't exist is what we call nonexistence. Cipriano Algor got slowly to his feet, his legs were still shaking, but, on the whole, his physical strength had returned. He said, When I was going down there, I thought at one point that I passed something like a wall and a platform, if you could just change the direction of one of those spotlights, he did not need to complete the sentence, Marçal started turning a wheel, working a lever, and the light spread across the ground until it came to the base of a wall that crossed the cave from side to side, though without touching the cave walls. There was no platform, just a passageway alongside the wall. There's only one thing missing, muttered Cipriano Algor. He walked forward a few steps and suddenly stopped, Here it is, he said. There was a large black stain on the ground, the ground was scorched, as if a fire had burned there for a long time. There's no point now asking if they existed or not, said Cipriano Algor, the proof is here, each person must draw his own conclusions, I've drawn mine already.

The spotlight returned to its place, as did the darkness, then Cipriano Algor asked, Do you want me to stay and keep you company, Thanks, but no, said Marçal, you'd better get back home, Marta must be worried sick, doubtless fearing the worst, See you in a while, then, See you, Pa, there was a pause, and then, with a half-embarrassed smile, like that of an adolescent who draws back at the same moment as he gives himself, Thanks for coming.

Cipriano Algor looked at his watch when he reached floor zero five again. It was half past four. The service elevator carried him up to the thirty-fourth floor. No one had seen him. Marta silently opened the door to him, and closed it equally carefully, How's Marçal, she asked, Don't worry, he's all right, believe me, you've got a fine husband there, So what have they found, Let me sit down first, I feel as if I'd taken a real beating, I'm too old for this kind of thing, So what have they found, Marta asked again when they had both sat down, There are six dead people there, three men and three women, That doesn't surprise me, that was exactly what I thought, that it must be human remains, it often happens during excavations, what I don't understand is why all this mystery, all this secrecy, all this security, the bones won't run away, and I shouldn't think stealing them would be worth the effort, If you had gone with me, you would understand, in fact you've still got time, What nonsense, You wouldn't think it was nonsense if you had seen what I saw, What did you see, who are those people, Those people are us, said Cipriano Algor, What do you mean, That they are us, me, you, Marçal, the whole Center, probably the world, Explain yourself, please, Pay attention and listen. The story took half an hour to be told. Marta listened without interrupting him once. At the end, all she said was, Yes, I think you're right, they are us. They did not speak again until Marçal arrived. When he came in, Marta hugged him hard, What are we going to do, she asked, but Marçal did not have time to respond. In a firm voice, Cipriano Algor was saying, You must decide what to do with your own lives, but I'm leaving.

Your things are here, said Marta, there wasn't very much, it all fitted easily into the smallest suitcase, anyone would think you knew you were going to be here for only three weeks, There comes a time in life when it should be enough simply to be able to carry one's own body on one's back, said Cipriano Algor, Fine words, but what I want to know is what you're going to live on, Consider the lilies of the field, they toil not, neither do they spin, More fine words, but that's why they never got to be anything else but lilies, You're a rabid skeptic, a disgusting cynic, Pa, please, I'm serious, Sorry, Look, I know it's been a shock for you, as it was for me, and I wasn't even there, I understand that those men and those women are far more than just dead people, Don't go on, it's precisely because they are far more than just dead people that I don't want to continue living here, And what about us, what about me, asked Marta, You must decide for yourselves what to do with your lives, as for me, I've already made my decision, and I'm not going to spend the rest of my days tied to a stone bench, staring at a wall, But how will you live, Well, I've got the money they paid for the figurines, that will last me a month or two, then I'll see, Yes, but I wasn't talking about money, one way or another you'll have enough to feed and clothe yourself, what I mean is that you'll have to live on your own, I've got Found, and you'll come and visit me now and then, Pa, What, What about Isaura, What's Isaura got to do with this, You told me that the situation between you had changed, you didn't say how or why, but that's what you said, And it's true, So, So what,

Well, you could live together. Cipriano Algor did not reply. He picked up his suitcase, I'll be off then, he said. His daughter embraced him, We'll come and see you on Marçal's next day off, but stay in touch, phone me when you get there to tell me how the house is, and Found, don't forget about Found. With one foot out of the door, Cipriano Algor said, Give Marçal a hug from me, You already gave him a hug, you've already said your good-byes, Yes, but give him another hug. When he reached the end of the corridor, he turned. His daughter was standing there at the door, she waved with one hand, at the same time covering her mouth with the other to keep herself from crying. See you soon, he said, but she didn't hear him. The service elevator took him down to the garage, now he just had to find where the van was parked and see if it would start after three weeks without moving, sometimes the batteries die. That's all I need, he thought anxiously. But his fears did not materialize, the van fulfilled its obligations. True, it did not start the first or the second time, but the third time it roared into action with a noise worthy of another engine entirely. Minutes later, Cipriano Algor was driving down the avenue, he didn't exactly have the open road before him, but things could have been worse, despite its slowness, it was the traffic itself that was actually carrying him along. He wasn't surprised that the traffic was so heavy, cars love Sundays and for the owner of a car it is almost impossible to resist the so-called psychological pressure, the car just has to be there, it doesn't need to speak. At last, he left the city behind him, along with the suburbs, soon the shantytowns will appear, will they have reached the road in those three weeks, no, they still have another thirty or so meters to go, and then there's the Industrial Belt, almost at a standstill, apart from a few factories that seem to have made a religion out of continuous production, and now the grim Green Belt, the dismal, grubby, gray hothouses, that's why the strawberries are losing their color, it won't be long before they are as white outside as they are beginning to be inside, which is why they taste like something that tastes of nothing.

On our left, in the distance, where you can see those trees, that's right, the ones clumped together like a bouquet, there is an important archaeological site yet to explore, I have it from a reliable source, it's not every day that you're lucky enough to get such information straight from the maker's mouth. Cipriano Algor wondered how he could possibly have let himself be shut up inside for three weeks without being able to see the sun or the stars, except by dint of craning his neck at the sealed window of a thirty-fourth-floor flat, when he had this river, smelly and shrunken it's true, this bridge, old and dilapidated it's true, and these ruins that were once people's houses, and the village where he had been born, grown up and worked, with its street down the middle and the square off to one side, those people there, that man and that woman, are Marçal's parents, this is the first time we have seen them in this whole long story, looking at them now no one would ever think that they were as black as they've been painted, even though they have given more than enough proof that they are, this is the dangerous thing about appearances, when they deceive us, it's always for the worse. Cipriano Algor stuck his arm out of the window and waved to them as if they were his best friends, it would have been better if he hadn't really, now they will probably think he was making fun of them, and he wasn't, that wasn't his intention at all, it's just that Cipriano Algor is happy, in three minutes' time, he will see Isaura and have Found in his arms, or, rather, have Isaura in his arms and Found leaping up at them, waiting for them both to give him some attention. He passed the square, and suddenly, without warning, Cipriano Algor's heart contracted, he knows from experience, they both do, that no amount of sweetness today can diminish the bitterness of tomorrow, that the water of this fountain will never be able to slake your thirst in that desert, I don't have a job, I don't have a job, he murmured, and that was the answer he should have given, with no frills and no subterfuges, when Marta asked him what he was going to live on, I don't have a job. On this same road, at this same place, as he had on the day when he came back from the Center with the news that they would not be buying any more crockery from him, Cipriano Algor slowed the van. He wanted both not to arrive and to have arrived already, and between one thing and another there he was at the corner of the street where Isaura Madruga lives, it's that house over there, suddenly the van was in a terrible hurry, suddenly it stopped, suddenly Cipriano Algor burst out of it, suddenly he went up the steps, suddenly he rang the bell. He rang once, twice, three times. No one came to open the door, no one called out from inside, Isaura did not appear, Found did not bark, the desert that had been due tomorrow had arrived early. They should both be here, it's Sunday, there's no work, he thought. Disconcerted, he went back to the van and sat with his arms folded on the wheel, the normal thing would be to go and ask the neighbors, but he had never liked other people knowing about his life, indeed, when we ask about someone else, we are saying much more about ourselves than we might imagine, luckily for us, most people when questioned don't have their ears trained to pick up what lies hidden behind such innocent words as these, Have you by any chance seen Isaura Madruga. Two minutes later, after further consideration, he recognized that sitting parked and waiting outside the house must have looked just as suspicious as if he had gone nonchalantly over to ask the first neighbor if she had happened to notice Isaura going out. I'll go for a drive around, he thought, I might come across them. The drive around the village proved fruitless, Isaura and Found appeared to have vanished from the face of the earth. Cipriano Algor decided to go home, he would try again later that afternoon, They must have gone somewhere, he thought. The van's engine sang the homecoming song, the driver could already see the highest branches of the mulberry tree, and suddenly, like a black flash, Found appeared at the top and came running and barking down the hill like a mad thing, Cipriano Algor's heart was a beat away from stopping, not because of the dog, however much he loves the creature, he wouldn't go that far, but because he realized that Found would not be alone, and that, if he wasn't alone, only one person in the world could possibly be with him. He opened the van door, the dog leaped up at him, into his arms, so he was, after all, the first to be embraced, licking his face and blocking his view of the path, at the top of which appears an astonished Isaura Madruga, stop everything now, please, don't anyone speak, don't anyone move, don't anyone interfere, this is the really moving bit, the van driving up the hill, the woman who took two steps and then could go no farther, see how she has her hands pressed to her breast, see Cipriano Algor who climbed out of the van as if stepping into a dream, see Found, who follows behind, getting caught up in his master's legs, although nothing bad will happen, that's all we need, having one of the principal characters stumble inaesthetically at the culminating moment, this embrace and this kiss, these kisses and these embraces, how often must we remind you that this same devouring love is begging to be devoured, it was always thus, always, we just notice it more at some times than at others. In an interval between two kisses, Cipriano Algor asked, What are you doing here, but Isaura did not answer at once, there were other kisses to give and to receive, as urgent as the very first kiss, then she found enough breath to say, Found ran away on the day you left, he dug a hole under the garden hedge and came here, and I couldn't get him to leave, he was determined to wait for you until who knows when, so I thought it best to leave him here and to bring him food and water and keep him company sometimes, not that I think he needed it. Cipriano Algor felt in his pockets for the key to the house, while he was still thinking and imagining, Let's both go in, let's go in together, and he actually had the key in his hand when he saw that the door was open, which is how doors should be when someone arrives back after a long journey, he didn't need to ask why, Isaura explained calmly, Marta left me a key so that I could come and air the house occasionally, get rid of the dust, and so, what with Found being here, I started coming every day, in the morning, before going to the shop, and in the afternoon, when I finished work. She seemed to have something else to add, but her lips closed firmly as if to bolt the door on those words, You will not come out, they ordered, the words, however, regrouped, joined forces, and all that modesty could do was to make Isaura bow her head and lower her voice to a murmur, One night, I slept in your bed, she said. Now let us make something quite clear, this man is a potter and therefore a manual laborer, with no elevated intellectual and artistic training apart from that required to carry out his profession, a man of more than mature years, brought up in an age when it was normal for people to repress their individual feelings and, indeed, other people's feelings too, to damp down any expressions of emotion or any bodily desires, and although it is true that not many in his social and cultural milieu could best him when it came to sensitivity and intelligence, however energetically he might be striding toward the house where this equivocal act took place, hearing suddenly like that, from the mouth of a woman with whom he had never lain in intimacy, that she had slept in his bed, would be sure to stop him in his tracks, to make him stare in amazement at this bold creature, men, let us confess at once, will never understand women, fortunately, though without quite knowing how, this man managed to discover in the midst of his confusion the exact words that the occasion called for, And you will never sleep in any other. This phrase was just as it should be, the whole effect would have been lost had he said, for example, like someone putting their signature to a mutually advantageous agreement, Right, then, since you've slept in my bed, I'll go and sleep in yours. Isaura had embraced Cipriano Algor again after what he had said, and it is not hard to imagine the enthusiasm with which she did so, but he had a sudden thought in which his feelings of passion apparently had no part, I forgot to take my suitcase out of the van, was what he said. Not foreseeing the consequences of this prosaic act, with Found bounding at his heels, he opened the van door and took out the suitcase. He had the first inkling of what was going to happen when he went into the kitchen, the second when he went into his bedroom, but he was only absolutely certain when Isaura, in a voice that struggled to remain steady, asked him, Have you come back for good. The suitcase was on the floor, waiting for someone to open it, but that operation, though necessary, can be left until later. Cipriano Algor closed the door. There are such moments in life, when, in order for heaven to open, it is necessary for a door to close. Half an hour later, at peace now, like a beach from which the tide is retreating, Cipriano Algor told her what had happened at the Center, the discovery of the cave, the imposition of secrecy, the increased security, his visit to the excavation site, the blackness inside, the fear, the dead people tied to the stone bench, the ashes of the bonfire. At first, when she had seen him coming up the hill in the van, Isaura had thought that Cipriano was coming home because he had been unable to stand the separation and absence any longer, and that idea, as you can imagine, warmed her yearning lover's heart, but now, with her head resting in the hollow of his arm, feeling his hand on her waist, the two reasons seem to her equally right, and besides, if we take the trouble to observe that in at least one respect, that of unbearability, both reasons touch and become one, there is clearly no evidence that the two reasons are in fact mutually contradictory. Isaura Madruga is not particularly well-versed in ancient stories and mythological inventions, but it took only three simple words for her to grasp the essence. Although we already know what those words are, we lose nothing by writing them down again, They were us.

That afternoon, as agreed, Cipriano Algor phoned Marta to tell her that he had arrived safely, that the house looked as if they had left it only yesterday, that Found was almost mad with joy, and that Isaura sent her love. Where are you speaking from, asked Marta, From home, of course, And Isaura, She's here beside me, do you want to talk to her, Yes, but first tell me what's going on, What do you mean, I mean the fact that Isaura is there, Don't you like the idea, Don't be silly and stop beating about the bush, answer my question, All right, Isaura is staying with me, And who are you staying with, We're staying with each other, if that's what you want to hear. There was a silence at the other end. Then Marta said, I'm really pleased, Well, I'd never know it from your voice, My tone of voice has nothing to do with those particular words, but with others, What words are those, Tomorrow, the future, We'll have time to think about the future, Don't pretend, don't close your eyes to reality, you know perfectly well that the present is over for us, You're both all right, and we'll sort ourselves out here, No, I'm not all right and neither is Marçal, Why, If there's no future there, there's certainly none here, Can you explain yourself more clearly, please, Look, I have a child growing inside me, if, when he's old enough to make his own decisions, he should choose to live in a place like this, he will be doing what he wants, but I won't give birth to him here, You should have thought of that before, It's never too late to correct a mistake, even when you can do nothing about the consequences, although we might still be able to do something about those too, How, First, Marçal and I need to have a long talk, then we'll see, Think carefully and don't rush into anything, A mistake can just as easily be the consequence of careful thought, Pa, besides, as far as I know, nowhere is it written that rushing into things necessarily has bad results, Well, I hope you're never disappointed, Oh, I'm not that ambitious, I just don't want to be disappointed this time, and now, if you don't mind, that's the end of the father-daughter dialogue, call Isaura for me, I've got lots of things to say to her. Cipriano Algor passed the telephone over and went outside. There stands the pottery in which a solitary lump of clay lies drying, there is the kiln in which the three hundred figurines are asking each other why the devil they were ever made, there is the firewood that will wait in vain to be carried to the furnace. And Marta saying, If there's no future here, there's none there either. Cipriano Algor knew happiness today, the open sky of a love which, once declared, was consummated, and now yet again the storm clouds are gathering, the malign shadows of doubt and fear, it's obvious that, even if they pull in their belts to the very last notch, what the Center paid him for the figurines will last for two months at most, and that the difference between what the shop assistant Isaura Madruga earns and zero must be very nearly another zero. And what then, he asked, looking at the mulberry tree, who replied, Then, my old friend, the future, as always.

Four days later, Marta phoned again, We'll be there tomorrow evening. Cipriano Algor made a few rapid calculations, But it can't be Marçal's day off yet, No, it isn't, So, Keep your questions for when we arrive, Do you want me to come and pick you up, No, don't bother, we'll take a taxi. Cipriano Algor told Isaura that he found the visit odd, Unless, he added, the roster for rest days has been upset by some bureacratic confusion caused by the discovery of the cave, but in that case she would have said so and not told me to keep my questions for when they arrive, A day passes quickly enough, said Isaura, we'll find out tomorrow. However, the day did not pass as quickly as Isaura thought. Twenty-four hours spent thinking are a lot of hours, twenty-four hours we say because sleep is not everything, at night, there are probably other thoughts in our head that draw a curtain and continue thinking unbeknownst to anyone. Cipriano Algor had not forgotten Marta's categorical words about her unborn child, I won't give birth to him here, an absolutely explicit statement, unequivocal, not one of those conglomerations of more or less organized vocal noises that seem to be doubting themselves even as they affirm. Logically speaking, there could be only one possible conclusion to draw, Marta and Marçal were going to leave the Center. If they do, they'll be making a great mistake, said Cipriano Algor, what are they going to live on afterward, You could ask the same of us, said Isaura, but do I look worried, You believe in a divine providence that watches over the helpless, No, I don't, I just happen to think that there are times in our lives when we have to let ourselves be carried along by the current of events, as if we didn't have the strength to resist, but then there comes a point when we suddenly realize that the river is flowing in our favor, no one else has noticed, but we have, anyone watching will think we're about to go under, and yet our navigational skills have never been better, Let's just hope that this is one such occasion. He would soon find out. Marta and Marçal got out of the taxi, took some packages out of the trunk, fewer than they had taken with them to the Center, Found gave vent to his excitement by running wildly twice around the mulberry tree, and when the taxi drove down the hill to go back to the city, Marçal said, I am no longer an employee of the Center, I've resigned from my job as security guard. Cipriano Algor and Isaura did not feel they needed to look surprised, which would, anyway, have rung entirely false, but they felt obliged to ask at least one question, one of those useless questions we seem unable to live without, Are you sure you've acted for the best, and Marçal replied, I don't know if it was for the best or for the worst, I just did what I had to do, and I wasn't the only one, two of my colleagues resigned as well, one external guard and one resident, And how did the Center react, If you don't adapt you're no use to them, and I had stopped adapting, the last two phrases were spoken after supper, And when did you feel that you had stopped adapting, asked Cipriano Algor, The cave was the last straw for me, as it was for you, And for those two colleagues of yours, Yes, for them too. Isaura had got up and started clearing the table, but Marta said, Leave it for now, we'll do it together later on, we need to decide what we're going to do, Well, Isaura, said Cipriano Algor, is of the opinion that we should let ourselves be carried along on the current of events, that there always comes a time when we realize that the river is flowing in our favor, I didn't say always, said Isaura, I said sometimes, but take no notice of me, it's just an idea I had, It's good enough for me, said Marta, besides it fits in very well with what's actually been happening to us, What shall we do, then, asked her father, Marçal and I are going to start a new life a long way from here, that much we've decided, the Center is finished, the pottery was already finished, from one hour to the next we've become like strangers in this world, And what about us, asked Cipriano Algor, You can't expect me to advise you on what you should do, Do I understand you to be saying that we should go our separate ways, No, not at all, I'm just saying that our reasons may not necessarily be your reasons, May I say something, suggest something, asked Isaura, I don't honestly know if I have the right, I've only been a member of this family for about six days and I feel as if I was still on probation, as if I had slipped in through the back door, You've been here for months already, ever since the famous water-jug incident, said Marta, as for the rest of what you said I think it's up to my father to respond, All I heard was that she had something to say, a suggestion, so any comments I might make at the moment would be completely out of place, said Cipriano Algor, What's this idea of yours, then, asked Marta, It has to do with that fantasy of mine about the current sweeping us along, said Isaura, Go on, It's the simplest thing in the world, Ah, I know what it is, said Cipriano Algor, What is it then, asked Isaura, That we go with them, Exactly. Marta took a deep breath, You can always rely on a woman to come up with a good idea, We shouldn't rush things, though, said Cipriano Algor, What do you mean, asked Isaura, You've got your house, your job, So, Well, just leaving like that, turning your back on everything, But I'd already left everything anyway, I'd already turned my back on everything when I clasped that water jug to my chest, you'd have to be a man to fail to realize that it was you I was clasping to me, these last words were almost lost in a sudden irruption of sobs and tears. Cipriano Algor shyly reached out and touched her arm, and she could not help but cry all the more, or perhaps she needed that to happen, sometimes the tears we have cried before are not enough, we have to say to them, please, go on.

The preparations took up the whole of the following day. First from one house, then from the other, Marta and Isaura selected what they thought was necessary for a journey that had no known destination and which no one knew how or where it would end. The two men loaded the van, helped by encouraging barks from Found, not in the slightest bit worried today about what was, quite clearly, another move, because the idea never even entered his doggy head that they might be about to abandon him again. The morning of their departure dawned beneath a graying sky, it had rained in the night, here and there in the yard there were small puddles of water, and the mulberry tree, forever bound to the earth, was still dripping. Shall we go, asked Marçal, Yes, let's go, said Marta. They climbed into the van, the two men in front and the two women behind, with Found in the middle, and just as Marçal was about to start the engine, Cipriano Algor said abruptly, Wait. He got out of the van and went over to the kiln, Where's he going, asked Marta, What's he going to do, murmured Isaura. The kiln door was open, Cipriano Algor went in. When he emerged shortly afterward, he was in his shirtsleeves and was using his jacket to carry something heavy, a few figurines, it couldn't be anything else, He probably wants to take some with him as a souvenir, said Marçal, but he was wrong, Cipriano Algor went over to the door of the house and started arranging the figurines on the ground, placing them firmly in the damp earth, and when he had put them all in their positions, he went back to the kiln, by then, the other travelers had got out of the van too, no one asked any questions, one by one they went into the kiln as well and brought out the figurines, Isaura ran to the van to fetch a basket, a sack, anything, and the area in front of the house gradually filled up with figurines, then Cipriano Algor went into the pottery and very carefully removed from the shelves the defective figurines gathered there and reunited them with their sound and perfect siblings, the rain would eventually turn them into mud, and then into dust when the sun dried the mud, but that is a fate we all will meet, now the figurines are not just guarding the front of the house, they are defending the entrance to the pottery too, in the end, there will be more than three hundred figurines, eyes front, clowns, jesters, Eskimos, mandarins, nurses, bearded Assyrians, Found has not yet knocked over a single one, Found is a very conscientious, sensitive dog, almost human, he does not need anyone to explain to him what is going on. Cipriano Algor went and shut the kiln door, then he said, Right, now we can go. The engine started and the van went down the hill. When they got to the road, it turned left. Marta, though dry-eyed, was sobbing, Isaura had her arms about her, while Found lay curled up in one corner of the seat, not knowing who to comfort first. After a few kilometers, Marçal said, I'll write to my parents when we stop for lunch. And then, addressing Isaura and his father-in-law, There was a poster, one of those really big ones outside the Center, can you guess what it said, he asked. We've no idea, they replied, and, as if he were reciting something, Marçal said COMING SOON, PUBLIC OPENING OF PLATO'S CAVE, AN EXCLUSIVE ATTRACTION, UNIQUE IN THE WORLD, BUY YOUR TICKET NOW.